AUTHOR

DELMAIN, J. BALMAIN

CLASS

G

TITLE

The meek inheritance

−9880

The Meek Inheritance

The Meek Inheritance

A Novel

James Balmain

Cranstone House
Publishing

First published by
Cranstone House Publishing
222 King Street, Aberdeen AB2 3BU

ISBN 1 898064 02 4

06049880

Collated by Waverly Press Ltd, Aberdeen.
Typeset by T.M.S. (Graphics & Design) Ltd., Aberdeen.
Cover designed by J. MacDonald, Aberdeen
Made and Printed in Great Britain by
BPCC Paperbacks Limited
Member of BPCC Limited

Forward and Acknowledgements

The information on AIDS used in the book has come from various sources both in the UK and Abroad; the author wishes to thank Graham Cronkshaw for his help in identifying and sourcing useful research material. What I have done with these statistics is, however, all the facts about AIDS in this book are correct; only the story is fictional. For the moment.

My thanks also to Keith Murray, Editorial Associate at Cranstone House, for his unfailing support and encouragement, and for his courageous decision to publish a book which contains so much information which has so far failed to reach the general public, for whatever reasons.

James Balmain
June 1993

CHAPTER ONE

June, 1994

The inside of the Daimler Sovereign was dark, sleek, private and comfortable: in the deep recesses of his heart, the Prime Minister wished fervently that on this occasion he could just stay there, tell the driver to take him back to Number 10 Downing Street, escape, and hide. He hated doing interviews in general, and he hated the Greg Sharp primetime morning radio show interviews more than all the rest. This was the beginning of his second term of office, and he had endured several Sharp interviews the first time round. With the Government's new majority being rather slender, he knew he would not get an easy ride of it from any part of the media.

He counted himself a good Prime Minister, but he knew he failed to come across well in the press, or radio, or television. He had never learned to love the assorted rabble of reporters with their insidious, devious questioning and their barely concealed hostility towards the Government.

Greg Sharp was well named: his jovial tones masked a rapier wit and a very well informed mind. You couldn't fumble or flannel on 'Sharp Shooting' or the bastard would gun you down in cold blood, smiling amiably all the while. But there was no escaping it: the public wanted it, and the Party recommended it. This was the biggest single radio audience of the week, every week; it was a golden opportunity to reach and persuade people.

The usual assortment of flunkeys took care of him from the impressive BBC entrance portals to the plain, padded, deeply inhibiting studio door. They waited until the 'Mic Live' light went off above the door, and quietly took him inside. Even the Prime Minister had to wait until Greg Sharp finished speaking and turned on the music. Most presenters (die rather than call them D.J.s!) had studio assistants and production assistants and technical operatives,

1

but Greg Sharp had started off in local radio and had got so used to doing everything himself that he now preferred it that way.

"Morning, Prime Minister! Back again!" He smiled pleasantly as he got the next record cued up for play, and fiddled with some paperwork. The Prime Minister was sat down at the guest desk, was fitted up with headphones, and was asked to chat about anything at all while Greg got his voice levels right on the mixing desk. During this, the flunkeys virtually bowed out backwards.

"Well sir" said Sharp, satisfied with the sound levels and with almost a minute to go before 'You Cute Little Devil, You' finished playing. "We'll be sticking to the agreed list of questions, of course, but equally of course you need to give me a little bit of leeway if any interesting ones get phoned in once we're on air. You'll get a copy handed to you at the same time I do, so there won't be any nasty surprises. We'll be fine." It was all very soothing and very friendly and very false. Greg Sharp didn't give a toss about his guests feeling relaxed; he cared about his audience, his ratings, his image.

"Shoobe doobe doway, OH!" wailed the record, and Greg Sharp opened his microphone fader, cut out the music, and smiled.

The Prime Minister had spent almost two hours with his Media Advisor that morning, going over the agreed questions and the appropriate answers. In front of him on the guest desk was a pile of papers, each headed with a question and then filled in with the answer he intended to give. He was prepared, he had been trained to survive interviews, he had done this many, many times, and yet still his throat was dry and his forehead damp.

The delectable Terry Aitken, his very skilled and able Media Advisor, had dinned it into him a dozen times that adrenalin was useful, that he was doing something he wanted to do, that the 'excitement', as she called it, would make him sparkle...he still felt like a naughty schoolboy on the carpet in the headmaster's study. Sharp, with sincerity oozing from every pore, went through his 'honoured to have you' introduction all too quickly, and launched into the questions with undisguised relish. Most of them had proved to be predictable, reasonably safe, requiring only the re nphasising of quotes from the Manifesto to clear the air. The cottish question, the Irish question, the National Health Service nd the plans to introduce payment for hospital stays, a question or vo about the environment, a few grumbles about bad council ousing and rising unemployment. With the answers in front of im, he could hardly fail to sound informed and convincing: it was te questions coming in on the telephone which he dreaded.

But even the 'safe' questions were hard going: Sharp rarely let im off the hook. Then, towards the end of the interview, a few lephoned questions were brought through, while 'The Golden ays of Your Love' was playing. The Prime Minister was already weating profusely, having just been skewered on the National ealth and the moral question of making little old ladies pay for aving their replacement hips when they'd paid into the NHS all teir lives and couldn't afford the operation. Now, he saw that the ext question, phoned in by a doctor in Somerset, was about AIDS. nd that was one subject he was not ready to talk about. Damn! here was scarcely time to start thinking about it before the record ded out and Greg Sharp pounced.

"Nothing in the Manifesto about AIDS, says Doctor Fenwick own there in Somerset: is anything happening? What are the overnment's plans for public education and the search for a cure: r is everything under control, is that why there was nothing in the lanifesto?"

"The Government" began the Prime Minister "takes the AIDS uestion very seriously indeed, of course..."

"Really?" asked Sharp, brightly. "How come there wasn't ctually a word about it in any of your election broadcasts or your lanifesto, or in the Queen's Speech either?"

The Prime Minister managed to sound as bland as if this uestion had been prepared and agreed.

"The reason for that is that we shall simply continue to do what re have always done; we monitor, we educate and inform, we ipport all the worldwide efforts to eradicate this tragic disease. Of ourse there are very few cases in this country..."

3

"The educating and informing bit seems to have died away recently, wouldn't you agree? Almost no advertising on the telly for almost three years now: why is that, exactly? And...you say you monitor. Well I'm sure that's tremendously reassuring for us all, but you might say Nero monitored while Rome burned...monitoring isn't actually DOING very much, is it?"

"I'm afraid I have to disagree with you there, Greg: unless we monitor effectively we cannot know what the situation is. Unless we know exactly what the situation is, we cannot deal with it. Monitoring is quite essential."

"So, Prime Minister: with AIDS expanding all over the globe, how exactly are you stepping up your response?"

Bastard. "In point of fact, we are in the early stages right now of setting up a Committee to investigate the whole picture, both globally and in the U.K."

"A Committee? Another Committee? Oh, splendid." The man skirted outright rudeness with such a smile in his voice he got away with it. "Well, I daresay we can look forward to hearing the report from the Committee, eventually. I'm sure that will be a tremendous leap forward in the treatment and prevention of AIDS. Thank you, Prime Minister, for a most interesting interview. And now, a real old favourite of mine...."

The next record played in, and the Prime Minister stood up, red in the face with rage, as Sharp smiled blandly at him and had the gall to say sweetly that he thought it had gone rather well.

"Perhaps" was all the P.M. could manage, from clenched teeth.

Went well? Well enough for you, you leech. That's the last interview you get from me, I can promise you that.

The bland smile faded slightly.

"So by the way, Prime Minister...are you really setting up that Committee or was that just spur-of-the-moment stuff? You deliver it so calmly it's hard to tell."

The implied compliment did nothing to dilute the explicit insult.

"Of course I am -we are. Do you think I would lie to sixteen million people? Whatever you think of me, I wouldn't do that."

4

The very barest of farewells were exchanged when the flunkeys returned. He refused a stopover in Hospitality, and raged back into the Sovereign. On the way back to Downing Street he informed his Private Personal Secretary that he wanted a meeting that afternoon with the Party Chairman and the Minister for Health.

"I have this working lunch with the Chancellor first; we should clear by about two-thirty. Put off my three o'clock; put them in the first slot available next week. So make the new meeting three sharp: and I mean sharp!" Of course he had lied to the sixteen million: he had had to say something. Now, he would have to make the lie the truth.

Before his lunch, he spent half an hour being debriefed by Terry Aitken and huffing about the fact that she had not prepared him adequately for questions on AIDS. She pointed out that she could only package and prepare information which the Party gave her, and the Party had, in this instance, not given her any information for months. While this was eminently reasonable, it was not the abject apology his ego wanted to hear, and he went into lunch in a less than receptive mood to listen to the Chancellor's fiscal maunderings.

His mood was not lightened by his lunch: he hated lunch in general, much preferring to be left in peace with decaff coffee and a sandwich, rather than picking gloomily at cool congealing plates of chicken a la King while attempting to conduct business with other diners. Working lunches at No. 10 had become markedly less festive since his occupancy; the Chancellor, like most regular guests, had had a quick shepherd's pie before coming. This enabled him to chew down the cheese and apples with some semblance of enjoyment, as they now constituted dessert, and he was able to get through the business part of the meeting without his stomach rumbling in anticipation of something more satisfying.

There was little satisfaction of any sort in his meeting with the Prime Minister today: but Ernest Faulkner was well used to the tetchiness, and merely put off asking any really trenchant questions until some more propitious moment. This rendered the luncheon somewhat redundant, a complete waste of time, really; by three o'clock the Prime Minister was fizzing.

Both of his three o'clock guests had heard the broadcast; having been telephoned by the P.P.S., they had thoughtfully got together over a very splendid lunch at their club, to discuss tactics and strategies for their meeting with the Prime Minister. They had a united front all worked out and ready to go. The P.M. liked united fronts; they smacked of Party cohesion, and intelligent cooperation. They also presented fewer difficulties than ramshackle fighting. But as those who worked closely with him knew, he did not like the united fronts to be prepared; what he liked most was a seemingly happenstantial agreement, a swift meeting of minds. So that was how Harold Sweeting, Minister for Health, and Alan Frensham, the Party Chairman, planned to play it. If the P.M. was in a particularly difficult mood, they might even chance suggesting that their proposals had been, originally, his own idea expressed at some meeting some time ago. That, they decided, was the surest way of getting the idea put through.

Frensham, a party hack from way back, was a polished, urbane, balding man of fifty whose manner was unctuous but whose loyalty was absolute. Sweeting, on the other hand, had cultivated a somewhat bluff and hearty manner in order to appeal to the electorate in his very working-class constituency in the Midlands. While Frensham affected his Home Counties accent, Sweeting did his best to conceal his own. Occasionally, the P.M. found them, in tandem, somewhat amusing.

Today was not one of those occasions. As he entered the Cabinet Room, the Prime Minister saw their faces and knew that they knew about his broadcasted lie, and knew that they knew what was expected of them this afternoon, and knew that they had got it all sorted out in advance and were pleased with themselves, and decided to whip the rug from under them.

"Good afternoon, gentlemen" he began in his most polite tone and noticed the slight droop at the corners of their mouths when they heard this. "Thank you so much for coming at such short notice; i is appreciated. I want to go over with you the proposals fo charging NHS patients. This has got to be watertight before it goe before the House. Do you have the latest draft of the draft Bill with you? Have my last corrections been incorporated?"

"Ah" said Sweeting, who had nothing at all with him. "The Freedom of Treatment Choice Bill....no, actually, I'm afraid not, sir. I thought...well, I didn't know that was what you wanted to see me about. The P.P.S. didn't actually say, you see. I do apologise."

"Hm." The P.M. affected perplexion. "Well, never mind. As you're here anyway, I might as well go over my proposals for a new Standing Committee I have in mind. On the AIDS question: did you by any chance hear the Sharp Shooting programme this morning? Good. Then you've heard about it already. Forgive me for going unilateral on you, gentlemen, but I do feel we have to do something. The public expects it. I propose, therefore, a crossparty standing committee headed up not by an M.P. but by a private citizen who can do the job properly."

Frensham brightened. "Yes, Prime Minister, an excellent idea. We could perhaps approach Sir Marcus Digby? A most able man, on several Boards of Directors, and a massive contributor to Party funds."

"What a splendid suggestion, my dear fellow" exclaimed Sweeting in tremendous surprise. "The perfect choice in fact, didn't you yourself, Sir, mention him in this context some time ago? Was it in Brussels, perhaps? I can't quite remember."

'Dear, dear, not that old ploy again, Sweeting? I'm sure you think it's a brand new idea, every time you have it. Tut tut.'

"I think not. I scarcely think I would have suggested a man whom I consider to be a perfect oaf for a position I had not yet envisaged as existing. Would I?"

"Ah...must be thinking of something else. So, do we have someone else in mind?"

"We do. You will remember Doctor Andrew Douglas, our Member for Perthshire Central? He has just lost his seat to some moronic pop star standing for the Scottish National Party. He's a clever man, a devoted medical chap, and well liked at Westminster. And he's out of a job. Gave up his practice when he became an M.P. oh, it must be fifteen years ago. Widowed. One son, all grown up, no ties, no tribulations. Ideal."

Neither Sweeting nor Frensham were under any illusion that they were living in a democracy.

"I shall be delighted to telephone him this very afternoon" smiled Frensham. "I'm sure he will be most honoured, most honoured." Sweeting nodded enthusiastically.

"If he isn't... most honoured...if you have any difficulty...I shall speak to him myself" said the Prime Minister dryly. "For all we know, he may be looking forward to his early retirement."

Andrew Douglas was annoyed to be called to the telephone on such a glorious day. He had been standing in his steeply sloping garden, which ran upwards from the back of the house, over a riot of rocks and pools of lawn and shrubs, about halfway up the hillside behind. Though it was a fine garden in late summer, when the roses were blooming, he always thought it was at its best now early in June when the rhododendrons and the azaleas flourished abundantly and profusely in a riot of colours. And though the rhodies and azaleas did not much perfume the air, the scent of newly cut grass was delightful and heady with lilacs from other gardens. The tourists who thronged St Fillans only in summertime missed out on this stunning display of colour; but then the majority of them did not stop anyway, in the one-horse, one-street village skirting Loch Earn. They were on their way to Oban, Perth, or Mallaig, and scarcely noticed the imposing Scottish Baronial sandstone houses, all turrets and battlements and gothic grandeur on a middling scale. Those few who were coming to stay were there for the water sports and the apreswater, up the road a mile or two at Lochearnhead. So though St Fillans was beautiful, picturesque and romantic, there were not too many gawping strollers in the average year. And Dr Douglas was always pleased to chat to anyone peering up at his garden with that particular gleam in his eye which a fellow gardener can spot at twenty paces. Conversations about ericaceous soil and limefree fertiliser would ensue, leaving all parties well content.

"Telephone, Doctor Andrew! London calling!" Isa had to yell to be heard above the Mendellsohn playing by the good doctor'

8

side, on a professional quality Walkman. She went back to her salad tossing in the kitchen, working quickly so as to get back to the papershop in time for the evening rush. Her husband didn't mind her doing the odd few hours for the doctor, but he didn't like to be left in the lurch, either.

"Frensham, my dear chap! How are you keeping? The ulcer behaving itself?"

"Actually Douglas, I was rather hoping you'd pop down and see me this weekend, spend a day with me and the family.."

"Frensham. I don't do house calls any more, and my fees for a house call in deepest Kent would be quite considerable!"

"No, no, not about the ulcer! I've got a fax punting through to you in a minute, it'll explain; there's a job the Prime Minister wants you to do, and Sweeting and I would really like to see you this weekend and discuss it. Are you free, at all?"

"You know I'm free, Frensham. All too free. What sort of a job?"

"Switch to fax mode when we've finished; when you've read it, phone me back, I'm at the office. I'll be waiting. See what you think. Okay?"

"Okay. Speak to you soon, then." He pressed the button and in seconds the fax appeared. Minutes later he was back on the telephone to Frensham, turning the job down. Minutes after that, the Prime Minister phoned him in person.

"I'm sorry, sir, but I honestly don't think I'm the man for the job; I trained about thirty years ago! Of course I've read the odd report in the Lancet and the B.M.J. and the Guardian and the Times, but really I hardly know more about it than the man in the street. There are dozens of highly qualified people currently working with AIDS patients, or working in research, who know far more about it than I do. It's most kind of you sir, but I do feel I must refuse, in all honesty."

"Andrew, Andrew, (*beware Prime Ministers using first names!*) do you think I don't know your capabilities? Your past history? We're not asking you to engage in virus research. We're asking; *I'm asking*; that you come and head up a committee and find out

9

what the overview is: there's nobody better qualified than you to do that. When you were in the Ministry for Health, you produced absolutely the definitive overview of the cancer research and treatment going on in the U.K. and all over the world: you achieved miracles. You got people talking to each other. You sorted out major funding from big business."

"I had a special reason for that, sir, as you know."

"I know, I know: Ruth. It was a tragedy we all shared with you. But out of your own personal sorrow came hope for millions of others. We need someone like you: no, dammit, we need YOU to come and do something similar with this hellish AIDS situation. You can do it. You can. I want you to do it. Please Andrew; a personal favour for me."

The weekend at Chequers was pleasant, but busy. Sweeting and Frensham were there, of course, and the Prime Minister's Media Advisor. She had never met Andrew Douglas before, and was expecting some ageing, bitter loser. She met instead a singularly handsome man who looked no older than forty, with a gentle expression and a bright intelligence in his eyes. On his part, Andrew found himself shaking hands with a mere chit of a girl, thirty years old going on seventeen, with a bright and winsome manner, glossy brown hair and a self deprecating smile. She was not pretty, nor particularly glamorous, but he was taken aback to find himself slightly dazzled by her, all the same. It was the first time any female had stirred his pheromones since he had married Ruth, twentyfive years ago: he shrugged it off to himself as the male menopause, and determinedly ignored the effect she had on him

He took the job, of course. He also negotiated a slightly different list of names than the one put in front of him by Sweeting a slightly different remit than that suggested by Frensham, and somewhat more reasonable budget than the one the Prime Ministe said the Chancellor had perforce delineated.

He tried also for a suite of offices at Westminster, in order to b out from under the permanent feet of Sweeting and his Permane Secretaries and UnderSecretaries, who had so strangulated t'

10

Cancer Committee in red tape that it had almost died of asphyxia before it was off the ground. Of course Sweeting would have been around at Westminster, dabbling and meddling, but at least the hovering hordes of bureaucrats would have had to phone to make appointments to come and irritate. But he had not prevailed. Three dismal green offices at the back of the second floor of Richmond House in Whitehall was his allocation; and lucky to get it, he was informed.

Within a fortnight the house at St Fillans was closed up again, with Isa set to come in every week and air the place, and Isa's brother to look after the garden, and Andrew was installed in a serviced flat in a big brick courtyard off Victoria Street, a short stroll from the Palace of Westminster, and Whitehall. He had stayed here before, during all his eleven years of being a Member of Parliament. Though it was not his usual flat, it was the same as all the rest: cleverly compact in design, the rosy chintz furnishings very elegant and clean, and the kitchen very space-age. But as always, the only greenery was one trough of pot plants, all made of silk. By the time he had installed his clothes, his books, and Ruth's photograph on the mantelpiece, he was as 'at home' as he was likely to get. The air outside was muggy, thick, dirty and full of noise; every time he returned to London Andrew was astonished anew when he first blew his nose and found his handkerchief blackened. He slept badly that first night, despite the liberal dose of whisky in milk he had prescribed for himself as a nightcap.

He awoke to find the morning unseasonably dark; storm clouds were gathering. Good. A dash of thunder and lightning would freshen the air, pump some negative ions into the atmosphere, make people feel alive for a time before the London microclimate reverted to its usual heavy June heat. Wilson, the courtyard doorkeeper, bade him a polite good morning as he stepped out into Victoria Street at seven fortyfive and, as if on cue, the heavens opened.

His early start was to permit him to indulge in one of the treats which London offers and St Fillans does not; a cafe breakfast of morello cherry pie and tea with condensed milk. Nowhere do you get a cherry pie like those you find in London; not too sweet, but delectably tart and juicy, with rich flaky pastry enclosing high piles of plump fruits. Joe's Sandwich Bar in Victoria Street went one further and offered double cream spiked with orange liqueur, vanilla and cinnamon, which ensured a plentiful supply of breakfast trade and a regular clientele. The seating was all through the back, in a room which was an oasis of calm on a busy London morning. Patrons sat mostly alone, and read the Times or the Mail or the Sun from the heap on the central table, and nodded pleasantly to each other as the other faces became familiar. Rarely did anyone speak. It was very civilised. And less lonely than breakfasting in the flat. Fortified, he emerged into brilliant sunshine and sparkling pavements; London smelled good. Ruth had always said London was at her best after a storm, with the brief supply of fresh clean air, and every window gleaming and the trees showered and aromatic, a bit like Paris...

Oh, Ruth. *If you are anywhere around me my dear, help me now. I have a feeling the next few months, or years, are going to be harrowing. And it is going to be so hard to do it alone.*

It was now almost three years since he had buried her, yet Ruth was as vivid to him now as she had been as a stunning, clever, elegant student at Edinburgh University. Up Victoria Street he walked, taking the long way round to enjoy more of the air, through St James Park, through Horseguards, and into Whitehall.

Sweeting (or some underling) had been busy: not only was there a secretary there waiting for him at Reception to guide him to the offices, there were two junior typists (sorry, Administrativ Assistants) already installed in the outer room, his name on the door, and a pile of paperwork already on his desk. He noted wit amusement that, according to the rigid hierarchy of Civil Servi carpeting allocation, he was apparently ranked equal now to Higher Executive Officer: the green carpeting very nearly reache the walls but the strip of brown linoleum around it was clear visible. And his desk, though wooden and not metallic (which w the apportioned lot of mere Executive Officers), was pine and r mahogany. You only graduated to mahogany when you became so elevated you hardly spoke to anybody except the Permanent Secretary, the UnderSecretaries, and God.

Judy Smith, his secretary, was courteous, middle-aged, welcoming, and clearly a capable sort. She introduced Peter Goonan and Sarah Kepple, the Administrative Assistants, and led Andrew through the middle room into his inner sanctum, showing him the filing system she had already set up, for his approval. He approved of everything so far.

They sat together and went over the mail and memos and faxes which had already arrived. Several people wanted to see him as soon as possible: these were ranked into a waiting list, with appointments to be made at varying degrees of urgency. Whole folios of information had arrived, and Andrew was extremely impressed by Judy's filing of them into categories including Virology, Aetiology, Epidemiology, and so on; this displayed a considerable degree of knowledge which he had not expected.

"I was a medical secretary before I joined the Service" she explained. "That's why I was seconded to you. That and the fact I volunteered as soon as I heard about this post."

He looked at her questioningly.

"There's such a lot of rubbish talked about AIDS, even here; ignorance, malice, prejudice, and sheer - forgive me - stupidity. I read all your Cancer Committee reports; I wanted to be part of what I think you will do here." She blushed a little.

"Thank you" he said, simply. "I am extremely glad to have someone of your calibre working with me." It was a good beginning to an important working relationship. Mutual respect. Excellent.

One of his first meetings was with Sweeting and Terry Aitken. He wanted to devise a policy statement on the Committee's work, for the P.M. to approve before she circulated it to the media.

"They're sniffing round already, have been since that Sharp Footing debacle - I mean broadcast. We need to toss them a bone keep them going in the meantime, till things start really happening."

Hm. *Yes. And to show that the P.M. is an honourable man...so are they all, all honourable men.*

A very bland short statement was agreed, describing the remit as being to form a crossparty committee with a watching brief, upon whose reports to Cabinet would be built the Government's ongoing response to the situation.

When Terry Aitken left Sweeting's sumptuous office, Andrew stayed on. Their private meeting was less affable than the one just finished; Sweeting made his first power play, and Andrew crushed him into the ground.

"Forgive me, Minister, but I cannot really allow you to dictate to me how I shall work, or whom I shall talk to: if you will recall our talks at Chequers you will remember that the Prime Minister asked you to render me every assistance; that is not the same as trying to tell me what to do."

Sweeting went very red in the face.

"Listen friend, I render my secretary every assistance; all the pieces of paper she needs to type on, all the words she needs to type, a pinch on the arse from time to time to raise her morale; but that doesn't mean that *I* am working for HER."

Andrew gave him a look of deep and genuine distaste, which he could not avoid seeing echoed in Sweeting's empurpled visage.

"Minister, this is a crossparty committee; I answer to the Cabinet. I feel sure the Prime Minister mentioned that, at Chequers in your presence. It is not exactly an abnormal procedure. It is in the press release we have just agreed. It is standard practice. I am not working for you. And if you feel that you will experience any difficulty in providing me with a supportive working environment then perhaps we ought to be discussing this with the Prime Minister perhaps he will be able to resolve our differences."

Game, set and match. For now. Sweeting climbed down so fast his shoes were on fire. But battle lines were drawn, all the same and both protagonists knew it. It did not alarm Andrew Dougl unduly to have such a powerful enemy: he was so used to Powerful enemies, powerful friends, lobbying and whispering, the appurtenances of politics were part of the daily scenery of his life, had been for years. Sweeting was just another integer in the equation; the first, but certainly not the last irritation, in this particular scenario.

The list of people he wanted had already been sent out to the relevant Party Chairmen, and the Prime Minister's Personal and Private Secretary, Jack Mullens, had received permission from each to approach the M.P.s whom Andrew Douglas had asked for. They had been approached, they had agreed with alacrity, and all three were assembled in his office on Thursday morning of his first week. As an ex M.P. himself, he would never ask them to be here on Fridays as so many Members travelled back to their constituencies and their families for weekends, and he knew how important and how precious that time was to them.

They were black and white, male and female, Tory and Red and Liberal Democrat; there was a doctor, a lawyer, and a man who used to fence for England. What they had in common was intelligence, a capacity for hard work, and a private belief that principle comes before party politics, every time. Two of them had been involved in the Cancer Committee, the third had doctored in Central Africa; the handshakes were warm, the intentions firm. All information would be collated and presented to Cabinet in such a way as to leave very few options open but that all necessary measures WOULD be taken. Weekly meetings were agreed, and each knew that many further separate hours of study and work would be required to prepare for each Thursday session and, before that, each would spend many hours on the telephone calling up old contacts, sourcing information, establishing credentials. This committee was no sinecure for anyone: it would be small, tight, and hard going. It was also likely to be distressing; less so, perhaps, for Dr. Jasmine Eliot, whose time in Central Africa had included a harrowing stint in an AIDS hospice and, next door, an orphanage for HIV positive children of parents who had both died of AIDS. For the others, the statistics were frightening: for Jasmine they were just the cleanly painted symbols of what was really frightening...the reality.

15

Judy had sat in at this first meeting to take notes; she also offered to go through the individual collections of information, crosscheck everything and incorporate it into the main filing system, with header files, all reports and all memoranda put into her Personal Computer, which was networked via the central processing unit at Whitehall to Westminster, and therefore accessible to each member of the Committee in their own offices when equipped with the overall file name. This had to be eight characters or fewer; they tossed ideas around which became blacker and blacker, from "Doomsday" through "Pocalyps", and finally settled on "Azaleas" at Andrew's suggestion. For their individual security entry codes, each scrambled another flower name, Jasmine choosing something completely different from her own. Hacking was such a popular computer sport...but few hackers would be equipped with an endless list of the Latin names of plants, so that with only a modicum of luck, even if they found "Azaleas" they would never crack the entry names.

"It's rather sad" commented Andrew as they all left the meeting room "to be spending time working up secure systems, when the whole point of the thing is to amass and analyse information so that everyone knows exactly what the situation is; still, we can't risk half-finished reports leaking out. Needs must. Thank you all once more; have good weekends; see you same time next Thursday.

But they would see him sooner than that, albeit not in person. Terry Aitken called him in the middle of a very intense meeting the following morning: Andrew, Judy and the Senior Administrator were crouched over Judy's P.C. examining the file header names of the Ministry's existing database of AIDS information and statistic. Whatever they wanted to copy into their own database had to requested, in triplicate, using the file name, the document number and the reason for the request. It was going to take days, especial as significant batches of AIDS statistics were incorporated in more general reports such as general practice returns, public health surveys, and so on, so that they would have to be identified, isola and evaluated before being incorporated into Andrew's figures. Judy's long service with the Department made her involvement invaluable.

Terry's phone voice was bright and charming.

"Good morning Dr Douglas! Lovely day! Well, it's started: requests all over the place for you or the members of the Committee. The Prime Minister has asked me to suggest to you that you might like to consider one particular request first: it's ITV's early evening chat show, Cross Currents. Have you seen it much? Good; Simon Bycroft is fairly genial, it's a mixed batch of guests usually, the audience is around nineteen million most evenings of the week. How do you feel about it? Great. They want you on Monday evening coming, would that be...? Grand. In which case, you and I should perhaps meet over the weekend to discuss...you know. Lunch? Sunday lunch? Excellent. If you could fax me over the sort of things you'd like to cover in the interview, we can go over that on Sunday. Do you like roast beef? Then let's make it the Tenderloin, on Piccadilly, shall we say two-thirty? Splendid. I'll book: see you in the cocktail bar. 'Bye!"

The Cancer Committee had sat for almost two years, and nobody had ever asked him onto a television programme on the strength of that: AIDS, he reflected wryly, was either more 'media sexy' or more worrying. Still, he had done several serious radio interviews and many talks, so he was only slightly nervous. Till Sunday lunchtime. In the nicest possible way, Terry Aitken shredded every item on his Friday fax to her, and 'suggested' instead some totally bland, featureless, contentless remarks he might like to prepare, to have ready'. It was clear from her total confidence that these came straight from Downing Street, and a cold feeling came into Andrew Douglas as he realised just how valuable a bland front man could be in his position: keep the public happy while somewhere else, somebody else was doing the actual planning. In absolute privacy. Seasoned trouper that he was, he smiled pleasantly at her, nodded affably, and kept his darkling thoughts to himself.

One of Simon Bycroft's assistants met him at the studio door at five thirty and led him straight to Hospitality to meet the man himself. He was not yet changed; his other guests were Mark Tyme, the rock star, already resplendent in a bodysuit of primrose stretch velvet and tumbling locks of shock-white hair, and Richard Makepeace, a mathematician who was enjoying a surprising success with a slim volume entitled "Damned Lies and Statistics", looking extremely nervous in a tweedy lounge suit. Bycroft, in jeans and jumper, was chain smoking and attempting to be hospitable, leading his guests to the coffee and sandwiches, calling them warmly by their first names, but staring through their eyes into some distant galaxy wherein the studio lights failed, the guests all died of apoplexy before coming on, and he was left with nothing to talk about. He left after twenty minutes, replaced by a perfectly cool and pleasant girl who went through the running order and the timings and all the details, then walked them down to the studio so that they could rehearse their entrances and be sure of which chair to sit upon when they mounted the dais.

After a short stop in Makeup (which Mark Tyme did himself to extreme effect, and both other men refused except for the mandatory powdering to stop their sweating brows and noses from gleaming like beacons onscreen) they were put into a small chamber near the studio, in which was only a television monitor and some none too comfortable chairs. "The sweatbox" announced their guide "Somebody will bring each of you out in turn, at the right time, to wait for your cues; don't worry if you've forgotten them, we remember them! Break a leg, all of you!"

The monitor was permanently tuned to Channel 3, so that they could watch the programme as it progressed; just as the previous programme was finishing, a man with headphones and a clipboard arrived and took away Mark Tyme.

Richard Makepeace turned to Andrew and remarked gloomily that he hoped the tumbril taking them to the studio would be comfortable. They grimaced at each other, and watched the screen anxiously. The quiet, thin, rather angular young man who had just left them suddenly erupted on screen as a glowing, dynamic, attention-compelling star. This did not help their self-confidence.

Richard disappeared next, and Andrew watched in some amusement to see how he would be transformed by the cameras. Somehow it was the other way round; the pleasant, quietly dressed, perfectly ordinary soul was now a rumpled, craggy eccentric who could hardly bring himself to look anyone in the eye. What, then, would happen to Andrew Douglas? Well, he'd see for himself on his video recorder, when he got home. But nineteen million, dear God, nineteen million people! would see first.

He was taken to stand behind the disappointingly tacky 'flats' which comprised the back of the studio set, where his right elbow was held by the young man with the headphones and the clipboard until at some cue which he himself did not hear, he was propelled encouragingly towards the long walk in from stage left, to thunderous applause, and a firm handshake from a suited, confident, charming Simon Bycroft.

"Well Doctor Douglas, let's get right to the heart of the matter: what are we going to do about AIDS? Or...are we all worrying too much about it? What do you think?"

"I think...that we need to know as much as possible about it, before we come to any new decisions." Terry Aitken would be proud of that one.

"And that, really, is what the Committee is for, isn't it? To find out. But what happens once we've found out? What do we do then? Obviously it depends on exactly what you DO find out. But what kind of measures do you think might be involved?"

The questions rolled on, none of them possible to answer definitively, all speculation until "How many cases of fullblown AIDS are there in Great Britain right now, Doctor Douglas?" to which he answered "Just under fifteen hundred, as of last month's figures."

A derisive snort came from Mark Tyme. "Excuse me for

butting in, but the good Doctor here must know at least as well as I do that it's not the AIDS figure that matters: it's the HIV positive figure. And that, as of last month's figures, which I happened to read, was just about two thousand five hundred and THAT is only the cases we know about."

"Interesting" said Richard Makepeace, with a small, apologetic laugh. "That means we've got about twelve years before every man, woman and child on the planet has got it, then, doesn't it?"

Not a word was heard. The studio audience went very quiet.

"You see" he went on, deferentially addressing his remarks to Andrew "to get the real public health figure from the number of known cases, you multiply by eight; that's on the conservative side, but let's be conservative, for the sake of argument. That gives us actually twenty thousand HIV positives in Britain right now. Cases double every year or so in the U.K. every six to eight months in the States, by the way, but let's keep it simple at doubling every year, here. So: next year, we have forty thousand cases; that means, after ten years, twentytwo point five million...twelve years, 90 million. More people than there are in the U.K. altogether! So somewhere round about the eleventh year, every single person in this country...and presumably in every other country... will be HIV positive. It's a rather simple calculation. I'm surprised you Government bods haven't worked it out before. Let's hope someone finds a cure well before Year Eleven, eh?"

The total silence in the studio which followed was echoed in nineteen million homes across Britain, and, for different reasons, in several Government offices. Simon Bycroft was, like everyone else, completely at a loss for words. Up in the gallery, the director stared wild-eyed at the various screens showing different angles of the four immobile, silent people on the dais. She was just about to shout "Roll credits!" and leave the continuity announcers to sort themselves out after a ten minute under-run, when Andrew Douglas finally found something to say.

He just pointed out, very gently, with a little quirky smile, that millions upon millions of the population are either too young, too old, too in love or too disinterested to be dashing about having sex with whoever takes their fancy... and are extremely unlikely to be sharing needles unless at a sewing circle. So however many years go by, there will always be millions and millions and millions of us around. Then, as if born to it, he turned and talked straight to camera.

"But that does not discount how serious it is, or how important it is to find out what is really going on. You, YOU watching, know more than I do about that, at the moment; I only get to see statistics....facts and figures about the known cases. We need to know about...well, what DO we need to know about? You tell me. Your experiences, your fears, your problems, your ideas. I promise I'll listen. And I'll make SURE things are done right. I have a family: I'm frightened for them, just like you. So tell me what YOU know, and I don't. Please. 79 Whitehall, London, is the address. Write to me. Any time."

Bycroft started to talk but was interrupted, and then drowned out, by a rising tide of clapping from the audience. And cheering. They rose to their feet and applauded and roared, louder than they had for Simon Bycroft's entrance, louder than they had for Mark Tyme's big number. They had found a champion. They trusted him. At No.10 Downing Street, the Prime Minister tore up the memo he had started only moments before, asking Andrew Douglas for his resignation. He was nothing if not flexible.

The end of the programme was scheduled to be Mark Tyme and his band playing out with their newest single release; but as the audience clapped, he slipped away a few seconds ahead of time, to have a quick word with the band. And as the spotlight found them, he announce that instead of "City Lights" they would perform a song only just written and due for release in a month; all royalties were earmarked for AIDS research, split between the AIDS Information Trust and Rock Against AIDS. The title of the song was to be "Keep Your Love Alive", and he asked the audience to forgive them if they were a little under-rehearsed.

Up in the gallery the director panicked anew. "Get ready to roll titles, get ready to cut studio sound on my command...if this bastard starts swearing, I'll slit his throat...this isn't the song we okayed....God knows what it'll say..."

But this song was not Mark Tyme's usual raunchy style at all. It was sad, sweet and haunting. It was a ballad. It was a plea for care and for caring. It said "one love is all you'll ever need" and it said "love is for living, keep your love alive" and though there was not one direct reference to sex or condoms or anything remotely offensive to an early evening audience, its message was pure, clear and simple: safe sex keeps your love alive because it keeps your lover alive. The director let it all through and rolled the titles on time. And now, even more dramatic than all the previous applause, the audience was silent as the band finished playing.

Afterwards, in Hospitality, Simon Bycroft was elated. The show had been a stunner, the audience rivetted, wonderful, wonderful, well done, everybody. All three of his guests looked at him curiously, wondering if he had absorbed anything at all that had happened tonight. He reddened slightly under the unified gaze, and burbled a bit about the real serious stuff and what good stuff it had been...he had, of course, been talking purely in television terms, but of course he realised that it had all been pretty...heavy. His guests helped themselves to wine, sipped quietly, looked at each other, waiting for someone to say something. Simon chattered inconsequentially, then, embarassed and out of his depth, and consequently getting rather ratty, left.

"I liked the song" said Andrew. "Very..."

"Sixties?" grinned Mark Tyme.

"Sort of...in terms of the rhythm and the sound...but not at all in terms of what you were saying. In my day we thought love was the answer to everything and we worried about the Bomb. Now...you have to worry about love. It's hellish. Listen; I know about the Trust, of course, but Rock Against AIDS?"

"Well, mostly we just raise money for the Trust...but we do a bit ourselves too. We get a lot of kids at rock concerts, you know? Young kids...young adults too. And a few geriatric hippies! We put leaflets inside the t-shirts and stuff we sell at the gigs...inside some of the album sleeves...that sort of thing. It all helps."

"That's...excellent" said Andrew, concealing his surprise as best he could. "A perfect target group, all collected together...excellent." Mark Tyme gave him a very oldfashioned look.

"And so surprising, too, eh?" he grimaced. "For a bunch of longhaired weirdos, gays, and druggies? Mm?"

"Not at all! After all" countered the good doctor, with alacrity, "gays and druggies are almost as much at risk as madly promiscuous heterosexuals!"

The two of them squared up to each other with wooden faces until Mark Tyme grinned infectiously and they shook hands, with a 'You'll do!' look on both faces. The little mathematician smiled aimiably at them over the rim of his fifth glass of wine.

Someone brought them their coats, someone else brought in Mark's band, the Tyme Machine, who evidently didn't quite merit wine and hospitality yet. It was clearly time to go. Goodbyes were exchanged, but somehow Andrew Douglas found himelf being driven home in a fluorescent yellow Transit with gothic decorations in scarlet and black.

He took home with him a card bearing Mark Tyme's real name and private telephone number, with an open invitation to come and talk about Rock Against AIDS, and the Trust, whenever he wanted: Mark (actually James Trewren) was fairly sure that the Trust could be persuaded to open its computer banks to Andrew, for more up to date street information than the Government probably had. It was a potentially invaluable link. In his other pocket was the business card of the little mathematician, who had pointed out that there are more than many ways to interpret statistics, and if Andrew ever needed a fresh viewpoint, to give him a ring.

As he turned the key in the lock he was conscious of immense weariness. It had been an incredible evening, and though it was only half past eight, he was really exhausted. He'd send out for a pizza and head for bed as soon as possible. After he answered the phone.

"Callum? Good to hear from you, son. How's college?"

"Great, great..."

"Results in yet?"

"No, a few days yet.."

"So to what do I owe the honour of this call, and how much is it going to cost me?"

"Dad! Mind you, if you've any spare...no, honestly, you've just bumped up my street cred here, we were all watching you in Halls....great stuff...and the other thng is, I've got a brilliant summer job on a hydroelectric scheme in Uganda! Fantastic money, guaranteed sunshine, and really good experience for an engineer, just great. Howzat?" The boy's voice was bursting with pride and excitement. But Andrew had difficulty keeping his own voice firm.

"Uganda, son? Well, that's...it sounds like a good job...just..."

"Oh Dad, don't worry! I'll get all my jabs! I'll look after myself! And before you give me any grief about AIDS in Africa, I know all about it and I won't take any risks, honest! Please Dad, be happy for me, won't you?"

"Of course, son. Of course. Congratulations. So, you liked the programme, did you? Were you listening to it as well as watching it?"

"Sure. Hey, imagine meeting Mark Tyme like that! I mean, you know, like in your day I suppose it would be meeting John Lennon or Mick Jagger...wow!"

"Yes. Actually he gave me a lift home. I rather liked him. We'll be meeting up again, sometime soon. A very responsible young man."

"Oh, Rock Against AIDS? Yeah, yeah. Just don't shake his hand, eh Dad? I mean, the guy's a raving...er...gay. Bring your own cup and fork!"

"Pardon?"

"You know...bring your own...oh come on Dad, don't cross examine me on every word, please!"

"Callum, you don't believe this kind of nonsense do you? You can't get AIDS from a cup or a fork, or from shaking hands either! And if you could it would come from a heterosexual just as easily as from a homosexual. Surely you know all this?"

"Oh, Dad. I'm sure you're right. It's just what people say, you know?" His tone was distant, his interest in the conversation finished. "Anyway; I'll be passing through London in three weeks, can I stay with you overnight before my flight? Thanks. Nice talking to you, Dad. 'Bye."

Damn. How did he manage to louse up every time he spoke to Callum? He ended up biting his own tongue afterwards, always having said the wrong thing, been too serious, too caring, too concerned. Ruth, how did you always say the right things so easily? He was always your boy, really. Now I'm failing him.

His musings were interrupted by the telephone ringing again; this time it was Judith, next it was Jasmine Elliott, then Harold Sweeting. Judith and Jasmine applauded him, but Harold Sweeting barely concealed his rage as he 'suggested' Andrew he might like to meet next morning for a 'debrief'.

"I'm sorry, but I have a very full morning tomorrow: three people coming to see me, and a lot of computer searching to catch up on. But I'm sure I can slot in a debrief later in the week...shall I buzz you tomorrow with some possible times?"

"Listen you supercilious bastard, you'll come and see me tomorrow nine sharp or I'll tell the P.M. you're being evasive. And as for your performance tonight, blue-eyed boy, just remember that people who play with matches sometimes get burned."

"And sometimes, they see the light" countered Andrew pleasantly. "If it's so important to you to see me tomorrow morning, dear chap, I wouldn't dream of disappointing you. I'm flattered, really." Okay, that was childish, but he was furious, and satisfied when the line went dead without any farewells.

He slept badly again.

And rose with a strong feeling that this was not going to be his day.

His principal Intray was swamped with faxes from people responding to his call for information, on Cross Currents. Yards of fax were arriving, and both the Administrative Assistants were already, by a quarter to nine, permanently manning the phones for incoming calls. Judy had his coffee ready, refused to let him get started on all this until after his first meeting, commiserated with him on his debrief with Sweeting and promised to rearrange his morning's appointments while he was upstairs.

"You can tell Him Upstairs that almost all this" she waved generally around at the piles of fast-accumulating messages "is extremely positive, welcoming, and encouraging: from scientists, researchers, Public Health bods, and Joe Public in his hordes. Your speech obviously went down very well, struck a chord. Oh, one call this morning in particular; chap who says you know him. He's in Health Administration in Kent now, says you were at Edinburgh University together and his name was Joseph...Cromwell, yes, and he said he wants his Kinks album back?"

Andrew very nearly giggled, and Judy saw in his face the young student he once had been. Though it was now five to nine, he insisted she gave him Joe's number, and called him.

"Joe Cromwell, you misbegotten beatnik you! How are you?"

"Pining for my Kinks album, thank you very much" came the soft Welsh lilt. "Saw you on the telly last night: nice to see your friends once every thirty years or so, even if it's only on the television. Even when it's people who steal your Kinks albums."

"Oh, bugger your Kinks album!"

"No thank you. The hole in the middle is too small even for me."

Andrew roared. "You really haven't improved with age, have you? Listen, I'm on my way upstairs to be carpeted for last night...I'll call you for a long talk later, just wanted to say hello for now."

"Okay, love to Ruthie: 'bye for now: good to hear your squeaky voice again!"

Ouch. Of course, Joe couldn't know about Ruth. It took the edge off his pleasure, knowing he'd have to tell him when they next spoke. Still, he was delighted to be speaking to Joe again: that roar of laughter had been the first for a long time. Joe was a natural comedian as well as a very bright young man....no, not a young man any more. Joe, fiftyfive? Impossible to imagine.

Somehow he was not surprised to see Terry Aitken waiting for him in Harold Sweeting's office. She looked like a day-old duckling in a temper, so young, so soft, so furious. He wanted to pat her head and say There, there...and he swallowed a grin imagining her reaction. He wasn't sure whether he was being paternalistic or just chauvinistic, but was quite sure he would be accused of both. It never occurred to him that he was already rather fond of this woman. He just knew that for some quirky reason he was quite looking forward to this morning's clash. The idea of fencing, of the clash of steel, of verbal thrust and parry, was quite enlivening. He didn't know he was smiling at her. And therefore didn't know why she blushed and rearranged her legs and looked away.

Sweeting was standing with his back to them, staring out of the window at Horseguards Parade. He turned and smiled icily and began to pace slowly, taking sips from his coffee cup calmly and quietly. His tone was measured, almost pleasant, certainly trying to be pleasant.

"Well well now. I hear you've had a flood of responses already, downstairs? Good, good. Perhaps it was all for the best after all. Your...performance last night. Not so much playing with fire after all, more...playing with the beam of a torch, which....illuminates us as a caring Government, a caring Party. It seems to be working out quite well after all. Don't you think, Miss Aitken?"

His body language was shouting rage; Terry, well trained in this, and Andrew, a doctor, both read him loud and clear. A brief glance of mutual uncertainty flashed between them. She opened her mouth but Sweeting cut across her.

"I'm quite sure you agree. So forgive me if I sounded a little hasty last night, old chap. It wouldn't do at all for we three to fall out, now would it? Miss Aitken is here to help you, and so am I. We're all on the same side, after all."

"The side of the public?" asked Andrew innocently. "Indeed we are."

"Yes, yes, them too, of course. Naturally."

"Can I ask a question?"

27

"Of course."

"What the mathematician worked out last night..twelve years till theoretically everyone on the planet is infected...did you know that already?"

"Well of course, for what it's worth: what you said in reply is perfectly correct; it's theory, not reality. My mother, who's eightyseven, is not going to get AIDS. Nor am I. Nor is anyone who's faithful to their spouse. There's no need to panic: sensible precautions are what's needed, not panic. You defused him beautifully. He was just a number cruncher, no idea of reality at all."

He paused, and the body language proclaimed that he was doing his utmost to contain and disguise his anger.

"However...from now on I would be most obliged if you and Miss Aitken here would kindly get your act together for your public appearances. On this occasion it did no harm that you departed from the approved script last night; nobody is trying to muzzle you or feed you your lines, but it would be helpful if what you said reflected, even just vaguely, what the Government's OTHER spokesmen on health were saying, don't you think? Both of you?"

The day old duckling hung her head in apparent contrition, and she and Andrew mumbled appropriate responses. Sweeting graciously permitted them to leave, and they retained their dignity until well out of his hearing, whereupon they snorted with mirth and grinned largely at each other.

"Ouch ouch ouch! My knuckles have just been rapped something awful! Daddy IS in a paddy today. I think I'll write a hundred lines 'I must be a better Media Advisor in the future' and hand them in to him tomorrow. He'd like that."

"Almost as much as he'd like my resignation. And he's not going to get that, either. Would you have time for a coffee in my office, Miss Aitken?"

"I would, and anyway I've a list the length of your arm here of people wanting to interview you. We can go through them and sort them out and..."

28

"Work out what I'm going to say?"

"DOCTOR Douglas! Would I waste my time? Twice? No. But we can work out perhaps what you'd like to say..."

"Look, I'm truly sorry if I got you into trouble last night."

"Don't be. Oh, SweetiePie roasted me a bit before you arrived this morning, but I can handle it."

"Roasted duckling? Dear dear."

"Pardon?"

"Nothing, nothing..."

There are few things lonelier on God's green earth than a weekend in London if you have no family or friends there. Andrew Douglas felt no great urge to spend time, effort and money travelling to St Fillans to be lonely there for the weekend instead, and so intended to stay put mostly, making desultory efforts to go to concerts and listen to the radio and eat particularly well. These few pleasant ideas were not enough to stop him accepting Joe Cromwell's invitation to spend the weekend at his farmhouse near Broadstairs.It was a 'sympathetically restored' brick farmhouse, with oak beams and an inglenook fireplace and children and dogs yawling around somewhere in the background, and clutter and cushions and ramshackle wooden sheds at the back which were allocated to general messing about with wood (Joe) and potting plants (his wife Shirley) and a gang hut/Wendy house (for the kids and assorted short visitors). Andrew was delighted by all the friendly family warmth, and was welcomed into it, yet at the same time it pierced him to the marrow when he compared Joe's home life with his own arid existence in the flat. Even the plump and rumpled Joe, the short balding middle-aged man with the dentures, looked the picture of contentment standing with his arm around the waist of his equally plump and extremely pretty wife. The two men eyed each other, and Joe grinned and said "Yes, you've worn better than I have, haven't you? And a suit, boy, on a Friday night? By, there's posh for you!" He himself had on jeans and a t-shirt with indecipherable Welsh words which he proudly translated as proclaiming that the English are a secondclass race - but he made an exception for

Shirley.

He introduced Shirley to Andrew as 'my present wife' and was genially thumped by her as she explained that she was in fact his second wife though he was her first husband, and she planned to get it right next time round by choosing someone with a modicum of decorum. The two younger children were swiftly fed and bedded, and the older girl, a tall and stunning brunette, left for the local disco around half past eight, whereupon the adults enjoyed a long and leisurely supper round the big farmhouse table in the kitchen. Shirley was very understanding about the men's spending large portions of the time wallowing in nostalgia for times long gone at Edinburgh University; she had already heard most of the good stories from Joe, but politely listened and laughed all over again when Andrew repeated them and anyway his versions were not as monomaniacally edited as Joe's, so that Joe did not always come out as the hero of the piece!

Of course they talked of Ruth: Joe had known her slightly, through Andrew, and had always liked her.

"So that was why you got involved in the cancer committee?"

"I suppose so. Yes, of course it was. I don't know if it helped, in the long run. Dealing with it every day of the week. She never left my mind for a moment. Every time I saw a mortality and morbidity report I saw her name on it. Even now the very word 'cancer' brings her back to me, every time I hear it on the radio or see it in a newspaper. I think that's the worst part: I do remember the good times, of course I do - but I remember the two years it took her to die, I remember that most often. It hurts. It still hurts."

He accepted another stiff whisky and soda. Shirley gave his shoulder a little squeeze as she bade them goodnight, instructing Joe not to keep his guest up all night but make sure he got some sleep.

They moved through to the sittingroom and sat in oversized overstuffed fireside chairs with their feet pointing towards the empty grate, where Shirley had installed a big board which the children had plastered with cutout flowers from magazines and

30

comics, to make the fireplace pretty over the summer months. It was mawkish and silly and delightful.

"Okay Joe: now you can tell me why you phoned me up. After all these years. And don't think I'm not enjoying this: I am. But you could have phoned any time during the last thirty years; so why now?"

Joe took quite a while to answer.

"Why I phoned now is upstairs sleeping peacefully except for Megan, out at the disco. Three kids, all girls: eighteen, fifteen and nine. All their lives in front of them. Good kids. Much the same as your Callum, I imagine; ordinary kids, decent kids, drive you crazy but you love them so much you could burst sometimes. Kate and I never had any children - she didn't want them, and I was too busy working to notice either way. I met Shirley two years after Kate and I divorced, and suddenly my world was upside down. From a smart flat in Canterbury to this...wonderful messy place. From expensive restaurant dinners to homebaked bread and big roasts and rice puddings. From an empty spare bedroom to a house that's always bursting at the seams with life. God, I love it. And I don't want to lose any of it; any of them. That's why I called you now. Because you might be able to help."

"How help?"

"Help keep us all alive, boyo. Simple as that. You're the first man they've put up that I've got any faith in: I was right, too. You bloody shone on that television programme. I bet you got royally carpeted for asking people to write in to you ? Thought so. I phoned instead of writing, that's all. Another whisky?"

"I think I might need it."

"I think you might." He poured out generous measures for them both. "How much do you know about AIDS at the moment, would you say?"

"Not a hell of a lot, to be honest. A bit more than the average citizen, but a lot less than anyone who's been working with it. I've got a pile of books the length of Princes Street to read, but I'm so busy with statistics at the moment I've scarcely had time to find out much about the virus itself or how it works. God, anybody who

31

trained when we did would have his work cut out to understand the damn terminology, before you start to understand the intricacies. It would be bad enough if I'd stayed in medicine all the time, but I haven't seen a patient now for over fifteen years. I've got a lot of catching up to do, even on the fundamentals."

"Like?"

"Like...what the hell is a retrovirus? The HIV virus is a lentivirus - I know that means it can take a while to manifest in any symptoms - but a retrovirus? We didn't have any of those in my day."

"Briefly, it just means that it causes persistant infections because it gets right into the host cells and forces them to replicate the virus, endlessly. They weren't discovered at all till the seventies. Very nasty little buggers indeed."

"Look. Your children. With you as a father none of those girls are going to get AIDS. And neither are you or Shirley."

"You'd be surprised who gets AIDS. Nice respectable people. Intelligent people. People who only ever had one lover, but that lover didn't know, or didn't care, that he was HIV positive. You saw Megan! She's a beautiful girl, and she's 100% normal, her hormones are leaping about just like ours did when we were eighteen, she goes out, she takes a drink or two I expect, and some likely lad smoothtalks her into bed...and a couple of years later she's dead? How the hell do I cope with that? And right behind Megan there's Briony, and then Jane, dear God." He drained his glass and got up to refill it. "I don't suppose you've ever seen someone dying of toxoplasmosis...or PCP - pneumocystis carinii pneumonia - or Kaposi's sarcoma. But I have. Last year I spent six months on secondment to the Shanti programme in San Francisco. It's a support group for AIDS patients. They buddyup one volunteer to one patient so the patient can be cared for at home for longer. The volunteers shop and cook and give medicines and befriend the patient...it's a marvellous system. My august employers wanted me to have some sort of overview of AIDS as a public health problem, they're really quite enlightened: oh and of course the

Shanti system does have one other cardinal virtue: it saves public money by keeping dying people out of hospital. Very neat and tidy. I'm bitching, I know: I'm the Public Health Advisor, I ought to be looking at the economics of all this as well as the human costs. And I do. But I can't get those people out of my mind any more than you can with Ruth. They do not die well. They get uncontrollable diarrhoea and waste away to living skeletons. They can't breathe because PCP is a particularly nasty pneumonia; their skin is covered with lesions; they can hardly eat because the white fungus in their mouths is so thick it's difficult to swallow. Of course they don't all get all these things; but most of them get several of them, and more besides. That's AIDS; not one disease, but legion." He drained his glass again and set it down beside him. "And those are the lucky ones. The Shanti volunteers never forget, however ghastly someone looks, that there's a human being in there, a whole person, someone with ideas and fears and opinions and intelligence. The unlucky ones are the ones in hospital: some of the nurses are pretty good, of course, but a lot of the staff think, well, they're going to die anyway, what's the point of bothering with more tests and more treatments? Some hospital staff won't even go in the ward: I know, I know, they won't catch AIDS that way but you can tell them a hundred times and they still won't believe you. They think there's something you're not telling them. Or something you don't know. They're terrified. And who can blame them? I can't. I'm bloody terrified and I know the damn virus inside out, aye, and all its works."

Callum. Uganda. Jesus. Joe's face was saying more than Joe's words, and they were black enough. The man had seen horrors, and brought them home with him. How could he not be frightened for his children?

"The laugh of it is" continued Joe, despairingly "that it turns out they might have a point after all! All these years we've spent educating people so they won't run out of the room if an AIDS victim or an HIV positive walks in... telling them you can't catch it like measles, it's not contagious or infectious... and now we have to tell them almost the opposite. The bloody rednecks are going to have a field day."

"But..."

"Oh, you still can't catch the HIV virus very easily, certainly not by breathing in someone's breath or touching them...but what you can catch easily from them might kill you just the same. Once someone's got pneumonia, it's infectious in the normal way: but the real bastard is the clutch of new varieties of T.B. So the AIDS patients really are dangerously infectious, believe me."

"But..."

"But nothing. Those poor buggers' immune systems are so wrecked they can pick up and hatch just about anything, out of all the viruses and other bugs that lurk everywhere. They can't fight off anything. So whatever they get, it flourishes and multiplies and occasionally mutates inside them and then yes, then you ARE taking a risk if they cough or sneeze near you. Millions of germs sprayed out, and not just ordinary ones that we can throw off with antibiotics or antiviral treatments: some of them are Multiple Drug Resistant. We can't touch them. Can't even slow them down. It's kids and old people that are dying of these infections, mostly. And sick people. Anyone whose own immune system is a bit depressed. And now we're seeing clusters of these diseases right here in Britain. They're small clusters, thin, for now; but they definitely correlate with the known numbers and locations of AIDS victims. I just had a feeling you might not come aross those particular statistics. Because believe me, if ever there was something we need to sit on heavily, it's this little tidbit of news. You haven't seen what I saw in the States: gays being beaten up, their homes set on fire, people shouting for concentration camps for just about anybody who might be a carrier...anybody who's suspected of sleeping around is in danger, it's bloody frightening. We can't risk that happening here. But what the hell do we do? What are the morals of the situation? Christ man I'm sorry: I meant to sort of lead up to all this with you, maybe over a month or two. I'm sorry. Let me give you more whisky."

"No, thank you. But let me get you some. Here.." *Callum must not go to Uganda.* "We must do everything we can, for a start, towards finding the cure. Whatever I can do to help that along, I promise you I will do it."

Joe gave a short, bitter laugh.

"A cure? Now that would be nice. No, Andrew, nobody's wasting time on that avenue any more. Didn't they tell you? There will never be a cure. *There can never be a cure.* Once the virus is in there, in the central nervous system or the lymphatic system, or the brain, it's there to stay. It is so interwoven with the fabric of that system that if you destroyed the virus you would destroy the patient. There will never be a cure."

The shock of this, the utter finality of it, rendered Andrew speechless for some minutes. Both men sat still, each sunk in his own private vision of hell.

"Prevention, then. A vaccine. People are still researching that."

"Oh yes indeed. That's another doozy of a moral problem. You'll love this one. You can't test out the vaccine on animals because animals don't get infected with HIV. So you have to test it on humans, when it comes along, IF it comes along."

"Well...?"

"Remember your History of Vaccination. You have to start with a lethal dose, and then work backwards to find the minimum amount required to do the job."

"Dear God."

"Gotcha. Who do you use? Prisoners on Death Row in the States? Not enough of them. Each research lab, each drug company, might need thousands of people to use as guinea pigs. And large numbers of those will die. Those that don't die of the vaccine may die later when we infect them to see if the vaccine works. And if we don't allow that to happen, there will never be a vaccine. No cure, and no vaccine. Nice one, isn't it? Whose kids will we kill off so that Callum and Briony and Jane and Megan can live? Any suggestions? There are millions of orphans in Central Africa at the moment, their parents have already died of AIDS, and

I can tell you that eyes are turning in their direction right now."

"I think I'm numb. I can't think of anything and I can hardly feel anything except shock."

"Welcome to reality. I wish I could say you'll feel better in the morning, but you won't. You'll never feel quite the same again, if you're anything like me. But you have to keep going. Smile."

Megan came home then, bright-eyed and happy, shouting goodbye to some boy at the front door. "Oh Dad, I think I'm in love!" she smiled as she raced upstairs. The ache on Joe's face was plain.

Andrew didn't envy him any more.

CHAPTER TWO

High above the waste ground, in a nineteenth floor council flat, big beefy Jack McLeod was deep in the beautiful body of a lithe, lissom boy. The boy's bedroom was a dream of blue silks, with a huge blowup of Marilyn Monroe occupying the entire bedhead wall, and, strategically placed on the opposite wall, a large, ornate gilt mirror. The sweet reek of patchouli filled the air from the glowing incense sticks, and everywhere there were lights...candles and lamps, spotlights, filling the room with brilliance, ensuring that every aspect of love was highlighted, an additional delight for the senses.

It was bliss for Jack to be relaxed and take his time, urgent though his needs were: a world away from the furtive fumblings he was more used to, outside in the dark behind clubs and pubs, or down in the stinking 'cottages', the public toilets. Jack was more than willing to pay the £50 the boy asked for, just for the sheer joy of time to spend, and the unaccustomed luxury of being naked and feeling the smooth skin of the naked boy beneath him. This was what he had dreamed of, since he had begun admitting to himself that he had longings for young boys. He did not count it as infidelity to his wife, for after all, he was not with another woman. He had little enough interest in his wife these days, and certainly none left over for another woman.

The boy was a young god, and well practiced in his arts: Jack was about to reach his third climax of the evening when the bedroom door burst open, a flash of light glamoured his eyes for a moment, and his ears were assaulted by the raucous laughter of three men.

"Dearie me, he seems tae have lost it!" gloated one of them. And he had. He saw two rough-looking individuals, one with a Polaroid camera, and one very different, respectably dressed, authoritative man of around thirty years, with blond hair cut neat, and a handsome face. As Jack hastily wrapped himself in blue silk sheets, this man spoke, in a sad, pleasant voice.

"Well now. This is a bit of a situation we have here, isn't it? A bit of a compromising situation, eh? You busy buggering my young friend here, and him only sixteen years old: tell me, sir, have you been to jail before?" He made a moue of excrutiating pain. "Not nice, sir, 'specially your first time. Not nice at all." He sat down on the bed beside Jack, looking friendly. The boy, who had never given his name, shrank back under the covers, looking frightened. The other two men were going through Jack's clothes, very methodically, and emptying the contents of his wallet and credit card holder onto the bedside table. The quietly spoken man continued.

"Really, it's our public duty to have you put away, isn't it, sir? A menace to society, I would say, someone to break the heart of every loving mother. A corrupter of innocence. Is that Polaroid developed yet, Sandy? Thank you. Ah, now there you are, sir, you see? Clear as daylight. You take a very good picture, sir, indeed you do."

Jack sighed. His physical size and strength had always kept him from being a coward, but he was outmanoeuvred here, and there were three of them: he didn't count the boy. And the two gorillas looked like they were almost hoping he'd put up a fight.

"How much do you want?"

"Oh, that depends. We're very fair. From each according to his ability, you know, sir? John, the credit cards? Thank you. My, my. Gold card. That'll do nicely, eh boys? You're not short of a bob or two then, Mr McLeod? That's nice for you. Photographs, boys? Thank you. Ah: this'll be the lucky Mrs McLeod, then? Quite a stotter. And two kids? Gosh, you're very flexible Mr McLeod, aren't you, or are they the milkman's? What a fine business card, very nice bit of paper, that. McLeod's Haulage: excellent. How much salary do you take out of the company, Mr McLeod?"

Jack sank his head into his hands, in despair. "About thirtyfive thousand."

"You're in the wrong line of business, pal! I make more than that myself! Of course the hours are very irregular; for example, I have

38

another appointment tonight, so we'll hurry things along a bit, if you don't mind. How much savings do you have, sir?"

"It's all ploughed into the business; there's only my salary."

"I'll believe you, since I'm in a hurry and you do seem like a fine, honest sort of character. Now. Is his cheque book there, boys? Fine. I'll tell you what you're going to do, Mr McLeod. You're going to write me six cheques for £300 each, dated on the day your salary arrives in the bank. And Sandy here will write your cheque guarantee number on the back. Okay?"

"But surely...?"

"You're saying you might be tempted to cancel the cheques? Oh I don't think so, Mr McLeod, really I don't. Because if you did, this Polaroid would have to be sent to the constabulary, along with statements from the three of us as witnesses, and a statement from your wee bum chum here about how you persuaded him against his better instincts; and they would have to prosecute you for having unlawful sex with a minor. And then you would have to go to jail. No sir, you won't cancel the cheques. I have every faith in you. Ah, thanks John: your driving licence, Mr McLeod. Queensferry Court? Now there's an address to conjure with. Number five, Queensferry Court. Write that down for safekeeping John, will you? Just in case we ever need to get in touch with the bonny Mrs McLeod, for any reason." He patted Jack's knee. "Now you get yourself dressed and write out the cheques, I'll just away through to the kitchen and get myself a snack. Take care of him, boys."

The blond man walked unhurriedly out of the room. Trembling, Jack pulled his clothes towards him and got dressed as best he could. Through in the next room, the blond and placid Frankie Dunn was switching off the video camera which focussed through the ornate, gilt, two-way mirror, and rewinding the tape, stopping it every so often to look at it, without interest, just checking the picture quality. When it was finished, he took a chinagraph pencil from his pocket and scrawled "F. D." on the black plastic casing. He heard the door of the flat closing, and his associates came into the kitchen.

"Cheques? Thanks. Did you keep one of his business cards?

Good lad. Here's the tape Sandy, looks okay; send it to the usual distributor."

Sandy snickered. "Wee Alec's starred in mair movies than Michael Caine! Short life but a merry one, eh boss? One of these days some pervert's gonna beat him up up real bad. They're like that, some o' them. Shame, eh?"

"Tragic" said Frankie. "Mind you, it's an ill wind: they pay a lot more for snuff movies, eh lads?"

Before leaving, Frankie handed over £50 in cash, and a small clear packet containing white powder, to the cowering boy.

"We'll try The Daisy Chain tomorrow night, son, in Dundas Street. Some very well-heeled homos there, I hear. Now don't you worry, we'll aye be right behind you." He grinned. "Not that close, of course."

And the three of them left. The lift was not working, as usual, and the stairwell stank of stale urine, as usual. John and Sandy were given their instructions for the rest of the evening, as it was now only eight-thirty.

"Alistair's in the Weeping Willow tonight, with instructions not to pull until you get there: I told him about nine. After you collect there, go to the Ruby Dazzle in Pilton, and tail wee Margaret. Shona's going to be doing the late shift, uptown, in Hudson's. She said could you be there before eleven thirty as she's needin' her sleep, she's got school tomorrow. We wouldnae like to keep weans out of school, now would we? Questions might get asked."

"Right, boss"

"Sure, boss"

"Good lads. And tell them all to take the weekend off; I cannae be bothered. Christ, what a way to earn a living. If I see one more limp dick falling out of one more hole this week, I think I'll puke. Well, goodnight. See ye Monday."

"Oh, by the way boss, I nearly forgot my wee sister Rena's got a pal wi' a bit of a habit, needin' dosh: d'ye want tae see her? She's only fourteen. No' a virgin exactly, Rena says, but looks like it."

"Fine, John. Tell her The Green Fig tearooms, four o'clock Monday. 'Night lads."

They departed, and he paid a young lad a pound for guarding his Volvo Estate, and drove off. He took the shortest route out of the housing estate, and headed across town to what had once been the picturesque village of Corstorphine, and was now an enormous sprawl of identikit middlemarket bungalows, each with an eighth of an acre of ground, and almost every one sporting a swing or an inflatable paddling pool outside, where children were noisily enjoying the warm June evening. These were the children who would be sent to Gillespie's High School, or the Royal High, or Heriots, or Watsons... Frankie felt a bitter loathing rising in him. Then, remembering where he was going, he relaxed again. He might not have had advantages of that sort, but he had had one hell of a happy home life, despite the fact that his father had never been named and his mother had run off when he was still a babe.

His wheels eased up the short tarmac drive of the little manse; the minister had no car, so he parked easily. This was no gothic stone edifice, this manse, but a very ordinary bungalow purchased by the Church when they erected the small church which they hoped would serve the spiritual needs of this, the less affluent corner of Corstorphine, which had a mixture of council flats and maisonettes sprinkled among the serried rows of respectability.

He was greeted with pleasure by the minister's wife, Gwendoline Spencer, and taken through to the lounge, where the Reverend Peter Spencer was playing chess with Frankie's grandfather. Both men looked up and smiled pleasantly at Frankie, before going back to their game.

It was something of a surprise when the Spencers' daughter, Flora, brought through a tray of teas and biscuits: Frankie had hardly seen her over the last ten years, as she had gone straight to Stirling University on leaving school, and then onto her job as a social worker in Inverness. She was not exactly pretty, or beautiful, but what used to be called a handsome woman; tall, slender, with a curving, womanly figure currently hidden beneath jeans and a loose cotton top, and a thick wavy mass of hair, that wondrous true auburn shade which only Highland women have.

"Frankie! Good to see you. Working hard and living sober?"

41

"Mostly. By, you look wonderful. She's a credit to you, Mrs Spencer. A real credit."

Gwendoline dimpled and smiled, and passed round the refreshments. Frankie couldn't believe how much he found he admired Flora. She wasn't what you might call his usual type: yet her energy, intelligence and good nature were spiced up nicely with a winsome charm, and her voice was a pleasure to listen to.

Grandad won his game, and the two men joined in the conversation. Grandad cottoned on very quickly to Frankie's having taken a fancy for Flora, and he made fairly skilful attempts to bring into the conversation just how wonderfully well Frankie looked after him, and just how kind Frankie unfailingly was, and again just how exceedingly well Frankie's insurance business was doing, and in general what a splendid grandson he was. Flora grinned conspiratorially at Frankie, who made self-deprecating gestures and grinned helplessly back.

Grandad's wheelchair was soon folded into the back of the Volvo, and they took a loop so as to include most of Princes Street in their journey, which Grandad always liked to see, even thronged with summer people as it now was. In minutes they were driving into the garage of Frankie's mews flat, tucked away in the elegant Georgian New Town. The lift took them upstairs, and as usual Grandad insisted on making supper in their specially adapted kitchen. Frankie took a shower and put on his pyjamas and dressing-gown, feeling good, looking forward to Grandad's cooking.

Over massive plates of spaghetti bolognaise, washed down with good quality chianti, they talked of this and that until Grandad forced him to talk about Flora, which he really did not want to do.

"Look laddie, it's about time you got yourself a good lassie and settled down. Lookin' after an auld mannie is no life for a chap, much though it's appreciated, aye, very much. You've been right good to me since your Grannie died. She'd a'been proud of ye."

"You and Grannie were always right good to me too, Grandad, so let's have no more of your blethers. It's you and me against the world, Grandad, just like always. We'll be all right."

"All right isn't good enough for you, Frankie, you deserve the best, son, and that Flora is just about the best I've seen in a long time. She's back to stay, did you know that? She's got a job at Radio Forth, doin' current events programmes or something, so she'll be lookin' for a flat, and a boyfriend too, more than likely. Now you go after her, boy, you go after her. I'm sure her dad would be just as pleased as I would be. Do you know that Mrs Spencer said you were a better Christian than some as turn up in church every Sunday? Well she did. Of course, it would be even better if ye COULD turn up...oh I know, I know, it isnae your cuppa tea. Pity."

Frankie groaned, in an exaggerated fashion, and rolled his eyes.

"Yeah, yeah, I know. I promised I wouldnae nag ye. Anyway, like I was sayin', you go after Flora and dinnae hing aboot too long neither. She's a good catch. And when ye get married, I want nae nonsense; Peter Spencer will get me a good place in a nice wee Church retirement home, what with me bein' an elder all those years before the accident, and I'll be -"

"You'll be here with me, Grandad; married or not. Nobody of mine is ever going into a home. Not while I'm alive and kicking. Now hush up and I'll get the coffee give me your plate."

Grandad held onto his side of the plate.

"Frankie, son..."

"You and Grandma never put me in a home when I was a nipper and Mum ran off; you could have. You didn't. And neither will I, and that's final. Give me your PLATE!"

Grandad gave up his plate and briefly touched his beloved grandson on the wrist.

"We'll see. Are we goin' up tae Grannie's grave this Sunday, then?"

"Of course: it's the last Sunday of the month, isn't it? Right well. When I pick you up after church, we'll go for a bite of Sunday lunch somewhere nice, then take a run up to Roslin. Take a wander round Roslin Chapel too, if you fancy."

"That would be nice, lad, lovely. Talking of church, the Reverend didnae seem quite himself, the night. Somethin's eatin' him. I don't usually beat him that easily..."

Supper at the manse had, indeed, been a somewhat less affectionate affair than in Frankie's mews flat. Flora couldn't work it out at all; they had both seemed delighted at her news, when she arrived that day, pleased about her job, pleased she would be living in Edinburgh again. Yet they seemed barely to be talking to each other, though both were speaking to her.

In the kitchen, over the supper dishes, Gwendoline gave in eventually and told her that there was a 'bit of a wee difficulty right now' between her and her husband. It was over Gerry Hansen; this was something of a shock, for Gerry had been Peter Spencer's blue-eyed boy for years and years, since he was a lad. Now that he was studying Divinity at Edinburgh University, Flora knew that it had become her father's fondest hope that he would one day hand over his church to Gerry.

"What on earth has Gerry been up to, then?"

"UP your father's nose about as far as it's possible for a human being to go. Except that according to your father, Gerry isn't a human being. Not a real one."

It transpired that Gerry had, just a week ago, shown his old friend and mentor a paper he was writing for his tutor, to get his reactions and perhaps some help, a scene which had been repeated many times in that lounge. This paper, however, had to do with forming a movement called "Gays for God" in the Divinity faculty, and later, in the Church of Scotland itself.

Peter Spencer, outraged, tried to explain to the boy that though helping the undeserving was all very Christian, these people deserved nothing at all, and he should not be wasting his time and efforts in trying to help those crawling ungodly sinners. With a good deal of nervousness, Gerry had explained that this was not an act of Christian charity he was trying to organise, but an organisation which he himself, as a homosexual and a devout Christian, could join.

"And your father threw him out" finished Gwendoline, crisply. "And quite literally told him never to darken either this door, or the church door, again."

"But Gerry's always been gay! I mean, I always knew it: I assumed you both did too."

"I sort of guessed he might be, but it didn't bother me...I suppose I thought your father knew too. Obviously not. Anyway we had a raging fight about it. He started quoting Scripture at me, and I quoted Scripture at him, and it got very silly. I mean, does a moral decision really rest on who can find the most bits of Scripture to fit in with his point of view? Seventeen verses and two lines on your side, and sixteen verses and four lines on mine, so you're right? It's pathetic. We were pathetic. It's nothing to do with Scripture, our argument; it's to do with personal attitudes. We were both using the Good Book to support our own corners, and I hope your father feels as ashamed about that as I do. But I doubt it. I always knew your father was a bit of a hardliner, but this...I can't accept. And I won't support him. I went to see Gerry to apologise. Since then, your father has hardly spoken to me, until you came today."

She sat down, heavily, on a kitchen chair.

"He's going to preach against homosexuality this Sunday. And for the first time in all our married life, I don't think I'm going to be there. And that is hurting both of us."

So Sarah went on her own. She had always attended her father's church, when in Edinburgh; it had been hard to decide whether to support her mother or her father, and in the end, her mother persuaded her to go so that her father would have at least one of them there.

The Church of Saint Andrew was, as usual, half empty. The Reverend Spencer's oldstyle preaching had not captured the hearts and minds and souls of either the maisonette dwellers or the bungalow people; the former because now that they had a maisonette in Corstorphine, they aspired to more modern and attractive styles, and the latter because they had already been brought up on the kind of soft and gentle Christianity which made fewer demands than Peter Spencer's kind. Nobody slept when Peter Spencer preached!

45

This Sunday, he did not so much preach as rage; and his rage was doubled when he saw from the pulpit that Gerry Hansen was on his usual pew. He departed from his prepared sermon, and pointed at Gerry, and denounced him as a son of Satan, a sodomiser, a spiller of seed, an abomination in the sight of the Lord. Flora was angry and humiliated as she listened to the father she had always loved. And as the tirade grew in pace and in strength, Gerry Hansen stood up to reply. Quietly at first, then more loudly, to drown out the vituperative screechings from the pulpit, he said that he was leaving.

"Not because of -" he gestured towards the Reverend " for this is not the voice of God you are hearing, only the voice of a man, speaking words wherein all of Christ's message of love, charity, forgiveness and compassion have been forgotten. I will leave because I see on so many of your faces that I am no longer welcome here. After all these years... I will say only one thing before I go; try to remember that there are more kinds of love in the world than one, and that every kind of love is good. For love beatifies; the lover wishes only the welfare and happiness of the beloved. Try to remember that you are Christians, not dwelling still in the dark and dreadful teachings of the Old Testament, but living now, in the clear light and warmth of Jesus Christ and His infinite love."

His eyes drifted sadly towards Flora for a moment as he turned and walked out.

"This house of God is purged and cleansed by his going!" ranted Peter Spencer. "We are uplifted by this exorcism of Satan from our midst! Our fight against evil must never cease!" To his horror, he saw several members of his congregation *and Flora* stand up and walk out. But he was gratified by the intensity with which the remaining people gazed upon him, looking suitably uplifted by his righteousness. His elders, all the church regulars, and old Jock Dunn, were all there...and all nodding with approval, between themselves and then to him.

He gathered himself up in his swelling pride, and he carried on with the sermon.

Outside, the small band of renegades talked in shocked surprise, shaking their heads and patting Gerry on the back. Flora hugged him, and shook hands with the others to quell their doubts about speaking like this in front of the minister's daughter.   They disbanded and went their separate ways...Flora was tempted to invite Gerry home for a quick coffee and a visit to her mother, but the prospect of her father finding him there was fairly bad and she abandoned the idea. Instead, they went to a nearby cafe, and talked. Flora told him of her new job at the radio station, and what she would be covering in her principal programmes and, which she had learned only the day before, that she would be presenting ForthRight as well as producing it.

She asked him for help in sourcing stories and information about the gay community, for a programme on gay rights she was planning.

"I know I've got a hell of a cheek asking anything just now, after what my father's just done to you. But my contacts in Edinburgh are very limited, after all those years in Inverness. Can you help?"

He promised to do so: they hugged again, comfortable with each other despite everything, and Flora went home to tell her mother of the morning's events, and await the homecoming of her father.

Frankie was disappointed not to see Flora when he returned to the church to pick up Grandad. She was such a lovely girl, and he was in such a good mood, this beautiful Sunday morning. Earlier, while Grandad had been in church, Frankie had used a hammer to break the little finger of the right hand of a publican who had not paid his 'insurance' money this week, on the grounds that takings were down and he could not afford it.

Frankie had explained that the payments constituted health insurance as well as fire and damage insurance, and it was amazing how the man found he did have enough money to pay them, after all, rather than have his other pinkie crushed.

The roast beef lunch at Eddlestone, and the trip to Roslin, were most enjoyable, marred (for Frankie) only by Grandad's recounting of the exciting doings at church. Frankie would normally not have cared, but the Spencer family schism meant that Frankie's good works with his Grandad, and his Grandad's close friendship with the minister, might not now give him an advantage in his pursuit of

Flora.

That week, Peter Spencer prepared a sermon on one of his favourite topics: honouring thy father and thy mother. He illustrated this theme with many Scriptural texts, and he also prepared a junior version for the Sunday School teacher he had inducted to replace Gwendoline, in case she continued her ungodly boycott. Miss Dinnie was not young, but she was fond of children, and a great admirer of the Reverend, so she had agreed instantly.

Gwendoline was very hurt. She had only stayed away from the previous service because of the specific content, as well her husband knew; he seemed to be ousting her from the church, and made several sarcastic offers to find someone else to lead the Mothers' League, someone else to do the sick visiting, and so on.

Since he had swept home on a cloud of victory last Sunday, he had been more difficult to live with than usual. The slight tendencies towards self glorification which Gwen had heretofore overlooked with a fond smile had become more marked; his intolerance of everything modern, which she had shared in part, became more rigid; and he now banned tea and coffee from the manse, as well as alcohol, as they were also drugs and therefore displeasing to the Lord. She kept a secret supply of both hidden away; but his other excesses were harder to overcome. It was now impossible to argue with him without being accused of supporting the Devil. If she disagreed with Peter Spencer, it would seem, she disagreed with God.

And of course this did not only apply to her, but to Flora in particular and the rest of the world in general. The sermon on honouring your father and mother stemmed directly from Flora's decamping from church; this was made very clear. The Reverend was not really speaking to either his wife or his daughter now, and would rather do without salt than ask either of them to pass it to him at the table.

Neither of them were sure about going back to the Church of Saint Andrew, and eventually, on Saturday evening, they asked him outright. His answer was that if a disobedient wife and an ungrateful child did not feel they would be mocking the Lord, and if they were coming in a spirit of true penitence, then they should come.

"Perhaps" suggested Flora brightly, in suppressed rage, "you would like us to dress for an auto-da-fe, and whip ourselves with flails on the way in, shouting 'unclean, unclean, we disagreed with the Reverend Peter Spencer?"

"Hush, Flora" said her mother desperately.

"It would do your rebellious spirits no harm to humble yourselves before God" said Peter, in stony voice.

"Before *you*, you mean" replied Flora, getting up from the table and leaving the room. Gwendoline tried to pat his hand placatingly, but he withdrew it from her as if she was leprous.

The end of love is not always signalled by one event; usually it crumbles bit by bit, unnoticed, till it is gone. But if there was one moment in which the reverend lost his wife, it was this one. And though he was not aware of it, his mind being on higher things, still, Gwendoline was aware of her heart dying within her, and she grieved. In the end, she and Flora went to another church, and so did not see that Saint Andrews was rather more full than usual, and redolent with expectation.

Peter Spencer, always sensitive to the mood of the congregation if not always particularly responsive to it, ditched the prepared sermon and launched once again into his moralistic tirade, to the clear delight of the assembly. He welcomed all the newcomers, told them that in this church they would find clear sight and an uncluttered worship of God and all His commandments. After consolidating his remarks of the previous week, he went on to gather into his arms all sins of the flesh and of the spirit, to denounce each by name and damn it to all eternity. Somewhere along the way, it ceased to be the sins which he damned, and became instead the sinners.

Skilfully he played on the fears and feelings of his congregation, bolstering their own pride and sense of worth by damning all who were different to them. And if any amongst them faltered for a moment as the hate went too far, none would voice or show his doubt when that doubt marked you down as a lover of Satan.

His wrath was visited upon every kind of person, every kind of sinner, until the only way left to be was to be married, monogamous, nonsmoking, non drinking, eschewing drugs of all sorts no matter how socially acceptable they were, from heroin to caffeine; and refusing even to speak to those who were otherwise persuaded. If you were female then you were subject to your husband's dominion (it is not difficult to find Scripture to support this) and if you were male, why, you were always right, for man was made in the image of God. Working mothers were reviled; it was better to live in righteous poverty than to mock the Lord. Best of all, if anything was wrong with your life it was certainly not your fault; it was the fault of all the sinners around you, fouling up the good earth with their poison, screaming in demented laughter on their way to the fires of Hell. Conveniently, as all sinners were corrupt, there was no compunction to be merciful, or compassionate, towards people in dire distress which could be traced back to some action, or inaction, of their own. The truly righteous thing to do was to ignore them if they pled for help or, even better, take the opportunity to castigate them roundly for their iniquity.

He had his audience in the palm of his hand: even the choir and the organist were suffused with glory, and barely repressed a cheer when he changed the hymns to "Onward Christian Soldiers", "Fight the Good Fight", and "Who would true valour see". A local pensioner, walking her dog past the church, was startled by the volume of the singing which had never before seeped out of the hallowed precincts and into the street.

One of the less lusty singers was the reporter who had come in response to a comment from a relative (one of those who had walked out the previous Sunday). He managed half a column on it all in the following morning's Scotsman. The tone of the article was very, very careful not to take sides; but the word 'fundamentalism' did appear, and somehow the throwing out of a homosexual was linked to the recent announcement of an 85% increase in AIDS cases this last year in Edinburgh.

The worthy Reverend was thrilled by the publicity given to God's word, and intrigued by the reference to AIDS. This was another platform for him, this was worth at least one more sermon. He tracked down the report on AIDS statistics, and started reading up on the syndrome. And as he read he heard the voice within him giving a great clarioncall; this was his mission. Here was a huge number of real, bad, corrupt sinners; drugtakers, homosexuals and adulterers, all neatly packaged together by their common virus. *They must be expunged.*

He put this view to the many parishioners and outsiders who telephoned him during the week, either because of his sermon or because of the article in the Scotsman. The reaction was gratifyingly positive; and when one of them, a quietly spoken man called Albert Kennedy, suggested that Peter Spencer should stand up, take a lead, and start a movement to purify society, the good Reverend could only agree; however heavy that burden might be, he must bear it humbly and patiently for the Lord's sake. As he replaced the receiver he felt his whole being fill with light.

The few lunatics who phoned to express their disgust as his activities were only agents of Satan, and he brushed them off his consciousness as one might brush a fly from a white shirt.

Gwendoline never answered the telephone any more; she would have nothing to do with her husband's parishioners, nor his fans, not even his detractors. She spent much time visiting friends, or just walking. Peter Spencer did not notice.

Flora started at Radio Forth on the Monday and found herself crash landed into a heap of work. Her desk was tucked into a corner of the newsroom, which guaranteed a nonstop hum of noise and bustle, making concentration very difficult until you learned to filter it out. This took some time, and so when on her first day two of the reporters were discussing whether they should drag in "this arsehole, the Reverend Spencer" described in the Scotsman, she heard them with perfect clarity. She wanted to ignore it, but logically it would be only a matter of time before they found out she was his daughter. She must, therefore, say something, but what? Shrug him off and agree he was an arsehole? Or defend his

51

indefensible behaviour and actions? She was caught between a rock and a hard place. But she had to say something, or, later, they would think she had been trying to hide her relationship to him.

"Excuse me..." They looked up, surprised. "The man you're talking about: he's my father. I don't agree with just about anything he says, but he is my father, so could you...you know...maybe not call him an arsehole in front of me?"

You could just about see the dollar signs in their eyes.

"Your father? Wow. Er - sorry about the - but - your father? Tell us about him."

"Oh no you don't" she said with as much good humour as she could muster. "You want info on my father, you ask him, not me." And she busied herself with some of the papers on her desk.

It made her think, though. And just before lunch she knocked on the door of the Programme Controller, and asked if he would mind her using another name when she presented ForthRight, and told him why. An ex-newsman himself, the P.C. was visibly intrigued, and visibly trying to look concerned. He thought about it for a moment, and then pointed out that if her father ever got any more publicity, people were going to find out that she was his daughter anyway, and so a stage name would be pointless. But he left it to her to decide, adding only that once people DID find out, they would think it odd, perhaps, that she used a different name. He cited Carol Thatcher as an illustration of his point. She sighed, and acceded, and left. And he gloated to think how much more punch ForthRight was going to have if it was part of a battle between father and daughter. Which, given her remit and his predilections, it was bound to be. You couldn't, he reflected, *buy* the kind of publicity this would bring the programme, and the station.

Flora had only two weeks before her first programme, and thereafter a programme must be produced every week for a run of sixteen weeks. Each programme was to be an hour long, which meant a heck of a lot of research, and besides producing and presenting ForthRight she was expected to lend a hand in researching and producing other current affairs programmes and programme inserts.

"What do you do here when you get bored?" she asked, despairingly, of one of the reporters. He grinned understandingly.

"Easy: you start catching up on all the work you haven't done yet!"

At least she wasn't starting 'cold': she had got the job because of her frequent broadcasts on Moray Firth Radio in Inverness. The Social Work Department had volunteered her to do the phone-ins and the programme inserts on social work issues in the area, so she was used to microphones and studios and trailing cables and deadlines and time pressures, and coping with difficult subjects and sounding concerned but practical, and...most of the aspects of the studio work. On the other hand, she had never driven a transmission desk; she had never interviewed guests; she had never produced a whole programme. She had to learn all this, and how to cope with commercial breaks, and how to bring in the news from the other studio at the end of her programme, and a myriad of other things. Still, she did have two weeks!

During this first week, then, she tended to stay quite late in the evenings. Which suited her very well; being at home was not pleasant just now. Dad was ice, and Mum was chilled. Thoughts of a flat of her own became uppermost, in leisure moments; preferably somewhere close to work. As Radio Forth was in Forth Street, not far from Princes Street, this was an attractive prospect; there were still straggly bits of New Town down this way, not quite as expensive or elegant as the centre of town but still charming, and much of it in quiet side streets where prices had not yet rocketed. Frankie Dunn would be able to get her a good deal on a mortgage, through his Financial Services company, and her salary was reasonable, so she should have no great problem, especially when her flat in Inverness was sold. She was looking forward to her new life immensely.

For now, she took the bus home each night, taking work with her to provide an excuse for hiding out in her bedroom. She felt guilty for deserting her mother, but she really did need every hour in the day for her job at the moment, and Gwendoline assured her she understood perfectly.

Late on the Wednesday evening, Peter Spencer felt the need for some company, and visited Flora in her sanctuary, bearing biscuits and a milkshake to ensure his welcome. He was feeling a little sad and bereft of family life, and wondered if perhaps he was not being too hard on his wife and daughter. He was prepared to be a little more magnanimous. Until, placing the tray on Flora's desk without invitation to do so, he glanced at the papers thereon. And saw the research for a ForthRight programme, to be called Needlepoint.

She saw where his eyes had travelled, and rallied for an argument. But she got none. Raging silently, pushing her forcefully away from her desk, he seized the papers, ripped them up, and threw them out of the open window onto the front lawn. She moved to protect the rest of her papers: then saw his face and was, for the first time in her life, afraid of him. He wrenched everything out of her grasp, ripped it, and sent it after the others.

Wild-eyed and staring, he began then to rage. And though the noise brought Gwendoline racing through, he hurled her aside and ignored her.

"How could you DO this to me? You are DELIBERATELY setting out to give aid and succour to those very people I intend to root out and destroy! Do you hate God so much that you would go to all this trouble just to make a fool out of me on the radio? Well you're not going to do this to me under my roof, my girl. Telling junkies how to get free needles? How DARE you?"

"It's better than letting them die" she retorted, and instantly regretted it.

"Better for WHO? For me? For God? For decent people who can't send their kids to school without worrying about junkies selling them drugs? Better for WHO? Better for your career, maybe. But no daughter of mine is going to make her living out of evil. Oh no. You'll not laugh at God, or your father, in MY house: now OUT WITH YOU. Get out now. And you will never come back to this house again."

"I am not going right now" she tried to sound calm. "I'll go in the morning with pleasure. Try to be reasonable."

"Flora, you don't have to go at all: your father doesn't mean it!" her mother implored. "He couldn't throw his own daughter out at this time of the night!"

"I have the strength of thousands for the Lord's work!" he cried, and began throwing everything Flora had there out of the window: her typewriter, all her clothes, her books, everything. And all the while his wife begged tearfully and was ignored, thrown off his arm when she tried to cling to it.

"Now get out of my sight! Henceforth, I HAVE NO DAUGHTER!" he screamed as a finale, and physically pushed her out of the room, out of the house, and threw her amongst her things on the lawn. Her weeping mother tried to go to comfort her, but was viciously held back, and then the front door slammed shut and Flora heard the bolt being drawn inside.

She stood, shaking with shock, rage and anxiety for her mother. It was almost midnight, but there were lights on in the house next door, and she saw the curtains twitching. The MacBrides would have a field day over this: they had never been friends of the Spencers. She shuddered to think that they had probably heard most of the argument, certainly most of the screaming.

Thank God her father had thrown her shoulder bag out; she had her credit cards and some cash in it. She scraped up as many of her clothes as she could stuff into the one suitcase he had thrown, and moved the other things into the garage. It was a long walk to the nearest telephone box, and a long wait for the taxi, but eventually she was settled into an hotel room. A very expensive hotel room, for the smaller places were probably locked and closed for the night, she reckoned, and in July, Edinburgh is booked solid.

On her way to the diningroom for breakfast she picked up a Daily Record from the hall table. On page three, another half column about her father and, this time, she was included. One of the damned MacBrides must have phoned the story to the paper, in great glee.

"Fundamentalist Rev. Throws Out Radio Star Daughter" was the headline. And though the story was very thin on facts, it was rich

55

in supposition, most of it wrong. Working in radio was enough to brand you as bigheaded, slick, amoral and condescending; it was assumed that the poor loving father, having tried to win his wayward girl back to God, had been obliged to ask her to leave. Her being physically ejected, her clothes on the lawn, was conveniently ignored. *"Daughter Flora is making her career out of junkies, homosexuals, lesbians and unmarried mothers, said the Rev. We can't have that going on in the manse!"* There was more but she had not the stomach to read it: nor to eat breakfast. And with a sinking feeling she realised that arriving at work this morning was going to be hell.

In the event, the reporters were very sympathetic and supportive, which she had not expected, and the female ones in particular were kind about offering make-up or tights or whatever she had been obliged to leave without. The P.C. even dropped by to say 'take the morning off to sort yourself out'. So she did.

She found her mother in tears at the kitchen table; her father was out, meeting Albert Kennedy. Gwendoline hugged her fiercely, tried to persuade her to stay and talk to her father, bring him round, change his mind...but Flora was adamant.

"I can't stand it when he takes this new tone of his, that if you disagree with him you mock the Almighty. I don't know how you can stand it either! How can you support him? If he finds out I've been here in this kitchen this morning, he's just as likely to throw you out as not. How can you stay with a man like that?"

But Gwendoline was not sure enough about this herself to make any convincing argument, so they got on with the sad business of packing up the things in the garage.

"Listen darling" she said, as they parted. "You phone up Frankie Dunn; he'll get you a place to stay, nice and quick."

"Yes Mum. I was going to, anyway. I'll just do it today instead of sometime soon. Mum...it'll be a two-bedroom flat. You'll always be welcome, for a night or for a fortnight, or for as long as you like. Remember that."

But it isn't easy to walk out on a marriage after forty years.

Gwendoline couldn't see herself ever having the courage. Still, she smiled warmly, and hugged her daughter tight before handing over the bulging suitcases. The taxi was already waiting outside, so there was not much time for talking. Which was probably a mercy on both of them.

As she waved her daughter goodbye, Gwendoline felt an aching emptiness which was entirely new to her, and very sharp.

It was standing room only in Saint Andrews, that Sunday. And as soon as the children were taken off for Sunday School, after the second hymn, Peter Spencer excelled himself. He was absolutely in his element, hectoring and lecturing, selling tickets for Heaven to the elect in exchange for their total commitment to everything he personally believed in. And in these uncertain times, in these troubled and dangerous times, he offered a way of life which would sweep away the ungodly and make the streets safe again for the righteous.

It was seductive stuff. He put things in such a way that you could scarcely disagree with most of it and even if you experienced a slight hesitation as he went further and further, it would have been unreasonable to withdraw your support, for you had already agreed with all the planks with which he was building the new Jeruslem...or possibly a gallows.

"Can you walk along Princes Street by yourself at eleven o'clock at night? No, you cannot! And why? You all know why, don't you?" He raised his eyebrows as he spoke, and he pointed at them, and he nodded his head, and they nodded back to each other and to him, and murmurs of agreement were heard. "The drunks and the junkies and the prostitutes, the lascivious young people and the muggers and robbers, and the homosexuals out of the bars in Rose Street, say you cannot! It is their territory! The main street of the most beautiful city in the world, and you, you the taxpaying citizens, may not walk there when you choose! Is this acceptable? Is it?"

He looked fiercely at them, then sadly shook his head, and watched as they also sadly shook their heads. "No! It is not acceptable! Of course not!" He leaned heavily on the front of the pulpit. "You send your children to school and what do they find in the playground? Conkers? Dolls? Skipping ropes? No. Hypodermic needles left behind by the drug addicts! Needles which might have all kind of viruses on them! Is THIS acceptable?" He looked around and shook his head sadly again, and they shook their heads sadly again. "Of course not! What kind of parents would you be if you wanted this for your child? And then what do they learn in school? Reading? Writing? Arithmetic? Things to help them go out into the world and make a success of themselves? No! They learn swimming, and finger painting, and drama, and Social Studies...like how to be nice to the corrupt and the evil people in our society. Half of them can hardly read or write or add up a column of figures when they leave school, but oh, they can tell you all about the social problems in Brazil or Australia. And then when you want to give your children a treat, and you let them go to the pictures...do you worry till they get home? Do you?" They nodded in swift and genuine assent. "Of course you do! Even if they're at the Scouts, or the Brownies, you can't let them go or come back on their own, can you? Because if you do, the degenerates will get them! They like nothing better than an innocent and helpless victim! Never a day goes by without a child being molested or raped or kidnapped and murdered. Is this acceptable?" He lowered his voice dramatically, to a hushed whisper. "Well it's not acceptable to me. And above all, it's not acceptable to God. Is there any parent here, any human being here, any Christian here, who feels as I do that maybe, just maybe, we ought to be doing something about it?" He looked around with eagle eye, nodding all the while. The response was almost 100%. "Is it time we did something about it? Is it?" The nodding became faster. "Yes! Yes! I agree with you! So..." he paused. "So what are we going to do about it? We must pray, my brothers, pray as never before. But we must also remember a very wise saying: pray to God, sailor, and row for the shore. We cannot leave it all to God to do, when He has graciously given us arms and legs and hearts and souls and minds. We must do something about it *ourselves*. If any of you here feel as I do, then I offer you the chance to DO something: come to the vestry after this service, and we will talk."

More of the martial hymns followed, and there were no church notices. As the organ swelled, some of the congregation began to file out, into the small crowd of demonstrators and reporters outside (no reporters inside, any more: Albert Kennedy had thoughtfully suggested that the elders checked people for cassette recorders or cameras as they handed out the hymn books). The rest of them walked gladly towards the vestry.

Up on the vestry wall was a massive array of sheets of white paper, and at the top, the name by which the new group would be known. The name, which had been suggested by Albert Kennedy, was "People for Purity". Beneath the white paper were half a dozen chunky black marker pens, with which to write up all the names. And addresses.

———— • ————

Peter Goonan and Sarah Kepple seemed to spend most of their days sorting the piles of incoming mail and faxes into trays marked "Facts" "Fears" "Ideas" and "Cranks". Though Doctor Douglas aimed to read all the letters, it made sense for Judy to skim through each tray and put the letters in order of importance before they went through to him. The "Cranks" tray only got read when there was nothing much else to do, which was not often.

But this bright Monday morning, Peter brought her a letter which seemed to have alarmed him, and suggested she might like to read it immediately. She did; and took it straight into Andrew. After ingesting the first two lines, he checked the address and told Sarah to phone the relevant police station and inform them.

'Dear Doctor Douglas' it began. *'By the time you read this, I shall be dead, and therefore past all shame. Once I have posted this letter I am going home to take my life.*

I was recently diagnosed as being HIV Positive, despite the fact that I am a virgin, have never used drugs, and have never had a blood transfusion. Lately I have been feeling very run down, feverish, and chesty: it would be logical to assume that this is due to PCP, or one of the other types of pneumonia which AIDS brings along (since my diagnosis I have read everything I could find about my condition). I do not intend to suffer bravely, nor indeed to suffer at all. I have received nothing but kindness from medical people and counsellors alike, but in one respect they are, alike, implacable: they do not believe my protestations of complete innocence. But I assure you, Doctor Douglas, what I have told you is true. You asked us, on the television, to write to you. So I have. Because I want YOU to know my innocence, if no-one else. You will believe me because I have nothing to gain from lying to you, as I shall never see or hear your reaction.

I have always thought that suicide was the coward's way out. I suppose, then, that I am a coward after all. I'm afraid I simply could not bear the humiliation of any more people knowing what is wrong with me. My remaining family is few and far between, but I do have one or two good friends. And I find I cannot now look them in the eyes. And I cannot face it, Doctor Douglas, I cannot face it, the prospect of them finding out. Suicide may be a shameful way to die, but to my mind, dying of AIDS is more shameful still.'

It was signed by a Miss Freda Hislop, of 18 Fernlea Drive, Streatham, London, and dated as of three days before.

There was something about Miss Freda Hislop's letter which spurred Andrew Douglas to take one of the pool cars and go to Fernlea Drive himself. He left Judy to telephone the Streatham police station, and to tell them to hurry. If there was even the remotest chance that she might still be alive...

But she was not. By the time he strove through the South London traffic to get there, Miss Hislop was being stretchered out of her house in a body bag. The paramedics were in full AIDS gear, having been warned by the police: their moonmen outfits so grotesquely out of place in that dapper little street with all the lace curtains and neat front gardens. The white rubber boots, the white coveralls, the big white headgear...clumping past Miss Hislop's roses and her one small garden gnome, carrying Miss Hislop sheathed in shiny black plastic. The rest of the garden was swarming with police, and a small crowd was already gathering, peering and oohing and aahing.

Andrew sought out the officer in charge, to find out what he could. But the officer was not very interested in a Doctor Andrew Douglas, excepting that if Doctor Douglas had the letter in question on his person, then it should be handed over as material evidence, and if not, he should send it to Streatham Police Station as soon as was convenient. And no, Doctor Douglas could not go into the house for a look round, as he had no authority to do so.

Disappointed, Andrew almost turned away before he was hailed by the Police Surgeon, who was watching from a window of Miss Hislop's house. The Surgeon recognised Andrew from his tv appearance, and warmly welcomed him to come and look round as much as he liked, though there wasn't much to see.

"Johnston Carmody" he introduced himself, shaking Andrew by the hand as they met at the foot of the stairs. "I'll give you a quick guided tour, anything you want to ask, fire away as we go. This is the lounge. Not a lot to look at from our point of view."

It was an achingly respectable little room. There were lace doilies on the mantelpiece, and antimaccassars on the chair arms, and a handstitched tapestry firescreen in front of the grate, patterned with bluebells and foxgloves. On the walls, pressed flower collages and photographs of various cats. There were no books.

"How old was she?"

"Oh, just about or just over eighty, I should say. We're trawling round the local G.P.s now, should come up with her doctor soon, get all the details. The kitchen's through here. Food cupboard..." many tins of catfood, and a few tins of human food. "...and the cats' dishes; they'll be off to be analysed soon." There was reeking food still in two of the bowls, with maggots starting to crawl in it. And sprinkled on top, a strange kind of lumpy greyish smear. "We reckon that's crumbled sleeping pills there: I think the old dear wanted to take them with her, but they weren't having any. Cats are wily creatures."

"Where are they now, the cats?"

"Away to the pound. Vicious buggers, both of them...I suppose they were near starving...they'd been fighting between themselves, and one of them just about took the face off W.P.C. Collins. You must just have missed the pound van." They continued their tour. There was, as Carmody had said, nothing much to see. Just the odd touching something, like the bottle of lavender cologne on the dressing table in her bedroom.

"Ye gods. I didn't know you could still even get that! It's so...little old ladylike, isn't it. So delicate, and...modest. Carmody, how the hell does somebody like that get AIDS?"

Carmody scratched the shaggy black hair behind his right ear.

"God only knows; we probably still won't know after the autopsy this afternoon."

"Could I have a copy of your autopsy report, do you think? Thank you. Will it be ready this afternoon?"

"Steady on old man! I'll only be done recording it this afternoon, getting it typed up and checked over usually takes a day or two...oh, all right, I'll do my best. Give me your fax number before you leave. Of course I shouldn't be doing it: but, well, I suppose you could get some sort of official requisition for it worked out, to cover me, could you? Good man."

Andrew was glad to leave; he found himself unaccountably moved by the almost tangible presence in the house of the lavender and lace Miss Hislop, who liked Earl Gray tea and loved cats, and had several copies of the more oldfashioned ladies' journals in her bedroom, and three lacetrimmed full length white linen nightgowns, much patched, in her wardrobe.

The press were already at the gate, panting. There's many a young police constable who earns an extra pound or two by letting a 'friend' on the local paper know what's going on. They hounded and chivvied him for a statement, but he was not ready to make one.

"Ladies, gentlemen, there is nothing whatever that I can tell you at the moment. Anything to do with the police side of this, you must ask the police. That is nothing to do with me."

"But she died of AIDS, right, Doctor?" called one at the back.

"We can't possibly say anything about that until the autopsy report is completed. I'm sorry."

"We understand" began the sweet, earnest, deep and trustworthy voice of the girl reporter with the tv camera behind her "that Miss Hislop was an elderly virgin; can you tell us how she managed to contract AIDS?"

"No, I can't. I don't know if she had AIDS. I told you, I cannot tell you anything at all, not at the moment."

"Then when?" And the cry was taken up: when? when? when?

"The...um...let me see. If you come to the briefing room at the Ministry for six-thirty tonight, I will have a statement for you then. Now please, let me pass."

There were murmurs of extreme disgruntlement; six-thirty meant that only Channel Four could have it on their main news programme, and the regionals would get it onto theirs...neither BBC nor ITV teatime news would still be on air by the time Andrew Douglas said anything.

He had hardly got back into his office when Terry Aitken was on the phone. Many a young reporter keeps him or herself 'in' with the Government Media office by letting them know what's going on... She wanted to see him, once the autopsy report arrived, so that she could help him put the press statement together. He did not really see the need for this, but as it meant spending some time in her company, he agreed, and fixed four-thirty as the time.

It irritated him immensely that he was supposed to let someone else construct, or at least edit, his speeches. But she was empowered by the P.M. to do so, and he had little choice. He had a sneaking feeling that he ought not to be doing the press conference at all without official sanction: still, if this was required, doubtless the efficient Miss Aitken would organise it. He did not foresee any great palaver...there was no way Frieda Hislop, or anybody else, could become HIV Positive except by the established methods. While she was doubtless correct about being a virgin, and never having taken drugs, it was a reasonable guess that she would have had a blood transfusion at some stage in her life, for some small operation which she had managed to forget, possibly in America, or Africa, while on holiday. It is easy to forget things, at eighty years old. He expected the autopsy report to include whatever was on her medical records that would support this. There was no other possibility, really. The reporters would be disappointed.

He remembered Jasmine Elliott telling the committee how difficult it had been in her clinic in Harare to tell parents that their babies were dying of AIDS. In almost every case, both parents denied strenuously that they were carriers of the virus. Many said that they were regular churchgoers, as if this conferred some sort of protection. Denial was most people's first reaction, and not only in Africa. It was more socially acceptable to have terminal syphilis than to have AIDS...no other medical condition had ever had such a nimbus of immorality surrounding it, and some victims would continue to deny the diagnosis, right up until they died of it.

Andrew Douglas remembered a similar syndrome with many cancer patients, too. The very word was enough to produce a kind of creeping horror of the mind. And for the same reason, so many people did not present themselves to their doctors till it was too late, preferring to bear the fear and the pain rather than have someone tell them they did indeed have the dreaded cancer. Many of them would also refuse ever to utter its name, referring to 'my condition', or 'my problem', never, ever, to 'cancer'.

And so, thinking of cancer, he became sunk in thoughts of Ruth, again. And thoughts of Callum, who would be arriving the following night, for his overnight stop with his father on his way to Uganda. Andrew was still hoping to change Callum's mind about going. He had signally failed so far, but at least he had been able to persuade his son to take a T.B. booster among his vaccination shots, as a precaution, and now felt a little easier in his mind. He had meant to ask Sweeting about having T.B. boosters included in the official lists of recommended vaccinations for going abroad, but pressure of work had meant they had not met for some days now, and he had almost forgotten. He made a note on his diary to do so soon.

It was like a breath of Spring air when Terry Aitken arrived, almost an hour early, stating baldly that she was bored, and needed some coffee and some intelligent conversation. Her summer suit was of white chintzy stuff sprinkled lavishly with flowers, and her skirt was short and floaty, and her hair was glossy, and her sparkling eyes drew him into their depths again. Judy, when she brought through the coffees, looked distinctly disapproving to find Terry perched comfortably on the desk, with her legs crossed.

She refused the proffered digestives: "Obesity lurks within every biscuit!" she said, and her slender figure mocked her words. Judy, who liked to think of herself as pleasantly plump, retreated in medium high dudgeon, and Andrew suppressed a chuckle.

"You had TWO puddings, that time we had Sunday lunch" he pointed out.

"Ah that's different; you can't get fat from puddings, I have decided. Only from biscuits. I don't like biscuits, you see. But I do enjoy my puddings. It's a very convenient philosophy, you have to admit. Utilitarian."

"I must remember that, if you ever come round to dinner" he said and then couldn't believe that he had said it. It had been his twenty-year-old self who had said it, not his fifty-one year old self. She gazed at him, unperturbed.

"Am I coming to dinner, then?" Her voice was soft, and pleased.

"Well...would you like to? I mean, it might be a little boring for you..." Yes, that was definitely his fiftyoneyearold self talking. Damn.

She waggled an imaginary cigar in her mouth, and drawled

"That'sh for me to know and you to find out, shweetheart." And relented. "Oh, don't panic, you can retract your invitation. I won't turn up on your doorstep unless you actually want me to. Honest. I'm a nice girl really, guv." She looked so demure he could not quite swallow his laughter.

"Did anybody ever tell you you look like a young Sean Connery?"

"Is this the intelligent conversation you came here for?"

"Oh no: I never claimed to provide intelligent conversation: only that I enjoy hearing it. You start, whenever you like. I'm listening."

It was a very long time since Andrew Douglas had flirted with anybody, and he enjoyed it inordinately, to the point that he actually felt guilty when Judy came through about twenty to five, to point out that the autopsy fax had not yet arrived, and would he like her to telephone Carmody and hurry things along? He harrumphed a bit and said yes, thank you Judy, and sadly, that little stab of reality punctured the bubble and reminded them both of what they were supposed to be doing. Terry went down to the briefing room to supervise preparations there, and Andrew sifted through his papers to see if there was anything urgent he could be getting on with in the meantime.

Despite several tactful telephone calls from Judy, the autopsy report did not arrive till almost ten past six, by which time both Andrew and Terry were starting to get slightly panicked, it did not leave much time to prepare a speech. They skimmed through the contents together, looking for the G.P.'s statement which Carmody had promised to append, looking for the blood transfusion in Miss Hislop's history.

There was none. Miss Hislop had never been out of the U.K., in fact she had rarely been out of London. Carmody had done his usual thorough report, and there was a lot in it, but the salient points, digested from his report and the doctor's statement, were these: Miss Hislop was a virgin, she had never had any kind of operation or a blood transfusion for any other reason, and her doctor would stake his reputation on the fact that she was not in the habit of injecting drugs, and never had been. In short, there was no apparent way in which she could possibly have become HIV positive. But she was, and she had been right about her pneumonia. She had moved from being HIV Positive to having fullblown AIDS. Her death had been due to a massive overdose of sleeping pills, but she would not have lived much longer anyway.

"You can't go down there and say this" said Terry, suddenly. "You really can't. I'll go down and cancel the whole thing." She rose from her chair.

"What are you talking about? Of course I shall tell them what's in this: I said I would.

"No! You know what they'll make of this: I can't let you. I can't get clearance for it: the P.M.'s in Brussels and not to be disturbed, Sweeting has gone walkabout: I checked earlier: there's nobody to give us clearance. We have to cancel it. We do!"

"You must have know that hours ago."

"Yes, but...I expected to find a blood transfusion in there somewhere, or SOMEthing that would explain it. I expected it to be straightforward, in fact I expected it to be a nice ordinary case of AIDS. But it isn't so you can't go down there. I'm sorry."

"Don't be absurd. I invited them, and I shall speak to them. It IS a 'nice, ordinary case of AIDS' it's just that we don't know yet how she got it. That's all. And that's what I shall say. Just that we haven't got all the facts in yet, but I shall get back to them when we have - if they're still interested by then. It could take months."

It sounded reasonable enough. But Terry was uneasy, very uneasy, and the hairs on the back of her neck were prickling as they always had when she had been a reporter and a really big story was breaking.

"It's nearly half past. I'm going down now. Are you coming with me?"

Oh, what the hell. She had a strong prescience of unemployment anyway: she might as well be hung for a sheep as for a lamb.

"Okay. Lead on, Macduff."

"Lay on. It's 'Lay on, Macduff.'"

"Good old Shakespeare. Never use an ordinary word when an obscure one will do."

"It wasn't obscure when he wrote it."

"No. Really? Gosh!" But the flirting had no heart in it now.

The headlines next morning were writ large, and they were not good. "MAIDEN LADY DIES OF AIDS" was the most restrained one. Possibly the least restrained was "MYSTERY AIDS DEATH: IS IT INFECTIOUS NOW?" And they were all there on the Prime Minister's desk, to welcome him home after his red-eye flight from Brussels, where he had just failed to persuade the other E.E.C. Heads of State that harsher labour laws were the way forward.

There hadn't been a morning like this in the Media office since anyone there could remember; the phone lines were jammed. The internal lines were red hot too, with Ministers and Junior Ministers yelling down the phone, and, of course, the Personal Private Secretary to the P.M., informing Terry that the Prime Minister would see her at precisely 10am. One of Terry's Press Assistants, an old hack almost three times her age, smiled evilly at her as she left to keep this appointment.

"Been nice working with you, sweetie" he said.

"S'funny: I don't actually remember you doing any work, Frank. Still, good of you to care. It's what I've always admired you for: nothing." It was childish of her, of course, but she was close to tears, and attack always feels better than defence.

Andrew Douglas was already waiting outside the sanctum sanctorum.

"You've seen the papers?" he asked, sounding incredulous.

"Yes - and watched the breakfast news on telly, and listened to it on the radio on the way in to work. I bloody TOLD you they would do this."

"But how could they? I told them it might be months yet till we knew...?"

"They weren't listening by then. All they heard was that she was a virgin, that she was eighty years old, that she'd never had a blood transfusion and almost certainly never done drugs. Their eyes lit up at that lot, and that's what they reported. More or less."

"But there are a lot of forensic test results not in yet..."

"They don't care about that. They care about headlines, and copy, and selling newspapers and raising the ratings on their news programmes."

"But it's so bloody irresponsible. Especially the idea that the virus might have become infectious. That's virtually impossible, even for the HIV virus, however dazzlingly mutable it is."

The Prime Minister called them in.

——— • ———

At that precise moment, Andy Harrison was holding the hand of his wife Meg, in their terraced house in Nottingham. They had just finished reading their morning papers, and had planned a day out in the country, as it was their summer holiday fortnight and they were spending this at home. Meg was shaky, and her eyes were very wet. Andy soothed her as best he could, holding her close, stroking her brow.

"Are you sure about this, love?" he asked.

"Yes. It's the right thing to do. It's important."

"We haven't taken the time yet to think it all through."

"We did that at the time; that's why we said nothing. But now, we have some kind of a chance of being believed."

"A lot of people will still think..."

"I know. I know. But I need to do this, if you...?"

"God, I'm not sure. We're only young, all our lives and our careers in front of us. This could hurt us, Meg darling. Permanently."

"Do you think we're not hurting already?"

"You don't need to ask that. But at least, just now, we've got jobs, and a mortgage, and insurance...have you REALLY thought through all the changes we might have to go through, if we do this?"

"But we can PROVE; and anyway; oh, anyway, I just think we should."

She waited for his final word. Which was that he couldn't decide, and would leave it up to her. He wasn't happy about the idea, but he did see her point, and if she honestly felt she had to do it: do it.

Trembling, she looked through the Daily Mail for the Newsdesk number, and telephoned.

"Hello? My name is Mrs. Harrison. My son Darren died of AIDS a year ago, when he was only two and a half. And...neither my husband nor myself are HIV Positive, and the doctors said they couldn't understand it...pardon? Oh, yes."

She gave their names and addresses, their doctor's name, the name of the hospital where Darren had died...it was a long conversation.

As she spoke, Andy slumped onto the sofa, remembering all the nightmare weeks and months, the horrific death which nobody could prevent, their toddler wasting away so desperately quickly from a romping, giggling child to a tiny skeleton who screamed with the pain in his head.

Though the hospital staff had been wonderful with Darren, they had treated both parents with cool detachment, as if they had deliberately killed their own child. That, on top of the awful sight of Darren himself, had almost finished Meg. It had taken her almost six years to get pregnant, since their wedding, and she had been as ecstatic about it as Andy. No child had ever been more welcomed or more loved, more cuddled or more played with.

The hospital doctors had tried to tell them that at least Meg, and possibly Andy too, must be HIV Positive, as there was no other way the child could have contracted AIDS. In fact, they said, as pregnancy tends to bring on fullblown AIDS more quickly in HIV positive mothers, Meg should have herself checked over immediately. The Harrisons couldn't believe what they were hearing. And the doctors didn't believe their protestations.

They both tested negative: no HIV virus in either of them. The doctors did not even apologise. As AIDS is not a 'communicable disease' they were under no obligation to notify any authority of the case, so beyond enjoying some speculative discussions in the hospital canteen, they did nothing.

The Harrisons, humiliated as well as bereaved, clung to each other and kept the world away, sunk in deep mourning. They had told their relatives and friends that Darren had died of meningitis, which was the truth. They simply did not add that this was caused by an opportunistic infection of the cryptococcus fungus, which he had no defence against because his immune system was ravaged by HIV, and they did not add that he was also blind before he died, as his lungs, gut and retinas had been attacked by cytomegalovirus.

They had picked up the pieces of their lives, slowly, as people do; but it was never the same, as it never can be. Both sets of grandparents were heartbroken, firstly by the death of their beloved grandson, and then by the death-in-life of their children.

Eating away at Meg and Andy, under their grief, was rage and fear; rage that they had been put through the humiliations they had suffered at the hospital, and fear that somehow, someone would find out why Darren had really died. If that happened, they thought they would probably have to move house, get away somewhere they were not known. To their shame, they realised that they themselves would have dropped any acquaintance who was suspected of carrying the virus and especially so if they had a child. Now, today, they thought perhaps they could tell the truth and be believed, because of Miss Frieda Hislop. It wouldn't make them miss Darren any less, but it might purge them of some of the hurt, the hiding, the rage.

They did not ask any payment for their story. Oddly enough, that was the reason why their story, after quite careful checking, appeared in the following day's Daily Mail and the dozens of others who had phoned in similar pleas for belief, to all the various newspapers, were turned down flat.

Callum, far too rushed and excited to have read the morning papers, and too busy travelling to have caught up on the news yet, had expected a rather more enthusiastic reception when he arrived at Gatwick and met his father. Andrew Douglas was very, very sober indeed. There had already been three deeply unpleasant events this day, and he did not anticipate much success in persuading Callum not to go to Africa.

The train to Victoria was crowded, as usual, so there was no opportunity to talk; and the walk from Victoria Station to Tudor Court was short. It was not until he had settled Callum into the spare bedroom, and set about making them a meal, that Andrew had a chance to talk to his son. Even then, the talk was desultory, as his mind roamed over the three happenings which had so much affected him.

Firstly, the interview with the Prime Minister had been extremely difficult. The man was obviously outraged, and furious that such contentious information had been released, and not interested in

71

listening to how Andrew's speech had been misinterpreted. He had fired Terry Aitken on the spot. Though she had been expecting it, it still hit her like a physical blow; she loved her job. Gallantly Andrew attempted to shoulder all the blame, and told the P.M. how he had brushed Terry's objections aside, and now regretted it; no use. As a last resort, he said that if Terry was fired, then he would be obliged to resign; he actually thought that would hold the man's anger in check. Instead, he was icily informed that his resignation would be extremely acceptable to this Government, and, were public opinion not quite so much on Douglas's side, it would in fact have been demanded. As it was...it was up to Andrew.

Terry tugged his arm and told him not to be so stupid. He was needed. He was the right man for the job ("if only you would learn a little discipline!"). He decided to keep his position, and begged afresh for Terry to keep hers.

"After all, Prime Minister, it would not look good if your Media Advisor was fired for allowing someone to tell the truth, now would it?"

The P.M. raged, but Andrew was right, and Terry's job was saved; but both of them had to swear that never again would anything about AIDS be released without official clearance. Which made Andrew feel as if he was walking with great iron shackles on his feet.

Secondly, as it was now very easy to find Sweeting, for Sweeting was hot on his trail over this morning's debacle, Andrew took the opportunity to ask him about putting T.B. vaccination boosters on the list of approved shots for going abroad.

"Don't be bloody stupid" was the haughty reply. "If there are AIDS cases here who are carrying those new superbugs, giving the booster ONLY to people who are going abroad would be pretty pointless, wouldn't it? I mean, in no time, some bright spark would be demanding boosters for every member of the population... and think of the expense of that! Quite out of the question. Even if we gave free boosters to the people who live in the cluster areas, the cost would be enormous. Simply enormous."

Oh well, of course, Andrew thought to himself. *If it's going to cost money to keep people alive, let's not bother. Fine.*

The third thing which had depressed him was a report from the British Medical Association on the rising number of general practitioners who were refusing to accept new patients onto their lists, if those people were HIV positive or in one of the high risk groups; and, moreover, were throwing anyone who became Positive off their lists and refusing to treat them.

Not, of course, that this was seen as any kind of moral judgement. Oh no, it was purely financial. Health Service budgets for G.P. clinics simply did not stretch to the enormous hospitalisation and other treatment costs of people dying of AIDS. At least, not to many; and it was seen as being morally preferable to refuse all such cases, rather than playing God and accepting a few for treatment. Unsurprisingly, those general practices which had made this decision were thickest on the ground in the very areas where there was most need.

Towards the end of the report, even more worrying, was the news that several of the Trust status hospitals had elected to withdraw their services for AIDS patients, and even for the regular ordinary treatment of the various diseases they were likely to present with, if the patient was HIV positive. And of course they had every right to 'specialise' in whichever kinds of treatment they wished to offer. Again, these hospitals were mostly in London, Edinburgh, and other places where the beds were desperately needed.

This meant that for those AIDS patients requiring hospitalisation, some other hospital would have to be found somewhere else, sometimes in a different town altogether, adding isolation and loneliness to the other miseries of their stays in hospital.

And now there was Callum; freshfaced, bursting with health and excitement, nineteen years old and, tomorrow, off to one of the worst-hit countries in Africa.

They sat together at the tiny diningtable in the cramped kitchen, and ate not well but fully, Andrew's cooking being of the plain-food-and-plenty-of-it variety. Once he saw his father relaxing a

73

little, Callum ventured to voice some of his enthusiasm for the trip; his eyes warned Andrew not to pull the plug on his happiness, for there was nothing to be gained.

So Andrew swallowed his worry, and tried to be happy for his son, tried to see it all through Callum's eyes. This job would help him on his course, being practical experience of some of the theory involved: it would give him something worthwhile to put on his curriculum vitae when it was time to go job hunting; it was six weeks in the sun not only cost-free, but with a whacking big paypacket every week thrown in!

The phone rang while they were washing the dishes. It was Terry.

"Um...got any spare puddings going cheap?"

"Dozens. Tomorrow evening?"

"Hm. How about tonight? I'm miserable."

"Ah...well actually I have..there's..."

"Oh, say no more. A lady friend is currently decorating your sofa. And it's doubtless a very small sofa. God, things are coming to a pretty pass when I phone up a bloke instead of waiting to be asked nicely, and THEN find I've been pipped to the post. I shall open a tin of macaroni cheese and never speak to you again till at least tomorrow."

"No, not at all, it's my son Callum here for the night, off to Africa tomorrow. Did I not mention?"

"Maybe. I never forget trivia, but I've a terrible memory for important things. He's about twenty, isn't he? Well then, should I come round and let the two of you fight over me? That might be fun, especially if you win."

"You are incorrigible."

"Not at all. I'm very easily incorriged. Well. Have a nice evening, and maybe I'll see you tomorrow. Take care. Oh, and make sure you watch the late news; I don't think you'll enjoy it, but I think you should watch it."

Andrew was acutely aware of Callum's delighted and very smug grin, as he replaced the receiver.

74

"Dad, you're blushing!"

"Rubbish!"

"Is she pretty?"

"Is WHO pretty?"

"Now that is the real question.   Tell you what, Dad: if you promise faithfully not to mention AIDS the whole time I'm here, I promise I won't tease you about her. Deal?"

He was about to say something rather pompous when he realised just how alienating that would be; instead he smiled, and agreed. The bond between them strengthened almost visibly.

They sat down to watch the news at ten o'clock together, and the pleasantries ceased immediately; the Government was in deep trouble. Every parliamentary trick in the book had been employed to force a debate on AIDS, and whether or not there was new evidence that the HIV virus had mutated to become infectious. The programme had live satellite links with experts in France, in Switzerland, and in America, all saying no, it was not now, never had been, and never could be, infectious or contagious in the normal way. But voters all over the country had been lobbying their M.P.s all day, demanding an answer. And now the M.P.s in their turn were demanding answers, and they were doing it loudly. Sweeting stood up and shouted them down, catcalling and insulting the Opposition as normal, throwing in denials every so often, sounding as categoric as possible.

The Leader of the Opposition was having a wonderful time. Half the Government back benchers were clearly on his side, and his own half of the house was a riot. The Speaker did his best, but things degenerated into a shambles.

Order was only restored when the Opposition leader called for a vote of no confidence in the Government, to be held the following morning. This was agreed. The rest of the news seemed supremely uninteresting, after that.

"God, Dad, were you involved in that?"

"Involved? Involved? I caused it! My incredible stupidity and trusting people to be sensible and responsible, that's what caused it..." and he outlined the story for his son, their 'deal' completely forgotten.

Callum looked doubtful.

"But surely...if she was a virgin..and no drugs, or blood transfusions...well how else could she have got it? Surely it MUST be infectious? What other explanation is there?"

"I don't know: but it ISN'T infectious. Yes, it's an incredibly mutable virus; if you examine a hundred and twenty-three corpses, you'll find a hundred and twentythree slightly different variants. But for it to become infectious would be the most horrendously difficult thing to do. It really can't happen."

Thank God Joe had given him all that bumf about the virus. Otherwise he might have got sucked into this madness himself.

"I see" said Callum, but he did not look convinced. And he did not look enthusiastic any more, when Andrew said brightly,

"Well, you'll be off out of all this tomorrow, away to the sunshine, eh?"

"I don't know. I mean, if it WAS infectious yes I know it's not, sure, but if it was...then Africa would be a bloody silly place to go, wouldn't it?"

"Now listen to me, Callum. I love you and I worry about you and yes, I didn't want you to go to Uganda, but that's because you're nineteen and I've no doubt your hormones are racing about like everyone else's at your age, and you're going to a country where prostitutes are cheap, and plentiful, and really deadly. BUT. But...if you keep clear of them, if you don't sleep with ANYbody, then you should be okay. Just keep away from anyone who looks sick: I told you about the new T.B. strains. More important, don't get drunk and - er - consort with prostitutes. Then you'll be fine."

"Well of course I'll be fine: there's Belinda, up in Aberdeen, anyway...I don't think I've told you about her, have I? Do you think I'd risk bringing her something nasty home with me? No way. We are reasonably intelligent, even at my age, these days, Dad. Honest."

"Then GO to Uganda. I can't believe I'm saying this! But go. Enjoy it. There is no possibility whatsoever of you getting AIDS by infection or ordinary contagion. Did you get your T.B. booster? Well then. You are on your way to the working holiday of a lifetime, with my blessing. If there was a millionth part of one doubt in my mind, would I be saying this?"

Callum sighed deeply, then caved in.

"Okay Dad. And thanks."

A millionth part of one doubt? His mind was full of doubts. The T.B. booster would only cope with the run-of-the-mill type of T.B. not the new superbugs. But if he made difficulties for Callum now, he knew he would lose him. And putting the small risk of T.B. against the absolute certainty of losing his son's respect...he kept his mouth shut about his doubts, and prayed that Callum would not suffer as a result.

Of course, every Member of Parliament had read his or her morning newspaper by the time the House assembled, the following morning. Those who did not read the Daily Mail were kindly handed copies by those who did, and every Member knew about Darren Harrison and his parents before they sat down.

Every nonIndependent Member was on a threeline whip, and the Government Whips were everywhere, busy, frantic to find quite this many stony faces turned to them. When the division of the House was called, and the numbers counted, the live television coverage of Parliament enjoyed an unprecedented viewing figure. Most people secretly believed that a vote of no confidence meant that there was something about AIDS which the Government wasn't telling them; a vote for the Government would mean that all was well, that Miss Hislop and the Harrisons were liars, or freaks.

The Government won, by a majority of three. And most people, regardless of political persuasion, breathed easier. Sure, it's a fine, logical thing, a human being.

That Sunday, the Corstorphine Church of Saint Andrews was bursting at the seams. The Reverend Spencer had decided to open the Lord's doors to the reporters after all, for good must not only be done but must be seen to be done. He had had several most

77

interesting chats with Albert Kennedy about the tone and style of his sermons. Mr Kennedy was something of an expert on language, and literature, and had been able to point out several effective little mechanisms which would make the message even more broadly appealing. For example, the more-in-sorrow-than-in-anger one; it made one seem less tyrannical, more caring. Peter Spencer liked that. It was a very Christian way of doing things. It had been Mr Kennedy who had suggested all the 'open questions' as he called them which the Reverend Spencer had employed the previous Sunday to such good effect. And it was Mr Kennedy who spent much time with Peter Spencer, polishing up his sermons with him, giving him feedback - "the breakfast of champions", Mr Kennedy called it.

The television cameras rolled, as the Reverend Peter Spencer gave of his very best. He did not stint himself, he did not cheat his audience of their very high expectations. A spontaneous response, carefully coordinated by Albert Kennedy, sprang to life during this sermon; every time Spencer uttered the name or description of a particular sort of evildoer, the congregation whispered back "We will root them out!". It was most effective.

Gwendoline saw some of her husband's sermon on the BBC teatime news. He was lauding the hard work and good heart of all the People For Purity, and inviting new believers to join, to work together with common cause, the benefit of all mankind and particularly Edinburgh mankind. To protect our children from the perverts (we will root them out!), to cleanse our schools of the junkies (we will root them out!), to demand the closure of gay bars and discos (we will root them out!) and sweep the drunks and the drugsodden from our streets, along with all the muggers and hoodlums (we will root them out!) and ensure that no more maiden ladies or poor little babies were killed by the foul disease of the adulterous and the homosexuals (we will root them out!).

The next item of news was that a discotheque near the city centre was currently on fire, and not expected to survive the blaze. It was not necessary for the reporter to specify that this was a gay disco: it was notorious as such.

"Oh God" she said softly, and it was almost a prayer. "How much longer can I stay under his roof?"

The acolyte stationed in the hallway to answer the phone, as Gwendoline was still on strike, was being kept busy this night, taking calls from people all over Britain...people who wanted to ask the good Reverend about starting up chapters of People For Purity in their own towns...and cities...and villages. Some of them, but not many, were ministers and priests. More of them sounded rather unintelligent, but even those were useful to God, after all, had they only the spirit and the energy required, and the courage of their convictions.

The seeds were sown all over the land. The soil was richly fertile, after this week's news programmes. The plants would flourish. But what manner of blooms they would produce, what fruits would ripen on them, no man could yet say.

CHAPTER THREE

It had been a beautiful wedding, she remembered; she had been sumptuously dressed in old ivory silk, with huge scallops and falls of handmade Brussels lace, and the same for her floorlength veil. Her generous father had not stinted; the wedding feast was for almost three hundred people, including mountains of Beluga caviare and seemingly unlimited champagne, all consumed under a giant marquee on the front lawns of the family home on the craggy Yorkshire coast.

Neither she nor Tony could stop smiling that day, they had been so in love and so happy. It could have been made better only by Chloe's mother having lived long enough to share the day with them. The bride hugged her father, behind a corner, alone for a moment, and they agreed that Mummy was watching from somewhere, smiling with them.

The honeymoon had been straight out of a storybook; two glorious weeks in the sundrenched Adriatic aboard a chartered yacht, sloping around the islands at a leisurely pace, drinking ouzo and retsina, eating squid, loving and lazing and lounging around.

In the four years since then, things had gone well. Her own job in her father's engineering works in Hull was a demanding and interesting one, working as the Human Resources Manager, taking care of the training, deployment and welfare of over five hundred employees. Tony had gone from strength to strength with his architectural consultancy, specialising in the restoration and extension of old country houses. Their own home was a snug four-bedroom Victorian mansion house, and both of them had taken pride and pleasure in bringing out the full beauty of every detail in the house...especially six months ago, when they discovered they were to become parents. The nursery was perfection, already complete with cot and rocking horse, with stencilled walls and painted furniture. That was where she was standing now, on the blue carpet with the creamy billowing clouds all over it.

A straggly dark red stain was spreading over those peaceful

clouds. It came from the shattered chest of her husband, whom she had just shot at very close range.

Chloe was good with a gun; her father had ensured she was a fine sportswoman, as befitted her station. She had shot rabbits, foxes, and deer. Perhaps that was why she felt so unmoved at the sight of Tony's corpse at her feet. Perhaps not.

She turned on her heel and walked calmly downstairs, putting on her jacket in case the late evening air turned chilly, checking that she had enough cartridges in her pocket for the shotgun she carried to the car.

She drove steadily and well, towards Hull, through the city centre, and down to the dockland area. She could not know, of course, which particular street corner Tony had favoured, but she knew he had a taste for skinny blondes, and had discovered only that day that his tastes also ran to the kind of sexual activities usually signalled by prostitutes wearing black leather, with metal studs. Not one hint of this had ever permeated their marriage: he had been a skilful and considerate lover, seeming to be as satisfied as she was by their sex life. Had she not taken the HIV test as a routine precaution of her pregnancy, and discovered herself to be Positive, she would never have suspected him of infidelity. He had been the only lover of her life; he had given her the virus. When she had challenged him, this morning, he had looked not shocked, or humiliated, but only disappointed. And tender; he hoped she would not be too hurt, but there were certain things he needed which a chap could not reasonably ask of his wife. It was no reflection on her, he said: she was magnificent. She was all the wife he would ever want. He loved her, he said.

"You have killed me" she had replied, quietly. "And our baby, too. All three of us are HIV positive. That's how much you love me, Tony."

His own shock did nothing to change hers. He did not even try to persuade her that it would be all right. He just went up to the nursery and cried. She had prepared a little lunch for them both, so that they could talk, but there was nothing to talk about. The keys to the gun cupboard were always in the bureau drawer, and the cartridges alongside the keys. She loaded the gun, she walked upstairs, and she shot him. She went downstairs and sat, numb and quite, until late evening.

The pump action shotgun, fully loaded again, and cocked, now rested alongside her, stock upwards, barrel down to the floor of the car. She drove round and round the maze of streets, peering through the light gloom at the various girls draped in doorways and under lamps. After twenty minutes she saw two thin blonde girls standing underneath the lamp above the lorry entrance of a ship's chandlery. Both were wearing black leather jackets and mini skirts, with thigh-high black leather boots. Most of the leather was thick with studs. She pulled up the collar of her jacket, high, and cruised past them once, twice, three times, staring appraisingly. On the fourth pass, she slowed down, and the girls wiggled across the pavement towards her. She lowered the kerbside window, and picked up the shotgun.

"Looking for business, dearie?" asked the first, as she bent towards the car. And then "Oh, shit!" as she saw the shotgun. Chloe fired twice in quick succession, killing the first girl outright and leaving the other screaming with a shattered shoulder and powdered splinters where the bones of her upper arm used to be. She drove on, considering, in a detached way, whether it would be kinder to go back and finish off the wounded girl rather than leaving her screaming like that in agony. But no, this girl was no wounded innocent forest creature; this girl might well be the girl who had sent her the little present, via Tony. The little gift which would spell virtually certain death for her baby inside five years. So she left her there, and continued to drive round until she saw the main dock gates. There was a crash barrier there, and a man sitting in a lit booth beside the gates, but she did not slow down. She raced through the barrier, and drove straight over the side, taking her car, her baby, and all her hopes deep into the freezing, filthy waters. All the alarm bells, the panic, the efforts to drag the car out in time, quite literally washed over her head. It was a mercifully brief struggle for her; she had chosen drowning because of the baby, because the baby was already floating in amniotic fluid, and perhaps, she had thought, confusedly, perhaps drowning would be less traumatic for the baby than being shot. She loved the baby dearly, you see; dearly.

Her father was wakened from his sleep by two police sergeants, at 3.45am. They told him, as gently as possible, of what had happened to his daughter and his son-in-law. In answer to his frantic questions, they said, hesitantly, that they were not, at the moment, looking for any other person. They asked him if there was anyone he could call, to come and be with him, or if he would like a policeman or woman to stay for a while, make tea, talk...

Tom Cannock did not phone his brother, or any of his relatives. He phoned Marsha, the woman he had been seeing for some years now, on a pleasant and platonic basis, and she came as quickly as she could. As it happened, she was one of the people who had telephoned the Reverend Peter Spencer's home about setting up People for Purity in her area.

Tom spent the night asking why? Why did his lovely daughter, so happy with her husband and looking forward with such joy to the birth of her first child, why did she how could she do this? The answer came, of course, from the autopsy reports. And that explained why she had gunned down the prostitutes (neither of whom were, in fact, HIV positive).

Before his one and only child was laid in her grave, Tom Cannock had made over his entire personal fortune to People for Purity. It amounted to just short of two million pounds. His first instincts had been similar to Chloe's, he had longed for the catharsis of revenge. But the fact that neither of the dead prostitutes was the guilty party (the second had died of massive trauma) stopped him from hazarding any more direct personal retribution. People for Purity, Marsha assured him, would spend the money wisely, on prevention rather than cure. On saving people, rather than killing them.

———— • ————

"We have to do something about this" drawled John Longfellow, at the next AIDS Committee meeting. "What with that girl who shot the prostitutes in Hull this week, and the gay disco in Edinburgh being set on fire last Sunday, and all the attacks in the streets all over the place..mostly gays, but some of them just young fellows fashionably dressed...I'm telling you, these rumbles of discontent are going to grow. It may not be directly in our remit, but... ?" He looked round the table for comment.

"It could be" said Jasmine, thoughtfully "if we class it as a requirement for Public Health Education. What do you think, Andrew?"

"I think that is an excellent idea. It's been far too long since this Government spent any real money on that: a disgracefully long time. I think we might be in with a chance but what do you all think should be the prime target, or the main message?"

"God" said Jasmine "There's so MUCH that needs to be told, and as for the prime target it has to be every man, woman and child in the country."

"They'll never give us the budget for that" sighed Jessie Adams. "Not in a million years."

"They might: remember the Patient's Charter? Every house in the U.K. got a leaflet. So it's been done before. And the AIDS stuff that went out years ago, everyone got that, too...so...it's a possibility. And we could support it with money from our own budget" But Andrew did not look all that hopeful. "What SHOULD our main message be, then, if we do get the go ahead? Ideas, everybody?"

"How about we take a coffee break and think it through?"

"Good thinking, Jessie; I'll buzz Judy."

The committee had grown since those first days; as the volume of work to be done grew and grew, more members had been co-opted in to help, and there were now nineteen faces round the Small Conference Room table in 79 Whitehall.

Inevitably this meant that everything took longer to talk about, longer to decide; but each member worked with goodwill and good manners, so that it was one of the pleasanter committees upon which to serve. On the other hand, what they were discussing was possibly the single most depressing subject in the world at the time. Andrew tried to soften the gutwrenching impact of some of the facts, some of the statistics, some of the stories, by keeping the actual procedures as friendly as possible, as positive as possible. Given that each member of the committee now knew that a cure was out of the question within the foreseeable future, and that the very idea of human vaccine trials was loaded with problems, and that T.B. was now surging forward in all the inner city areas of those countries which reported such things, it was difficult to find much that was positive: Andrew had to major on the individual efforts and contributions, on the helpfulness of correspondents, on the valiant work being done in the field by so many people.

He stood talking to Jasmine Elliott as they had their coffee and biscuits. He told her of his abortive attempt to get Sweeting to consider T.B. being put on the list of vaccinations recommended for people travelling abroad. She merely shrugged as he recounted Sweeting's reactions.

"Did you really expect otherwise?" she asked softly. "He's right about the money, you know: there will never be enough to do all that needs to be done. Every person in this country, in every country, should be having a T.B. booster shot or a vaccination, if they've never had one. But you can imagine what that would cost."

"A lot less than treating them for ARC or AIDS!"

"Maybe. I mean, if you calculate how much a mass booster programme would cost here in this country, right now, and then calculate how much the treatment of AIDS-related T.B. patients is costing this year, in this country - I don't think Sweeting would see your plan as being much of a cost benefit."

"But"

"I know, I know: and so does Sweeting. But that man is set on the Treasury as his next post, everyone says so. So he must show himself strong on budget controls. The Treasury next, and then after that, Number 10. He's an ambitious man, our Mr Sweeting."

"I see. As long as he can keep the lid on his budgets here at the Ministry for Health, he'll be looking good for the Treasury next time round."

"Exactly."

"Pity so many people will have to die to get him the job, of course."

She laid her hand on his arm gently, reassuringly.

"Andrew, Andrew...we have to deal with the world as it is, not as we would make it. We are doing what we can. We can't change human nature. And anyway, you know that a booster is not a guarantee against the new strains. Look, everyone is sitting down again."

The discussion on the contents of a new Public Health Education programme went on for a very long time. There were, as had been said already, so many things people needed to know. Though when it came down to it, the populace already knew the principal thing: that the only sure way to avoid dying of AIDS is not to get it in the first place, and that avoiding getting it is done by not sharing needles and by not indulging in unsafe sex. People knew it intellectually, but they did not accept it emotionally. As Jessie Adams (an experienced clinician from a Special Unit which dealt with sexually transmitted diseases in Central London) pointed out, since the beginning of the AIDS scare in the 'eighties, there had actually been a massive upsurge in the number of STD cases reported, and numbers were now higher than at any time since the turn of the century.

"It's ridiculous" she said. "People are absolutely thrilled when we tell them they have terminal syphilis, because it isn't AIDS! Even though they're going to die, they're happy just because they don't have AIDS! You'd think fear at that level would make people careful not to get anything at all, but people are actually taking risks MORE than they used to. Have you all read the report I circulated about the psychological profiling of these people? It's terrifying.

'Young ones especially; they feel that if they don't acknowledge the dangers, they won't be prey to them. Except for the ones who think it's more fun when there's a bit of risk. Fun? These are crazy people! You can't lock them up, but they are crazy...risking their lives so as to get a little more kick out of sex. Unbelievable. How do you educate people out of that attitude? Can we inject them with extra I.Q.? Can we make them grow up ten years early? I don't know what we can, possibly, achieve."

"We have to get round the schools and colleges.." began Alan Shaw, the committee's senior member, and an exDean of the Faculty of Medicine at Aberdeen. But Jessie interrupted him with a despairing wave of her hand.

"You think we don't try? I stood up in front of a whole school once, with the teachers on the platform with me, and tried to tell them the risks. They didn't believe me. This was the teachers I'm talking about, not the pupils. The teachers. They thought I was scaremongering. The children? They just thought I was a killjoy. A boring old fart. I was booed off the stage! And this was a good school, people, this was a school which cost money, a school for very bright kids. It was much the same at the other schools I went to, and the colleges, and the universities too. It was a waste of time. I took slides, graphs, figures, proof of what I was saying. But it's like people smoking, you know; everyone thinks, it won't happen to me. So they carry right on."

"What about last year's alcohol abuse campaign on television? It was very good. Maybe we could take a leaf out of their book. The way they made drunks look stupid, funny, pathetic...very effective. My own kids tell me it's not looked upon as being quite so smart any more, getting drunk. They make jokes about the ones at school who boast about having hangovers. And I believe it's the same in workplaces...the old soaks are not respected any more, they're sneered at. I think that's a good tactic." This was the maiden speech of a rather timid lady who had been coopted because of her stint at the European Parliament.

There was a general murmur of approval, and nodding of heads.

"How would you see it being applied?" asked Andrew, in an encouraging tone. Mrs Bishop ventured to speak again.

"Well, er...the way people boast about their conquests is about the same way they boast about the vast amounts of drink they have consumed. Maybe we could show some people at work, and this man, a fellow worker, comes in and starts boasting about the women he's had at the weekend, and maybe the other workers could sort of move away from him a bit and jokingly, jokingly suggest he brings in his own towels in future, and his own cutlery for the canteen?"

"No, no, Mrs Bishop, we can't do that; not at the same time we're telling people that AIDS isn't infectious! Conflicting messages, you see?" Jasmine was squirming.

"Oh" said Mrs Bishop. "Of course. Yes, I do see. Of course."

"I think we're going to have to leave this discussion there, for the moment" said Andrew. "What I propose is that we each go away and think about this individually, come up with some ideas about how best we can use the media, and any other vehicles that come to mind. Perhaps we should get hold of an advertising agency, for example, and discuss it with them? If we could all come back here next Thursday with concrete ideas down on paper; even better, if you could get them in to me by next Tuesday, so that I can get them copied and circulated, we can discuss them at the next meeting. Does that meet with your approval? Excellent. I want to move on to the question of hospital bed provision for the future. Mr Longfellow, I believe you have something to say about this?"

Having been Senior Administrative Officer at a major London teaching hospital for some years, John Longfellow had been keen to join the committee, and had already proved his worth as a clever and competent worker. Had you been forced to find some little fault with him, it would have been his pomposity; but he meant well, and so his ego was accommodated along with the rest of him.

"Yes, thank you, Mr Chairman." He rose, although that was not the custom of the Committee. "I do indeed. I'm afraid this is going to mean asking for even more money, ladies and gentlemen: more than our Public Health Education ideas, considerably more. Yes." He shuffled papers importantly. "Now then..."

His point was that as the geriatric population of the country continued to expand, with medicine keeping people alive for longer and longer, there was every possibility that by 1995 between one-third and one-half of all hospital beds would be occupied by geriatric patients...and by the turn of the century, that fraction would have increased. This in itself would have been a considerable worry, but with the introduction of a growing population of AIDS victims, most of whom would require several stays in hospital during the terminal phase of their illness, the picture was getting even worse.

"By early next century - and please remember, ladies and gentlemen, that we are talking here of only a few years from now - we may be faced with a situation where only around a third of all hospital beds are available for ALL the ordinary treatments of ordinary patients. Waiting lists are going to grow and grow, and not just for the non-urgent cases. That would be bad enough; but what will happen is that only emergency cases will be dealt with immediately, and not even all of those. The number of people who will die while waiting for even quite a small and easy operation is going to increase quite dramatically. The number of people who will die while waiting even for their very first appointment, to be diagnosed, is going to increase quite dramatically. In order to accommodate all the people we think will need hospital treatments, we would need to build...the same number of hospitals again as we have now. And I believe I hardly need to tell you that, financially, that is simply not possible."

In an ordinary place, with ordinary people, dealing with ordinary things, this information might have caused shock, or outrage, or at least a big stir. Here, in this room, with people who were rapidly becoming inured to shock, it merely caused the shaking of heads.

"There is, I am afraid, more. As you know, the AIDS syndrome is causing many dormant diseases to spread out again...T.B. is only one of them. People have no natural resistance, and in many cases the new diseases are Multiple Drug Resistant. You know this, I know this, and a lot of hospital workers know this too. We have a growing number of members of staff who refuse to deal with AIDS patients because of this. Now, we have whole hospitals turning them away. From the contacts I still have, I learn that this is a trend which is likely to grow. Every Trust Status hospital is considering it, right now, including my own. Partially because of the fears of personal contagion among the staff, and partially because they too can see that their services to their other patients must necessarily suffer more and more over the years.

'If I may condense this for you: as AIDS spreads, so the services available to deal with AIDS will contract. The more hospital beds are needed, the fewer will be available." He sat down. And stood up again.

"The actual figures and forecasts are in my report, of course; I shall be giving it to Doctor Douglas at the end of this meeting, for circulation."

"Thank you, John" said Andrew, still sitting. He was weary to the marrow of all this. What was the good of a toothless Committee, in the face of all the imminent disasters and the public apathy? Still, all anyone can do is try. "It is going to require very delicate handling, as that situation develops: I can foresee howls of outrage from the general public...when little Johnny can't get a bed in the Isolation ward when he has whooping cough, because it's full of AIDS victims...when Mum has to wait maybe five years for her hysterectomy...when Auntie Jill needs a mastectomy and can't get one until some date at which she is likely to have died...and Gran can't have her hip replacement until she's 92. When it really comes home to the average family that their health is under threat, that their lives are under threat, because of AIDS...God knows. We will keep taking National Insurance contributions, indeed we will certainly have to increase them; and while we are increasing the charges, we will be offering less and less of a service. And, of course, as more and more young workers die of AIDS, we'll have fewer and fewer people contributing." He looked around the gloomy faces, and he could take no more.

"My friends, I don't know about you, but I am beginning to suffer from doomsday fatigue. That's not meant as levity; it's just a statement of fact. Unless anyone else has anything very urgent they wish to say, I would like to declare this meeting over. All reports to Judy as per normal, for copying to the circulation list. I will see you all again next week, our last meeting before our first report to Cabinet. But right now, I need to go outside and see some grass and earth and flowers, to restore my sanity. Thank you all for your contributions; and goodbye for now."

They dispersed more quickly than usual, without the customary subgroup huddles and chats with Andrew. Partly because they were all beginning to suffer from the same emotional exhaustion as he, and partly because they were concerned for him. He was better liked, and better respected, than he knew.

What he needed, he thought, was a walk in the park with Terry. *With Terry.* It was the first time since Ruth had died that he had ever found himself wishing for the pleasure and comfort of...anyone but Ruth. He immediately felt guilty; then chastised himself. Terry was very much alive: and so was he. Ruth had made it very plain, when she knew she was dying, that he was to go on and have a life after she was gone. That it would not be infidelity, nor betrayal, but a celebration of life. Those words had cut him deep at the time, but now, as he remembered them, he looked out of the window and saw birds, trees, and people...and he called Terry.

"Are you booked for dinner tonight?"

"No, Dr Douglas, I believe I have a table free!"

"Good. How about lunch today? A sandwich in St James's park, and feed the ducks?"

"A sandwich...and cakes?"

"And cakes. Big cream ones. With pastry. And jam."

"You make my mouth water. Still, I have hinted that to you already, I believe."

"The feeling is entirely mutual."

"Oh good. I mean, I knew that. I just didn't think YOU knew that. Are we having dinner at your place, then, like you promised?"

"Yes please."

"No haggis, though. In fact, why don't you let me bring stuff and cook it? I can cook, you know. Rather well, in fact. May I?"

And so on. God, flirting with Terry was the best tonic a man could wish for. He found himself panicking suddenly about the state of his pyjamas, and giggled inwardly. Any man thinking what he was thinking, in June, with the temperature soaring, and still worrying about pyjamas...didn't deserve Terry Aitken!

———— • ————

Flora Spencer's first programme went fairly well: she remembered everything she had to do, sitting at the broadcast desk, and her live interviews were reasonably interesting, she thought. Her mother thought they were wonderful, of course; the Programme Controller was not quite so biased, the next morning, but still basically complimentary. But she needed a bit more angst, he suggested, a bit more raw emotion and real trauma. He was looking forward to her programme on Gay Rights, how was that coming along?

"Oh, pretty well" she lied. "A bit more polishing up to do." Hell, she had hardly started it! How many hours in the day did these people think there were?

She phoned Gerry Hansen, and arranged for him to come into the station the following day. He suggested dinner that evening, but she was already tied up with Frankie Dunn, and rather regretfully had to decline.

Frankie was waiting for her outside the front door at five-thirty prompt. He was really rather a stunning-looking man, Flora thought to herself, careful not to let this thought show in her eyes. He led her to his Volvo, and opened her door for her, politely.

"I've a very nice flat to show you tonight; just down the road, in Bellevue Street. On the edge of the New Town, where the money ran out! I think it's very possibly just what you're looking for. I have the keys..." He started up the car, pulled away smoothly. They were there in less than five minutes.

The street was an odd one, with slightly crumbly New Town tenements down one side, and harled villas on the other. But the flat, on the first floor, was of perfect proportions, and virtually unchanged since first it was built. There were marble fire surrounds with cast iron insets and Dutch tiles...the cornice was egg and dart, the floor boards were beautifully waxed. Two huge bedrooms, a big kitchen, a perfect lounge with big double windows complete with shutters, a large cupboard in the hall, and a cute little bathroom: it was indeed just what she was looking for, but she dreaded to think what the price would be.

The Scottish system of starting with an "Offers over" price, called the "Upset" price, was a swine. You might offer far too much...or you could miss the house by a whisker. "Upset" was the right word for it.

Frankie told her not to worry. This flat had only just come in, and he had persuaded the seller to go for a fixed price, as this would hasten the sale.

"Fixed price of what?" said Flora, still worried. "About seventy?"

"No: fifty two."

"You're kidding! What's wrong with it?"

"Nothing! Look, I've had it surveyed already." He passed her the report. It was almost flawless. One window cracked, and needing repair; and polystyrene ceiling tiles to be removed (which she would have done anyway) from the kitchen ceiling. That was it. The survey value was £65,000.

She looked at Frankie, puzzled. His tone was bland and reassuring.

"The seller is emigrating next week: needs a quick sale. He's got loads of money, he really doesn't need all the profits. Anyway, he bought it in 1982 for about ten thousand: so forty two thousand profit is high wide and handsome as far as he's concerned. I have to confess, I've not actually shown it to anybody else..."

"Oh, I want it: but my flat in Inverness, any sign of a buyer there yet? I hate to think what a bridging loan would cost on this lot, even at fifty two thousand!"

"That's where my nice surprise comes in. We sold it yesterday, and did very well on the price. You'll have around fifteen thousand clear profit. Which means your mortgage here will only be around thirty eight thou. Is that affordable for you?"

"Affordable? It's brilliant! Frankie, you're wonderful! Can I really have it?"

"Really, really, it's yours if you like it. I thought you would."

"And you can sort out a mortgage for me and everything?"

"And everything. All you need to do is get me a letter from Radio Forth confirming your salary, then come and fill in a few forms. And seeing you're you, I'll waive my commission on the insurances. Have you thought about redundancy protection, for example? These days, it's kind of a sensible thing to do. For everyone."

She could have hugged him. But something held her back, she didn't know quite what. Still, when he invited her to come and find something to eat, she said yes. He took her to a Chinese restaurant, and they talked with a kind of artificial ease. Although they had known each other off and on for a good many years, they had never really talked, never really got to know one another. By tacit consent they did not discuss her father, or his grandfather, or the Church of Saint Andrew at Corstorphine.

They seemed to be spending most of their time talking about her: she did try to steer the conversation on to other topics but Frankie always brought it back to her again. If she hadn't known better, she'd have thought he was courting her. He couldn't be, could he? Though then again, why not?

And after he had dropped her at the cheaper bed and breakfast to which she had now moved, and after he had walked round and opened the car door for her, and not even attempted to kiss her goodnight (which was something of a novelty for Flora, though not as much as it was for Frankie), she thought to herself again, why not? She was not a snob, except perhaps about intelligence. And Frankie was far from unintelligent. So he didn't have a classical education, nor had he gone to university...but his wits were sharp, and he spoke well enough, and what he said was usually informed and to the point. And there was a certain something about him, an element of not-quite-tamed wildness, which was definitely attractive. As she undressed, she imagined what kind of a lover he would be. She imagined the two of them, dining in her Bellevue Street flat, looking into each other's eyes over the food and the candles, their eyes saying different things to their mouths, and later, their mouths and their hands affirming what their eyes had promised.

Frankie, in his own bed, was also thinking of Flora. But not of her eyes, or her mouth, or her hands. He was thinking of her respectability, her acceptability, and her consequent desirability as his wife. Frankie wanted to go legitimate - on the surface, anyway. Frankie wanted to join golf clubs, and have two point four children and a labrador. These were the things which he reasoned would keep him out of Saughton Prison, firstly by taking him out of the circles from which police drew their suspects, and secondly, if all else failed, by making him the kind of man who got a few months in an open prison instead of a few years in Saughton. Only after he had convinced himself that marrying Flora was an entirely selfserving move did he allow himself to dwell on the fact that he was immensely attracted to her. This second point was, distinctly, secondary. But it was all that saved him from being a fullblown psychopath. He preferred to think of himself as a sociopath. It had a nicer ring to it, and more modern. After all, his reading on the subject had informed him that the true psychopath does not experience love, except as a variety of hatred. And he did love his grandfather, and had loved his grandmother equally. So he could not be a psychopath. So he could allow himself to love Flora, at the same time as using her. Yes, he felt quite pleased with his reasoning and his plans. He would never hurt Flora, for that would diminish him in her eyes and he might lose her. She would be safe with him. The idea did not occur to him that for other men, not hurting their wives was simply a part of loving them and caring about them. Frankie Dunn was only able to love those who were useful to him.

Gerry Hansen was most helpful to Flora next morning. Among his suggestions was that she get in touch with Doctor Andrew Douglas, to see if he would consent to an interview, round which she could build a separate programme about the Civil Rights of AIDS victims and HIV Positives.

"I doubt it but I could always try. I mean we're not Capital Radio in London, or the Beeb...I should think we'd be too smallfry for a man in his position."

"He can only say no. And he'd be good I saw him on television a few weeks ago, with Mark Tyme...he came across well. Serious, committed, concerned, all that good stuff and articulate, too. Try the Government Press Office."

Later that day, she did. And spoke to Terry Aitken. Terry was rather dismissive of her chances, but promised to speak to Doctor Douglas and get back in touch: Flora was to fax Terry details of the planned programme, and in particular the names and backgrounds of the other guests. This was a bit on the previous side: Flora had no other guests in mind for the programme yet!

She mentioned this to her mother over their salad lunch in town, grimacing at her own incompetence.

Of course Gwendoline reassured her, praised her, loved her very obviously. But Flora was quite ashamed of having gone as far as phoning Terry Aitken without having a thought in her head yet about the format of the programme.

"I should have thought all that through first: it's obvious now it's been pointed out to me. Flora Spencer, the compleat professional, eh mum?"

"Have some gateau from the trolley dear...and stop talking nonsense. Did you have your job in Inverness down pat inside three weeks? Does anybody? Well then. Behave yourself."

"How are things with Dad, Mum? The truth, please."

"Um...not too good. From his point of view, terrific, of course; we have heaps of letters every day addressed to People for Purity. I am SO tempted to burn them before your father sees them! But I don't touch them; his secretary arrives at eight-thirty six mornings a week, and takes them away into the study, and that's the last I see of them. Oh, and he's got a new telephone line put in, for People for Purity. So I can actually use my own phone for things like telephoning you, if I want to. That's a great step forward."

Flora had never heard her mother sounding so bitter before.

"Look, Mum...it's got two bedrooms, this flat I'm getting: remember that. One of them is yours if you want it, for as long as you want it. Any time."

Gwendoline gave a tight little smile.

"It's like that, for your generation, isn't it dear? When things get difficult you just...what's that phrase?...cancel and move on. It's not like that for your father and me. No really, think about it. If I had got multiple sclerosis or something, do you think your father would just have walked out on me and left me to it? Well then. Your father's disease is different. But I'm still his wife, theoretically anyway. He may get better, and need me again. He may get worse, and need me again. Either way, I should be there when he wants me. But I appreciate your offer, I do. Anyway, you don't want your mum around, cramping your style! I can't see Frankie Dunn being thrilled to see me if you have him round for a meal!"

"It's not like that! I'm going to his office tonight to sort out the mortgage, that's all."

"That's not what the twinkle in your eyes is saying, my girl. This is your mother speaking, remember, the one that knows you inside out!"

"Och, MUM. Well...he is kind of...nice. Protective. Kind. Polite. I like that in him, I must admit. He does make me feel cossetted. And sort of safe."

At that precise moment, Frankie was having a meeting with his two staunchest sidekicks, Sandy and John, in the Volvo, down on the seafront at Silverknowes. The battered Morris Marina which the other two shared was parked alongside. From time to time in their conversation, they threw bits of sandwich out to the screeching gulls.

"You did a nice job at The Purple Pansy, lads. Well done. Bit of a public service, you might say, eh? A right old poofters' parade, that. Still, it does leave us one place short to put wee Alec and his chums out to graze."

"Aye but" ventured Sandy "You couldnae let thon auld fucker away with it, could ye now? Four weeks behind wi' his protection money? Fur a thrivin' wee disco like thon? Naw, naw, ye did the richt thing boss. As usual. The others is fair dyin' tae pay up now, so they are."

"Arson was a nice touch, eh lads? Bit of wit, eh? Naw? Arson, boys, arson...for a place with a lot of arsin' around going on? Oh, never mind boys, ye'll get it eventually. Maybe. Is there any more tuna sandwiches? Oh, thank you kindly John. Very nice too. So: anything else to report?"

"Well, yes an' no" began Sandy, hesitantly. "It's maybe nothing, but...I was driving through the Grassmarket the other day and I saw wee Alec goin' into the V.D. clinic. I'm a bit worried about him."

"That's handsome of you, Sandy my lad" said a rather surprised Frankie. "But I'd leave the wee snotter to take care of himself."

"Naw boss, I'm no' worried FUR him, I'm worried ABOOT him. Thon clinics dinnae only have tae dae with the clap an' the syph ony mair; they do AIDS as well. D'ye think he's got it? Maybe?"

Frankie pondered for a few moments, but only a few. Alec was the kind of person who was more or less guaranteed to get AIDS one of these days. If Alec himself saw grounds for worrying, Frankie was not going to disagree with him.

"Waste him" he said, briefly. "We're not taking any chances for the likes of him. Wear gloves. No; wait a minute, I'm not thinking right here; hold on. Do you remember that guy we interrupted beating the crap out of Alec a year ago? A farmer's son from out Penicuik way?"

"The bampot? Oh aye; we made a few hunner' oot o' him" said John, eagerly. "That guy was really mental: he'd a' killed him if we hudnae' got there when we did."

"That's the one. I've never forgotten his face, the look on his face when he was hitting Alec, just before he saw us standing there. I never saw a man so happy. I wonder how much he'd pay us to be allowed to kill Alec?" Frankie had read somewhere that a sadistic homosexual psychopath is the cruellest person in the world. What he had seen on the man's face that night had confirmed this. Unholy joy and wild sexual excitement, contained in a face which offered no compassion and no possibility of reprieve. A man like that would pay much to be let loose on such as Alec, and then protected from the law afterwards. Perhaps even thousands. The boys were lost in admiration. This was what made Frankie a leader of men. The man had real vision.

"Of course it would be a shame to waste the event, so to speak;

with the video camera already there, you know, boys? Remember what I was saying about snuff movies and how much money we can get for one? I do believe it's time for wee Alec to star in his last film. His farewell performance. Only, unlike Frank Sinatra, wee Alec'll not be staging a comeback later."

"Fuckin' brilliant, boss" said Sandy. "Jist fuckin' brilliant."

"Leave it to me, boys: I'll tell you when and where to have Alec in place for the bampot to meet him. It'll maybe take a week or so to set up we've got to leave that homicidal maniac enought time to organise himself an alibi - unless of course he'd like us to organise it, for a small extra fee. I tell you what, lads: when it's over, why don't you take the body and dump it in the yard of Macleod's Haulage? I feel sure Mr Macleod would gladly pay us a wee bit extra then, for us not to send that Polaroid of him and Alec to the police."

Sandy was lost for words, and could only repeat his previous evaluation of Frankie's genius.

"Fuckin' brilliant."

Frankie felt as if a new vista had opened before him, with a great deal of money sparkling at the end of it. The farmer's son from Penicuik could not be the only one of his kind in this area...and there were plenty of wee Alecs to be culled.

"I mean" mused Frankie "we don't want bampots like that guy wandering the streets killing just any innocent passerby, do we? Not if we can make a buck out of directing their attention to suitable candidates. Candidates who are better off out of it anyway. Who wants to die of AIDS? No. Wee Alec should be grateful, really. It'll all be over in a few hours. I'll better make sure and tell the bampot not to stretch it over more than four hours, that's the longest tape we can get.

'Well boys, is that it? I'll need to be getting back to the office. By the by, Sandy, how's Rena's pal Susie doing?"

"Not bad: a hunner' a night usually, of course she only does weekends, Fridays and Saturdays, 'cause she's got her homework the other nights. Not too talented, but enthusiastic enough, you know."

"Yes, I do know. And I agree. She's got potential. But she needs a helping hand: show her some of the copy videos of Shona at work, give her some ideas. And yes, you can devote some of your spare time to educating her, if you like, Sandy. You too, John. Free of charge. I like my people to get the odd perk from time to time. She gives great head, by the way. But she doesn't like taking it up the ass. She needs a bit of encouragement there."

"Thanks boss" they chorused, as they left the car. "See you soon."

'Dunn & Company, Independent Financial Advisors Ltd' was in a basement in Frederick Street, right in the city centre and damned expensive, basement or not. There was a pretty receptionist, not too dim; and two very hardworking young men who did most of the actual work. Frankie had never seen the need to sit the arduous examinations required to obtain official registration, when he could just as easily employ people who already had.

Frankie nodded to the staff as he went through the back to his own office, where he entertained the more wealthy and/or promising clients. It was here that he had converted many a blackmail client into a straight insurance client. No point in wasting good contacts, especially of the quality of Jack Macleod. They didn't come along all that often. Macleod's Haulage now had Keyman policies on all senior staff, plus a fat pension fund, plus private health insurance for all staff. Jack Macleod himself had changed his mortgage, changed his insurance company, and generally been very accommodating. Most of the converted blackmail people were only able to afford a very small pension plan, and of course a new mortgage if they had one already or were looking for property. And with Dunn & Company being also estate agents, Frankie could always find them property.

He opened his personal safe in the wall, and placed there the special books of accounts which John and Sandy had just filled in for the month of June, up till the twentieth, which was how they did their accounting. Those books were bound in red: the legitimate books in blue. Frankie had found an excellent accountant (literally found him, found him and photographed him with his penis in the mouth of a thirteen-year-old girl Frankie used to run.) He was very helpful, with both sets of books, and never charged a penny.

Frankie chuckled, remembering the accountant's face when he had first come across the receipts for the pornographic videos.

"But surely these aren't...? People like me? On film? Distributed?"

"'Fraid so, old man. Actors are so expensive, you see? And not as whole hearted as people like you. I tried them once; it was a disaster. Limp dicks all round. Not like you, Charlie, what a stud, eh?"

Charlie had cringed, bright red with embarassment.

"That mole on your arse came out particularly well, I thought. Would you like to see the video, then? Maybe you and your wife could settle in at home one evening with a box of chocolates and Charlie on film? No? Just an idea."

The afternoon was spent pleasantly enough, with Enya wiggling through with coffee from time to time, trying to catch his eye, wearing a very thin lemon yellow shirt you could see her bra through, quite clearly. He was, as always, not interested. There was never any shortage of females eager to please him and eager to bed him. He knew he must be handsome, or at least magnetic, but it did not please or excite him to know this. He could get laid by any of his whores any time, and they were a great deal more skilful than any wriggling receptionist. They were trained. They were professionals. And even then, he rarely availed himself, except to try out a new girl and see what she was good at. Frankie was so steeped in his life of selling sex that he really had lost his taste for it.

With Flora, when they were married, it would be so different. She would be a virgin, of course, and he would instruct her gently, carefully. It would be pure and lawful and respectable, and Flora was a lady. If he ever needed more spicy fare, he could soon get it. But loving Flora would be a sweet and soothing loving. A perfect loving.

She arrived after the rest of the staff had gone, at six o'clock. She brought the letter from the accountant at Radio Forth. They went over various possible types of mortgage, and settled on an endowment. He explained very carefully what this involved, and that if she ever moved she could take the mortgage with her, and that it was very important not to just drop it and start another one with the next house, for she would lose money. He selected the company which he knew was giving the best returns at the moment, and they set about filling in the forms.

"New ones, just arrived today by courier, so I haven't had time to look them over yet, but I shouldn't think there's much difference. Let's see now..."

They filled in her name, her address, her employment, her earnings, her date of birth, and then they came to the Medical Details section.

"Now then. Sorry about this, but it says here...have you ever had a test for the HIV virus? Of course you haven't. Ah, here's the new clause: if you contract HIV after signing this declaration, and die of AIDS, the policy is null and void. Wait a minute, that can't be right. Yes, yes it is: oh well, it shouldn't be any worry for you, should it?"

"Does it really say that? Let me see, would you? Good grief. Listen, Frankie, would you mind, could you give me a spare blank copy of this? I'm doing a programme on the Civil Rights of HIV Positives and AIDS victims soon, and this did you say it was new? right, this is dynamite."

"I don't see why you shouldn't have a copy - they're not exactly secret. As this is one of the biggest companies, I imagine the other companies will be following suit right away. Here you are."

"Thanks."

They continued until the forms were completed. Frankie would get one of his men to finish and process them the next day. When their business was done, they looked at each other, slightly awkward about the leavetaking, each wondering if the other was going to suggest a drink or a meal. As a kind of halfway measure, not too personal but still quite friendly, Flora asked if she might go down to Bellevue Street and take another look round the flat. So of course he offered to escort her, and of course she accepted.

Even though the electricity was switched off at the mains, the house was full of soft evening sunlight, and it was beautiful. They wandered from room to room, and Flora expounded on her ideas for decorating and furnishing. Frankie listened, entranced. Flora, it seemed to him, had incredible taste and style, and a surefooted understanding of just how to bring out the best in this particular flat.

"I wish I'd seen your Inverness place" he said, wistfully.

"Oh, it was a modern flat; nothing like this. The decor completely different, modern, bright and airy, but hopefully comfortable and restful all the same. I always seem to finish up with jobs that require a restful home to come back to at night! And a cat: I gave my ginger tom to a neighbour in Inverness. I can't live without a cat. Maybe I'll treat myself to a cream Persian this time."

Frankie took mental note of the fact that a cream Persian was obviously an expensive cat: perhaps it would make a suitable engagement gift?

They sat down together on the window seat in the lounge, gazing around them, outwardly contented. But he had brushed her fingers accidentally as they sat down, and to Flora's amazement she was seething with desire. Those black eyes of his...that unfathomable expression...his tall, wiry body...the heat from him, the smell of him. Her nipples were getting hard and prominent. As the evening cooled down around them, she hoped he could not see those nipples pushing through the thin cotton knitted jumper she was wearing.

Of course he had seen. As they chatted, casually, of this and that, he knew. But Flora was a lady, and so he did nothing.

Flora was on full heat by now, and had seen his pupils expanding as he had looked at her, and had glanced downwards and seen the bulge in his crotch. She waited, and he did nothing. So she stood up and asked him to move while she tried the shutters on the windows, to see if they worked. She closed them and turned to face him in the gloom. Only the light coming through the kitchen window filtered through to them. Without a word, she lifted off her jumper. And then took off her bra.

Even then, he did nothing. And she did not understand the dying of the expression which had been on his face up till now. She did not understand that she had, in that instant, ceased to be a lady and become, instead, just another whore. Frankie was terribly disappointed in her, and felt she had made a fool of him by pretending to be what she clearly was not.

Frankie was angry. His dreams of respectability and two point four children and a labrador had been put off, possibly for some time, till he found a real lady. Still, standing there looking at her, he saw that she had really sensational breasts. Big and billowy, they were. She must really have crammed them into tight bras up till now, for he'd never noticed the size of them. Her nipples were standing proud, and her eyes were huge and her mouth was slightly open. Her knickers must be creamed already. So why not? He wanted her, right now, and she was, as all whores always are, available. There was no reason for him not to fuck her. And after that, he would never see her again. There were enough whores in his life already, and Flora was an amateur.

"Suck me" he said, coldly.

A shock went through her and left her shivering but still desperately aroused. She had not expected him to be like this...except deep in her heart, there, there she had not only expected it but wanted it. She dropped to her knees and unzipped him, took him in her mouth, sucked and tongued him, caressed his balls, squeezing gently, pulling upwards with her teeth only just touching him, until she felt his legs begin to shake and tasted the saltiness of his juices.

"Get up, whore" She stood, aching with desire, before him. "Take that skirt off. And everything else. I want you naked. NOW."

She stepped quickly out of her clothes. He had not removed anything. She tried to undo his trouser belt but was pushed back forcefully.

He reached out and pulled the hair between her legs, worked his fingers inside her, rubbed her, stroked her, all without saying a word, until he felt she was ready to give him maximum pleasure. She was shaking all over, her head flung back, lost in exquisite sensations. She would have done anything he asked. And he knew it.

"Turn round and bend over; hold the edge of the window seat." She obeyed. And now she heard the trouser belt being slid off, and she trembled afresh, but the trembling was still lust. Her hair, dripping with sweat, fell over her face. And with each stroke of the belt across her backside she flinched and convulsed inside and the moistness of her ran down her thighs. Then he opencd her again with his fingers, pushing and fingering, until she was almost ready to come and her knees were buckling with the pleasure of it. Only then did he thrust inside her, only then did he give her what she ached for, and when he did, he drove it so deep and so hard that she gasped, over and over again, until she gurgled and screamed as she climaxed, orgasming over and over as he continued to ram into her, on and on, as she slid helpless from the window seat and lay face down on the floor and he lay on top of her, his hands underneath her crushing her breasts, tugging her nipples, as he drove into her over and over and on and on, till he was finally satisfied and she was almost unconscious.

When he had come, and they had breathed deeply for a moment, and she began to feel human again, he turned her over. He was still fully clothed. He pulled and pushed on her breasts until they were sore, until her clitoris started to throb again, softly, and then he stroked that and pulled at it too, till her back began to arch and she sought him with her hands, to guide him into her. But he was limp. He continued to rub and finger her, and she arched and bucked and moaned towards another climax. And just as she was about to come, needed only one stroke more to come, he stopped.

Her eyes were closed, and she waited for the coup de grace, she needed it, she waited...and it did not happen. She looked up to find him casually zipping up his trousers and putting the belt back through its loops.

"Whores always want more" he said, in a dreadfully normal

voice.

"Please" she whispered "No more games...come back.."

"It wasn't a game. It wasn't even a particularly satisfying fuck, to be honest." He threw the keys of the flat down to her, there, naked on the floor. "You can see yourself home. You never know: you might pick up some extra business, on the way. Your poor father. Poor old Rev., with such a whore for a daughter. Such an untalented whore."

And while she gaped with astonishment and hurt, and tried to cover her nakedness with her discarded clothes, he turned on his heel without another word, and left.

Alone in the deepening night she dressed, and left, humiliated and shocked. She got to the bed and breakfast about five minutes before her mother called, and it was difficult for her to sound normal for she was on the brink of tears.

"About your programme on AIDS victims and their rights, dearest" her mother began, all bright and chatty. "I was thinking, this afternoon...why don't you ask your father to participate? It would get you two together again, and you know he is an excellent speaker, and he would give your programme what did you call it? editorial balance. (Your father has just walked past me, dearest, and I think he looked interested!)"

"I don't think so Mum. At least I'll think about it. Thanks for suggesting it, though."

"Are you all right, dear? You sound a bit shaky. Did your meeting with Frankie go all right?"

"The meeting went fine, Mum. The mortgage is all sorted out. I - I went back down to the flat afterwards for another look round, and...I'm not sure if I want it any more, that's all. I'll make up my mind tomorrow."

"But you were so in love with it!"

"Yes. I think maybe I was. More than I knew. Look Mum, I'm awfully tired... would you mind if I....?"

"Not at all dearest. You get a good night's sleep."

But of course she did not. And in the morning she had to get through her work as best she could. But by lunchtime, her humiliation had transmuted into rage, and she went to the basement in Frederick Street, hoping to find Frankie there and hoping to throw the keys in his face.

He was there. And at the sight of him, her resolve changed. This was someone she remembered from way back, this was someone she had liked, and trusted.

"Your office, now" she said, and Frankie, surprised in front of his staff, agreed without a murmur. Once the door was shut behind them, he waited for her to speak. He hadn't stopped kicking himself yet, for losing such a good prospect as Flora, all for the sake of a quick rut which was neither here nor there in the scheme of things.

"You stupid little boy!" she began, and he was startled. "You're one of those monolithic prehistoric morons who divide women up into those on pedestals and the other ones, the other ones, the whores, who are less than the dust beneath your chariot wheels...aren't you?" For once he was unable to think of a reply.

"*You cretin!* Did you think it was any different for us than it is for you? You had sexual feelings towards me last night, but oh, that's fine, because you're a male, one of the lords of creation, you can do no wrong. But for me to feel it too, well, that makes me a miserable creature you can afford to humiliate and insult. I trusted you, I felt safe with you, I was halfway towards being in love with you! That's why I felt all right about making love with you! You're not the first man I ever had sex with and I'm not your first woman either. But it's okay for you, is it, Frankie, but not okay for me? That makes you worse than a slut: it makes you a fool. Still, I wasn't a virgin, so by God you're right, what a whore! Oh Frankie, you stupid bastard. You went and spoiled it all. What on earth *for*, Frankie?"

He still couldn't think of quite what to say. He was in his office mode, his respectable mode. So he couldn't just smack her in the face, which was what he generally did if one of his whores got uppity. As his anger towards her grew, so did his lust for her. And his visions of marrying her began to swim back into his mind.

107

Perhaps, after all, he could tolerate her the way she was? Yes. If he could get her back, he could tolerate much.

Now he knew what to say.

"I'm sorry." He put his arms round her and squeezed her towards him so that there was no mistaking the hardness in his groin. "I went too far with the bitch routine last night. It's just me. Sex brings out the beast in me, I suppose. Sex with you certainly does. I want to fuck you right here, right now. But only if you'll agree to have dinner with me tonight. And tomorrow night. You set me on fire, you know that: you know that. I do think the world of you; I do respect you; but not while we're fucking."

She was struggling quite seriously against him, which excited him more. He stopped her mouth with his, and she could hardly believe it when she felt him lift her skirt and his hand went into her panties and he groped around and fingered her, roughly, insistently, until she stopped struggling and leaned back gasping for breath.

"Jesus, Frankie!" was all she said. "This was NOT what I had in mind when I came here."

He grinned. "You haven't come, here, yet. But you're going to."

And he pulled her panties down to her knees and left her sweating there for a moment while he locked the door. The carpet was all wool, and very thick and soft. And what they ate for lunch was each other.

Afterwards, she walked back to Radio Forth in a daze. He had handled her and treated her almost as roughly as the night before, but this time, when they were dressed, he had kissed her chastely on the cheek before she left and promised to collect her from the bed and breakfast around eight o'clock, to take her for supper.

What kind of man was he? The question was becoming academic. She was hooked. She could see what the future would be like: a sweet and gentlemanly man for a husband, a tiger in bed. It was hard to wipe the smile off her face as she sat at her desk. She wondered how long it would take Frankie to get the smell of sex out of his office, so he could see his clients there.

The phone call from Albert Kennedy surprised her. He was asking if she would consider him as a guest on the programme with Doctor Douglas. As her father's appearance would embarrass her, he hoped he might be acceptable as a substitute, allowing her proper balance without personal upset. He was very smooth. She still wasn't at all sure that People for Purity constituted real editorial balance alongside a Government spokesman, and she said so: he answered that as they were now a national organisation, secular and multi-party, with views diametrically opposed to the government's, they were indeed equal and opposite. So she consented, with the proviso that Dr Douglas had not yet agreed to come and it was only if he did that Albert would be invited on air. Along with a spokesperson for one of the highrisk groups, she added, thinking of Gerry Hansen. He had no choice but to agree, but he did not sound happy.

She immediately faxed those two names to Terry Aitken. And Terry ran them, as a matter of course and normal procedure, through her personal computer terminal, using a programme to which only she, in the Media Office, had access. And Terry found Albert Kennedy's name there, together with some details which she could not pass on to Andrew Douglas or anybody else. She telephoned Andrew and suggested that if he was going to Scotland for the Parliamentary Summer Recess, he might consider an interview with Radio Forth.

They had not yet discussed the summer recess, but this was as good a time as any for Andrew to suggest what he had in mind.

"On one condition, O Media Guru Mine: that you come with me to hold my hand. And then come on with me to St Fillans and spend a week or two lazing in picture postcard country. With me. Will you?"

"It's all right for some. I don't get the entire summer off, only three weeks. And I've already booked...that is to say...oh, why didn't you ask me sooner? You really want me to give up a fortnight in Turkey in favour of a fortnight in Perthshire?"

"I really do."

"Okay. Do you guarantee the weather?"

"Unconditionally. I guarantee it will rain. But there will be" he continued, in his best broadcast voice, "sunny spells."

"As long as it's you that's weaving the spells, I'll be there. Thankyou. So do I tell Radio Forth it's a goer? Good on you. See you tonight."

He could not quite figure out if there was something not quite right with her voice or not. But as she volunteered nothing, he said nothing.

The 'yes' from Terry Aitken rounded off Flora's day nicely, especially when she told the Programme Controller. He was very nearly excited, and set about phoning the rest of the Scottish independent stations to sell the programme to them, as a live phone-in, sent by landline as it happened. As they already owned Radio Tay, there was only Clyde and Northsound and Moray Firth to get round: Clyde said yes immediately, Northsound bargained him down on price, and little Moray Firth apologetically asked if they could have it for nothing. Still, it was an achievement, the first programme of its kind to be networked in Scotland live. He just caught Flora as she was leaving, to tell her how successful he had been.

"That'll up your audience a bit! The whole of Scotland! We'll move it into prime time in the morning, I think; the evening audiences are too small for something like this. So you'll have around fifty times your usual audience listening; have fun!"

She tried to look pleased. The whole of Scotland, listening to a rookie? She would dry...she would corpse...she would forget all her questions...she would get obscene phone calls...she couldn't do it! Then she thought of what her mother would say if she heard Flora whining like this. And she smiled, and she rallied, and she began to look forward to it. She caught the bus to the bed and breakfast and had a long bath, prior to getting ready for eight o'clock, and Frankie.

Out at the manse, Frankie was just arriving to pick up his grandad, who was now a member of People for Purity and, being wheelbound, the perfect choice for answering the telephone. He did several shifts a week, and was glad and proud to be useful again.

110

The Reverend was at home, and came out smiling from the kitchen, to say cheerio to Mr Dunn.

"Stalwart work, Jock, as always, thank you so much" he beamed, and shook Grandad's hand warmly. Albert Kennedy glided out of the kitchen behind Peter Spencer. "Frankie, you haven't met Albert Kennedy, have you? Frankie Dunn, Albert: Albert, Frankie. Jock's grandson, and a good boy."

The two men shook hands. Albert looked casually enough at Frankie, yet Frankie had the distinct impression that Albert had just scanned his soul, and recognised something in it. He put it down to imagination.

"And are you going to be joining us then, Frankie?" asked Albert.

Jock spoke up hastily in his defence. "No, my Frankie's not much of a church-goer, are ye, Frankie? But he's a fine lad all the same."

"But my goodness, People for Purity is quite separate from the church" said Albert. "We have agnostics and atheists and Hindus and Baptists and Jews and Muslims and just about everybody. We have middle-class people and working-class people and one or two extremely rich people and one or two very poor ones. What we have in common binds us all together."

"Well" said Frankie "Grandad's been very enthusiastic about it all, but I must admit I haven't quite cottoned on to what it's all really about yet."

"Wiping the scum off the face of the earth" said Albert, quite calmly.

"And the scum would be...?"

It was Peter Spencer who replied. "Junkies and drunks and homosexuals and rapists and murderers and muggers and thieves and in particular, in particular, people who are spreading the worst plague since mediaeval times. That scum. That dangerous scum."

"AIDS? I see." Frankie was thinking fast. What with the potential for mortgages and insurances and pensions from all the members of this organisation, and the piquant idea that he might possibly gain access to names, the names of various sorts of 'scum' which the more psychopathic of his clients might pay very well to be allowed to eliminate, People for Purity was beginning to sound like something Frankie Dunn ought to be getting into.

"It's a right good cause, Frankie" interjected Grandad, proudly.

"Well nobody in his right mind could disagree with that" said Frankie affably. "But I'm not much of a one for joining things, really. And my business does take up a fair bit of my time. Still...I could be tempted. But what could I possibly offer you?"

Grandad looked up at Peter Spencer with pleading eyes. "Frankie's got such a good head for business, and for money, and for advertising campaigns an'that, haven't ye Frankie? Well what aboot the two million? We need advice on that, and how tae spend it for the biggest possible result. I mentioned our Frankie tae ye already in that connection, didn't I: maybe he would be willin', now?"

He couldn't possibly mean two million POUNDS, could he? Where did people like this get money like that? It made Frankie's heart beat faster just thinking about it.

Peter Spencer knew how well Frankie's business was doing, and had heard how astute he was at managing finances. He was very keen to have Frankie on board, especially as it would gladden the heart of his old friend Jock. He had already mentioned this idea to Albert, but Albert had said, could we wait till I meet him, me being a disinterested party, as it were? So now Peter turned and raised a questioning eyebrow at Albert, and Albert nodded.

"Why don't you take a day or two to think it over, Frankie my boy: we would be delighted to have you, but you must think it through properly. We don't want to be taking up too much of your time. He turned once more to Albert. "We're all very proud of Frankie, aren't we, Jock?"

Jock smiled, Frankie looked modest, everyone shook hands again, and Frankie wheeled his grandfather out to the car.

"Will ye do it, my lad, d'ye think?"

"Why" smiled Frankie, fondly "Just so you can keep it in the family, like?"

"Well now the minister has been more of a father to you than your own father, whoever he was. So I suppose I do think of him as family, yes. Nothing wrong wi' that, is there?"

"Of course not, Grandad. Not a thing. I remember him quite well from when we lived in Roslin, before you retired. He always had sweeties when he came to the house! Grandad...are you sure my mother never even hinted who my father might be?"

"Oh, Frankie, I'd cut my arm off to be able to tell you. She wouldn't say a word, didn't even put anything down on your birth certificate. I'm so sorry, my boy. When she took off, when you were just a bairn, she didn't even leave a note. I don't know what went wrong: we never blamed her, never gie'd her a hard time, we were as helpful as we knew how. But we must hae failed her badly somewhere along the way, else she'd no' have run off. It was a terrible blow to yer Grannie, right enough. Me too. But at least we hud you, Frankie my boy."

Son of a whore, he thought, and looking to marry a whore. Still, with two million pounds to play with soon, and a new operation making victims available safely to highpaying maniacs, and a nice highprofile bit of public service as Treasurer and Communications Manager of People for Purity, things in general were looking up for F. Dunn Esquire.

And that, after all, was all that mattered in the world.

CHAPTER FOUR

On the following Thursday morning, Andrew Douglas woke to the smell of fresh pancakes, bacon, and strong coffee, wafting from his galley kitchen. There was also Terry's voice humming a bright, summery pop song. He turned in the cool cotton sheets and stretched luxuriously, wiggling his toes and smiling. Memories of last night wafted to him from Terry's side of the bed, and he smiled some more.

Remembering Terry's comments on his dressing-gown, he wrapped himself in the top sheet, toga-style, and wandered through to the kitchen in his bare feet. The floors were already warm from the sunshine pouring through the tiny windows.

Terry, wearing an entrancingly silly short thing with big flowers splashed all over it, waved her spatula at him menacingly.

"Get back! No men allowed in the kitchen! You can set the table if you like, though. After all, you're the one who knows where everything is. It defeats me: I can't find the pepper, or the maple syrup, or the eggs."

He leaned against the doorway and smiled fondly at her.

"The maple syrup and the eggs are still in the shops. The pepper is on the top shelf behind you."

"Still in the shops? What kind of a house is this? Get thee hence, Sir Douglas, and bring back the aforementioned. Or it'll be a pretty devoid sort of American breakfast."

"There's ordinary syrup, won't that do? And we can do without eggs, can't we?"

"Hm. All right. But this is the second breakfast I have eaten here, and I can tell you, they are nothing to write home about. Next time..."

"Next time I shall take you to Joe's, and you can gorge yourself on morello cherry pie with scented cream. I promise."

"Okay. As long as they do big portions."

He folded her in his arms and she did not complain.

"You are the most appalling glutton I have ever met" he

114

mumbled approvingly through her hair. She moved against him so softly, so gently, so sensuously that it took the distinctive smell of burning bacon to drag them both back to reality, and his toga had developed an interesting projection down the front.

Over breakfast she demanded to be told all about St Fillans, and his house, and the countryside.

"We'll go to Oban too" he promised "And take the boats to Barra and Tiree and Mull and all over the place."

"And will your housekeeper disapprove of me tremendously?"

"You'll be the talk of the town in no time. The women will go into huffs, and the men will envy me. Especially when they see you."

"Couldn't we do without a housekeeper while I'm there? I can do things. I'm not entirely useless. I wield a mean Hoover, for example. And you should see me with a feather duster."

"And nothing else?"

"Maybe just a garter."

"We'll do without a housekeeper, then."

"Stop looking at me like that. We'll never get to work on time. I warn you."

"You stop looking so gorgeous, then."

She pulled a gargoyle face. He affected delight.

"Why, Miss Smith, you're beautiful!"

He couldn't remember ever feeling so happy. But, life being what it is, it didn't last. By ten o'clock he was back in the Small Conference Room at 79 Whitehall, facing the committee, trying to hammer out their first Report to Cabinet. Although the Report had first to be given to Sweeting, he had no power to bluepencil one dot or comma: it was simply a courtesy so that he would have his comments ready for the Cabinet meeting.

Every man and woman in the room had strong convictions that their own personal major concern should form the principal meat in the report, along with recommendations which they themselves had worked out. It wasn't a Committee today, he reflected grimly, it was a rabble.

Yet every one of them had a perfectly valid point, there was no doubt about that. The simplest solution would have been to incorporate them all into a massive report which covered all the known angles, with all the known information, all the intelligent projected statistics, and all the ideas for tackling each area of problems. This he was determined not to do. It would be an indigestible, unwieldy report so seething with information that it would give Cabinet a perfect excuse for sitting on it for months on end, deliberating each fine point till it was no longer current. He had no intention of allowing this to happen.

So after waiting and listening for a while, he offered the sensible solution: that each of them compile a very short one-page report on his or her area of particular concern and expertise, and that they jointly choose one pressing concern to ram home effectively as the principal ingredient of the report. This was immediately agreed upon, with relief on all faces. The next problem was to identify the most pressing case, the most urgent necessity.

"Each one of you this morning" Andrew began "has been emphasising one aspect, one common aspect, of the information you hold: each one of you has said, in these or similar words, 'when people realise....'. I contend that this means that we have already agreed upon the principal recommendation; that we push very hard for a massive Public Education Programme, as we discussed last week. How do you all feel about that?"

They looked at each other' faces, and nodded. Yes.

"And now to the difficult bit: what is it we are to recommend that the programme be designed to achieve? I have received all your separate suggestions, for which many thanks. They are all worthy. They all contain information which, yes, we wish every living soul on the planet would take on board. But after what we heard last week about the reaction of people, and especially young people, who are the highestrisk group, to the most praiseworthy efforts...well, I am very worried that we may be proposing a great deal of money be spent on a complete waste of time. If they won't listen, if they won't believe us, how can we get the message across? If the principal message is safe sex, which it really has to be, how do we make that message persuasive, how do we cross the huge barriers of apathy and disbelief out there?"

There followed many suggestions as to how to sell safe sex to a disinterested public who did not truly believe that anything very bad was really out there, and if it was, it certainly had nothing to do with them.

Jasmine Elliot was especially pressing on this issue, having spent three years in Central Africa dealing with the results of the unstoppable, incurable virus.

"Denial is the keynote all the way through" she said. "People deny that there's a problem, people deny that they are promiscuous, they then deny that they have the virus, they deny they are dying of AIDS...their relatives, especially their parents, deny that the diagnosis is correct. Whatever we tell them, they just won't believe it: look at the way S.T.D. cases are increasing everywhere."

Andrew tried a new tack, one which had just occurred to him.

"This may sound like a rather stupid idea...or even quite wrong, quite almost criminal...but if people disbelieve what we tell them on principle, because we are seen as representing authority, couldn't we...lie to them? Then if they disbelieved us, they would be reaching the truth, themselves. And then, because they had thought of it themselves, they would believe it. Am I making any sense?"

John Longfellow and the other more conservative members of the committee were outraged and amused. But one or two, Jasmine among them, looked at him and thought it through and began to look much less stressed.

"You mean...do a Mark Anthony?" asked Jasmine, almost smiling.

"That's the one: 'I come to soothe your spirits, not to fright them'...or something."

Dawn broke on many of the faces round the table.

"After all, not many of you will die..in the first few years, anyway" shrugged one committee member.

"And there'll be more jobs left for the rest of us" added another, grinning.

"So really, don't panic" finished a third. "That's our

117

recommendation."

They looked round at each other, with a certain amount of glee.

"It worked with my children" Jasmine volunteered.

"And mine" chorused several of the other ladies.

"Yup. For example, I remember...I'm sure it won't really matter if you don't take this medicine: I'm sure you'll get better all by yourself, eventually. I expect this medicine really won't be any use. Let's throw it out, shall we?" She grinned. "Little swine took his spoonful like a hero, after that, and no more complaints or whining."

"Exactly" said Andrew. "I think any advertising agency worth it's salt should have quite a good time with this one. It's novel, if nothing else! But do we all really agree that this is the tack to take? We do? Excellent."

The rest of the meeting went very smoothly, and had a distinctly end-of-term feeling about it. Andrew had arranged for Judy to organise a buffet lunch for them all, and the chat was all supportive and pleasant and, for once, with some hope in it. Jasmine was slightly less cheerful than some of the others, and Andrew drew her quietly aside to ask what was the matter.

"It's not committee business, don't worry...just personal stuff." She clearly did not want to be drawn, but Andrew liked and respected her and wanted to help if he could, so he gently persisted. Eventually she sighed and said

"It's my family. My husband, really. He wants to take our daughters out of school and keep them at home in purdah. He's never been that orthodox before, but he's as scared as the rest of us about AIDS. Every man walking the streets is a threat, now. Every male schoolteacher, every male schoolchild. Some of the men he knows at the mosque have been talking about this new group they are joining...'People for Purity'."

Something twitched at the back of Andrew's mind.

"I think I'm sharing a radio programme with one of that lot, up in Edinburgh, quite soon. I don't actually know that much about them."

"You don't want to. From what my husband says, they make

118

fundamentalist Moslems look like liberals. Well no, that's an exaggeration. But only just. Some of the Moslem men are taking it up because it agrees with what they secretly believe but can't really get away with in this country. It's not so much the don't drink, don't smoke, don't have sex outside of marriage...all that is reasonable enough I suppose, given the dangers. What worries me and most of my Moslem women friends is the way they provide almost an excuse for the fundamentalists to insist on taking us women back a few centuries, to where we had no life as well as no rights. Of course it's all done in the name of protecting us. Once, it was protecting us from the depredations of men. Now, it's protecting us from the virus, and the Multiple Drug Resistant T.B. But it amounts to going back into purdah, cut off from the world entirely and never being allowed to see a living man except your husband and your young boy children. For those of us who have gone ahead and made a life and a career for ourselves, it is very worrying."

"I always felt - forgive me - that that kind of attitude presupposed the fact that all men are weak, unselfcontrolled rapists. To me, it's an insult to men as well as to women."

"Quite. And even for a fundamentalist, the man is held equally responsible; if a man even harbours lustful thoughts towards a woman, he is censured and disciplined by the mullah. Yet they, the men, they are not kept in secret courtyards: it's easier, you see, just to remove all temptation from the poor petted darlings, and lock us all away. Turn us back into nothing: nothing but convenient machines for reproducing boy children. And cooking and cleaning, of course, and agreeing with everything our menfolk say, however inane."

"Surely not now. Not in Britain, anyway."

"Think again. There's a pressure group building up to force the authorities to allow Moslems to follow all their customary religious practices; and that includes purdah. Look what happened in Iraq, Iran, even Algeria, over the last few years: as fundamentalism increased, women who had earned their living and run their own lives for years were taken away and draped in black and locked into courtyards.   Not people any more, but possessions.   It's very...convenient."

"Dear God."

She smiled, sadly. "It's not your problem. Except as a sideline, one of the many things that are happening because of AIDS and now, the T.B. scare. I feel quite certain that it won't only be Moslem women who are kept out of circulation; I can see quite a backlash against women's liberation, all over. In fact, there is already a groundswell of opinion that it is principally women who are at fault for the spread of AIDS, because of the fact that it is easier for a woman to infect a man than vice versa. So although it takes two for this to happen, it is the woman's fault. It has a dreadfully familiar ring to it, does it not? Still, at least it's a change from homosexuals being to blame. It's a more socially acceptable way to think; you see blaming women will appeal to a much greater cross section of the public than blaming homosexuals. Homosexuals are still men. And men much prefer to blame women, for anything and everything. In general terms I think you'll find women who are promiscuous have a particularly hard time of it. In the particular situation of being a Moslem woman, it means...back to arranged marriages and the locked courtyards."

"Surely you won't allow this to happen to you personally?"

"I have few choices. If I leave my husband I become a pariah in my own religious community. I will be ostracized, spat upon in the street. And I would never be allowed to see my children again. Maybe I could take that; maybe not. I have a lot of thinking to do. I am only telling you this so that, if I am not here when the Committee reconvenes after the summer recess, you will understand why. If I can, I will write to you. Or you may get a letter from my husband."

"And if you are here, it means...? Oh, Jasmine. Is there nothing I can do? Put pressure on your husband?"

"Please, no: things are difficult enough between us already. You see my husband is the son of a Moslem mother and a Christian father. He took his mother's religion; but as a convert, and because he is a halfcaste, he is more fanatical about it all than most. He feels he must be seen to be more devout, more dedicated, more wholehearted, than anyone else.   Please don't think he is an unpleasant or a bad person: he is not. What he is doing he does out of genuine conviction, and a real desire to protect me and our daughters and our granddaughters still to come. Not all Moslem husbands are like that, but he is. I am one of the lucky ones."

Andrew felt as if he was living in a timewarp. He had difficulty in believing that a modern, educated, experienced doctor like Jasmine could actually be contemplating the kind of death-in-life she was describing, and contemplating it with a certain amount of equanimity. She saw his thoughts on his face, and grinned.

"I quite enjoy sewing, you know. And I can weave. Maybe I could look upon it as an extended holiday; a retreat. Or very early retirement. There are positive aspects of it too, honestly. Peace, security...and a lot less stress than the way I am living right now. It's not hell on earth, Andrew: it's just different. And as a Moslem girl, I have always had it in the back of my mind as a possibility. It's not the culture shock to me that it is to you. Of course it will be very different for the younger ones. Very hard. That bothers me more. There will be terrible rifts in many Moslem families.   Girls and young wives are not so fatalistic any more. Or so obedient. I am nearly fifty: I was brought up to unquestioning obedience. That's the difference."

It was plain that she had already made up her mind, even if she had not admitted this to herself yet. Andrew had a strong impulse to hug her, but restrained himself and merely took her right hand in both of his.

"Take care of yourself, my dear. Always. Either way."

He sent Sweeting's copy of the report to his office, rather than taking it by hand. Perhaps this was discourteous, but he really did not want to see the man any more than he had to. Judy and the team had done a fine job on it, typing and proofing and correcting and binding it so that it looked, and was, very professional, despite the fact that the presentation to Cabinet was just under a week after the last Committee meeting, on the last Wednesday before the end of July and the beginning of Parliament's summer recess. A list of the topics covered in the report was also circulated to those members of Cabinet who would be present at the meeting at Downing Street, so that they would have a chance to formulate questions and opinions.

Andrew and Terry managed to have lunch together that day, before Andrew went into the lion's den. Terry was optimistic: 'He's in good form today, the P.M. I even persuaded him to do another radio interview with Greg Sharp. Full of beans, he is. Wonder who's bed he fell out of on the right side this morning?!'

"What an uncouth youth you are" he remonstrated teasingly. "Can't a man be happy without having just come from a sexual hotbed?"

"No, not really" she replied smugly.

"You may have a point there after all" he acknowledged.

"You should know about my points by now! Now please stop talking dirty over lunch, it's very unbecoming in a gentleman of your advanced years. Ouch."

"You deserved worse."

"I know. I think you should give me a severe talking to. Tonight at your place, for example."

"Are your bags all packed for the train tomorrow?"

"Yup. I packed my gold lame halter top and my itsywitsy bikini and my most lowcut cocktail dresses and...oh, don't panic. I don't possess a gold lame halter top, honest. Oh, you should see your face!"

"I didn't mean...I mean I wouldn't care if people...oh, you know."

"Yes you would care, and so would I. God, it's half one already: you'd better get going. And remember, keep it simple. Some of the Cabinet went to public schools. And try to get out of there by five; I really want to cobble the press release together myself with the P.M., before we two head for the hills."

She drove him to Downing Street, as her own office was not far distant. Even so, he was two minutes late turning up, which flustered him. The Prime Minister and all his merry men (or a considerable number of them) were waiting for him, and for once, the atmosphere was quite relaxed. The heady prospect of a holiday enlivens even sober and industrious Ministers of the Crown.

Unfortunately, it also made them less than willing to listen seriously to an endless flow of doomladen information. They shifted in their seats as he talked, and they exchanged glances with upraised eyebrows, and they looked out of the window at the sunshine, and they thought of their appalling children and how they would be forced to spend many tedious hours entertaining them over the holidays, and they daydreamed of silver sands and turquoise waves, and they shuffled over to the coffee table more often than usual, just to be doing something.

The only exceptions were Sweeting and the Prime Minister. They listened at full attention. Sweeting looked angry, but the P.M. merely evinced interest.

John Longfellow's report on the potential difficulties of finding hospital beds and treatment for AIDS sufferers, and his predictions on the shortfall of hospital treatments for everybody else, provoked the first spoken reaction from the P.M.

"Excuse me, Doctor Douglas: Harold, this sounds right in line with our own current thinking, doesn't it? It's good to know we're all pulling together on this very important issue."

Andrew did not quite know what he was talking about, except for a small suspicion that it was going to have something to do with the current proposals for payments by National Health patients for some hospital services. He was right.

"Indeed, Prime Minister" began Harold Sweeting in his most unctuous voice, letting the full plum shades of his true patrimony colour his tones. "It's quite clear from this report that we must forge ahead as soon as possible, if I may say so. We cannot allow our good citizens to find themselves untended when they need treatment, just as we cannot allow them to have their treatment dictated to them by the State."

"Are you going to be building new hospitals, then?" asked

Andrew.

Sweeting smiled at this gross naievety.

"Hardly. That would be more State interference in health care provision, wouldn't it? That's not our way, Andrew. No. Our plans are well known and well documented, but if you would like me to condense them for you...let's just say that free enterprise and the market economy are being allowed into health care in a much more vigorous way than before. And, more importantly, the people themselves are to be given much more reponsibility for their own health. It is a good system: it worked very well in America, when the idea was promoted that the individual must take primary responsibility for their health. Coronary episodes were cut by almost a third over ten years. Most encouraging. We are going to adapt and extend that idea."

He leaned forwards, clearly enthralled by his message.

"The proposal is not entirely a new one; it is something which the British Army has always recognised, and we are simply extending it to all our citizens. The concept of "self-inflicted wounds", Andrew. Why should Joe Public have to pay for the treatment of diseases which people bring on themselves? That's the idea. Lung cancer, for example, in smokers. They will have to pay for their operations, and the aftercare, themselves. Heart attacks in people who stuff themselves with grease and cream and sugar, and take no exercise. They will have to pay for their treatment. And so on. And of course, as you so rightly point out, promiscuous young people who contract AIDS because they couldn't be bothered using a condom: well. Another clear case of self-inflicted wounds, wouldn't you say, Prime Minister?"

"But these treatments cost thousands and thousands of pounds! Nobody is going to be able to afford it! Are you going to let them die?"

"How can you stand there and accuse us of such cold-hearted villainy? Our proposals ensure that that will never happen. We are going to make it mandatory for every citizen to take out separate medical insurance to cover these eventualities. Nobody will die untended. This is Britain, after all."

Andrew's head was swimming. He was thinking of his medical school days, and his friends there. All so eager to be part of the finest health care system in the world, all proud of it, all keen to serve. He wondered how they would react to this.

"And which insurance companies will give such cover to smokers? To obese people? To young unmarried people? And how much will they charge them?"

"They will charge them enough to have a twofold result: one, people will realise that it's time they took better care of themselves. Two, the profits will go to building hospitals to cater for these diseases. So that as the money comes in, so the need for the services DECREASES, while the provision for them INcreases. You see?"

It had a certain logic to it, yet Andrew could see a dozen different scenarios in which this system would fail people. And not just a few people, but many. Many. He could not take the time to go into all this now, with his own report still largely unread, but he resolved to do something about it, when he could.

In the meantime, he carried on. He had expected many interruptions, queries, comments...even derision. But nothing more was said until he came to the principal proposal for the health education programme, by which time he had become enraged by their apathy and his voice and manner were beginning to show the strain a little, despite his best efforts to the contrary.

"...which will cost, to our best current estimates, approximately sixty-five million pounds. As to the creative content; " he got no further. A general snort of cynical derision was heard, and the figure was repeated in rising tones of disbelief all round the table till it reached an incredulous crescendo at the Chancellor of the Exchequer, Ernest Faulkner.

"My dear doctor, you cannot seriously expect us to agree to a figure of that size?"

"Of course not: we anticipate taking a sizeable chunk from our own budget, what we can afford, you understand, and ask the Treasury for the top-up amount. Of course with our own budget being somewhat small, we can only offer about an eighth of that total cost. But we do offer it, as a gesture of cooperation and goodwill more than anything else, to get the ball rolling. You cannot doubt that such a programme is needed; and of course my first attempts to get costings from advertising agencies may not be accurate. It's also worth bearing in mind that even at that initial figure, we are only looking at just over a pound per person, to reach every home in the country. Every person who then takes action to avoid AIDS is saving the Health Service...."

"But he's not, is he?" enquired Sweeting pleasantly. "Not after we introduce the Private Health Care bill. It won't save us the Government - the taxpayers - one penny piece, will it?"

"Then at the very least" and there was ice in Andrew's voice now "at the very least, you will save face in the world community. By looking as if you give a damn about the people who vote you in and then rely on you."

The Prime Minister's good mood had now completely evaporated. Terry had been wrong about his bonhomie being caused by good sex the previous night: it had been caused by his looking forward to good sex all weekend, when his wife took the children away to their cottage in Wales, while he 'worked on various urgent reports' before joining them on the Monday. And Andrew Douglas was spoiling the whole day.

"No tantrums" he said, sharply. "No childish digs and implications. This is too serious an issue."

"Thank you, sir."

"Don't thank me. I'm warning you both: I will not tolerate any dissent. We are here to reach agreement, and we will do so."

Rhubarb and harrumph noises and a bit of thumping approvingly on the table was heard, from all except the two protagonists.
Sweeting spoke with the heavily patronising generosity of victors:

"Never mind, Andrew. Better luck next time. The rest of the report is excellent, really good stuff."

The Prime Minister turned to fix Sweeting with a gaze of utter disinterest before turning back to address Andrew.

"Your suggestion will be taken up. The money will be made

available. If the rest of Cabinet agrees, and in particular of course Mr Faulkner here. Ernest?"

There is nothing so fast on its heels as a politician in full volteface.

"I am delighted to say I most heartily concur with Doctor Douglas. Sixty-five million is, compared to some other budgets I get proposed to me, extremely modest. And money well spent."

Sweeting's face was a picture. Quite which picture, it would have been hard to say. But it certainly wasn't The Laughing Cavalier. The Prime Minister continued.

"You must forgive us if we seem a little preoccupied today, Doctor Douglas. It wasn't the happiest choice of dates for you to present to us: there is no time before Parliament dissolves for the summer, for us to examine your proposals in any depth. We will, all of us, take the report with us back to our constituencies, and study it at home over the summer. If you would be kind enough to make an appointment with my Secretary, once we reconvene....?"

He was being dismissed, before he had even finished reading the report. He should have felt indignant, but he was so elated about the success of his principal proposal that the summer sunshine had already entered his spirit, and he smiled at them all, even Sweeting, and quite understood and wished them all a very pleasant recess.

He paused only to say 'Gentlemen, I beg you to remember that while you are deliberating, another 5,000 people a day are becoming HIV positive, in the world. By the time Parliament resumes, that's... around a third of a million." Then he picked up his papers and walked out, head held high.

He bumped into Terry before he reached the front door. She was on her way in, for her meeting with the P.M. to write up the press release based on Andrew's meeting. She looked at him questioningly, and he allowed his face to light up and took a bow. She grinned back at him: she did not know the contents of his report, and so had no opinions either way as to the obviously successful outcome of his presentation; she was simply glad to see him happy.

Uncertain of the wisdom of kissing in public, they merely shook

127

hands, for a fraction longer than was absolutely necessary. Their arrangements to meet later were already made.

"Have a good holiday, Ms. Aitken" he waved cheerily, while the policeman waved him through the door.

"You too, Doctor Douglas" was her airy reply, while she walked away from him and wiggled her fingers behind her just like Liza Minelli in Cabaret (she hoped) only minus the green nail varnish.

He walked the couple of hundred yards back to Whitehall and his final end-of-day wrap-up meeting with Judy. She was delighted with the success of their proposals, and produced a miniature of whisky for putting in their pot of tea, to celebrate. Slowly they went through the piles of incoming mail, which was still pouring in day after day.

"Still no follow-up from Johnston Carmody about the forensics on Miss Hislop?"

"'Fraid not. I sent him a reminder the other day, in case he'd forgotten, but nothing back from him yet. That reminds me..." she fished under one of the piles and produced a handwritten letter.

"This came second post today. Another non-drug-taking, no-blood-transfusions HIV Positive and hopping mad that nobody believes him. It's his mother that's HIV, by the way, but the letter is from the son."

"So she's not a virgin, then, unless she's claiming that as another miracle!"

"No - but from the sound of it she is the very pillar of respectability."

"Pillars crumble. I still don't see how anybody can get it any other way than the usual. Perhaps I'm being overhard?"

"You haven't been through the Cranks pile recently, have you? Well, there are another half dozen miracle claims since Miss Hislop." She did not mention that photocopies of those particular letters had been quietly sent to a certain person who had specifically requested any such letters after the Miss Hislop incident. What he was going to do with them, she had no idea. But his seniority to her rank was immense, even if he did not work for the Ministry of

128

Health but for another Ministry, whose interest she could not quite understand. And of course the money he had promised for her silence would come in very handy.

"No thanks. You hold on to them. I can think of better reading for the holidays. I suppose we ought to organise some sort of investigation into such claims, but it can wait a couple of months. Well Judy, enjoy your break. You've worked very hard here. If it was in my power, I'd make sure you got the whole summer off. What are you going to do with yourself after your three weeks in France?"

"Oh, Sweeting will find work for idle hands to do, if there's nothing doing here. But I've plenty to do in your absence; I want to go through all the computer files again, make sure we've got everything we need. Make sure that you've got hardcopy digests of everything relevant on your desk the day you get back."

"Now remember: anything of interest, you have my home phone and fax numbers. Don't hesitate. For example, if you manage to compile that estimate we just talked about, the average cost of treating an AIDS patient..."

"Of course."

"Have un beau Calva et cafe complet for me while you're there."

"Have a Drambuie for me in Scotland!"

He made a mental note to bring her back a bottle of the stuff.

"And good luck with your radio interview on Monday: wish I could hear it!"

He had almost forgotten his appointment at Radio Forth, as his mind was full of summer and St Fillans and Terry.

By the time he had walked home, he was brimful of delight and good spirits, a schoolboy, free for the holidays. He bought champagne for their evening meal, and another to make Buck's Fizz for their breakfast. That should shut the wench up about the quality of breakfasts provided Chez Douglas! Once home, he set about preparing dinner for them, with half an eye on the intercom all the time. He expected her around nine, after her work at Downing Street and then home to Battersea to pick up her cases and water her garden and check with the neighbours about taking care of her lovebirds while she was away.

But he had scarce peeled a potato before she arrived, with taxi driver in tow and five bulging suitcases between them, and she looked upset. He paid the driver, ushered her in, enquired anxiously.

"Bloody Frank bloody Ainsley's going to bloody handle you from now on. The P.M. knows about us - you and me - and he's taken me off your case. Bloody useless bloody Frank bloody Ainsley was waiting for me in the corridor after I came out of the Cabinet room, about three minutes after I went in. *Bloody Frank bloody Ainsley!"* She shook her head in disbelief.

"Who is this Frank Ainsley?"

"A yellowing old hack in the Media Office. Straight from the gutter into the gutter press, and then, God help us, he came to work for me. He's useless after lunch time every day, and he's still hung over first thing in the morning. I keep trying to fire him, but I keep getting told to be more charitable. And now he's been brought in over my head. I am livid! Livid! I'd like to say I've never been so insulted in all my life, except of course I have been, often. Ooooh!"

She looked up at him suspiciously.

"I don't hear any poor-little-you noises. And you appear to be smiling." Her voice changed to a dangerous purr. "Why is that? And I warn you: if you say I am beautiful when I'm angry, I will rip out your liver. I mean it!"

"I cannot tell a lie. I'm delighted you've been taken off my case. Delighted. No more skulking around, no more feeling ashamed of being rather unprofessional... I'm relieved. It should be a load off your mind too: you won't have to play pig-in-the-middle between the Prime Minister and me, or Harold Sweeting and me, any more. No more...divided loyalties."

"Actually, and I do regret the blow this is evidently going to cause to your ego, I didn't have any divided loyalties. My first loyalty was always to my profession. To my work. Not to my job, you understand, but to my work. But as the Prime Minister clearly didn't think I was capable of that, and as you clearly think that my little female heart would go all aflutter because of our relationship, and perhaps you believe that the application of sperm to the vagina causes the immediate dissolving of not only the backbone but also the brain...well, I'm glad I shan't be an embarrassment to you any more. Little woman trying to do a man's job can be indulged for a while, eh?, but when LURV comes along, well, she reverts to being treated like a woman again, not a journalist, not a professional, not a person. Perhaps you have a frilly apron I could borrow, to wear twenty-four hours a day?"

Hot tears were running down her cheeks, which made her even more angry. She dabbed at them perfunctorily with her handkerchief, and turned away from him. She expected to hear apologies spilling from his mouth, yet something in the atmosphere was not quite what she had anticipated. When he spoke, his voice was cold, and she knew immediately she had gone too far.

"Grow up" was all he said, as he rose and walked towards the kitchen. "Beef Stroganoff? Or shall I make you fish fingers and beans?"

She opened her mouth to protest, but the telephone rang.

"Hello? I can't hear you! Ah, Callum! Everything all right? Good, good! Oh fine, fine. Thank you son; I will. One way or another. Yes: see you at St Fillans, last week in August. In fact no, let me know your E.T.A. and I'll pick you up at Glasgow Airport. Okay? Great! Love you, son take care!"

He turned to find her picking up two of her suitcases and trudging sadly to the door. She looked at him in mute misery, and he strode across to her and wrenched the suitcases out of her hands and pushed her back onto the sofa.

"I said" he repeated, but in much gentler tones "grow up. That means staying here and sorting this out, not running away."

"I'm hurting, Andrew."

"Yes well you shouldn't be. There WAS a potential conflict of loyalties, and the P.M. was perfectly proper to do what he did. He'd have done that whatever the mix of the sexes happened to be

131

between the three of us. Margaret Thatcher would have done the same thing. Anybody would. You haven't been insulted, or given a row: things have been adjusted to take new information into account. That's all. It would be extremely unrealistic to imagine that feelings don't matter, don't affect judgement. In men and women and children and probably everything that breathes. So don't allow yourself to feel singled out for vindictive treatment...it's just...a logical policy."

"Shit. I handled it really badly, then, if you're right. When he started in on me; no you're right, dammit, he was just stating his case...I got good and mad. I blushed. I must have looked as angry as I felt. I thought they were all laughing at me."

"I doubt it."

"Hm. They don't all think like you do, unfortunately. Some of them, the ones I've trained in the past, the ones I've had to nurse through press releases and interviews, those ones definitely WERE laughing up their bloody sleeves. But not all of them. And you're quite right, dammit. The P.M. was perfectly calm and wished me happy holidays with some semblance of sincerity."

They hugged, and she sighed and rested against him. He stroked the damp hair from her forehead, and smiled quietly to himself.

"Your're smiling again; I can feel it. What's funny?"

"I was just thinking. About logic and feelings. After all I've just said, and I meant every word of it...I want to go and punch him on the nose for upsetting you."

She snuggled closer into him, like a kitten seeking warmth.

"That's because you love me" she said, with peaceful confidence, not really thinking what she was saying. Then she realised, and stiffened, dreading his reply. But he was still relaxed, still stroking her hair, and she could not see that his expression was first shocked, then thoughtful and then, nuzzling into her hair, profoundly gentle.

"Yes, I do" was all he said, and she curled up on his lap and they said nothing at all for a considerable time, not moving, not kissing, just being.

They slept in. Andrew had patted the alarm clock and gone

straight back to sleep, and when they woke up it was less than an hour till their train left from King's Cross. There was no time for Buck's Fizz in the ensuing panic, so they took the champagne and orange juice with them.

"I'll get that morello cherry pie from you yet, Andrew Douglas!"

At least the minicab was on time, so that they arrived at the station calmed down, beginning to look forward to the day and starving. The Branson Pullman was luxurious and welcoming, and the uniformed attendant led them to their seats with a respectful smile.

"Have you travelled with us before, sir?"

"Yes indeed."

"Then I'll just leave you to it and go make out your luggage receipts, sir, if I may. Welcome aboard."

Terry had not travelled by the new Pullman coach before, and was decidedly impressed.

"It's nice to see you travel first class!"

"Oh, this costs considerably more than first class. But it's worth it. No drunken oilies on their way to Aberdeen...no children screaming up and down the corridors...just rest and comfort and extremely good food in the dining car. Oh, wait till you see the dining car. It'll gladden your piggy little heart, so it will."

He showed her all the buttons and controls for her light, for her seating position, for fresh air. She squirmed her way into the most comfortable possible position for sleeping, squirmed back up again and leaned across the mahogany table between them, and pronounced herself well pleased but hungry, and when could they visit the famous dining car and admire the architecture?

"We'll be called. I booked first call for breakfast, seeing you were going to be with me. I'm getting to know your major weaknesses, you see. The little foibles, we can investigate at our leisure in St Fillans."

"My goodness but you know how to flatter a girl. Pity that wasn't an example of it....ratbag" she added comfortably.

Breakfast was announced within minutes of the train exiting from the long tunnel which leads from King's Cross to the rail route north. The dining car was panelled in mahogany, with pink plush seats and pink velvet carpeting, white linen tablecloths, silver cutlery and pink napkins and crystal glasses. More to the point, the breakfast was delicious, and enormous, with unlimited quantities of mushrooms and bacon and eggs and tomatoes and fried potato scones being pressed upon you by endless streams of waiters whose only wish seemed to be to see you dying happily of cholesterol poisoning before the day was out.

"May I never get an ulcer" said Terry fervently, as she pressed another forkful of highly peppered mushrooms into her mouth.

She managed to make breakfast last almost an hour before she was full up and they ambled back to their seats.

"We'll be in Edinburgh by four o'clock" he reminded her. "You might just cram in lunch and then afternoon tea, before we get there. I've booked us into the Caledonian, at the West End, through till Tuesday morning. Then it's train to Perth and taxi to St Fillans. After that, we'll have my old boneshaker to take us out and about. I plan to show you as much as I can. It is truly beautiful, I promise you."

"Your boneshaker? Is this some marvellous vintage Bugatti or something?"

"Not exactly. More of an out-of-date Vauxhall."

"Oh. I rather fancied myself, for a moment, in full Isadora Duncan getup, long veil flying in the summer breeze...ah well. An anorak in a Vauxhall will have to do."

"I'll take you to the motor museum at Scone. And take pictures of you sitting in a Bugatti with an Isadora hat on. How would that be?"

"You're such a lovely man."

"We aim to please, modom."

"Oh you do please modom, very much." The look that grew between them was such that his neck started to sweat under his collar. At this point, a man of about sixty, expensively suited in summer linen and with a thick head of pure white hair, stopped as he walked past them with the newspaper he had just picked up from the attendant's table.

"Pardon me, but aren't you Doctor Andrew Douglas? Of the AIDS Committee?"

"Oh no DON'T' thought Andrew. 'Don't want to sit down, don't stop, don't talk to us, I want to spend this time with Terry, PLEASE..."

"Would you mind awfully if I sat down for a few minutes? I was intending to write and ask for an appointment with you, but...fortune seems to have accomplished it for me. My name is Jan van Elsen, by the way."

"The Chairman of I.C.I.? Please, do sit down: he may, mayn't he Andrew?"

"Delighted." He stood and shook hands and introduced Terry, subduing his annoyance as best he could.

Van Elsen talked about the weather, about the luxury of the new Pullman class, until he had danced around the roses long enough to decently bring up the reason he wanted to talk to Andrew. Which was, of course, the business of the Committee.

"I also chair a Committee, you see" he explained "and my Committee is most interested in what yours is doing. Because it affects us."

"Mr van Elsen is the current Chairman of the British Manufacturing Industries Board" said Terry, helpfully.

"I have that honour, yes. We represent most of this country's manufacturing companies, from the biggest to the smallest. Of course we are no longer the biggest employers in the United Kingdom, the service industries have that position; but still, as that sector is so fragmented, we do represent possibly the largest single body of employers. I am sure you would rather I did not ramble, Doctor Douglas, and so I will come straight to the point...well, to one of the points upon which I would appreciate your comments."

The first point was only a precursor to a stream of points, a list of concerns which the B.M.I. had recently expressed relating to the spread of AIDS and the new strains of T.B. The manufacturers were principally worried about the two effects of the plague which most directly involved them: a shrinking labour force and a shrinking marketplace. Combined, they would lead to collapse. Not just of these particular industries, as van Elsen pointed out, but to the economy in general...not just in the U.K. but all over the world.

"Already we have 20% of our workforce in Kenya, 27% in Uganda, infected: and on and on, smaller and bigger numbers in other African countries, in Europe, the Middle East, everywhere we operate. Skilled workers and management as well as the blue-collar and secretarial people." He spread his hands helplessly. "If the figures that statistician quoted on the television show you were on are right...it can only get worse."

Andrew grimaced. "If he was right, then the death of industry and even the economy will be merely byblows of the collapse of the human race, and, as such, hardly worth worrying about."

"Yes" said van Elsen "and if that kind of talk becomes generalised, our shareholders are going to pull out and start buying cottages in the country to stock up with canned foods and bottled water. Which means our industries will collapse long before the population has shrunk. And the death of the economy will be unduly hastened."

"Ah. I see. You want me to stop spreading fear and gloom because your profits are starting to hurt. Is that it?"

"Our profits create jobs. And the vast majority of investors are small investors; ordinary people living off the small returns they get from modest holdings of a very few thousand pounds. I refuse to feel guilty for worrying about them. If you're some sort of anticapitalist, fine. I'm not."

"Oh, sit back down again, keep your shirt on. I just get fed up from time to time with everyone interpreting this - this disaster through the filter of exactly how it's going to affect *them, their* lives, *their* jobs, *their* families. If we don't get together and look at the broader picture, we don't deserve to survive this."

"I disagree. Self-interest is the only reliable motivation."

Andrew's eyes opened, and he looked at the man with new respect. He spoke slowly, reluctantly.

"You may have something there. Sadly."

"I truly didn't mean to take up this much of your time. Or to leave my wife sitting alone for quite so long. We're on our way to fish in the Dee, just outside Aberdeen. This is supposed to be a holiday, and here I am talking shop as usual. I'm sorry.' He rose, not in haste this time, and bowed politely to Terry. 'I expect we will meet again sometime. I would only ask you one thing' and he brought his business card from his inside pocket. 'If there's anything we can help with; a health education programme for our workers, anything at all; please get in touch with me. Maybe our reasons are less lofty than yours, but we are every bit as concerned. Anything we can do to help, we will. Enjoy the rest of your trip."

He went back to his seat, leaving an uncomfortable silence behind him.

"Just the radio interview to go" said Terry, softly. "Then you can forget all about it, for three weeks anyway."

"How did you recognise him?"

"Oh well, if you read the papers more often, particularly the business ones, you'd have seen his picture plastered over them. Every company represented by the Board has now got a company doctor on retainer. The doctor will be involved with every recruitment, testing applicants for the HIV virus. Then there will be routine checks on all members of staff every year thereafter. Testing Positive will mean automatic dismissal without reference."

"But that's an incredible workload for the labs!"

"Nope. They're using that instant-assay card, where they print the reagent onto the circuit, drop in a little bit of blood, and get a virtually instant reading, no possibility of error. I remember reading that they the Board were pressuring Sweeting to let them buy the cards themselves, but he insisted that only doctors could have them. Every doctor in the land must be rubbing his hands with glee at the money."

"How come you never told me any of this?"

"It was only in the papers yesterday. You were busy yesterday."

"Then why the hell didn't Sweeting tell me? I'm supposed to have ALL information pertaining to AIDS and how people are reacting to it."

"It'll be in your In tray, I expect."

"Mm. You know, it's a hell of an intrusion into people's privacy, as well. Hasn't there been any backlash from the Civil Rights people?"

"Hasn't been time yet. Anyway, I don't know that there would be. I don't think they'd get much support. People want to feel safe, don't they? By the way, there was speculation in the article yesterday that all Civil Servants and Government employees might be put through it regularly too. That means you and me, doesn't it? So you do YOU feel about it?"

"A good question. Sort of irritated...but...I do understand it. Even though it's totally pointless."

"How can it be?"

"Simple. If somebody tests Negative today, they can get infected tomorrow. By the time next year rolls around, who knows how many people they'll have slept with?"

"Dammit, you're right. Again. Oh Andrew, let's not talk about it any more just now. In fact, let's get the champagne and orange juice out. And toast each other and our holiday. Look: the sun is shining. The countryside is beautiful. And I love you. Let's be happy?"

"Can I just get one of those newspapers and check out bloody Frank bloody Ainsley's press release, before we start being happy?"

"NO."

"All right, all right! On with the motley!"

"Inappropriate use of a quote. You lose ten points. That means you have to buy me two puddings at lunch."

"You mean I wasn't going to have to anyway?"

She pouted, then blew him a raspberry. A very small, ladylike one, of course. The dark clouds rolled off his shoulders again, and he relaxed.

———— • ————

To Flora's relief, the special programme on AIDS was to be broadcast from Studio B, not the normal on-air Studio A. Studio B had a glass wall dividing the performers from the broadcast desk,

138

where an engineer would sit and drive the proceedings, bring in the commercial breaks, and thus enable her to concentrate on the business of conducting the interviews and the discussion.

This, she reckoned, was going to be quite difficult enough without fiddling with volume controls and gainpots and faders. She had spent some time on writing her introductory remarks, and had wanted to prerecord these and put them on cartridge, so that this could be played for a few minutes at the beginning of the broadcast, on the basis that at least this short segment would sound good. But the Programme Controller had firmly refused her permission to do this.

"You can always tell when something's being read, or it's prerecorded" he said. "The audience will feel cheated, especially when we've promoted this as a live programme. No, you'll just have to go over and over your notes until you're confident you'll do it well. Sorry."

Frankie had wanted to be around for the programme, partly, he said, to see how a radio programme was made, and partly because of his new involvement with People for Purity. They had given him the title of Financial and Media Manager, and as Media Manager he felt he ought to know how these things went, especially on this occasion, with Albert Kennedy participating. Flora had gently suggested he do some of the courses at the local Enterprise Trust, as she could not possibly smuggle him in to the radio station whenever he, or she, wanted and she had no influence at all to get him into Scottish Television or the BBC.

He was not pleased, but did not show his anger. He might ride roughshod over her at night, but he knew better than to seriously alienate her during the day, and he was well aware how much she wanted to be truly professional. So there was no way he would insist, or humiliate her by turning up on the day and demanding favours because of his relationship with her. In any case, his anger was fleeting, as life was getting sweeter by the day at the moment and he was in rare good spirits most of the time. The farmer's son from Penicuik way had been tracked down, and though at first he had been highly suspicious of Frankie's offer to take his time murdering the young rentboy, his mounting excitement had convinced him that this was a straight business deal and one which he might never be offered again. He had sold his car to raise the money to pay Frankie the five thousand pounds he had set as the price, and he had casually pointed out to Frankie that if there was any suggestion of blackmail money later, he would be round to see Frankie some dark night.

They understood each other.

Frankie had negotiated a fat fee from his video distributor for the snuff movie, and had already identified another prospect to replace Alec in his organisation. His men had informed him that it was never going to be difficult to replace these boys, as the amount of gay-bashing in the city had increased again, and the prospect of a safe house to operate from, with endless lovers, endless dope and endless cash, was more than enough to attract them. And despite the gay-bashing in Edinburgh, there were still lost young boys coming in to the city from all round, as their sexuality made them even more vulnerable targets in their own smaller communities.

Alec's demise was fixed for the following Saturday night: Frankie wanted it all out of the way before he attended the People for Purity meeting on the Sunday, after church.

The more he thought about it, the more he realised that rent boys were worth a lot more to him a lot quicker this way. If there was indeed an endless supply, why run them as prostitutes when it could take months to reach an income of five thousand pounds from one? Better just to let him operate just long enough to find the next psychopath. A much more businesslike proceeding.

Yes, Frankie Dunn was well pleased with life at the moment. Flora was putty in his hands, and he felt it would not be too long before he could ask her to marry him without fear of rejection. Grandad would be pleased. Jock, too, was happy at the moment, working hard for the movement and pleased to be one of Peter Spencer's key men again. Grandad thought the world of Peter Spencer, and his pleasure was doubled now that his beloved, successful, goodhearted Frankie was part of the organisation.

Because of the minister having thrown out his daughter, Jock never mentioned about Frankie and Flora walking out. But he was bursting to do so, sure that Peter Spencer would be glad and happy and that Flora's marriage would sort out the family problems. After all, how could anyone go on being difficult when they were getting Frankie Dunn for a son-in-law?

On the Sunday before the Monday special programme on Radio Forth, the Church of St Andrews at Corstorphine was packed, as it always was nowadays, and the faithful were told to tune in to Forth at 10am the following day. The same message was being relayed in churches and meetings all over Scotland. This was a grand opportunity to let the public know that People for Purity were here, were big, and must be listened to.

"If you have a point of view, telephone the radio station! If you have a question, telephone the radio station! If you want to support us, telephone the radio station and say you think Albert Kennedy is right in everything he says! Make sure the public know you're there!"

One or two of the congregation were slightly troubled by Peter Spencer using pulpit time to promote his organisation, but as the two areas overlapped to such a degree, perhaps it was all right. It was all God's work, after all. Peter Spencer said so.

On the Monday morning, Radio Forth's Managing Director called the Programme Controller into his office.

"I want you to pull the plug on Flora Spencer, after this morning's programme, I'm afraid, Jim. I'm sorry."

"But the ratings! Her programme on Gay Rights polled almost a daytime audience, at half past seven on a Wednesday night, with Coronation Street on the telly!"

"I do know that."

"Yes of course you do. But why? Why kill off what promises to be one of our biggest evening shows? If this morning's show works out well, I had planned to make it a daytime show every week...the audience would be enormous, especially if we syndicated it every time."

"We kill it off because we can't afford to run it. I had Grease Ball in here on Friday." Grease Ball was the nickname in the station for the Head of Advertising Sales. "Since Flora's programme on Gay Rights, almost every advertiser whose commercials ran in the breaks phoned in to say never again. Then the agencies were on the phone, insisting that their client's ads be kept out of any programme Flora put together or presented, or any other programme which was likely to cause offence. They don't want to be associated with...liberal sentiments, not in the middle of an AIDS scare. It's bad for business. So it's bad for our business. We just can't afford to lose these clients, Jim. You know that. If they got sufficiently pissed off with us, they'd just as likely cancel all their contracts and put more ads in the Evening News. I should mention that this isn't only the local advertisers we're talking about, but the nationals too."

"How the hell would a London agency know their client's ad went out in a programme about Gay Rights?"

"They didn't. It's just a coincidence. B.R.M.B. and the other booking houses have all had circulars from the national agencies saying keep our stuff out of any contentious programming, and *in particular*, in particular, Jim, keep it well away from anything about homosexuality, promiscuity, or AIDS whether it's drama, films, current affairs programmes, documentaries...anything at all."

"Jesus."

"I saw Michael, from S.T.V. sales, at the weekend. They've had the identical message delivered to them. And so have all the other tv and radio stations, and presumably the papers too. Interesting, isn't it?"

"But that means only Auntie Beeb will be able to do anything at all...keep people informed."

"We can ignore them, of course, the advertisers. If we don't mind being unemployed within weeks. You know how tight our margins are."

Jim Finnegan felt rage begin within him.

"Come to think of it, how did the local advertisers know their stuff went out in the Gay Rights programme? These guys don't usually listen to the station all that much."

"People for Purity. They've started writing to every advertiser asking if they know what kind of programme their ads are appearing in, and if the public are to assume that they, the advertisers, support the views expressed in it. I gather Channel 4 have had a hell of a time with them."

"So what are you saying here, Ken? Drop everything worth doing and punt out more pap all the time? Or perhaps you'd like us to expand the Godslot on Sunday right across the week? That would make rivetting listening, eh?"

"Calm down. We'll find some way of dealing with it. The Independent Radio Operators Association is talking with its lawyers in London right now, looking at all our advertising contracts. But in the meantime, we'll have to bend with the wind. Go with the flow."

"Give in, you mean. So we let Brian McShoogle and his Used Car back lot in Leith dictate our programming policy, according to his mediaeval whims? Bloody brilliant. And we just lie down and let him and his kind walk all over us. Christ. I thought the days of Senator McCarthy were over. Wrong again."

As he rose to leave, he had a thought, and turned for a Parthian shot.

"You are remembering that we've got one of these sanctimonious bastards on the programme this morning? Albert Kennedy? Nice to know you'll give him the airtime, when he is making sure you're not allowed to give airtime to anybody worth listening to. Nice editorial balance."

Ken sighed. "Being savage with me is pointless. I've got to keep the station on air. There are about thirty of us working here, and all the freelancers, and the shareholders, all depending on it. If you find you can't live with whatever editorial policy becomes necessary, well, I'll understand. You'll let me know, eh, Jim?"

The chill air of unemployment wafted through him as he closed the door carefully behind him, bumping into Flora immediately, who was on her way through from the newsroom to receive the first guest to arrive: Gerry Hansen.

"Break a leg" he said to her, pushing past into his own office. And his tone made it plain that he did not mean what that usually meant in radio stations. He meant 'break a leg'. But she didn't have time now to wonder what had caused his abrupt change of heart. She had a programme going all over Scotland, live, in under half an hour.

As there was no space for a Green Room in the cramped confines of Radio Forth, Flora had to take Gerry through to the tiny Board Room, then get him coffee with her own money, out of the machine in the News Room. He was fairly nervous himself, so they were little help to one another. Terry and Andrew arrived next, and Albert Kennedy only seconds behind them. Each was welcomed and taken to the Board Room and given coffee and then left, while Flora got all her notes together for the umpteenth time and took them down to Studio B. In the Board Room, everyone said hello; Albert Kennedy refused to shake Gerry's hand, but was icily polite otherwise. It was not a promising beginning.

At ten minutes to ten. Flora went back upstairs, brought her guests down to the studio, introduced them to the engineer, and sat patiently through the soundchecks.   Terry Aitken, as a fairly highflying Governmental type of person, was allowed to sit behind the engineer in the control room.   Within minutes she had 'accidentally' dropped the fact that she used to work in the Production department of Capital Radio in London, and the engineer had gladly accepted her offer of manning the phones for any incoming calls.

"How much of a delay do you use?" she asked him.   The engineer shrugged wryly and explained that although they did have a three-second delay button, they didn't usually use it.   It was up to the engineer to cut off anyone who sounded like they were about to swear. On the whole, he said, it worked. She was not impressed. Nor did she think that this kind of programme could get through a whole half hour without some swearing, blaspheming or libel being attempted, all of which was illegal on the airwaves. Still, it was not her show, so she shut up and stationed herself by the small phone exchange, with notepad and ballpoint at the ready.

Three minutes to ten, and Flora's heart was hammering hard. Andrew Douglas was charming but very formal, Gerry was very nervous, and Albert Kennedy was going to be difficult to handle. She had already explained the format to each of them by post, but went through it again. They would start after the news, at three minutes past ten plus twenty seconds for the intro music; go on till ten twenty, at which point they would take a commercial break; and stop twenty seconds before ten-thirty, to allow the music to play them out. They nodded, still saying nothing to each other. The first part of the programme, up to the break, would be the three of them in discussion; after the commercials, the phone lines would be opened up. They nodded, silently, again.

"Mandy's Morning Show" came to a prompt halt at ten, and the news started. More pressure was being put on the Pope by the bishops and cardinals to allow the use of condoms for the prevention of disease. An Edinburgh banker was in court for misuse of investment funds. A pair of twins had displayed amazing feats of telepathy. Edinburgh District Council were pulling back on all funding of Council projects. The engineer had the intro music on cartridge, and his finger was poised on the play button while with his other hand he prepared to switch the on-air feed from the newsbooth to Studio B.

"...and that's the news this morning, from Radio Forth." Flora's ident music started, and her voice on the cart announced "This is Forthright, and this...is Flora Spencer". The engineer cued her from behind the glass, and she went into action.

"Good morning. And a special good morning to all our listeners all over Scotland...Northsound listeners, Tay, Clyde and Moray Firth listeners, who are hearing this live through their own local radio stations. This morning's programme is all about AIDS. In a minute, the number to call if there's something you want to ask, something you want to say. But first let me introduce my guests this morning..."

She was more professional than she knew, and her voice was

warm, confident, authoritative. Terry listened appreciatively, and saw the engineer nodding and smiling; high praise, as she well knew, from an engineer!

Flora had hardly announced the phone number when the calls started to come in, and Terry was kept constantly busy taking calls, phoning people back to check their numbers, finding out what they wanted to say, sifting through them for interesting questions, listing those on paper, and taking new calls. She scarcely heard the discussion.

The first few civilised lines from each guest were soon exhausted, and Flora set about putting them at each other's throats with deft accuracy. Agreement does not make good radio. The one thing she hoped and prayed for was that Albert Kennedy would not disclose her identity as Peter Spencer's daughter, and because of this she was unconsciously kinder to him than to the others, even though she despised him most heartily.

He was well aware of this, as was Gerry, and kept it as his ace up his sleeve in case she needed to be demolished. If she gave him reasonable airtime, he would not refer to it: not to save Flora's blushes, but those of Peter Spencer.

"So" Flora looked at Albert. "What exactly do People for Purity want, Mr Kennedy?"

"Safety in our own homes, our own streets, our own cities, our own country. Freedom from being mugged and murdered, freedom from being infected by this deadly virus we're here to talk about today. What we want is a truly civilised society. Can anyone object to those aims, would you say?" His voice was very mild, polite and likeable. Which made him much more dangerous, Flora recognised, than her ranting father.

"That would depend on how you proposed to obtain them" said Gerry. "And who had to suffer in the process."

"But we don't ask that anyone suffer! Where did you get that idea from, Mr Hansen? All the bad guys have to do is stop being bad guys. Behave themselves like the rest of us. Are you saying that's impossible for them to do? I'm sure they can do it. Our aim is to reduce the suffering in our country, not to increase it."

146

"That's a childishly simplistic hope, Mr Kennedy. No country in the world has ever managed to eradicate crime. And I'm sorry, but I don't believe that a man of your obvious intelligence and sophistication would believe in that aim for a minute." Gerry was still smooth, but a slight tremor of anger in his voice weakened his words.

"Oh but I do. And so do the millions in Britain who have already joined us. We extend a welcoming hand to any wrongdoer who is willing to stop hurting people."

Andrew interrupted. "Excuse me, Miss Spencer, but I understood we were to be talking about AIDS this morning, not crime. And I would like to point out to Mr Kennedy that the grief caused by illness and death is much more widespread than that caused by crime. Everyone alive suffers from those natural griefs."

"We trust in our doctors and research people to set about alleviating those griefs, Doctor Douglas: except in the case of AIDS, of course, where there is no cure possible. How do you plan to protect us from the AIDS carriers, Doctor Douglas?"

"We cannot protect you. Only *you* can protect you, by having only safe sex. As long as you have safe sex, Mr Kennedy, and do not share infected needles, or get a contaminated blood transfusion, or get it from your mother while you are still in the womb, you cannot be infected by the HIV virus. It is really very simple."

Albert affected shock. "What are you saying? The Government, in all its might, cannot protect us? How can you sit there and say that, and not weep for shame, Doctor Douglas?"

"Possibly because I am not a member of the Government, but a doctor. And as a doctor, I am telling you, you must protect yourself. If you do so, you will not get the virus. In this country, there are no more contaminated blood supplies. There is nothing we can do to save a baby from getting the virus in the womb. But for the vast majority of people, if you don't inject drugs with a dirty needle, and you practice safe sex, you will not get the virus. I do apologise Mr Kennedy, but I cannot think how I can express it any more simply so that you will understand."

The heavy sarcasm did not perturb Albert Kennedy in the least.

Indeed, he winked silently at Andrew and grinned, as if to congratulate him on scoring a good point. Then he spoke:

"It makes me sad, Doctor Douglas, to hear that you think insulting our intelligence is a good way to win our hearts. Perhaps, of course, your arrogance is just covering a terrible awareness of your own inadequacy. We must forgive you."

Gerry Hansen had had enough. "You sanctimonious... "

Flora got in before 'bastard' quite made it out of Gerry's mouth.

"Thank you Mr Kennedy. But I feel we should drag ourselves away from personal animosity, don't you, and get back to the point? If I may repeat it, how exactly do you plan to achieve your aims? Assuming for the moment that all the bad guys are not about to turn into good guys overnight, to accommodate you."

"Why, simple. We believe profoundly in the traditional methods of dealing with pockets of infection or evil. You isolate them. Criminals are taken out of circulation, out of harm's way...and so are carriers of fever. We are very conscious of the difficult lives led by many HIV sufferers. More and more, they are being attacked, fired from their jobs, ostracized by their families and friends. What we want is to offer them an alternative way of life, for the rest of their lives...away from civilisation. Safe. Relaxed. Living with their own kind."

"Prison camps" said Gerry dully.

"No, no, not at all. It isn't a crime to carry the virus, now is it? What we have in mind is more like a holiday camp. For HIV carries, for AIDS victims, and for those high-risk groups such as yourself, Mr Hansen. After all, you are well known for being...homosexual. You'll get the virus one of these days, won't you? Don't you think, as a Christian, that it would be kinder of you, more responsible of you, to take yourself out of circulation BEFORE you infect some innocent person?"

"Wait, wait" interrupted Andrew, angrily. "You're talking nonsense, man! You don't know what you're talking about! Just because someone is homosexual does NOT mean to say they'll get infected! In fact the infection rate among homosexuals is dropping like a stone, it's in the heterosexual population that it's rising, even

148

in America. Do try and get a grip on reality, here!"

'Oh, Mr Kennedy' thought Flora 'You are very, very good.'

She tried her best to keep things on an even keel, after that, but Andrew was enraged and Gerry was afraid, and Albert Kennedy simply took over. Flora did not have the experience to control him. Upstairs, listening, Ken Cameron doubted if any of their presenters could have done so. In his quiet, reasonable, pleading-for-understanding voice, Albert Kennedy steamrollered over al of them, and used the airtime like a free advertisement for People for Purity.

At the commercial break, Terry raced to the photocopier she had seen in the corridor, took two copies of her final list, raced back to the studio, gave one copy to the engineer and took one through to Flora, who was looking very strung out. Flora skimmed through the list, bluepencilled some whose points she didn't want to cover, and ground it down to a manageable size before handing it back to Terry with thanks.

"Back in in five...four...three...two..." said the engineer's voice in Flora's headphones.

"Welcome back, and welcome to our first caller..." she began, "Mrs Anderson, in Kirkcaldy...what's your question?"

On it went. Caller after caller for Albert Kennedy, asking him questions which allowed him to give out more and more information about his kind and concerned organisation, about his care and love for ordinary people who were fed up of being pushed around and threatened by junkies, by gays, by the bleedingheart Government. Terry was doing her best to keep things balanced, but Albert's supporters were jamming the lines. When the last caller was banked up and waiting to be put through to the studio, she finally swivelled her chair around and sat back to listen.

"...and what can we do if they refuse to go to the camps, Mr Kennedy?" asked the man who was currently on air.

"Well, I think we ought to consider having HIV Positives tattooed, don't you? Oh not in some obvious place, we don't want

149

to cause anyone distress or embarrassment. Maybe...on a shoulder. Then if they were applying for jobs you could tell right away. And they couldn't make love without their partner knowing. And we'd know who to avoid on the beach, or at the swimming baths!"

By now everyone in Radio Forth had given up all pretence of work and was rivetted to the speakers which were all through the station and usually ignored.

"May I come in here, Miss Spencer?" Terry had never heard Andrew rage before. "There is no point in tattooing any more than there is any point in concentration camps because that's what we are talking about here, make no mistake. An HIV Positive person can be around and sexually active for years before they know themselves they're Positive. Tattooing some people will NOT prevent the spread of the disease by other people who don't know they're Positive. This is patently absurd, and very, very evil."

"I'm so grateful to the good doctor for making my point for me" said Albert, his voice still whipped cream. "That is why we want to see compulsory testing for everybody, every six months. Every month, if necessary. We must protect the innocent, Doctor Douglas, however much you and your Government cronies object."

Flora was lost and foundering, by now managing to control only her own voice, and certainly not the programme.

"We'll take our last caller now; from Glasgow, Sandy MacIntyre. Sandy, you're concerned about something?"

"Aye, I am that. My question is for Doctor Douglas, Flora; Doctor Douglas, what about all they folk that are gettin' AIDS by some mysterious method, not by sex and not by blood and not by needles? Thon Miss Hislop in London, and that poor wee boy in Nottingham. How can ye say we're safe if we practice this safe sex? Miss Hislop didnae have any sex..."

Andrew leaped in.

"The autopsy report on Miss Hislop is not yet complete, Mr...MacIntyre. As to young Darren Harrison, as he was cremated, we cannot investigate any further. But I assure you, if all the facts were known there would be nothing new. Both these people..."

Kennedy cut across him.

"Oh come now Doctor Douglas, it's not "both" these people, now is it? Why are you talking as if there's just the two people who mysteriously got AIDS some other way we're not being told about? I mean I presume you've read the World Health Organisation's statistics recently?" And he pulled a folded report from his inside jacket pocket. "Let's see now...yes, here we are. Reports on deaths from AIDS where no normal infective mechanism can be determined...for us ordinary people, that means, people who've died of AIDS and we don't know how they got it. America, twenty-nine three years ago, two hundred and fifty-three last year, almost a thousand in the six months of this year so far. In Britain,..."

"Where did you get those figures from?" raged Andrew. By which he really meant, 'how the hell do you have figures I don't have?' But it came across loud and clear as 'how did you get hold of secret information?'. And Albert Kennedy smiled.

"Ident music out coming up in ten seconds" said the engineer's voice, and Flora had to stumble through thanking her guests and saying goodbye to the audience very quickly. As the music played them out, Albert Kennedy sat back in his chair, beaming, delighted.

The other three were hunched forwards, or had their heads sunk on their chests, the picture of despair.

Albert tapped Andrew on the shoulder. "Would you like a photocopy of this W.H.O. report, Doctor Douglas? I'm sure you like to keep yourself informed."

Andrew's fists were clenching under the table and he made no answer, not trusting himself to speak.

"Oh come come now, gentlemen, Miss Spencer: it was a good programme, I think? You must agree. Lots of disagreement...the stuff of democracy, eh, Doctor Douglas? You must defend to the death my right to say what I believe in, after all." He rose, tucked the report back into his jacket, and tried to kiss Flora's hand, but she jerked it away. "Ah" he said. "I see which side you're on, Miss Spencer. No wonder you have caused your father such intense grief. Well, I think I can find my way to the front door. Thanks for all the free airtime." And he walked out, humming a merry tune, oblivious to the scathing stare of the engineer as he passed him.

Andrew looked at Flora, musingly. "Spencer...the Reverend Peter Spencer's daughter? Good god, lass, this must have been difficult for you." The sympathy in his voice very nearly broke her last bits of self-control, and tears pricked at the back of her eyes.

Terry came through to the studio, and clapped Flora on the back. "Bloody well done! You handled that incredibly well. That bastard would have demolished most people...you kept your cool. Bloody well done!"

Flora did her best to rally. "Would you two and Gerry - would you like a cup of coffee or anything before you go?"

Gerry was about to accept before Terry surreptitiously tugged at his sleeve and shook her head violently behind Flora's back and mouthed "Leave her alone for a bit" at him. So she escorted them upstairs and through Reception and they wondered why a cluster of staff was standing inside the front door and peering out. Flora followed them, curious, as they pushed through the cluster and walked out to face a very ill-assorted crowd of shouting, placardwaving demonstrators. To their annoyance, television cameras were filming the whole thing.

There were soberly-dressed middle-aged people who were pumping Albert's hand like there was no tomorrow, and cheering...there was also a group of ludicrously dressed young men who looked like cartoon versions of gays: lavender and pink and orange and scarlet silk trousers and yellow and turquoise and emerald silk shirts and earrings and permed hair which looked suspiciously like wigs and thick stage makeup and jewellery clanking everywhere. None of Flora's guests, including Gerry, had ever seen anything like it. The gays were bearing placards which read "GET OFF OUR BACKS!" and "PEOPLE FOR PERVERTS" and "FAGGOTS FIGHT BACK!" but the sober citizens had no placards and were behaving impeccably. The silk-clad young men were mincing extravagantly but using the clenchedfist salute, and calling out "Enough is enough! Faggots fight back!" over and over again. Nobody made any move to speak to Andrew, or Gerry, or Flora; Albert Kennedy was the target for both groups and the groups were the target for the television cameras and their boom microphones. Terry and Andrew quickly shook hands with Flora and Gerry, and strode off along Forth Street, avoiding the television reporter who was beginning to look at them with interest.

They spoke little as they walked, each deep in thought, each perturbed. They had planned to walk back along Princes Street, to admire what Andrew had assured her was the most beautiful street in Europe. But neither had any taste left for sightseeing, and in any case Terry had spent a reluctant weekend being dragged round all Andrew's old student haunts, pretending to have a good time. So they grabbed a taxi and headed back to their room in virtual silence.

Andrew ordered lunch from room service, as neither of them felt much like joining others in the dining room, nor like going out. And they began to pack.

Standing folding her frothy little nonsense nightgown, Terry looked at Andrew with profound seriousness.

"You do love me, don't you, Andrew?"

Her tone was not flirtatious, and for answer he went and held her face cupped in his hands, and nodded down to her gently, affirmingly, and whispered 'Oh yes my love. I do."

"Okay then. Sit down. There's something I want to tell you. Something I'm not supposed to tell you. If they find out I did, I can get up to twenty-five years in prison for breaking the Official Secrets Act."

"Maybe you shouldn't tell me, then. I would never want to be the cause of any difficulty for you...and twenty-five years is one hell of a difficulty. No, my love, don't tell me."

"You need to hear it. I need to tell you." She sat down beside him, so that he had to turn to see her face. They held hands.

"I know how bad you're feeling about the interview. About Albert Kennedy. But; oh, this is difficult: you did better than you think, given...given who he is. Believe me."

"I did appallingly, whoever he is. I never met such an expert verbal manipulator in my life, not even in fifteen years of politics. All of us fell at his feet and made asses of ourselves. I love you

153

dearly, but I can't think of anything you can say that'll make me feel better. Though it's dear of you to try. And even if I'm feeling a bit shamefaced, it's not that serious. Not twenty-five years' worth, certainly."

"It's only partly because I love you that I'm going to tell you. The other part is that someone needs to find out who is running Mr Kennedy this time - and stop them."

The look of enquiry on his face was her permission to start talking. And she did. She told him what she had found on her computer when she screened his name, and Gerry Hansen's, for the radio programme. And she told him about the D-notice which had been put upon the life, history or provenance of Albert Kennedy.

"He's a Public Relations specialist. Of a very specific and unusual type. Not ever quite criminal, not quite...yet whenever he represents any organisation, that organisation's rivals tend to fall apart. Usually under some kind of scandal. While officially he's legitimately promoting the organisation which hires him, in reality he achieves much more by demolishing the opposition. And he rarely does this in a fair or equable way. Allegations of insider trading get thrown around like confetti...sexual and personal scandals come tumbling out of the closet...any whisper of something not quite right with a company suddenly appears all over the media until that company's shares are tumbling. In short, he's a hit man. A very expensive hit man. He's got villas all over the world, two yachts, everything a man could want. His fees are astronomical, but he spends money like water. People for Purity couldn't possibly afford him. So who's paying for his services this time?"

Room Service arrived with their lunch under silver covers on a trolley. Andrew sent the waitress away, saying they would serve themselves. But neither of them made a move to touch the food.

"Well what do you think?" asked a very puzzled Andrew.

"I don't know. The D-notice was only dated two months ago just before he seems to have joined People for Purity."

"So he's working for the government."

"Or he's under covert investigation by the government. It could be either, and they're kind of diametrically opposed to each other. So I just haven't a clue. Whoever it is, they're spending a lot of cash. More than his usual fee."

"Why do you say that?"

"You know 'Day of the Jackal'? The Jackal asked a huge fee for bumping off de Gaulle because he wanted to retire afterwards because he could never work again, because every policeman in the world would be watching out for him. It's the same here: Albert Kennedy has never actually gone on camera, or given an interview, or been publicly known, ever before. He's pinned his colours to the mast in full view of the world this time, which means his usefulness to gray quiet men in secret rooms is pretty well defunct. To do this..."

"...he'd have to charge enough to retire for life."

"Exactly. And as he's only just over forty, that could easily run into millions, to keep up his lifestyle. So who's paying him, and what are they after?"

Andrew started pacing the room.

"If it IS the government...oh God, a million questions. Why have they set up him and me in opposition...and...which department is running him...and...look, Terry, you're the one with the access to the famous computer. You can find out, surely?"

"You overestimate my importance in the scheme of things. As far as the Prime Minister is concerned, I'm some kind of overpaid window dresser. I have no access to anything secret or important, beyond occasionally bumping into a D-notice on the computer. There's no way I'm going to be able to find out anything. And even if I did, with the D-notice, I can't get the story carried by anyone. I doubt even The Grauniad would tackle this one. Though they might, they just might."

"Your department runs a clippings service for any Government office, don't you?"

"Yes. I've offered our services to you a dozen times."

"Don't remind me. When we get back to London: when YOU get back to London, can you start one up, please. Anything and everything to do with AIDS. Anything and everything to do with

People for Purity. Any events like muggings of homosexuals, or by homosexuals. Any murders or other crimes which seem to be linked to the general subject. And send it all both to St Fillans and to my Whitehall office."

She looked at him with admiration shining in her eyes.

"Attaboy, Andrew. We'll nail that son of a bitch yet."

But Andrew was still very serious and very sober.

"Somebody had better. Before too many citizens start howling for those concentration camps, and tattooing. Dear Lord, who'd want to live in a world like that?"

Terry sagged gloomily onto the sofa. "Any fascist. Anybody so afraid of AIDS they've lost their common sense. Anybody who doesn't have any common sense to begin with. Anybody who is easily influenced by rhetoric a la Kennedy...and that's one hell of a swathe of people. In Australia, they had their first 'holding centre' for HIV Positives about three years ago. Sweden had an island with just one prostitute incarcerated on it, four years before that. Mayors in America are riding for election on a single-issue ticket right now: put the gays into camps. So don't think it can't happen here."

Andrew sat down beside her and took up her hand again.

"It mustn't happen here" he said.

CHAPTER FIVE

They left the hotel on the Tuesday morning and were soon aboard a very ordinary train to Stirling. The raging sun did nothing to help the heaviness of their mood. Terry slept most of the way, and Andrew sat and looked at her, sadly, fondly, wonderingly. Such a young thing, he thought, to be caught up in all this. Such a lovely young thing. Such love. But for how long? Well. He'd relish every day of it and waste no time on regrets afterwards, but rejoice for all the happiness.

He wondered how Terry would take to St Fillans. She had never visited Scotland before, and so far had really only seen Edinburgh, which was enough like some of the Georgian parts of London not to excite much interest or comment from her, excepting how relatively clean it was.

And he felt her holiday was spoiled in advance by their situation and their problems. They were not two innocents abroad, smiling and gawping and laughing and loving. They were two professional people caught in a difficult, stressful and complex scenario of intrigue and self-interest and massive fears for the future, and their chances of a really relaxing holiday were minimal. But by God he'd try for it! He looked at her brow furrowing in her dreams, he saw an anxious expression flit briefly across her face, and he determined to keep London, and AIDS, and Albert Kennedy out of her consciousness as much as was humanly possible for the next three weeks. He would fill her time with delights, with fresh air and mountains and lochs, with good food (lots of it!) and sweet talk and walks on the hills.

London, and AIDS, and all the rest of it, would still be there three weeks later, after all. It would keep. They both needed rest and recuperation to deal with the next batch, the next onslaught, the next chapter.

At Stirling, the doughty Isa met them in Andrew's big black 1955 Vauxhall Wyvern, which was immaculate and a deal more impressive than Terry had been led to believe. Isa had made the house ready and put up enough food for Andrew and a guest, as per his telephoned request, but had not expected said guest to be young, female, and attractive. Though Isa smiled and was pleasant to them both, Andrew could feel her withdrawing from him by the minute as they loaded the cases into the boot. Perhaps her support and helpfulness had all been built on the rock of his being a solid and respectable widower. Now that he was back in the fray, so to speak, he had a feeling he would be left to get on with things himself. She might work for him still, but she would not mother him any more. One of these days, he reflected wryly, it would be nice to have even a momentary glimpse into the female psyche.

She would not be going back with them but visiting her sister in Stirling for the day and returning by bus later on. They all shook hands and smiled, and Isa wandered off.

"Wow. Does she not like me, or does she not like me!"

"Nonsense! How could she not like you?"

"Because she nurtureth a little tendresse for you, my dear."

"She what?"

"She's fond of you. She thought she was fond of you in a motherly way, which made it all right, but now I'm on the scene I've taken you over and she's retiring from the field, wounded. I'm awfully sorry."

"Ach, lass, you're full of blethers." And he kissed the top of her head.

"Whereas by contrast" she said sweetly adoring and worshipful "your mind makes me think of the Grand Canyon. Your head's full of rocks!"

She enjoyed the drive. The scenery and the townships were beautiful. As they entered Callander, Andrew solemnly requested that she spit out of her window. An ancient and honourable tradition, he informed her. With a little prodding, he heaved a sigh and explained that they were now in Doctor Finlay's Casebook country; and he seemed to think this would mean something to her. As it didn't, he told her of the stories by A J Cronin of his idyllic country village practice, and how when it had been filmed for television it had been set here in Callandar, and from then on everybody expected their G.P. to be like the characters in the series and it was a monstrous burden for a young emerging chap such as he had been at the time.

"Naturally, I was cast as the gawky Finlay, and my father as Doctor Cameron, the lovable, testy old rogue."

"Ah, so your father was a doctor at St Fillans before you?"

"Briefly."   He was naturally reticent about himself, but she encouraged him to elaborate. They had in fact lived in Chester most of his young life, but his father had bought the combined practice and house in St Fillans in 1959, just when Andrew was looking to go to university. So he had gone to Edinburgh, and afterwards come home, with Ruth, and settled in with his father. His mother had died long since, in the war, bombed while working as a volunteer fire fighter in Manchester.

"Being in general practice in St Fillans was a busy life, but a good one. Dad was always involved in politics, always had been. He was great chums with Graham Patrick, the local M.P. So I was always fairly involved too. You don't want to hear all this."

"But I do. I want to get to know you, of course I do. Please carry on."

"Well...Ruth and I finally decided to have Callum when we realised we were twenty-nine and still childless. Ruth wanted to have some time to ourselves again while we were still young enough to enjoy it, after our sprog would have grown up and gone away." He was silent for a moment, and she hugged his arm. "Anyway.   Callum was born in 1973, and Dad retired soon afterwards. We took on a junior partner, I've told you about him, you'll meet him at the house when he's taking surgery.   Graham Patrick was always after me to get more involved, and finally succeeded; I was elected to Parliament for the first time in 1979.'

'Poor Callum. I think he got the short end of the stick all along the way. First of all I was never there, because I was in London...then when Ruth decided she was coming down too, Callum had a big change to cope with, and then when Ruth died in 1981, there was only me and I was far too busy to take care of him. We had a

159

succession of nannies, till both of us got fed up with that and he decided himself he'd rather go away to school. He wanted to go home to Scotland, too, so I packed him off to an excellent school in Aberdeenshire, and we met at St Fillans for the holidays."

"No wonder he's such an independent and resourceful boy, then. You should be proud of yourself, Andrew."

She could not know the effect of her words. Andrew had castigated himself down all the years for neglecting his son, and yet here was someone telling him he had done all the right things? That he should be proud of himself? And he thought about Callum and yes, he was resourceful, he was a sturdy, quite reasonable kind of human being...enterprising, too. He would be all right. Andrew had not, then, completely failed him. Or failed Ruth...that was another thought of midnight solitude, that when Ruth left Callum to his care he had let her down.

"I mean" she continued "When you couldn't possibly look after him, you went through burning hoops to make sure he had the right kind of quality care, and you spent time with him yourself when it was humanly possible. He's a lucky boy. My parents more or less left us to bring up ourselves if we felt like it, or die if we didn't. Four of us. And all the budget went on booze. Ah well. You wouldn't believe how talented we all became at shoplifting. And moving house by moonlight, to escape irate landlords. All over South London."

And as she continued her own story, as she told him how, when she started working, she had had to put a lock on her bedroom door or her parents would have pawned or sold her work clothes to get money for drink, he felt great anger rising in him. In the face of their parents' neglect, Terry as the oldest child had spent her own childhood taking care of her three brothers, and much though she loved them all, she resented it.

"Which is why I never want to have kids myself. I've done my share."

Something in him leaped with joy to hear that. It was the probability that she would want children which had most convinced

160

him their relationship could not last; he would never want to start all that dreadful haul through sleepless nights and dirty nappies again, not at fifty years old. Of course she knew perfectly well that he thought that, and that was why she had said it, and she smiled to herself when she saw his face brighten and then his swift change to his former look of sober concern.

The scenery changed dramatically after Callandar...from impressively manicured estates to rough hill and wild heather. The real Scotland, she thought to herself. Picture postcard country. She began to feel better, for the beauty was real and eternal and deeply refreshing. Moreover, and less loftily, the Wyvern was exceptionally comfortable, and she was revelling in the unaccustomed luxury of not having to wear seatbelts. Also there was the novelty of the benchlike front seat, covered in bright red leather, along which she could sidle and tease Andrew with kisses on the cheek and nibbles on the earlobe. At Lochearnhead, they turned down to the right and followed the banks of Loch Earn till they came to St Fillans. Terry had already decided this place had definite potential, before they turned up between two majestic houses and passed two passable new bungalows and finally, at the end of the steeply climbing lane, found the red sandstone turreted and wonderful house with the sign outside headed "Surgery Hours".

Red gravel crunched satisfyingly under the Wyvern's wheels as Andrew pulled it smoothly round so that Terry's door was right at the entrance portal: a broken pediment atop a panelled oak door. When they were out of the car and stretching their legs, he looked up at his home and saw the comfort, the security of it, the pleasing proportions and elegant windows.

"Cor" said Terry. "This is one of your three-million-pound jobs, anywhere in London or within barking distance of it."

"It was your appreciation of architectural form which first drew me to you, no question about it" remarked Andrew mildly.

"Please. I'm doing my Visiting Smart-Ass Cockney, and you're spoiling the effect. Over lunch, you can tell me the one about all the haggises having two short legs and two long ones so they can stay on an even keel when they're running round the mountainside."

"I apologise for whichever Scot tried to unload that one on you. Now: get your very delectable Cockney smart ass in gear, and let's get organised."

She loved the house from the minute he unlocked the front door. Black and white marble tiles on the hall floor, ancient wooden staircase, even a wrought iron chandelier...it was, she informed him, a bit of all right. Her heels clicked pleasantly on the marble as she wandered about exploring while he lugged the cases into the house and headed her in the direction of the kitchen to see what victuals Isa had left them.

Chicken salad. Ah well. Still, the chicken was cornfed and plentiful, and the salads were colourful, fresh and delicious. And there was trifle; a real Scottish trifle, with sherry in it, and smothered in cream, decorated with the traditional solitary cherry in the middle. Isa had left enough for four people, so Terry was very nearly full by the time they drained the last of the Vinho Verde.

They took their coffee in the drawingroom, which had views up the hilly garden. Terry glued her nose to the windowpanes.

"Ericaceous soil, I would imagine? Great for those azaleas and rhododendrums."

"Drons. Rhododendrons."

"Oh yes, that's right."

"From the word Dendritic, meaning, having roots, from the Greek."

"Showoff."

"Showoff yourself. What's all this about ericaceous soil, for God's sake? You don't know an azalea from a pint of Guinness!"

"Not convincing?"

"Not at all convincing."

"I confess. I've been reading up, to impress you. We never did Latin at our school, but I do have a highly retentive memory. For example: Acer palmatum dissectum purpurea. Howzat?"

"Excellent. And do you see one in the garden?"

"Um...well...not from here. I don't think. Mind you" she gave

162

up completely "I think I see a pint of Guinness up in those rocks there."

"Does it resemble a Japanese maple with reddish purple leaves, at all?"

"Why yes!"

"Then you've got it. That's the acer. Pretty, isn't it?"

"All right all right, it's a fair cop. I'll come quietly."

Oh the temptation to make a pun out of that one! He almost did, but didn't, and she almost did, but didn't, and then they caught each others' eyes and giggled and snorted and of course finished up kissing.

"Take me to the pub."

He groaned. "I'm exhausted. I was half-hoping to grab forty winks in the armchair, just this once. Aren't you tired at all? Okay then, we'll go out."

"No no, you slouch the afternoon away, I'll take myself off and show myself the sights."

"In that case, wake me up when you come back in around seven minutes. It's a very small place, St Fillans."

"You should have gone into sales, you know. Your silver tongue, your gift of the gab...wasted in politics. Wasted."

From Andrew's drive it was a steep walk down the twisting lane, past the two other sandstone edifices and the two modern bungalows, to the main road. This has shops, hotels and houses on one side, and Loch Earn on the other.

Loch Earn is a storybook Scottish loch, with hills all around and ice-cold water of unfathomable depths. But it is also a busy loch, with fish-farming and water sports, and Terry found pleasure in just leaning on the wall, watching the splashes and hearing the shouts of all the people motorboating and yachting and just plain paddling. Across the water, on the farmost hill, a little village of caravans nestled amongst the pines. It all reminded her of a lake in Austria two years ago...which reminded her of the young man who had stood by her side on that occasion. The young man who had been the one and only love of her adult life, till Andrew came along.

Charlie. Charlie of the laughing eyes and the tousled hair and the come-day-go-day attitudes of a latter-day hippie. Charlie, who sang her songs on his guitar, sitting by the fire in their rented log cabin in Kitzbuhl, who took her horse-riding in the Camargue, who got her drunk on sherry in Jerez and on Calvados in Normandy, and all without ever seeming to have any money at all. Charlie, who sang nothing but Leonard Cohen songs for two days before he told her, ever so kindly, that it was time for him to move on alone. When she burst into tears, he had sung "Hey that's no way to say goodbye" and dried her tears and walked out, leaving her penniless in Paris, without the ticket home. Charlie was like that.

Her mental pictures of Charlie, the only souvenirs she had, were all of Charlie with the sun in his hair, or Charlie naked and glowing in the firelight; at this moment, though, thinking of Andrew, she suddenly remembered Charlie's mean little mouth and sly expressions. Charlie, she realised with a start, had been a total bum, an expert working his way round the world for nothing by exploiting romantic girls.

Europe on no dollars a day he used to say, grinning.

She looked at the hills across the loch through misted eyes. 'Goodbye, Charlie' she thought to herself. 'I hope you get the clap. It's the only applause you deserve. What is the sound of one right Charlie clapping? Why, it's me, cheering!' Seeing a passing bus, she hailed it and was very quickly at Lochearnhead. Shivering slightly as the afternoon cooled, she amused herself by peering in the blatantly touristy windows at lambswool sweaters and tweed skirts. On a chuckling impulse, she went into one of the shops and had herself kitted out in the whole caboodle, including a rope of fake pearls and some frightfully county brogues, and a tweedy Inverness cape which made her look like an anorexic Margaret Rutherford.

The sales assistant could not see the joke when Terry looked in the full-length mirror, which only made her chuckle more.

Smirking all the way back in the bus, she strode manfully back towards the house, enveloped in tweeds, hidden under a mansize fore-and-aft complete with unlikely fishing fly in the brim. She tiptoed into the drawingroom backwards, still snickering with glee, and turned and said in her best (worst?) Scottish accent "Is Dohctor Finlay here then, the noo, och aye?" And then noticed that Andrew was not alone.

God bless him, he didn't bat an eyelid.

"And this is she" he explained to the young man now rising from the other armchair by the fireside. "Terry Aitken. Terry, this is Doctor Hamilton that I told you about. We're just having some tea before he starts five o'clock surgery."

"Delighted to meet you, Miss Aitken."

For one wild moment she wondered if she should carry on with the accent and brazen it out. But good sense prevailed over her dire embarassment. She shook his hand and threw off the cape and the fore-and-aft and went for a cup and joined them, finding them this time laughing out loud and then refusing to tell her what it was about, but both looking at her very merrily.

"It's the soft Highland air" offered Andrew, solemnly. "Goes for the brain, every time. Would you like a Rich Tea biscuit, dear?"

"Would you like a sock in the jaw, dear?"

Fred Hamilton grinned, approvingly, and left, reluctantly, after promising to bring his wife to dinner the following night.

Terry cringed. "God, what must he think of me?"

"Fred's all right. He's been known to laugh from time to time, I believe. Stop being so hyper about what people will think of you! It's not like you!"

"Yes but I'm on your territory here and I don't want people to think you've gone slightly crazy..."

"I'm not the one dressing up like Harry Lauder in drag. And don't say Who was he? or I really will have to do something extreme to you."

"I'm counting on it. Later. For now, I'm starving. Did I see a chippie on my travels, or was it a Cockney mirage?"

"It must have been a psychic flash. There's an excellent chippie in Comrie, not too far; let's go."

They dined splendidly, in the kitchen again, on very thick fresh haddock and mountains of chips. It wasn't quite how Andrew had intended to impress her, but she seemed well pleased. Everything went beautifully until bedtime. Isa had of course made up the bed in the guest room, as well as in Andrew's room. For a moment, when he was showing her round the upstairs, Terry wondered if he was going to let her sleep alone. And when the time came for them to undress, in Andrew's room that still had Ruth's dressingtable set and Ruth's choice of eiderdown and Ruth's presence still strong in it, they were very quiet with each other and only lay down in the bed and cuddled a little. Andrew was, he said, very tired. And he kissed her and rolled over and she felt very secondary to him, not just second but secondary. And perhaps temporary. And very miserable. It took her a long time to get to sleep.

It took him a long time after she fell asleep, for him to fall asleep. He knew she was upset, and he cursed himself for hurting her, but he could not make love to her in the bed he had shared with Ruth. He awoke in confusion from a deep erotic dream in which Terry was...to find Terry really was licking his toes! Still sleepy, he tried to speak but she shut his mouth with kisses, firmly, and said only 'Don't talk; lie back and let me love you'. He lay back, soundless, but shrivelled and unhappy. Opening his eyes he saw her kneeling naked at his feet, looking at him with such love in the early sunshine, looking so happy in her love and so innocent, that he relaxed, closed his eyes, and let a myriad delicious sensations begin. Like many men of his generation, Andrew had always thought it was his job to initiate sex, to begin it, to encourage it, to start arousing his partner. No woman had ever made love to him before, and, briefly, he was embarrassed. Then he was floating on a warm ocean, drifting, lazy, while a host of mermaids licked and stroked and nibbled and soothed his legs, his arms, his ears, his face. And then he was drowning in the warmth, he was sinking, and the ocean grew warmer and warmer when her kisses strayed across his belly and his thighs, and her fingers touched his rising manhood just in passing, just lightly, then back again and a little more, a little more, while her

166

lips and tongue explored all the soft sensitive skin on his body. More than once he reached for her and his arms were gently put back to his sides. More than once his back arched as his penis strained to find her wandering hands, but when he did that she moved to another part of his body till he quieted again. As he became more and more aroused, he had to learn to control his urge and lie passive. At once it was against his nature and yet perfectly natural. She sniffed his skin here, and there, and said he smelled like newbaked bread in the mornings but like warm new tar at night. She pulled lightly on his ears, opening them to put her tongue deep inside, wet and hot, while her hands stroked his chest and his stomache.

When her mouth took him at last, he bucked and reared inside it, almost unable to hold back; but he held back. And here, she said, he tasted of salt, of the sea, of eternity and the cradle of all things. She ran her tongue up the underside of the shaft of him, and he quivered and thought he was lost but she moved quickly away, and he felt her unrolling the sheath down over him as if it was precious silk, as if she was honouring him, and then she sat astride him, plunging him deep into her warmth and he found she was quivering, then clutching, and clutching, and together they met the supreme moment and for the first time in his life he knew what the word ecstasy truly meant.

And thus, together, they exorcised him and the room and made it their own and filled it with their own light.

When he lay, quiet at last, holding her close and breathing in rhythm with her, the doorbell rang. He shrugged on his infamous dressinggown and disappeared to the front door, then came upstairs and snuggled and kissed her and told her she really wanted to come downstairs for breakfast now. She was already half asleep, but she meekly consented, to please him, and there on the kitchen table, in a box marked 'Joe's Cafe, Victoria Road, London', was a whole morello cherry pie, just arrived by Datapost, along with a large carton of Joe's special scented cream.

"Oh Andrew you lovely wonderful man. I'm lost for words!"

"Then fill your mouth with pie, beloved thing. As much as you like. With half a gallon of cream. And I will feed you every morsel."

"How about I feed me every morsel and you make some coffee?"

It was ridiculously difficult to leave her side even for long enough to make coffee, and he kept making little trips across the kitchen floor just to run his fingers through her hair, or bite her neck, or open the top of her short housecoat and run his hand downwards over her breasts, and generally completely fail to distract her from the flaky rich pastry and the tart delicious sweetness and the light and luscious cream.

After breakfast, they retired, burping slightly, to bed, this time to sleep till almost noon, nestled into each other like spoons, happy as children.

Their idyll lasted almost two whole days; on Friday, just before lunch, Sarah Kepple telephoned from Andrew's office. She'd just heard that all British universities and colleges were sending out letters to all students from central African countries, and certain parts of America, telling them not to come back next term or in the foreseeable future; remembering that Callum was in Uganda, she thought Andrew would want to know.

"It'll hit the papers tomorrow, probably be on tv and radio by late this afternoon...there may be no reprisals, of course, but the Foreign Office says it's probable all our students will be sent home from those places, pronto."

Damn. He thanked her, went and told Terry, and their joy collapsed.

"Here we go" said Terry, glumly. "I'd hoped this wouldn't happen for a couple of years yet."

"You were expecting it?"

"Of course. There's nothing so insular as the Brit mentality. If something nasty is coming here from over the water, pull up the drawbridge. The universities are just first to do it, that's all. You wait; there'll be more to come. Now what about Callum; are you going to pull him out?"

"I won't be able to get hold of him till around four our time...six o'clock in Uganda, and even then he might not be finished work and home. God. So much for the working holiday of a lifetime. Poor Callum. Still, if he gets the next possible plane home, he'll be okay. I don't see any riots starting over this, or anything like that, do you? No, of course not. Why would they?"

She let him comfort himself as best he could, while pacing the floor. It was going to be a long afternoon. To help it pass she suggested they do a bit of phoning round, to find out what else they could about this 'ridiculous bit of paranoia' as Andrew called it. First off, he called his own alma mater in Edinburgh, and angrily asked the Bursar what possible reason they could have for barring innocent students from AIDS-heavy countries, especially students bound for medical faculties, who were so desperately needed back home when qualified.

"My dear Doctor" purred the Bursar "it was not exactly our decision. The parents, you see, and a lot of our potential students...started asking us how many students we had enrolled from Uganda, Kenya, even San Francisco and New York. When we started quoting numbers, we starting losing customers from within the U.K. You must remember that we are now subject to market forces, and must keep our heads afloat just like any other business. If our customers want things this way, we have to give in, whatever we might feel about it ourselves."

"But the whole thing is absurd! All your paranoid students from the U.K. have to do is not to indulge in unsafe sexual practices with these people, and nothing can happen! Don't they realise that yet, with all the publicity about AIDS over the years? And these are supposed to be the more intelligent of the population - the top five per cent, for God's sake!"

"Well now: that used to be our answer and it used to work. I'm afraid your Miss Hislop, and the Harrison child in Nottingham, have rather changed public opinion. I have to tell you, Doctor Douglas, that there is more than a little suspicion in many people's minds that somehow or other, AIDS has indeed become infectious, or perhaps contagious, and that the government is not telling us the truth. Then of course there was your own interview with Mr Albert Kennedy, and the statistics he quoted from the World Health Organisation...and all the reporting of that interview in the Scottish and the national papers. That certainly didn't help. And of course there's the T.B. now; the unrest about that began right after your television appearance with that young rock star and the mathematician. You have certainly made a significant contribution to this decision. The idea of a Multiple Drug Resistant T.B., which assuredly IS infectious and can be got from any AIDS carrier, well, that is not very acceptable to many of our students, or indeed their parents. Or to people who favour us with endowments. Or to any of the industrial bodies who engage the various departments to do research.

'Please, I'm only quoting other people's opinions, not necessarily my own. But, that's the way things are; and we have to live with the way things are, not the way they should be. I'm sorry. There's nothing we can do."

The conversation was clearly at an end. Andrew was furious with himself for not buying a newspaper since the Radio Forth interview. He and Terry had not even watched television or listened to the radio since that time, in an effort to make this a real holiday for both of them. Now that the Bursar had mentioned it, he remembered that he had meant to investigate the report which Kennedy had quoted, and find out why he himself had not got a copy, the minute he got back to London. But he might as well do it now. The holiday was over, at least for the moment.

He called Sarah Kepple and asked her to chase up the report. It took almost an hour for her to call him back, and though she was able to give him an answer, the answer only threw up more questions.

"That report should be with us in a few days. The thing is, Doctor, when I asked about it, it turned out that it had only gone to the printers in Zurich the day before your Mr Kennedy seems to have had a copy in his hands. The printed and bound copies have only just arrived back at H.Q. in Geneva today, they'll be sent out

170

tomorrow. The World Health couldn't understand how he got his copy... though they're investigating it right now. They're no more happy about the premature leak than we are. Oh, and another thing, Doctor: the Department of Agriculture have requested a copy of our copy when it arrives, will that be all right?"

"Of course...but why? Why do they want it? Oh well, never mind; by all means run them off a copy. And could you print other copies for all the Committee members please, Sarah, and distribute them? Thanks. "

It was just before one: they reluctantly put on the lunchtime news on the BBC. There was nothing yet about the embargo on foreign students from high-risk countries. Just the usual parade of misery and disasters.

They ate bread and cheese washed down with chilled beer, and went out to walk away the three hours yet till Andrew could get hold of Callum.

Andrew drove to the south side of the loch, where the walking was quieter and lovelier, with low mossy dykes and thick naturally mixed trees and not so many walkers and almost no traffic. The noonday sun sparkled harshly off the wavelets, and the overhanging branches of oak and birch and willow drooped sleepily in the heat, dappling the sunshine on the grassy banks.

They held hands as they walked. The ditches by the sides of the road were still clogged with last year's autumn leaves, squelchy and muddy even in the aridity of this summer's day. They met nobody. In the silence, the squeaks and calls and songs of the forest inhabitants were loud and sweet.

"We might be the last people on earth" said Terry, absentmindedly, entranced. Then her own words stopped her stone cold chill and stock still and she turned to Andrew and said "We won't be, will we? Us and a few more? It's not really going to happen, is it?"

He did not attempt to soothe her like a child, with hugs and kisses and 'there, there's. He wanted to, but she was a grown woman and wanted an answer of reason and facts and intelligent extrapolation. Nevertheless, she was gripping his hand a little harder.

"No. It won't happen. Every instinct in my guts tells me it won't happen. We may have done some bloody stupid things to ourselves, the human race, but we can't be so suicidally stupid as to wipe ourselves out when preventing it is so incredibly easy. Easy, simple and cheap."

"There's something I want to ask you, something else, something specific. Andrew, how did Miss Hislop get AIDS? And Darren Harrison? And all the other ones Albert Kennedy seems to have found in that W.H.O. report?"

"I don't know. You know that I don't know!"

"Doesn't that fact frighten you? That you don't know? It scares me to death. What if it is infectious? Or contagious? Hell, the average person doesn't even know the difference between those, never mind how to cope with either."

"That can't happen. It's virtually a physical impossibility for the virus to mutate to that extent. Even though.."

"...I know, I know, it's a highly mutable virus. You said it was VIRTUALLY an impossibility. Is that as far as you can go with being sure about it? Darling, it just isn't that convincing. There are millions of people walking around with thousands or even millions of slightly different variations of the virus in them. Can you honestly say that out of millions there really isn't a chance that one, just one person, has a mutation that makes it infectious?" She took his other hand in hers, and looked him straight in the eyes, demanding his complete attention. "Andrew, would you stand up in a court of law, with your hand on the Bible, and swear - *swear* - that it isn't possible?"

He tried to say yes, and found he could not. He lowered his eyes but would not let her hands go. He saw the look of despair on her face and the beginnings of her not trusting him and this was bitter anguish to him.

"Listen to me; really, really listen. Before I answer you I'll tell you WHY the answer is what it is. In all our knowledge of viruses, there is not one thing that tells us this virus is likely to do this. Not one. It is about as likely as that yellow dress you're wearing suddenly turning into a white suit with pink stripes. It's as likely as an infinite number of monkeys actually one day writing the complete works of Shakespeare. As likely as all these trees around us falling down at the same time with no wind.   It's not ABSOLUTELY impossible but it's as near as makes no sensible difference at all. Your dress; it could have been made with an unstable dye that might fade completely in the U.V. of the sunshine, and the pattern of the branches here might make a striped effect of the fading, and maybe there's a thin thread at the waist and it might rot when the dye fades and so split the dress into a suit. It's that likely. It's that unlikely. So now I tell you no, I couldn't stand and swear on the Bible that the virus will never become infectious, any more than I could swear your dress will not turn into a suit. Because they are both POSSIBLE. But neither of them is very probable."

Her mouth was working strangely and he could not tell if she was yet convinced.

"And there's another thing; viruses mutate in all sorts of ways. It is also possible that the HIV virus will mutate so that it is no longer virulent, so that it becomes more or less inert, doing no damage any more, ever again. And that is MORE possible than it's becoming infectious, I assure you. Much more possible.   For all our ignorance, and all our failure to produce a vaccine or a cure, the virus might just lie down and quietly die inside a couple of years. Okay it's not VERY likely, but it is possible."

Her reaction was not at all what he had expected. She raised her eyes heavenwards and gave a small mock scream.

"Where's my cassette recorder when I really need it?!"

"Pardon?"

"We're going straight home so I can write all that down and change it from my yellow dress to...something universally understandable...fish changing into chips or something. Andrew, by the time we get back to the house the phone is going to be blowing off the hook with press calls. And what you've just said is so wonderfully sane and reassuring; THAT's how you're going to defuse all this panic."

"All what panic?"

"All the panic that's going to start up when people hear about what the universities have done. The panic that would make people start being paranoid about going to work, or using public transport, or just going out into the street. The panic that started in me about AIDS becoming infectious. You're brilliant! Come on, let's head back..."

"Oh my sweet, do you ever stop work?"

"This isn't work; not for me any more, remember? This is life. Now get going!"

To their surprise, the first caller when they returned was Callum. He and other student workers were being kicked out, he'd be on the plane that evening and in Heathrow the following morning. Although disappointed, he was perfectly relaxed and hastened to reassure Andrew that the individuals he'd been working with were sorry to see him and the others go, they'd been made very welcome and there was no question of any unpleasantness. He didn't want to go back to Aberdeen yet, nor to St Fillans, and Andrew agreed instantly to his having the flat in Tudor Court for the summer.

"I'll phone the doorman, get him to give you a key; and I'll put money in your hole-in-the-wall account this afternoon. Listen, son, this must be costing you a fortune: I'll phone you tomorrow night at the flat, okay? Great. Take care!"

After that, the press calls began. And continued. Terry's reconstruction of Andrew's speech to her was faxed to a dozen newspapers, a dozen news agencies. And by teatime they were both thoroughly hacked off with the intrusion. Andrew suggested they throw some clothes into the back of the Wyvern and head for the hills - literally.

"Argyll is full of hotels and bed-and-breakfasts. We can get away from everything and just be tourists and enjoy ourselves for the next fortnight. We can call Callum just as easily from anywhere else...and we can buy the odd newspaper to keep ourselves informed. Well?"

"You betcha. A real holiday? You're on!"

It took them only half an hour to get organised, inform Fred Hamilton and Isa of their departure (but not of any destination, on Terry's insistance "You don't know the hounds like I do, darling; tell nobody nuffink!") and get on the road. Andrew was full of relief...relief that Terry was no longer frightened, relief that Callum was not in any danger, relief that they now had some chance of a real old-fashioned holiday. They drove off in high hopes.

———— • ————

Alec was thoroughly frightened, though less than he had been the day before. Since he'd been diagnosed as having the beginnings of fullblown AIDS, his principal fear had not been of dying from AIDS, but of dying from Frankie finding out he had AIDS. Frankie struck him as the kind of man who would not take kindly to this information, as he had most probably infected half a dozen regular good clients, and many casual one-offs. Frankie would not like to have dissatisfied customers: and Frankie was quite likely to take his revenge. If it had been possible to escape, Alec would have done so. But since his visit to the clinic, he had been locked in the flat. Nobody lived above or below or beside him, so calls for help would have availed him nothing. This was a tower block with only five flats still inhabited, and those only by drunks and druggies, who were rarely there and who did not interfere with each other, whatever they heard or thought they heard. Besides, those flats were all on much lower floors.

Frankie's men had brought him food and drugs and clients until yesterday evening, when Frankie paid one of his rare visits. He seemed in high good humour, and even patted Alec fondly on the knee, sitting on the bed beside him right after they'd 'discovered' him being buggered again and put the bite on the man and the man had left and the sidekicks were sorting out the videotape in the next room.

"Aye, Alec, you've done me proud over the last year son, so you have. Quite a bit of money, you've brought in. But all good things come to an end. For me as well as for you, eh? Frankly, Alec, you're losing your looks. Too much of the old drugs, eh, boy? Fair does you in. So me and the boys have come to a sad decision, but I think you'll be quite happy with it. It's time to part company, laddie, you and us. Just one more wee job for us, tomorrow night, and that's you unemployed, I'm afraid. Still, we've decided to give you a golden handshake, as it were: two thousand pounds to set you on your way. How does that strike you, boy? Mm?"

"That would be jist lovely, Mr Dunn, sir...but...but why have I been locked up?"

"Ah well, I haven't told you yet what the wee job tomorrow night is, now have I? You're not going to like the sound of it, Alec, but I promise you it'll be all right. You remember that bampot that started in on you that time, and we came in and found him just about tearing your fingernails out?"

Alec shivered uncontrollably. "Oh JesusGod Mister Dunn don't let him back in here, oh please Jesus Mary Mother Of God don't do that!" He was on the floor, on his knees, still naked, shaking, trying to clutch Frankie's ankles. Frankie booted him out of the way. His tone was still mild.

"Now son: you don't get the two thousand for nothing, you know. But you can understand why we've had to lock you in. We couldn't take the risk of you maybe going for a wee holiday, or getting run over maybe, when we had such a big job for you to do tomorrow. You understand, don't you, Alec?"

Alec sat huddled in the foetal position in the corner, rocking.

"Please Mr Dunn sir, don't you worry about the two thousand pounds, just if you could let me go sir, please, for God's sake sir, please let me go, don't let that Tommy Bain back in here please sir please sir Mr Frankie Mr Dunn sir please, no' him, don't do this to me, please, I don't want the money, just..."

But Frankie had stood up and walked across the room and now booted Alec until he was quiet and only whimpering.

"We'll be next door, Alec; there's nothing for you to worry about. Now get yourself back into bed and decently covered and I'll explain to you. I don't want you all frightened when he gets here, I want you all pouting and strutting your wee buns and looking forward to a magnificent fuck. That's what Mr Bain wants, and that's what he's paying us for. He has promised there'll be no rough stuff this time; but just in case, me and the boys will be next door watching and listening, and if there's any nonsense we'll be right in here to help you."

The blue silk covers showed he was still trembling, but trying to get a grip on his facial expressions. "Yes sir" he managed. But he obviously did not believe Frankie for a minute.

"Look" said Frankie in his most fatherly tone "I can't afford to have you hurt, now can I? Because I'm wanting you to be the one to find your own replacement. You know all the boys around, eh Alec? And if you got duffed up, well, you wouldn't hardly recommend us to anyone now would you? You've been well enough treated up till now, haven't you? Well then. Didn't we stop Tommy Bain last time? We'll stop him this time too, only quicker, 'cause we'll be right here. Look:" and he pulled a thick wad of twenty pound notes from his pocket and deposited it on the bedside table. "Here's your dosh. Tomorrow night, after Bain has finished with you, you're to take this money and away up town; we've got a room booked for you in a nice hotel for a few days. Of course you'll have to pay for it yourself out of the two thousand, I'm not made of money, but you see we'll know where you are and we can phone you and you can tell us when you've found a good lad. About thirteen or fourteen years old, well broken in though we can always help with that: and willing. Okay, Alec?"

The bit about Alec paying for the hotel room himself was a master stroke. The boy believed him.

So, on the Saturday afternoon, Alec was thoroughly frightened but not so much as he had been the day before. He knew he would die of AIDS, but the hospices in Edinburgh were famous and he knew he would be well treated and not in pain. What's more, he would be able to buy himself some new clothes, and give maybe a thousand clear to his Mum before he died; she'd always wanted a wee holiday in the South of France, and his father had never made it possible. Maybe then she could forgive him. Maybe she would come and hold his hand for a bit, in the hospice, maybe, if she could

177

do it without his father finding out and beating seven bells out of her. So the business of dying would not be so bad, might even have a good side to it. And with the boys being next door tonight, even Tommy Bain would not be able to do very much harm before he was stopped. Still, he was nervous. The only thing which cheered him was remembering that Tommy had not used a condom; with luck, Alec would infect him with the virus, and take his revenge posthumously.

Tommy Bain's mother could not understand what her son's jocularity was all about. Normally he was a dour, uncommunicative man, who went out of the farmhouse in the morning without a word of thanks for her breakfasts, and came home from the fields at night to a huge meal which he devoured in silence. But today, he actually smiled at her, sniffed the lunchtime casserole appreciatively and asked if she would mind leaving a nice big macaroni cheese pie in the oven for him to come home to that night, as he might be late and would certainly be hungry? She was delighted to comply with such a civil request. Oh, she hoped he had fallen in love with some nice local lass. It would be good to have another face about the farmhouse, someone cheery to gossip with and share the housework. Maybe that's why he'd sold the car, to have money to take her out with. And it would explain, too, why he had bought a whole new suit of clothes which he was putting on by six o'clock. Things had fair changed since her young day, she reflected; Tommy was now kitted out in his new suit, but it was a suit of jogging clothes; in her day, it would have been a real suit, with a good tie, that a man put on to take out his lady love.

She'd been so worried about him when she found the magazines under his bed. But he had explained that they were just for showing him what he could develop his body into. And he certainly worked out with weights and things. Now, with a lass in the offing, Mrs Bain felt she could relax. Her son was not, after all, a homosexual. Her dead husband had been dead wrong.

"You make sure and enjoy yourself now, son" she ventured, as he left.

"Oh I will tonight Ma, no problem." She did not remember ever seeing him with such an air of happiness and excited expectation about him. Her motherly heart was full.

She watched him climb into the taxi at the back door, and briefly wondered what was in the sports holdall which bulged so and seemed so heavy.

Four hours he kept saying to himself. Four hours. It'll be work of art. A slow symphony of pain. I wonder why they're insisting on four hours and not any more than that? Ach, who cares. Probably some old bag in the flat above comes home at eleven, and the noise would be a problem. He had devoted considerable thinking time to devising ways of stretching the torture and death over four hours. It had become a matter of pride to him, calculating things so that Alec would take exactly four hours to die, without ever being out of pain, or unconscious, for one minute after Tommy had had his first ejaculation.

Subsequent orgasms were timed in advance, as they would coincide with the peaks of Alec's agony. Yes, the plans were excellent. This might be the only time in his life he could really let himself go, and he intended to enjoy every single second of it. He got the taxi to the centre of town, where one of Frankie's men picked him up and took him to the tower block. As he walked up the stairs to Alec's front door, he was whistling softly.

Alec opened the door wearing eyeshadow, mascara, one earring, a pale blue silk galabea. And a nervous smile. The fear in that smile gave Tommy an instant erection, and within a minute Alec was splayed face down on the bed enduring a brutal buggery which he honestly believed was going to be the worst thing that happened to him that night. So he gritted his teeth and he thought about the new clothes and his Mum holding his hand in the hospice, and he was as brave as he'd ever been in his life.

At three forty-seven on Saturday morning, 'Hawkeye' Pierce, the night roundsman from LockStock Security, walked his alsatian round the transport company yard off Leith Street. The dog seemed restless; Hawkeye knew this to be unusual, and so became a little

179

watchful and on edge. Even at this time, the summer dark was not absolute, so the shadowy corners were less menacing than they might have been in midwinter, but there were many potential hiding places between the serried ranks of artics. He could hear no shuffling of feet, or talking...there were no lights showing in the Portakabins which served as offices...but Sheba was definitely on to something, and he gave her her head. She picked up speed as she hauled him across the yard, between the still and silent lorries, till she yelped and started pawing frantically at a large and shapelessly lumpy black polythene bag lying at the foot of one of the perimeter walls. He pulled her off and commanded her to sit; she did, but she was high as a kite.

Gingerly, he took off the rope which tied the top of the bag shut, and shone his torch inside. Meat! Great hunks of meat. No wonder Sheba was going berserk! He relaxed. Some drunken yobbo had done over a butcher's shop, then got cold feet, or been chased, maybe, and chucked it over here. Was it beef? He peered closer, and immediately vomited both into the bag and all around it. There were strips of clothing...blue silk clothing...adhering to some of the lumps of flesh, and fingers protruding between two of the lumps, fingers which had no nails left on them but bloody pulp instead.

It was several minutes before he could collect himself sufficiently to radio headquarters. They followed standard procedure, phoned the police first, then called Jack Macleod from a deep and peaceful slumber to suggest he go down to the yard, as the police would certainly want to see him as there had been an incident on the premises, an incident which sounded like murder.

By the time he got there, the yard was brilliant with floodlights, there was a tent being erected close to the perimeter wall, and yellow sticky tape laid all around it, clearly marking off a closed zone. There were policemen everywhere, and one of them tried to push him away.

"Look, I'm Jack Macleod: this is my yard!"

"Ah, well then sir you'd better wait and meet Detective Inspector Turnbull, when he gets here. He'll be in charge, sir, and he's on his way. I suggest you let yourself into the office, sir, and make yourself a cup of tea."

"Fine, fine, but what's happened here?"

"I'm very sorry sir, but I think you'd better wait for Detective Inspector Turnbull. Perhaps you might like to invite the security man to come inside for a cup of tea too, sir? He seems pretty distressed and we've got to hang on to him till the D.I. comes."

"Of course; tell him to come in." He fumbled with his keys and got inside, put the lights on, filled the kettle to the brim: there seemed to be at least a dozen police out there, maybe more. When Pierce stepped in, he was still stinking of vomit, and still in shock. He'd never seen a dead body except for his Grandma, and that had been all lace and silk quilted coffin and this was... this was something that would haunt his dreams for the rest of his life. Jason 'Hawkeye' Pierce was only twenty seven years old.

Jack showed him to the toilet and put on the water heater so he could clean himself up a bit, then set about making a pot of tea. Then, looking outside at the hordes of police, he filled the urn instead. It was likely to be a long night. He phoned his wife, who was too sleepy to take in most of what he said but dimly understood there was something up at the haulage yard and he would not be back for a long while, and gratefully sprawled across the whole of the double bed, to make the most of it.

The tea was only just infused when Detective Inspector Turnbull and Sergeant Paterson arrived. Turnbull took Hawkeye Pierce away to interview him, and Sergeant Paterson detailed a constable to make and distribute the teas while he stayed and chatted with Mr Macleod.

"Well sir, is there anything you can tell us about the body?"

"No, I'm afraid not; first I knew about it was when the Security people called me up. I don't know a thing."

Paterson had a pleasantly mild and respectful manner.

"Must have been a bit of a shock to you, sir, I expect. Not the sort of thing you imagine ever happening to you, is it? Something you read about in the papers, more like."

"Exactly" said Jack, ruefully. "It still seems unreal. All these lights, police everywhere, me up in the middle of the night. Very strange. Disconcerting."

"More disconcerting for the poor soul that was found in the bucket bag, though."

This was the first scant bit of detail Jack had heard so far, and it did not sound nice.

"A bucket bag? Oh."

"Yes, sir. Though by the time the body was put in the bucket bag, sir, the person concerned was way past caring what sort of shroud, if you understand, sir. Way past caring."

Jack was consumed with curiousity but did not want to appear ghoulish by asking about the body, or the murder itself. Still;

"Was it a man or a woman, in the bucket bag?"

Sergeant Paterson shrugged. "Can't really say, sir."

"Oh, you've just arrived, haven't had time to find out yet?"

"Not that sir; even the police pathologist hasn't taken a guess yet, you see, sir. You can't tell by looking. Not at this particular corpse, anyway, sir. The murderer was very...demented." He looked carefully at Jack through lowered lids. The man's face was going white and he looked nauseous, and Sergeant Paterson was quite satisfied that this man was not the murderer. Nobody could fake shock and disgust like that - nobody except a complete psychopath, of course, which this murderer quite probably was. No. Most likely the choice of the haulage yard was at random, nothing to do with this Macleod character; he'd hardly have done this bloody deed and then casually chucked the bits into a bag in his own yard, would he, for the security man to find?

Unless of course that was what he thought the police would think. Sergeant Paterson decided to keep his mind open a bit longer.

"So, sir; were you out last night, Saturday on the town, anything like that?"

"No such luck; the family was round. The wife's family. Came for a barbecue in the afternoon and stayed till nearly one o'clock in the morning. God, I'm tired."

The point of the question suddenly hit him, and he looked up at the sergeant.

"Was that - am I a suspect? Just because it's in my yard?"

Sergeant Paterson merely shrugged again, and raised his eyebrows quizzically as if to indicate well, it's a silly old world isn't it, but routine is routine. Jack relaxed.

"Either way there are about a dozen people who can corroborate my alibi, if needed."

"And why do you think you might need an alibi, sir?"

Confusion and unease. "I thought; oh, I don't know. How do I know if I'll need an alibi? I was only saying..."

"Quite, sir."

"Something like this...it throws you. It's like a bad dream. And that poor kid with the alsatian...his nerves are really shot."

"Understandable, sir, given what he saw."

He didn't get home till half past five in the morning, after visiting the station to make a statement. He was dog tired. And there was still this unpleasant tickle at the back of his mind that he was a suspect. Still, he knew he was innocent, so he was not unduly worried. He kissed his sleeping wife fondly, and snuggled into bed, heaving her gently across to her own side, and slept deep. He had already called Reg, the office manager, to come in for the day and keep the police supplied with data and tea and whatever else they wanted.

At which time, precisely, Frankie Dunn was rising from Flora Spencer's bed, pulled back by her warm arms for one last kiss, which he gave reluctantly. She was hurt by this and showed it.

"I'm not much of a one for slobbering...sorry. But I'll make you a nice cup of tea, shall I?" He did this most mornings for Grandad. She nodded, trying to look pleased. As he wrapped himself in her dressinggown, she reflected that this was the one area in which Frankie failed her. The - she struggled for the right phrase - the interface between the courtesy of daytime and the unbridled lust of night. She would have liked more cuddles, more hugs, more kisses, but Frankie did not care for these and doled them out meanly, like rewards when she was specially pleasing to him. She was certainly learning how to please him in bed: he still called her a whore, but nowadays it was to praise her, a sort of certificate of merit for her new accomplishments. Oh, how Daddy would convulse if he could see his good little girl now!

He brought the tea through and sat on the bed beside her to drink it.

"You'll never guess where I'm off to this morning" he said. 'Your Dad's church!"

"Frankie do you have to? It's a bit sick, isn't it, right after crawling out of my bed?"

"I have to; well, I think I should. The whole congregation is in People for Purity these days, and I'm the only one that doesn't attend the church. It's been noticed. It's not good."

She sipped her tea slowly.

"I still think that organisation is deeply worrying. You're not an extremist, Frankie; it's not your sort of thing."

"I told you; strictly business. I invest their money, make a nice commission on it too. I advise them about local media schedules. I sell pensions and mortgages. I do very nicely out of them. But I pull my weight as well."

"Don't you find it difficult, working with my Dad and never saying anything to him about us?"

"Not in the slightest. Would I want to say anything? What would I say? 'By the way, Reverend old chap, I am screwing the arse off your daughter on a fairly regular basis, and a damn fine fuck she is, these days. You brought her up a treat, thanks, old mate'?"

Flora did not rise to the bait this time. She was beginning to get to know him.

"No. I did think, though, that one of these days you might be saying 'Your daughter and I are going to get married, and we would very much like your blessing.'"

He looked at her in genuine surprise. He had been planning to ask her to marry him, in a few weeks, or maybe months; it simply had not occurred to him that she would ask him.

"Was that a proposal?"

"No. Well yes, I suppose so. I think we should get married quite soon. If you'll have me. Because I'm about a month pregnant.

You're going to be a Dad, Frankie."

"But how?"

"The usual way. That first time; remember, in the lounge, with the shutters drawn? Or in your office, the next day. I'd only just gone back on the Pill after a year's break, and...it obviously hadn't settled into my system."

The teacup in her hand rattled slightly in the saucer. She half-expected him to get dressed and walk out on her. She fully expected him to give her mouthfuls of abuse at her stupidity. What she did not expect was the way he took the saucer from her and set it down by his own on the bedside table and then moved close to her and took both her hands in his and then stroked her hair, gazing at her in wonderment while he still clasped both of her hands in one of his, close to his chest.

"You're the mother of my child?" And she smiled, a little tremulously, and nodded.

"Look at you" he said, in an entirely new tone, full of reverence. "Madonna" he said, and then "My love" as if it surprised him.

"My wife, yes, my wife. Will I have you? I'd die for you." He stood up, suddenly full of glee, clenched both fists in the air and yelled "YES!" and jigged for joy.

"Damn, damn, I have to go - I need to be going - Grandad'll be getting up in half an hour. Oh, Flora! Look: stay in bed, be lazy, I wish I could stay here right now but I can't. All day, I'll be busy all day...can I come round at tea time? Right and don't you move a muscle, I'll bring something in with me for both of us."

She got up, dressed in nothing but the warm morning air, and this time she got a very satisfactory hug, very chaste considering their mutual state of undress and his normal reaction to this, but still, very close and loving. She brushed her hair while he dressed, and he watched her covertly, delighting in the eternal nature of her movements. The butchering of Alec, the hours his boys had spent cleaning the blood spatters from the walls, could not have been further from his mind. They kissed when he left, and he walked to the car, every inch the proud new father, looking forward to seeing the special smile on Peter Spencer's face when he heard his wayward daughter was caught and tamed at last.

Driving through the empty West End of Princes Street, he just missed seeing Albert Kennedy driving his blue Ford Escort through the same area, on his way out of town. Half a mile behind Albert, very discreet, a large unmarked Rover carried the two plain clothes policemen who were following him.

It was an easy job for a Sunday morning; tail the Escort and see where it went. No interception required, just a report. And the Escort was easy to follow, with its white gofaster stripes and the tall whiplash aerial. The policemen chatted about this and that, having nothing much to say about Albert because they knew nothing about him and cared less.

Up Lothian Road they went, following the Escort right out of town, out past Glencorse Barracks, out through Penicuik and on towards Eddlestone, through Eddlestone and on towards Peebles, which they approached around seven-thirty. They were still hanging well back, as the roads were not busy and they were not to let the subject know he was being tailed. The Escort turned right towards the High Street, out of sight for a few moments. When they turned the same corner, they were relieved to see the blue Escort with the white go faster stripes and the whiplash aerial just pulling left into the High Street, at the T-junction traffic lights. Unhurried, they carried on half a mile behind it.

Another blue Escort with white gofaster stripes and a whiplash aerial then emerged from one of the sidestreets off the road leading to the traffic lights; it turned right at the lights, then left, then swung off the road at the bridge, down to the little car park, and Albert Kennedy stepped out of it.

He walked down to the bank of the River Tweed, and walked along it for a hundred yards, to where a man was standing feeding chunks of bread to the ducks, whose furious babbling kept the few swans gliding hopefully at the back of the crowd.

The man was tall, conservatively dressed, and moved with graceful elegance. He nodded as Albert came alongside him.

"Good morning" he said, with the faintest trace of a soft Irish accent.

"Good morning" replied Albert, and the man threw the last of the bread in a great wheeling arc, so that the swans finally got some, and the two men walked along the riverbank together.

"You've seen the papers, yesterday and today?" asked Albert.

"Yes. We are very pleased. Well done. How are things progressing?"

They talked easily enough together, not like old friends but certainly old acquaintances with a good deal of mutual respect between them.

"Very well, on the whole. A little faster than we had anticipated, even, but I don't think...prematurely."

"The Reverend Spencer?"

"Sobering down a little. For the public, anyway: but it's still his energy that drives the machine. I just hope I can keep the lid on him."

"And if you can't?"

"Then...as we agreed."

"Good. Any other potential problems?"

"Only one; a psychopath friend of Spencer's, called Frankie Dunn. It's tempting to think he could be useful in a tight situation, but he's deeply unstable. His grandfather is the only thing that keeps him linked to the human race."

"And in what way could he be a problem?"

"In discrediting the organisation, if he goes haywire."

"Don't let that happen, Mr Kennedy."

"I shan't. What's happening Stateside just now?"

"It's going very well. Reuters and Cable News Network picked up on the British university story, of course, and carried it worldwide. Public opinion in America is heavily on the side of the universities. They're pushing hard for a similar ban there; and it's the same story throughout Europe, particularly in Germany and France. When will you be moving this out of the arena of the ivory towers, and into business?"

"A week or so. Not too soon, or it might be regarded as reactive hysteria. Not too late, or the impetus generated by the universities

187

will have dissipated."

"Excellent."

"There's something you're not happy about; I wish you'd tell me what it is."

The man sighed, a very small sigh. "It's the slang you chose; that's all."

"It was not I who chose it; it honestly was already a grassroots piece of slang. I had to build on what was already there, already causing the right kind of reaction. I regret it, but there was no alternative."

"Fair enough. But if you get a chance to change it, do so."

"I doubt that will be the case, I'm afraid. But on to better things; I have been informed that the new Clause to Section 5 will be instituted very soon, as we discussed. And towards the ends that we agreed."

The man was visibly pleased by this.

"Splendid! That's sooner than we hoped for; anything else?"

"Apart from the fact that I am being followed, no."

"Well now that's nothing new to you, Mr Kennedy! I have no doubt you are coping admirably as always. Now do you need anything? Money, for example?"

"Not just now, no, thank you. The normal monthly amounts are quite adequate at the moment. I may need more later on, but I can let you know nearer the time."

"Is there anything else, then, for this morning?"

"Only thank you for the World Health Organisation report; it really was the creme de la creme. I don't mean to sound flippant, I know how serious it is, I just mean in terms of my own end of things, it was wonderfully useful."

"No problem, it was brought in a diplomatic Bag. But you're welcome, anyway. Well, goodbye, Mr Kennedy. A pleasant day to you."

"And to you. Enjoy your journey."

He drove back, in good time for church.

———— • ————

Neither Terry nor Andrew had yet seen the Sunday papers. Not because of any deliberate decision not to read them, but because they were in the depths of Argyll, where the Sunday papers do not arrive until late lunchtime. They had not seen the Saturday papers either, and that *was* because of a deliberate decision. They were determined to relax.

They were breakfasting in a small diningroom with a wonderful view, through plate glass windows, down Loch Awe. The hotel sat squat and hidden at the end of a steeply descending track which barely deserved the title 'road' and which gave it a romantic atmosphere all its own. Water lapped at the foot of the garden, and there were small boats for hire and fishing if you wanted to. It had been their first stop since their flight from St Fillans on Friday, and their plans to tour round had died on them when they found it. It was perfection, in a comfortable, slightly shabby way, and they were enjoying themselves immensely. The hotel had neither television nor radio in the rooms, only an old tv in the residents' lounge, which was rarely switched on these summer evenings, as most of the guests were out walking by the loch or in the hills.

"You know something? I have such a ridiculous dream" said Andrew, long finished his grapefruit and patiently waiting for Terry to get through her monstrous four egg omelette with wild mushrooms and fresh herbs. "A paddle steamer on Loch Awe. All white paint and bunting, just paddling round the shores at your ease, drinking in the scenery."

"Oh yes. Not ridiculous at all! The public would flock to it. It would be gorgeous!"

"Bugger the public" said mild Doctor Douglas, hotly. "This would be for ME and maybe you, if you're good. I meant, to live on, not a floating charabanc."

She considered, as she swallowed. But she did not answer, because the uniformed policeman who had just walked into the diningroom was making straight for their table.

"Miss Aitken? Doctor Douglas? I'm sorry to interrupt your meal, sir, but I wonder if I could have a word?"

He had his word in the Reception area, so as not to disturb the other diners, and his word was 'pack'. They packed, they paid their bill, they followed him through the front door. He drove them to the airstrip at Connel, just outside Oban, where a helicopter was waiting to take them to Glasgow Airport. He knew nothing, he said, about the reason for their recall to London.

"You'll be on a scheduled flight from Glasgow, sir, much more comfortable than the chopper." He was polite and even apologetic as he let them out and walked them to the waiting helicopter, making them duck under the rotors, which were already beginning to whirl. "Sorry to disturb your holiday, madam, sir."

They climbed aboard, aided by a young man in camouflage gear and shiny black glasses who sat them down in boneshaker seats and strapped them in. There was room for another dozen passengers, but passengers there were none. Only them. And then, when the pilot had gone through to the cockpit, another man emerged from it, a middle-aged man with thinning hair and broken veins all over his nose, and came to strap himself in beside them. Andrew did not know him, but Terry did.

"Bloody hell" she breathed, just loud enough for Andrew to hear. "Bloody Frank bloody Ainsley!"

CHAPTER SIX

As the rotor blades circled ever faster the noise made conversation difficult, but Frank Ainsley did not attempt any. With the merest nod to Andrew and a raised eyebrow to Terry, he handed them each a bundle of Sunday newspapers and a headset of ear protectors, then sat down and strapped himself in across the aisle from them. Andrew and Terry squeezed each others' hands comfortingly, exchanged looks of consolation and support, and settled down to read. The newspapers did not make happy reading, and after a few shocked looks, each settled into a private and absorbing horror which quite eclipsed from their minds the little matter of lift-off and sloping and veering which otherwise might have at least interested them a little, as neither had ever flown in a 'paraffin budgie' before.

The front page stories were almost all about the universities' decision to bar students from high-AIDS-risk countries, but the language was far from academic in the majority of papers.

"UNIS SOCK IT TO DEATH STUDENTS" was one. *"STAY HOME, SAY OUR UNIVERSITIES"* screamed another. *"U.K. WORLD'S FIRST AIDSFREE ZONE!"* claimed another, with xenophobic pride and total disregard for the truth. It continued:

"Typhoid Marys trying to come into Britain were warned off this week by all our universities and colleges. The message was clear and strong: stay home and keep Britain clean! British young people can rest easier from today, and so can their worried parents." The newspaper kindly went on to explain about Typhoid Mary, the infamous carrier of deadly typhoid who had so loved to cook that she had killed off several whole families in America for whom she had gone to work even after she knew she was the reason they were all dying. A new version of an old nursery rhyme was offered. The parallel with modern day HIV Positives who might all unwittingly (or not) infect those around them with tuberculosis was all too close, and had given rise to the slang term for Positives: Marys. The revamped nursery rhyme was a model of perfect

191

scansion and perfect hatred.

> *Mary, Mary, thin and scary,*
> *How does your virus grow?*
> *With AIDS you see, and now T.B.,*
> *And little graves all in a row.*

Even the more upmarket papers, with the prominent social consciences and the barely hidden agendas of party political whiplines, were united in praising the 'courageous move of our academics'. One or two of them went farther, in their editorials, by pointing out that those selfsame students could still come here and infect our innocent youth, as long as they did not actually attend university and perhaps something should be done about that? One major heavyweight actually solicited readers' opinions on this matter in a kind of unofficial referendum. They had printed a voting slip, which they invited the reader to complete and cut out and send to the editorial offices. For choice of response, there was only 'yes' or 'no'. Nobody was to be allowed to put in a 'don't know' vote. And the way the question was phrased left little room for doubting which answer was being solicited: "DO YOU WANT INFECTED AIDS CARRIERS TO BE ALLOWED INTO THIS COUNTRY?"

And on, and on. For a leavening, Terry glanced over some of the advertisements. There was a quarter-pager which quite tempted her on sight. It was on behalf of the Government of Australia, and it offered free passage and a two-year mortgage moratorium to anybody with a)certain specified skills and qualifications and b)anybody displaying an ability to reach those skill levels and qualifications, if they would just come to Australia and help them build on their new boom economy. The jobs they seemed to want filled spanned most of the construction trades and professions, and many service industry sectors. Moderately curious, given the extremely exigous nature of her present life, she scanned the column to see if journalists and/or P.R. people were wanted. They were not. Ah, well.

A boom economy, she thought. What a pleasant idea. It seemed to be happening almost everywhere except in the U.K. these days. Now that the exUSSR states had pretty well settled down and become Europeanised, the whole of Europe seemed to be hitched to the wagon of the German economy, and was thriving. Even those countries where fundamental Islam was rising, and insisting on a return to mediaeval practices, were surviving. Only Britain, and her very weak pound, was failing. Turning the pages she was surprised to see very similar advertisements offering very similar blandishments to come and help the Canadians...the Americans...the Russians...build on their boom economies.

But none of them wanted her, either. So she settled back down to reading the catalogue of hysteria which was being presented as news. It was, as propaganda usually is, peppered with genuine facts, facts she recognised from the various conversations she had had with Andrew. One in three people in Zambia, between the ages of twenty and forty, were seropositive. One in four in Namibia, two in five in Kenya and 'incalculable numbers' in certain other countries notorious for their reluctance to publish their figures, such as India, China, and several Asian states. These numbers were given as ample evidence to support the universities in their struggle to save the youth of today, and as ample reason for right-thinking people to beware of foreigners. The connection with T.B. was well to the fore; she felt uneasy herself, reading those articles. In countries where T.B. had been virtually unknown for decades, it was now wiping out whole families.

And it had already started to affect families in Britain. Which, of course, meant it was no longer merely an interesting set of statistics, but something which actually mattered. A million families in Africa wiped out equals marginally interesting; one British family affected equals headline news. This was the first time anybody had bothered reporting that T.B. patients had been routinely screened for the AIDS virus since around the end of 1992.

There were also reports which clearly relished the amount of violence erupting onto the streets; mobs of youths, some of them

193

armed, were out to kill, and their targets were, excepting in Edinburgh, any men who looked effeminate. In Edinburgh they had two targets: homosexuals and drugtakers. Drug abuse had always been the primary cause of the spread of AIDS in Edinburgh. This made it a different case to the others; everywhere else, the rampaging youths were working class boys who in other times would have been called yobs. In Edinburgh, some members of the gangs were reputedly well-educated and from more middle-class families, and those gangs went into the worst housing estates and broke into flats known to be used as shooting galleries and kicked hell out of the hapless occupants, often torching the place before they left.

The editorial tone was, in every case, one of the mildest possible reproof, with admiration and encouragement only barely concealed. There was also, in 'The Sunday Scot', a Stop Press paragraph about the horrific murder of a person unknown, whose dismembered corpse had been found in a transport yard in the early hours of the day.

Within an hour, Andrew, Terry and Frank Ainsley were aboard the shuttle to London in the VIP section, which was empty apart from themselves, having been booked in its entirety. Here, conversation was possible, and therefore unavoidable. And bloody Frank bloody Ainsley was in bloody mood.

"Jolly super to see you, Frank" said Terry, with amiable sarcasm. "Just what we needed, really."

"We'll have less of the sarcasm, Madam" he replied, and not in tones befitting an underling addressing his boss. "I don't work for you any more and I don't have to take any more of your crap." Terry was disconcerted. "What do you mean? Since when have you not worked for the Media office, then?"

"Oh, I still work there; in fact I run it now. But *your* bum is out of the window, in a big way. You've been fired. For sending out those ever-so-cute faxes from Strathfillan, or whatever, without permission. After being told, quite clearly, that you were not working on the case any more. Tough titties, little one."

Andrew's voice was ice cold. "You will not use those tones, or those words, to any lady in my company. Unless you are prepared to back up your words with your fists, of course; which I shall instantly report to every major news agency in the world. Maybe you would keep your job after that; it's up to you to decide whether that risk is worth the extreme pleasure of behaving like an ill-mannered lout. Now you will apologise."

"It's all right, Andrew, really!" Terry was embarrassed, being used to this kind of language and far worse too, from her days in newspapers. She was quite used to giving as good as she got. And then some. "Shit-for-brains here can't think up a whole sentence without expletives in it. It's a congenital malady, inherited from his mother, a wellknown waterfront whore in Liverpool."

This left Andrew looking rather foolish. Which she regretted instantly. And Frank lunged in at her weak side.

"Must be nice for a little trollop like you to have Sir Galahad here on your side. Clearly he doesn't know about your worldfamous reputation as a foul mouthed brat with an inflated ego and a tiny talent."

"Well now dear" said Terry with aspartame sweetness. "Better that than a deflated ego and a tiny prick. Still, them's the breaks. Now can we get down to business, or is it too late in the day for you to be compos mentis?"

Rather late, Andrew realised that this sparring was their lingua franca, and quite enjoyable for both of them. They did detest each other, and he had to admit it must be quite pleasant to be so open about it, unlike the honeyed arsenic of the talk between Parliamentary colleagues.

"Firstly" began Terry, crisply "I didn't send those faxes; Andrew did. He's allowed, I believe, being somewhat senior to yourself. So we'll have my being fired rescinded, prontissimo, as soon as I get to the P.M. Secondly, I rather think you have just blown any chance of Andrew ever agreeing to work with you. Thirdly;"

"Oh, put a sock in it for God's sake! I thought you said something about getting down to business?"

"Okay; thirdly, why the hell are we on this plane, on our way to London?"

"Like I said, a tiny talent: you've read the papers. They weren't intended as inflight entertainment."

"So? Okay, it's bad; but it could have waited till I'd - till we'd had our holiday, surely. It's not going to go away, in a fortnight."

"SO sorry dear, but your little love nest comes way down the list of important things on the world stage. If the Prime Minister can break into his holiday, you sure as hell can break into yours. Both of you; Doctor Douglas, it is principally you that the P.M. wants to see. We just thought you'd prefer to have...Miss Aitken...along for the ride?"

"Oh" said Terry, suitably squashed.

"Is anyone else going to be in on the meeting?" asked Andrew, soberly.

Ainsley looked at him with a modicum of respect. "Yes, sir, there is someone else; Jim Brettles. He's been recalled too."

Terry broke in. "The Minister for Agriculture? What the hell has HE got to do with this?"

"I'm afraid I can't tell you that. But you'll find out soon enough, whatever it is. And that peripatetic doom monger from the World Health Organisation is at the meeting too; rumour has it he's just come from the States, and before that, central Africa. But if anybody knows why, he's keeping his mouth well shut about it. You'd think there was a bloody D-notice on this guy and no, there isn't, not that I can find on the computer anyway." He shrugged.

"Which particular peripatetic doom monger are we talking about?" asked Andrew.

"Juan Romero de Boca Negra. The AIDS collator."

"And Jim Brettles?"

"That's it. Well, you won't have long to worry about it. Couple of hours from now, Doctor Douglas, you'll know more than I do. You, on the other hand, Madam, will still know less than I do. You're not invited to the meeting."

"Then why ? I don't buy the bit about being along for the ride. This Government does not pay all this money to bring someone along for the ride."

"Oh, what a nose for news we have, all of a sudden! Okay, you ARE invited to a meeting: the whole Media office is to stand by for the end of the P.M.'s meeting. Seeing as how you're supposed to be out of a job, I don't know what they want you there for at all. But, ours not to question why... Big stuff in the pipeline, by the sound of it. And don't bother asking, 'cause I don't know."

"Situation normal, then" said Terry, subsiding.

Andrew was very quiet for the rest of the journey. Something his old friend Joe had told him was nagging at the back of his mind, almost coming into view and then sinking down again. Something about rabies...

At twelve-thirty, Senor Romero de Boca Negra informed his audience of three that the World Health Organisation had completed its covert investigation of the cases of Miss Hislop, Darren Harrison, and all the other people, worldwide, whose infection by HIV could not have been by any known method.

"I regret to inform you, gentlemen, that the result is not a particularly pleasant fact. But it seems to be indisputable. The cases varied so much in personal circumstance and medical history, you see, so it was a very difficult job to try to pinpoint a common denominator. We had copies of every autopsy report, we interviewed every family doctor involved, and still we drew a blank. Then we began the lifestyle investigation. There was only one common factor, but it was present in 100% of cases.'

'Every one of these people had a cat. And every one of those cats is now dead. Except for two in France and one in America, in households where, again, the route of infection seemed impossible. Those cats were tested; they have AIDS."

"Feline AIDS, you mean?" asked Jim Brettles.

"No, Senor Brettles. Not feline AIDS. Human Immunodeficiency Virus...with just a very small mutation so that it can be carried by cats and transmitted by cats. Whether it will in fact affect the cats, being human-specific, we do not yet know. Frankly, it is low on our list of concerns."

This was not the first small audience to which he had delivered

197

his speech, and he knew to stay quiet for a time while the people attempted to digest what was happening, and what had to happen next.

"There is more. After this discovery, we caught and tested several wild varieties of cat; lynxes, lions, pumas and others. A small percentage of these were also HIV Positive. They have been humanely destroyed, of course." Just in case any of them was missing the point, he laboured it: "A bite from any infected animal would be quite capable of transmitting the virus. Quite capable; because of the assortment of flora and fauna in the average feline mouth, the virus is present in larger quantities than in a human mouth. Indeed the saliva of infected cats is swarming with the virus."

Jim Brettles did not look so surprised as the others, but more as if what had been said confirmed his worst suspicions. He looked at the W.H.O. collator.

"You have saved my people much time, Senor. We have been researching this precise thing for some weeks now."

The Prime Minister was even more surprised now. "Really? And under what directive did you authorise this?"

"We have our own procedures, Prime Minister. As you know, whenever an infection which involves animals arises, our vets are informed immediately and begin a full investigation. In this instance, we had a small suspicion that what Senor de Boca Negra is saying might, possibly, be the case one day or even now. It is a relatively small and easy mutation for the virus, as he says. We, too, tried to check up on the appropriate cases. And we too found there had always been a cat involved. Unfortunately we never got hold of the corpse of one of these cats, or a live one. But the necessary procedures have already been dusted off."

"The necessary procedures?" The Prime Minister was puzzled. He had not got this far in this thinking yet. But Andrew had, thanks to a chance remark of Joe Cromwell's.

"Yes sir; Mr Brettles is talking about the procedures which have been on the files for many years now, in case rabies ever got into Britain."

"Oh, shit" said the Prime Minister, with real feeling, once he had remembered what those procedures involved.

The four men looked at each other in mute and mutual misery.

"I am so sorry" said the man from South America. "We all feel the same way about it. It is going to be expensive, and difficult, and most unpopular. But it has to be done."

"Yes, of course" said the Prime Minister, wretchedly.

"Every single cat in the world must be rounded up and destroyed. Every single one, gentlemen. Every last one. The species must be eradicted from the face of the Earth."

"Jesus" said Andrew. "Why in God's name can't we just get people to use condoms? Wouldn't that be simpler than killing millions of innocent creatures?"

"Of course it would senor. But people are not logical. They will not do it. And as long as they are not logical they will continue to keep cats as pets, even if we tell them of this new development, and some of them will die because of it. Many of them will die. And as the cats breed, and fight, more and more people will die of the virus and more and more and more people will die from the tuberculosis *they* carry. You know we cannot allow that to happen. We must stop this infection wherever we can. Whatever it takes.'

'Your Reserve Forces, your police and your vets all have their orders and plans for the event of rabies, I understand? Then everything is in place. But if I may suggest you do nothing just yet...? Not every country is as ready as yours. If you would please await our signal to go? We do not want panic spreading before necessary. You are so lucky here, being an island. You can contain things so much better. And of course D-notice any word of this, instantly, if you would be so good."

"Of course" said the P.M., dully. The good Senor rose to leave them, and shook hands all round. "Perhaps next time I will be the bearer of better news" he said. "Though I find myself saying that every time. And so far there is no good news."

Andrew rose to shake his hand, but clasped it and held it for a moment.

"Senor, may I ask you a question?"

199

"Of course, Doctor Douglas. Anything."

"What is happening about the search for a vaccine? I mean, what is happening that we are not hearing about? Are any companies trialling vaccines in Central Africa?"

The man retracted his hand too quickly. "No, senor. I can tell you that much. No. The moral question is too difficult. If anything happens, you will be informed. Well, I have a plane waiting at Heathrow. Thank you for your time, gentlemen."

He paused by the door. "I meant to say: what your universities have done... it is causing some interest and some concern in various countries. You already know the immediate reactions of the Central African countries...I fear there may be more recriminations there. They are very...exhausted...with being cast as the dragons in this business. But in America and Canada and Europe and Australia (and also in China of course because they did it years before you did) there is much sympathy for these universities, and I think we may see more of the same. Of course this business of the cats may wipe it out from people's minds. Cats are much loved. Well. Goodbye." And he left a large silence behind him, as he closed the door.

"Prime Minister" ventured Andrew at last "I recall that you have the entire Media office standing by...perhaps we should be putting a statement together for them? They seem to know that something major is in the wind today."

"I know they do" said the P.M. gloomily. "I told them myself. When Boca Negra asked for Jim Brettles here to be present, I had some foolish idea that they'd found a cure for AIDS in wheatgerm or something. Now, we can't give them one solitary thing to broadcast. This has got to be put under wraps a mile high for the moment. And D-noticed to the hilt. I suppose I'd better go and tell them. Gentlemen, I want you to collect your thoughts and be back here at nine tomorrow morning, if you would. Tony, I want the full rabies round-up plans with you when you come. Andrew, your job will be to decide how we can use this frightful business to push home the message the AIDS message. You know; today, your kitten - or tomorrow, it'll be your son and your daughter."

"Of course, Prime Minister" they said, and nodded, and watched him as he left to face his Media people.

"I can't believe this" said Andrew. "I keep having this mental picture of a little girl in a frilly pink party frock cuddling her kitten, and the kitten is licking her face and she's smiling, and then some great walloping Territorial sergeant clumping in in hobnail boots and ripping the kitten from her arms and dashing its brains out on the mantelpiece. I know it won't be quite like that: but it will be a bit like that. People are going to go crazy about having their pets taken away."

"Not if they care about their children. We'll have to make sure people KNOW why we're doing it, BEFORE we do it. Once they know it's their cats or their families, they'll understand. Of course the finking for fivers will help...of course you don't know about that bit. It's always been anticipated that if rabies DID get into a port city and we had to round up all the cats and dogs, some people would hide their pets. So part of the plan is to advertise for people to rat on a neighbour for money; save your neighbour's life, make yourself some money; inform on them."

"Interesting times" said Andrew, reflectively. Then in response to Jim's querying look, "An old Chinese curse; 'may you live in interesting times'. I begin to understand why it's a curse, and not a blessing."

———— • ————

Frankie had found little of interest in Peter Spencer's sermon, partly because of not being made from a hysterical mould and therefore not being swayed unduly by rhetoric, and partly because his mind was full of happy thoughts about Flora's pregnancy.

The meeting afterwards, in the church hall, was more to his taste not least because here, he was part of the platform party. Peter Spencer was more subdued here, being tired, and Albert Kennedy seemed to occupy rather a lot of the platform party's alloted amount of speech time. He was proposing a rally in Edinburgh, hiring the vast Usher Hall, and bringing the faithful from People for Purity groups from all over Scotland and down as far as the English Midlands while at the same time, hiring the Albert Hall in London for all the southern English groups (which were many) and the Irish and the Welsh.

"Friends" he said, in that soft, pleasant voice which effortlessly filled the hall right to the back rows of standing people "we are now many thousands, and we are ready for the next step. What that step is, is up to you. But we now have the funds, the organisation and the will: most importantly, *the will* to start making a real difference in this country. Will you come to the Usher Hall with me?" The roar of assent made it clear they would have gone to Timbuctoo with him, had he only asked.

"Mr Dunn, our Treasurer: will you give us the funds for this great venture? I do not ask it of you - they ask it of you!" It was pure theatre, and Frankie responded in kind. He stood up and opened his arms wide, embracing the whole crowd.

"Gladly! All you need and more! The money is yours! You need only ask! And I shall be there with you, in that great Usher Hall, to listen to you, and marvel at your courage!"

They roared again, but, modestly, Albert broke in, took the floor again.

"My friends, my brave friends, we have much work to do. Some of our helpers are now among you, passing out forms: we want every one of you to fill in that form and send it in to our Reverend Spencer here, at the manse, before next week's meeting. You'll find it contains some suggestions as to things you might want to consider for our agenda at the Usher Hall meeting. And we are asking you to propose speakers. These same forms are being passed out today among all our friends in other groups, all over the United Kingdom..."

He went on about the democratic amalgamation of the completed forms, and the consensus which would therefrom emerge as to the agenda. Frankie didn't believe it for a moment, which enabled him to enjoy Albert's performance all the more.

Afterwards, in the anteroom where the platform party met

briefly each time to discuss the outcomes of the meeting, Frankie made a beeline for Peter Spencer, with a proud smile on his face, but was headed off very neatly at the pass by Albert.

"Are you lunching anywhere, Frankie?"

"I'm just away to speak to the Reverend just now, actually..."

"I wonder if I could tempt you to a spot of lunch somewhere quiet and expensive so we could have a chat? There are a couple of things I'd like to discuss with you, and you alone, if you have the time. Reverend Spencer will be at the manse all afternoon, you could catch him there later."

There's nothing like a sniff of intrigue, gilded by an expensive lunch, to tempt the unwary - or the very wary, either, come to that. Frankie sent his Grandad home in a taxi, then he and Albert went to the Fingal, a glitzy riverboat moored in the Forth near the Royal Forth Yacht Club, and drank cocktails while they waited for their table.

"So, young Frankie. How do you feel about being part of the movement? Or are you just in it to sell lots of insurance and pensions.."

"Right to the point, eh, Mr Kennedy? Well then, I'll be equally honest with you. That was part of my reason for volunteering, but now, I'm more with you heart and soul, you might say." He was thinking about his child, and the absolute need for a world for that child to grow up in safely and securely. This in no way conflicted with his other plans, to expand the psychopathic murder side of his business. That was purely financial, nothing to do with family life.

"I'm glad to hear that, Frankie. And you must stop calling me Mr Kennedy, as if I was your schoolteacher or something. I'm far from being anybody's schoolteacher."

"Aye" said Frankie, watchfully. "I imagine that's true."

They looked at each other, engaged in a delicate, probing fencing match with their eyes and their wills and their facial muscles.

"And you, Frankie, strike me as perhaps being a bit more than some mealy-mouthed do-gooder. You strike me as a man of action. A man with some guts about him. Some balls."

"What exactly are you getting at, Albert?"

The waiter interrupted them to lead them to a porthole table and seat them most deferentially and depart to bring the starters they had ordered. They delayed their conversation until the prawns and the melon had arrived. Albert watched Frankie look quickly at the array of cutlery on either side of his place mat, and quickly picked up the appropriate implements, to give him a lead. And Frankie watched Albert doing this, and seethed. And Albert saw Frankie seething and had the key of him at last.

"You ask what I'm getting at? I'll tell you. But you'll not tell anyone else, Frankie; I'm speaking to you because I see something in you which I need. Something you don't find among those weedy, overfed, overeducated gits in People for Purity." He saw he had hit home, and smiled inwardly. The rest was going to be easy.

"Those people want a lot, but they won't get their lilywhite hands dirty to get it. They might want clean streets to walk in, but you don't see any of them out there with brooms and shovels, do you? They'd rather talk, and go to meetings, and write minutes and resolutions and play at it. But some of us...some of us, Frankie, want it enough to do something about it. Are you one of the few, Frankie, I wonder? One of the special few?"

"How few, exactly?"

Albert smiled. "Good point. A reasonable question. Okay; half a dozen in London, a few in Birmingham, a couple in Manchester, one or two more here and there. A very few, like I said. And still nobody in Edinburgh. I need someone here I can rely on."

"And what exactly do they do, these extra-special people?"

"They do what I ask them to do."

"And what do they get, for doing what you ask them to do?"

He had been asked this question by every single one of them, and he had not yet given the same answer twice. Each man was led to the slaughter by his own individual need.

"Power" he said, on this occasion. He looked casually at Frankie and saw he needed one more hook to land him. "And the knowledge that your own special talents are valued and important. Oh yes, and you'll need your own choice of handpicked men

204

working under you."

Frankie could not quite hide the sparkle in his eyes.

'Gotcha' thought Albert, and sat back to await his rare and bloody steak.

Over the entree they talked, still dancing round each other a little, about civil unrest, about changing mass opinions, about ways of doing that. Frankie was a willing pupil.

"Ever heard of a book called 'The War of the Flea'?" Albert continued. "I'll get you a copy. It's banned in this country, but there are ways...it'll take a few days, that's all. You'll find plenty of useful stuff in it. Psychological tricks...little fleabites that can infect a nation before it knows what's happening. Infect it or, in our case, protect it. By marshalling its own common sense and energy. By harnessing that energy to push the Government into acting."

"You mean like...irritating the country until it scratches?"

"Nice one. Exactly that."

"Like...running cartoons of big fat Jews eating Christian children, before starting the pogrom? Oh aye, Albert, I can read. And learn. I'm a fast learner."

'Thought so; reading about dictators and tyrants. Typical of the species; always seeing themselves in the shiny shoes of the tyrants, not in the rags of the victims.'

"One thing though, Albert, one question, and I would like a straight answer. Who's paying for all this?"

"Sorry, Frankie; no can do."

"Is it the C.I.A.?" This was delivered with a nervous chuckle, as though to indicate how ridiculous the question really was.

'Why do they always think it's the C.I.A.?'

"It might be. Then again it might not. I told you; I can't tell you. Security reasons."

"I'll need expenses. Some of the boys will do things just for the fun of it, of course, but some of them will want paying."

"Of course. But I depend on you to keep the expenses under control. No creative accountancy, Frankie. And anyway, plenty

205

of what needs doing comes free; talking to people, people who are centres of influence, getting them onto your side. Getting them to foment their own bit of rebellion, their own bit of disruption, out of conviction like you and me, Frankie. Men who will do it because it needs to be done. Men of strong will and strong principle."

"And strong right arms?"

"Not often, Frankie. The pen is mightier than the sword, as somebody once said. And the spoken word is even more effective than the written word. It gets spread faster."

"Just the same, I don't think I'd be sitting here right now unless you wanted a few skulls broken along the way."

"Perhaps, but only occasionally, only when necessary, and only on my direct instructions. You must keep strict discipline with your boys, Frankie. Rabbles have their place, but not yet, and not unless we are controlling them."

"Don't you worry, Albert, I can keep order. That will not present a problem."

Over the luscious coconut cream ices with fantail wafers, they talked of the end result of their labours; a country where vice, corruption and infection would be contained and then eradicated. And only then did Albert talk of exactly what he wanted Frankie to do. It all sounded pretty tame to Frankie, but he realised that in the first instance he would be being tested, sounded out, on trial. Only when he had demonstrated his loyalty would he be given the hard stuff to do. Well, he'd do it. If for no other reason than that his curiousity was now thoroughly piqued, and he wanted to know more.

Albert drove him back to Gloucester Mews, as Frankie had decided the Reverend Spencer could wait a while yet for the good news about Flora. In the meantime, having sent Grandad home in a taxi for once, Frankie was anxious to make sure he was all right.

"One last thing, Frankie" said Albert, as Frankie unbuckled his seat belt. "You must keep out of the public eye, and out of trouble. If you've anything... delicate....on the go just now, it'll have to be dropped. We can't afford to lose someone like you, or have them banged up in jail, out of circulation. You understand?"

Frankie looked slightly annoyed.

"Of course if that's going to involve you in any financial losses, see me about it."

'Five thousand a time to let the psychopaths go to town...that's a hell of a financial loss, if I have to let that go. But why should I?'

"No, thanks, nothing like that at all. You're okay. So: when do we meet again?"

Albert handed him a small white card.

"Call me only when you've anything urgent to report. Or any questions you need answered immediately. But don't speak on the phone just say, usual place, such and such a time. The usual place will be different each week, and I'll sort that with you at the People for Purity meetings each Sunday. For this week, we'll make it...Chamber Street Museum. Near the entrance, by the bust of Nefertiti. But if it isn't urgent, don't phone at all, wait for the meetings. Good to have you on board, Frankie."

Grandad was so pleased to see him. He got lonely sometimes, did Grandad, and the sight of Frankie gave him such immense pleasure, every time, every day. Frankie opened a couple of bottles of beer, and they sat down for a game of chess.

"Well Grandad, I've some news to cheer you up, I think: me and Flora's going to get married. How's that for an opening gambit, eh?"

Grandad's face lit up with every Christmas in the world in his eyes. He nodded his head, inarticulate, and pumped Frankie's hand in mute congratulation. The tiny piece of Frankie's heart that was not stone was warmed to see it.

"And...I know it's a bit previous, but...Flora's pregnant. Another wee Dunn on the way, Grandad; and a legitimate one, this time. By God, that wee wean's going to have everything money can buy, I promise you that."

"Oh laddie, what a shame: not about the pregnancy, just the timing. Still, what a day to look forward to - well, two days! The wedding and the christening. The Reverend must be chuffed to bits,

207

is he not?"

"I haven't told him yet: you saw me away for lunch with Albert Kennedy there wasn't time today. I'll go round there tomorrow and tell him then."

"By jings son, he'll be thrilled. He couldnae ask for a better son-in-law, now could he? He'll have tae forgive Flora now, now she's goin' respectable."

As the chief reason for marrying Flora was to obtain the respectability she would confer upon him, this was a new and entertaining idea for Frankie, and he could not suppress a smile. Grandad's innocence was so endless, so almost deliberate.

———————— • ————————

The Managing Director of the Birmingham Cardboard Box Factory was surprised at the appearance of the two gentlemen he met at ten o'clock the following morning. It was not usual for his customers to be quite so blandly featureless or so soberly dressed. Nor did they usually bear a copy of the Official Secrets Act which he was to sign before the discussion even began.

It was an odd start to a Monday morning, and it got odder. The two gentlemen were most meticulous about explaining the terms of the Act, how serious it was, and how not one single detail of anything they might or might not agree with him could ever be discussed with anyone at all, not his wife, not his Board of Directors, not his pet poodle. When they were fully satisfied as to his having imbibed this, they set about explaining their requirements.

The design they wished to have costed was simple: a box two thousand millimetres long by nine hundred millimetres wide by six hundred millimetres deep. A very plain box, they said, and not necessarily sturdy, not made for repeated usage. Just a box that would safely carry a weight of, say, around a hundred kilos, without breaking up. Supplied flat, with interocking tabs.

"A coffin, you mean? A disposable coffin? For cremations, then."

"If you could just cost it out for us, Mr Brown."

"And what sort of quantities would you be after?"

"Quote us for runs of a hundred thousand at a time."

Mr Brown felt uneasy.

"Are these for export, then?"

"If you could just cost it out for us, Mr Brown."

"Oh, wait a minute now; this is ringing a bell with me. Wait a minute..." Eric Brown rose and paced the office, thinking back.

"Yes; my father told me about this; Second World War, wasn't it? We made thousands of the bloody things for the Ministry of Defence then. In fact they're still in storage; they were all paid for, you see, and the Ministry said, not to destroy them. So I could let you have them at a good rate, if you like. I don't know the dimensions off the top of my head, but they can't be much different I don't suppose."

The obvious thought finally struck him.

"Are we going to have another bloody war, then?"

"If you could just cost it all out for us, Mr Brown. And if you have already been paid in full for the previous order, we would not expect the idea of a price to apply at all." They rose in unison. "Thank you for your time; you have our card. Please send your best estimates as soon as possible."

"Just a moment lads: the old coffins; I'd have to charge you for storage all this time, of course."

"Very well. Goodbye, Mr Brown."

"Wait on; what about delivery dates? And transportation?"

"Just as soon as possible. And we will arrange uplifting and delivery ourselves. Goodbye, Mr Brown."

What the hell did the Government want with hundreds of thousands of coffins?

———— • ————

Andrew was not in his best humour when he arrived at Downing Street that morning to meet the P.M. and the Minister for Agriculture. For a start, Terry was very irritated by his steadfast refusal to discuss the visit of Senor Romera de Boca Negra. Then there had been the visit to Callum last night; the flat was a shambles, all the dirty dishes and empty pizza boxes were still in the sink, and the odour of

Callum's socks was everywhere. It had rather tarnished the happy family reunion, which was still further dented by Andrew's discovery that Callum had not a penny in the world. His wages were to be paid on an end-of-contract basis, with only his housing, his food, and a little 'fun money' doled out to him before that. Having been ejected from the country, he did not now expect anything further to be arriving from Uganda.

"So you'll be getting a job for the rest of the summer, then. No, that wasn't a question. Yes, I do know the employment situation at the moment. And I appreciate you're a bit shell shocked right now, yes. No, I don't think you'll need a month living off me to recover. I think you'll go round the various London hospitals tomorrow and get yourself a job as a hospital porter, that's what I think, because I happen to know they're in short supply, and the money's pretty good."

Callum had been expecting a hero's welcome from his Dad, and was angry at being put through the parental mincer. Andrew had been expecting his resourceful, intelligent son to have already decided about getting a job, and was angry at having his flat desecrated and his hopes disappointed.

"Christ" said Callum. "You leave a couple of socks lying around, and your Dad sends you off to die of AIDS or T.B. Charming."

Andrew was incensed. "Don't you EVER joke about that again! If you had any idea at ALL of what you were talking about, you'd cut your tongue out before making such jokes."

"Hey, hey" interposed Terry "You two shouldn't be allowed out! Andrew, you come and spend the night with me, and we'll sort things out tomorrow. Come on."

And she dragged him away and sat him down in her own pretty little feminine flat in darkest Battersea, where he felt completely out of place, and he knew that her annoyance with him was running fairly deep. He knew, too, that the annoyance was the coverup for the hurt she felt at his not telling her about the meeting; and he knew his own flareup at Callum was mostly about what Senor Romero had said. Knowing all this did not help undo any of it, and he slept badly, after the most perfunctory of goodnight kisses.

She woke him with bacon and eggs at seven-thirty, having already been to the local shops. There was even cream for his coffee, but there was little warmth to her smile. She was doing her best, but her faith in his love for her and his trust in her was badly fractured.

"I love you" he said, at the breakfast table.

"I know" she said, and it was the first time she had not answered 'I love you, too', and it hurt him.

So he felt wretched. Still, he was in good company; neither the Prime Minister nor the Minister for Agriculture were exactly sparkling. Sweeting, recalled from his holiday and briefed by the P.M. last night, was equally depressed.

When Jim Brettles started to read out the procedures for rounding up all the pet cats in each town, the mood got a good deal grimmer. All vets would be involved, and the local police forces, including every Special Constable available, and the local Territorial Army. The whole procedure had been designed to scoop up and quarantine every cat and dog, if rabies ever succeeded in breaking the British cordon, so all that had to be changed was to replace 'quarantine' with 'destroy'.

It was obvious that there would be considerable resistance, and it was hoped that the uniformed presence of the police and the Terrys would tend to avoid any major unpleasantness. Vets would be issued with large quantities of the lethal drug used to kill domestic pets, and all corpses would be incinerated; this would be too large a task for the average town practice, so the Terrys would take the sacks of corpses to the various incineration facilities available principally council rubbish burners and any remaining sacks would be burned far from town on bonfires. All slaughter and burning would be supervised by teams of Government vets. The task of the police, which nobody envied them, was to be the 'collection' of any animals not voluntarily relinquished by their owners. Feral cats were to be the province of the Terrys, with their trained marksmen. The lions of Longleat and all other big cats in all parks and zoos were to be killed by Territorial marksmen too. It would have been a difficult enough task with dogs, this rounding up and carting off to vets - but cats, with their more universal tendency to scratch and bite when irritated, were much more to be feared; especially when those bites could lead to the handler's death from AIDS.

As the logistics were long established, and every branch of the relevant organisations knew exactly what their task was to be, it could all be set in motion at the drop of a hat.

"We would anticipate that the whole business would be over in about two months, for the most part. Rounding up the ferals, and checking up on reports of hidden cats, would go on for longer...a month or two more, perhaps. And after that, constant vigilance. Especially with the ferals; if we get the mother, we may miss a litter of kittens somewhere." Brettles looked slightly sick as he read his own notes. They had been academic yesterday morning; now they were real plans to find and destroy millions of animals, beloved animals, warm, furry, softwhiskered little things which right now were purring in their owners' arms, or lapping milk from a saucer with innate elegance and delicacy.

"Every town is going to smell like Belsen" said Andrew, sadly. "You can't burn thousands of cats without causing an awful stink."

"In every sense of the word" said the Prime Minister. "This is going to be one stinker of an exercise."

With a start, Andrew realised that there had been a tinge of relish in the Prime Minister's voice. Why? Did he hate cats? Even if he did, he surely could not be contemplating this horrible affair with any kind of satisfaction? Apart from anything else, it would take the public a long time to forgive this political party, which surely was most heavily counter to the P.M.'s interests. No, he must have been mistaken.

"Actually no" said Brettles. "We have a chemical treatment which enables us to burn corpses without producing that smell. We were using it way back in the sixties, in the Foot and Mouth epidemic."

"My wife has cats" interrupted Sweeting, dreamily. "Three

sealpoint Siamese. She's entering them in the local show, next week. Will she have time to do that before...?"

"Yes" said the P.M. "She'll have time. You do understand, Harold, that you can't tell her about this?"

"Of course. God, she's going to blow her stack when she finds out. She loves those things like children. No: she loves them more than children. She's never done grooming the damn things, or making silk cushions for their baskets, or cooking chicken fillets for them."

"Do you think she might try to hide them, rather than give them up?" Brettles was genuinely interested; after all, Mrs Sweeting was no more fond of her cats than millions of other people.

"Like a shot, if she thought she could get away with it. Given half a chance, she'd run off and hide in the bloody woods, cats and all."

Brettles persisted. "Is there any way you can think of that we could persuade your wife about the dangers sufficiently powerfully for her to WANT to give up her cats?"

Sweeting considered. "No. She'd as soon die for those things as lose them. And anyway, there's nothing wrong with OUR cats, is there?"

"And that" said Andrew "is what everybody is going to say. There's nothing wrong with OUR cat. Take away her next door's cat, but not mine. You're not getting mine."

"So how do we run the press releases and the advertising campaign? We're going to need absolute blanket saturation coverage in all the media, to reach as many people as possible. How do we convince them that giving up their cats, when the call comes, is the best thing to do?"

There was a long silence.

"Perhaps we could ask Terry Aitken" Andrew suggested cautiously. "I understand she has her job back. She knows a fair bit about swaying public opinion."

He got a real oldfashioned look from the Prime Minister, but he did not blush.

"Okay, Andrew. You can brief her this afternoon, and bring her to tomorrow morning's meeting, back here, ninethirty again. While you're at it, you can tell her she's head of the Media Office again. It was wrong of us to fire her over those faxes; they were damn good. So she's reinstated. She's too good to lose."

"Yes, I think she is" said Andrew, smiling.

The P.M. grinned at him, welcoming a little light relief. "Hmm. Well *that's* been bleeding obvious for a long time, round here!"

Tuesday morning's Scotsman, the Scottish major national daily, contained an interesting report on the developments in the Body in The Bag murder. The victim had now been identified, from his fingerprints. His name had been Alec Jamieson, once convicted of a minor shoplifting offence, and lately believed to have been working as a homosexual prostitute: a rent boy. It was also revealed that Alec Jamieson had been HIV Positive, and already dying from AIDS when he was murdered.

Several people in Edinburgh took a keen interest in the story. Frankie Dunn was one, and his interest was a fatherly one, as he had caused the story to be born and was rather proud of it. Pity he couldn't boast about it to anyone, really. He made a guesstimate at how much the journalist had got for writing it, compared it with how much he had got for creating it, and smiled broadly. Flora took an interest in it too, at Radio Forth, where her job was now strictly research. It was a brutal footnote to her programme on the rise in crimes against gays.

Jack Macleod was so interested in the story he took himself a long coffee break in the morning and went to the G.U. clinic in the Grassmarket to be tested for the virus on the spot. He tested negative, but was told to come back every week for three months, just to be on the safe side. He was not happy; but he had used a sturdy condom when buggering Alec, one intended for rectal intercourse, and so was not very afraid of having contracted AIDS. He would just have to feign disinterest, or exhaustion, at home for the three months. His wife would not notice, nor suspect anything, their sex life was so sporadic and unsatisfying at the best of times. Still, though he rarely desired her, he had no wish to inflict the virus on her. They were reasonably good friends, he and his wife, and he still quite enjoyed her company. Despite his complacency concerning his likely HIV status, though, he was most assuredly made afraid by the story. For it seemed unlikely that the long arm of coincidence would pluck Alec Jamieson from Granton and bring him all the way round the coast road and up Leith Walk and into Macleod's Transport yard. The dim but dirty hand of Frankie Dunn seemed to hover somewhere in the background, and Jack was uneasy.

Would the police have any way of connecting him with the dead boy? Or was Frankie's ploy just to sink his teeth more deeply into Jack's bank account? Either of these possibilities would make life difficult for him; he hoped most fervently that it was the latter which was Frankie's plan but, given the atrocity of the offence, Frankie's bite was likely to go clear to the bone this time.

But the person who took the most profound interest in the story was a certain young farmer from out Penicuik way. And though a visit to a G.U. clinic was on his list of things to do, having read the article, a visit to Frankie Dunn came higher up that list; it was right at the very top.

He took the bus into town and made his way to Frankie's office, where he announced himself quite calmly and asked to see the manager. Enya wiggled through to the back office, said the visitor's name, and was surprised to see the boss blench a little; it was not like the boss at all. But he said 'bring him through', so she did.

"Tommy, my man" said Frankie, warm sincerity oozing from him. "How's it going then?"

Tommy Bain ignored the proferred hand. "Cut the bullshit, Frank. Ye've set me up, ye wee shite. Five thousand pounds to get AIDS? I could have got it for nothing. Yer price is too high, Frank. Way too high. It's goan' tae cost you dear yourself, Frank. I'm goan' tae enjoy maself wi' you. I'm goan' tae take ma' time, wi' you. No' jist four hours. Much, much longer."

Frankie had never been so afraid in his life, and did not know how to handle it. He was sheet white and shaking.

"That is, Frank, that is, if I test Positive. If I'm goin', Frank, you're goin' an' all. Fair enough, eh?"

"I'm sure you'll be just fine..."

"Maybe. Maybe no. There wis an awfie lot o' blood cam' oot o' the wee bugger. I hud tae throw a' ma claes away. But I got some on ma skin, Frankie, an' maybe in ma mouth, tae. You promised me protection, Frankie, an' ye havenae delivered. So Ah'm off tae the clinic. An' if there's ony trouble, I'll be back. Dae ye unnerstand me, Frankie?"

"Look, look, how about if I give you your money back? Listen, you can have it back, whether you're Positive or not. I'll get it for you. 100%, Tommy, eh?"

"I wis comin' tae that. Yes, a refund is on the cairds all right, Frank, whether I'm Positive or not. But it changes nothin', son, nothin'. I'll be back fur the money at closin' time, whit is it, six? Richt then, six o'clock. An' dinna try nothin', Frankie; if ye run, I'll find ye."

He made for the door, taking his time, enjoying the effect he was having.

"An' I hope ye're nae stupit enough tae go tae the polis, Frankie? Naw, o'course ye're not. Cheerio, then!"

I'm not stupid enough to let you frighten me again, though, either, thought Frankie, his mind still working perfectly well even if his body was overcome with this unusual emotional disturbance.

Grandad phoned him.

"I've just been talking to the Reverend, Frankie, and I kind of let slip there was something you wanted to see him about hud on, here he is..."

"Frankie? Peter Spencer here. Are you well? Good, good. Now what can I do for you? You can always talk to me, Frankie, any time at all. What is this about?"

Frankie ground his teeth in the effort to sound placid and normal.

"It's kind of personal, Reverend Spencer. I'd rather not talk about it over the phone..."

"Well now, if you can get away, why don't you come early to pick your Grandad up tonight, and have a cup of tea with me? It's been a while since we had a private chat, I'd enjoy that. Say around five?"

"I'm not sure I can make that, sir. But if Grandad wouldn't mind waiting, I could probably be there around seven, seventhirty. Would that be okay for you?"

It was agreed. But Frankie had too much else on his mind to feel good about it. Still, it would be a memorable occasion, his adoption into ultra respectability (assuming Tommy Bain had not killed him by then), and to celebrate, he thought he'd buy Flora that cream-coloured Persian kitten she'd mentioned once she wanted. He set Enya to phoning round the various local breeders and shops. Enya sighed as she began her task, thinking what a lovely romantic man the boss was, as well as sexy as hell. She daydreamed of seducing him, just once, before he got too entangled with this lady love of his. She thought of his pinstriped trousers, and she imagined a thrusting bulge at the crotch when she bent down low over him with his coffee, having perhaps first accidentally left the top button off her blouse again, and this time maybe she could arrange for her breasts to brush over his shoulders, very softly. If he had his jacket off, he would even feel her engorged nipples hard on his flesh. Then...oh, then she would stand in front of his desk with her legs slightly parted, talking of office work, letting him see the red on her cheeks and the large pupils of her eyes. She would pout a little, and falter in her speech a little, and the heat coming off her in waves would drag him across to her, and he would he would - um - well maybe she'd have to open another button on her blouse, so he'd be sure to understand, and then she would bunch her breasts together with her hands, and finger her own nipples, pulling them out of her lacy bra, and leave them hanging there, ripe and full, for him to admire. No man could resist a great pair of breasts, she had been told, and she had also been told on many occasions that her own breasts were unbelievable. It was the same daydream she had about Frankie most days, and it never went further than having Frankie admiring her naked breasts, possibly even handling them, gently, gratefully.

She could not know how good her timing was, today. Frankie was erect already, before she came through with the coffee. The prospect of death sometimes has this effect on people, and Frankie was pulsating. He saw the button open at her cleavage, and he saw the erection of her nipples right through her blouse, and he knew she'd been after him for months, and then she did brush her breasts over his shoulders and he waited till she'd set the hot coffee on the desk and then stood up, close to her.

"Lock the door" he said. "Then come back here."

Her eyes were enormous, and shining, and her breathing was very shallow. She stood in front of him, her breasts rising and falling, and her lips parted. He drifted the backs of his fingers over her nipples, saying nothing, and those nipples became even larger, poking through the thin fabric. He ran his hands roughly through her thick auburn hair, which tumbled in waves to her shoulders, and used her hair to force her head back. He used his free hand to undo all her blouse buttons, then pushed the garment off her shoulders but did not take it off her arms...he moved his other hand from her hair to the blouse, using it to trap her hands behind her back, then pulled the bra upwards, leaving it crumpled above her bosom, and now his fondling was much coarser, and he teased and pulled the nipples till he heard her gasping.

"Take everything off except your knickers: I'll take those off when I decide."

Like a good little secretary, she did as she was told, as best she could in her trembling. Frankie watched. The lacy froth of her lingerie was delightful: Flora's tended to be more ordinary. The little underslip came down along with her skirt, and she stepped out of them, now wearing nothing but a white lace suspender belt, white stockings, and the tiniest Gstring of white lace, which was already darkening with the moisture between her legs. Round it peeped curls of reddish blonde, already soaking. She leaned on his desk for support, for she was in an ecstasy of fantasy come true.

Frankie had no time for preliminaries today. He turned her round, ripped the Gstring off her, unzipped his fly and shafted her immediately. He expected to come quickly, but this erection was made of granite. He fucked and fucked her, he turned her round and fucked her some more, he lay her down on the floor, with her legs in the air and wrapped round him, and he fucked her more, and more, and still he was massive inside her. Her innards clenched and sucked him, she rose and arched and climaxed again and again, shrieking, muffling her cries against his chest, and still he drove into her, over and over, in a relentless tempo.

And then he rolled her over again, and fingered her arse, and she was so far gone she did not protest, and he rammed his cock up her; the tightness of it was excruciatingly erotic, and he finally shot, and collapsed beside her.

She was in agony, and sobbing, clutching her sore bottom, moaning. The telephone rang, and Frankie gathered himself together enough to get to it. Enya lay on the floor, huddled and miserable, and heard him talk lovingly and respectfully to Flora, telling her that he would be seeing her father tonight, and talking to him about their marriage. Out of breath? Oh yes, he said, he'd just been doing some exercises. Get himself in shape for taking his son out to the park and playing football. Yes, he said, his eyes on Enya, he loved her too, very much. He was, he said, a very lucky man.

When the call was over, Enya was crawling around picking up her clothes, her tears still wet on her cheeks. Frankie sipped his coffee, zipped his trousers.

"Did you find me a cream Persian kitten, yet?" he asked in his normal business tones. He actually expected a reply, so she shook her head as she dressed and he told her to get on with it, and not to take all day about it.

When she had left, he locked the door behind her again, knelt down at the corner of his carpet, and lifted it up. There was a small handle set into a section of floorboard, and from inside this cavity he removed a package wrapped in oilcloth. Carefully replacing the flooring, he set the package on his desk, then sat to unwrap the

Smith and Wesson .357 Magnum snubnose. He flicked the chamber open, checked that all six rounds were in place, then with a flick of his wrist, closed the chamber. It was ready. He hid the oilcloth at the back of the files in his lower desk drawer.

Next, he took Tommy Bain's file from his cabinet and looked through it, seeking inspiration. Roselea Farm. What a sweet address. He remembered driving there, to make his splendid offer to the bampot. It had turned into something of a sentimental journey. After leaving the Bain place, he had turned his car towards Penicuik, where his early boyhood had been spent, and meandered round the country lanes he remembered so clearly. The old back road to the reservoir at Carnethy, near Roselea Farm, had been one of his happy hunting grounds, with his boisterous pals, when school was out. It was quiet and lush with trees...beech, elm, birch. Daytrippers rarely went there.

What a perfect place for a murder.

In seconds, he had it all worked out. It was flawless. He was lucky that he knew the area Tommy Bain lived in, knew it intimately.

At twelve o'clock, he telephoned Roselea. Mrs Bain said Tommy was not back yet, but she expected him soon and could she get him to call...? Mr..? Frankie thanked her, but said he'd call again. He phoned at twelve thirty, and just caught Tommy coming in the door.

"Ah, Tommy, my man; good news. I've got your money, in cash, all ready in a plastic bag, right here in my office."

"Oh yes?"

"So how was your news at the clinic, Tommy? Everything okay?"

"Just fine. Negative. Just as well for you, eh?" And Frankie knew he was lying.

"That's magic, Tommy, just magic. But I want you to have your money back, just the same. Just as well for us to stay pals, eh? Right then. I don't want you bothering to come back into the office well, to be honest, I've got somewhere I want to go, tonight, so I was

220

thinking, pick some quiet spot, I'll bring the money to you right now. How does that sound?"

Tommy heard Frank put his hand halfover the mouthpiece and say 'Thanks, Enya, just put it down there, will you?'

"Okay pal" said Tommy. "Somewhere quiet. That'll suit me fine."

Frankie grinned to himself. "Right what I was thinking, that old back road up to the reservoir...could you be there in an hour? I'll meet you there."

"You'll be on your own, Frankie? Right. An hour, then."

"We could go into Penicuik afterwards for a bit of lunch, if you like?"

"Fuck off, Frankie. You and me's no' pals. We don't 'have lunch'. You just give me ma money and then bugger off and I don't care if I never see you again, right? Right." He put the phone down.

Dear Lord, thought Frankie, it was as easy as shelling peas. And he'd done lots of that at his Granny's knee, contentedly chewing the sugarsweet pods as he popped the peas into the big bowl of vegetables for Granny's wonderful Stand your-spoon-up-in-it broth.

Christ, thought Tommy, the man's a fucking moron. Pity I don't fancy him. Too old for me. Still, I can still have a bit of fun with him; he's terrified of me, that's the main thing. I'll make him sweat a bit, before I tell him the test this morning was Positive. Then, he'll learn what real fear is. Him first, then a few others I can think of that deserve it. My bloody mother, for a start.

Yes, it would take Frankie about an hour to drive from the middle of Edinburgh, and it would only take Tommy twenty minutes to walk it. He went through to the kitchen table, where his mother had laid out a large cold lunch for him, as he'd said he'd want one today. Though she was sitting at the fireplace, knitting, he did not address one word to her, nor did she expect him to.

Ten minutes later, in plenty of time to arrive first at Carnethy, he left the farmhouse and walked down the lane to the main road. He turned left, walking along the beech hedge, sheltered from the warm wind by the trees across the road which had been planted by

221

his grandfather. The old red telephone box was gone, now, and the modern green one installed.

It never occured to him that it was from here Frankie had telephoned him.

The beech hedge rose from four feet to almost eight, just out of sight of the farmhouse, at corner of the T-junction. Tommy didn't even bother looking up the junction, as you could hear any cars approaching and this was a fairly rare event. He walked out to cross the road, and Frankie took one short sharp step forward, held the cocked pistol to Tommy's temple, and shot him, twice, the execution technique known as a 'doublecapper'. Frankie had read quite a lot about the Vietnam war.

Tommy never knew anything about it, which was a pity, thought Frankie. Considering what this heap of shattered bone and flesh would have done to Frankie, given half a chance.

In Roselea farmhouse, Tommy's mother heard what sounded like a shotgun echoing across the fields. Poor wee birds, she thought, or rabbits; can you men not leave anything alone?

The three men went back to the car parked just up the road, and took from the boot a five-gallon drum of water and two scrubbing brushes, and several extra large plastic bags. Gagging slightly, they scooped up the big bits of Tommy's head into one of the bags, and then placed the rest of Tommy in the same bag, using another to cover him from the waist upwards. The two bags were then taped together with strong paperbacked tape, and the body carried into the boot of the car. The men then meticulously scrubbed the blood and spattered brains and morsels of flesh from the pavement and the roadside, down the drains, to the annoyance of the rooks, who were already wheeling and cawing above. Soon there was no trace of anything having happened there.

Tucking the five-gallon drum and the scrubbing brushes under the beech hedge, the men then drove to the reservoir and used the heavy-duty chains lying coiled under the body, swirling them round and round him, weighting him thoroughly before throwing him in the water.

Lastly they returned to the beech hedge and collected the drum and the brushes, before heading back to Edinburgh. During the whole operation, not one word had been said. Frankie dropped the men off in George Street, and handed each two hundred pounds.

"Thanks, boys. See you later."

He stopped to buy a sandwich from the stall at the carpark, which he crammed down before walking to the nearest Crawford's and buying a large box of fresh cream cakes.

This he deposited on Enya's desk when he walked into the office, smiling broadly to all his staff and proclaiming the deliciousness of the large lunch he had just enjoyed with a friend in the Balmoral hotel. He hadn't wanted to take the time for a sweet, he said, so he'd brought cream cakes for everyone and would Enya make him a nice cup of tea and bring him through a meringue?

Christ, it's as if this morning never happened, she thought incredulously. The bastard. The bastard! She did as she was told, took Frankie through his tea and meringue.

"Thanks, dearie" he said absently, as he pored over some insurance papers.

Her written resignation was on his desk by five o'clock, and she was gone. The resignation had two typing mistakes in it. He was laughing as he dialled the nearest Temp Typists agency. Easy come, easy go; there were a million Enyas in the world, and some of them could actually do their job.

He worked late, then drove out to Corstorphine in good time and in high spirits. He was out of the mire, Enya had vanished along with any potentially embarassing incidents, and Tommy Bain was off the face of the planet, probably never to be found.

Peter Spencer welcomed him in, and took him through to what had been his private study and was now the busy U.K. headquarters of People for Purity. Grandad beamed, switched the phones through to the extension in what had been Flora's bedroom, and left them to it. There was no sign of Gwendoline Spencer, and nobody mentioned her, all as usual.

Peter poured tea, offered Digestives, smiled at Frankie.

"So; Jock's been all mysterious smiles today; what's the big secret, Frankie my boy?"

It was Frankie's proudest moment. He rose. There was a faint crust of dried semen on the fly of his trousers, but the Reverend did not notice.

"Sir, I have the real honour to tell you that your daughter and I are engaged to be married." He paused, waiting for the delight to show on the man's face. It did not. What appeared on the man's face was horror.

"What?"

"We are having a child..." Frankie's proud tones were tailing off into uncertainty. This was not the reaction he had expected. "I know we've jumped the gun a bit, but we are very much in love, and I promise you sir, I will take great care of her. I truly love her, Mr Spencer."

"She's pregnant? BY YOU?" Peter Spencer was ashen, and his hands flew to cover his face. He slumped back in his chair, fell slightly forward, and began to rock.

Straining, Frankie caught some mumbled words; So there's no forgiveness, after all. No forgiveness of sins. No forgiveness.

The Reverend looked straight at him. His face had crumpled, his voice was weak.

"Get it aborted. She can't have your baby. You can't marry her. She's your sister."

"She's not! How could she be? She's your daughter oh my god. You're my father. It was you. You dirty bugger." And Frankie, too, subsided.

"Don't use that kind of language in my presence" said Peter Spencer, automatically.

"There's no kind of language foul enough to suit your presence" Frankie replied, slowly. "My Grandad worships you. And you had it away with his daughter. And dumped her. My god, you stand in that church every Sunday and preach purity? Christ. Jesus Christ."

"It wasn't like that!" The man was in anguish. He got up with difficulty, but sat heavily down again. "It wasn't like that at all."

"I don't want to hear what it was like. I don't want to hear anything about it. How you were tempted, eh? How you succumbed. How she wanted to protect you, you and your ministry, you and your wife, and how...how she ran away and didn't put your name on the birth certificate, to protect you, and she ran away to protect you, and left me behind, to protect you. You miserable old hypocrite. Does your wife know? No, I thought not. Nobody knows, eh, Daddy? Except me."

More pictures came to his mind; the gentle Reverend coming round to Grandma's house, soothing her distress over her daughter's unmarried pregnancy: such a public shame, in those days. The Reverend who cared so much. Who held Grandma's hand, possibly while Frankie's mother sat nursing her baby, looking at him. The good Reverend who presumably gave Frankie's mother some money to take her on her way.

"Where is she?" He wasn't sure if he wanted to meet his mother, but he might.

But the Reverend didn't know, had never heard from her. Frankie was relieved.

They sat without speaking for some time. Then Frankie knew what to do.

He said "You'll call the banns for us this Sunday."

"What? Didn't you hear me? You can't go ahead with this!"

"Really? Why not? Nobody knows we're brother and sister except you, Reverend Spencer. And who are you going to tell, hmm? Nobody. So call the banns this Sunday, like I said. She's having my child; I'm going to marry her. And you are not going to fuck it up."

"Frankie, you must get that baby aborted. It's incestuous; it could be terribly affected. Surely you don't want an abnormal child?"

"Well, I've got an abnormal father...haven't I?"

"You're hysterical. I understand that. You don't mean what you're saying."

"Call the banns this Sunday."

"You can't!"

"Oh, but I can. It'll be a nice little family scene, won't it? The

225

father standing there marrying his son to his daughter. And later on, the proud grandfather christening the result. Dropping holy water on each of its two heads. Lovely. People for Purity, eh, Dad?"

"I suppose the baby might be all right" said Frankie's father in a whisper, weary from his pain. "After all, you're only her half-brother. But you can't marry her. And you can't ask me to do it. Dear God, Frankie, have mercy."

He was asking the wrong man for that.

CHAPTER SEVEN

Terry was getting that uneasy prickling at the back of her scalp again, the sign of a major story about to break. She was now getting it every time she read a newspaper, and it had started with that batch of Sundays on the helicopter. What was in them had been bad enough, but she could not shake the feeling that there was a lot more that wasn't appearing - yet.

Andrew had cheered her considerably by telling her she was back in business with him and would be going to Downing Street this morning. He had told her about the cats; that was horrific, but it didn't scratch the itch. There was something more, something even bigger, in the wind. She could almost literally smell it. She had kept it to herself, and talked seriously to Andrew about the media preparations for the feline roundup. She had also reminded him that Mark Tyme had offered his services and those of Rock Against Aids, and perhaps it was time to draft him in. She had done everything she could to convince him that their relationship was what it had always been, and that the previous day had been a temporary glitch. She had persuaded him to phone and make his peace with Callum (which was easy, as Callum had already got himself a job in Streatham General as a porter, at a salary which delighted him). She was extra-attentive, extra-calm.

Andrew too was making strenuous efforts to reassure Terry, while still feeling that she should have understood, and also still feeling distinctly ill at ease in her Battersea flat. So their entire conversation and being together was quite ridiculously polite and over-effusive and over-reassuring and sweet and loving.

By bedtime they were both exhausted by it all. And all the cubes of sugar were building a higher and higher wall between them. They sat up in bed together drinking hot chocolate with cream in it, smiling away at each other like anything.

Then Terry slammed her empty mug down on the bedside table.

"Oh, sod this for a game of soldiers! I am furious with you; if I'd been your wife, or just even your official girlfriend, but NOT involved in the media, you would have told me yesterday about the cats, wouldn't you?"

Andrew shook his head vigorously. "No, I wouldn't."

"Yes you would! Anybody would have! I bet Sweeting is away home telling his wife right now! I bet the P.M.'s wife knows all about it; I bet Jim Brettles' wife knows all about it! But not me, oh no, not me, because you just don't trust me not to go running off to my old newspaper pals and spill the beans, DO YOU?"

Andrew refused to conduct a major argument lying in bed stark naked with the person with whom he was arguing. It did not make for dignity. So he had risen while she was raging, and donned his trousers, and now sat at her side of the bed, looking at her severely.

"You're not the only one that gets angry; I was extremely annoyed last night too, at your forgetting what my job is like. I have to maintain confidentiality on everything I hear, and YOU KNOW IT. How could you want me to be dishonourable? Okay, maybe Sweeting's wife DOES know all about it already, but would you really want me to be like Sweeting? Well, would you? You can't trust that man as far as you could throw him; is that how you want me to be? Just so you don't feel left out in the cold?"

"That's not the point!"

"Yes it is; it's exactly the point."

"No it isn't."

"This is getting silly. What is the point, then, if I have missed it?"

"Well I don't know exactly but it's a bloody sharp point, I can tell you!"

They glowered at each other. Andrew's mouth twitched first, and then Terry's grim visage wobbled a bit, and in a minute they were giggling and rolling about in each other's arms on the bed. He finished up on top of her, kissing her. She gazed up at him.

"Sex doesn't solve anything, you know" she said in a mockingly prim little voice.

"I know"

"But I think we should give it a try, just in case, don't you?"

228

"Well, if you insist."

"Oh, I do."

And then they were all right again. Mostly. But Terry remembered what an old boyfriend had once said to her: that every relationship has a limited number of such events built into it, which it can tolerate without breaking. That number might be a million and twelve, or it might only be three. And you won't know until you've just gone through the last one.

Still, for now, they approached Number 10 Downing Street feeling refreshed and ready for battle, arriving prompt at nine-thirty. To their surprise, they were met by a receptionist who told them that the meeting had been put off, as something urgent had come up; they were requested to return after lunch, at one-thirty.

They wandered out again into the sunshine. As they descended the few steps onto the pavement, a sleek black limousine drew up. Neither of them paid much attention; such visits were commonplace. They scarcely looked as the chauffeur opened the passenger door and a tall man, conservatively dressed, came out and walked up the steps, moving gracefully.

His eyes met Andrew's briefly, and Andrew felt that the man recognised him; and was equally sure he had never met him. He would have remembered that particular face; aristocratic, with an expensive quality to the tan, and an aquiline nose between two piercingly blue eyes. The man walked into Number 10 as if he owned it.

Andrew felt a slight shiver of premonition. He did not mention it to Terry. She was engrossed in her own thoughts. She turned an annoyed face to him.

"Well? Where do two redundant political superstars go to pass a summer's morning in London these days?"

"You're the Cockney Sparrer, aren't you? You choose."

"Okay. Let's be frighteningly original and go and take a boat out on the Serpentine?"

The tube journey was unpleasant. Both of them were used to taking taxis, and had thought the tube would make a change, and be

229

fun. But they were wrong. The stairways, corridors and platforms were full of beggars; not colourful buskers, but straightforward beggars, most of whom looked lost, as if they did not quite know what they were doing. Nobody seemed concerned, from which it could be deduced that this was an everyday sight, nothing new or alarming.

Then when they were aboard their tube, a group of skinheads with "PFP" tattooed on their foreheads was stravaging through the carriage, stopping and staring at anyone who did not look like an ordinary character. Andrew watched in chilled fascination as they picked out young men wearing flamboyant clothes; young people who had long hair; anyone with a beard which was not neatly clipped; young women wearing short skirts and/or a lot of makeup. They did nothing, these louts; they just stopped and stared at their victims so long that every one of them got off in a hurry at the next stop. Then the new incomers were weeded out. All without a word or a gesture, just that cold hard stare.

Most of the other passengers pretended it wasn't happening, burying themselves in their newspapers or very interesting things they found in their pockets or handbags; a few were looking on with approval, and some even put money in the hands of the louts as they passed by, muttering "Good on you, son" and similar encouragements.

One of the louts came up and stared briefly at Andrew, who caught his arm, to Terry's horror, and smiled at him.

"Excuse me" he said, in the broadest Scots voice he could muster. "Me an' ma lady here are just down from Scotland fur the day. I've no' seen people doin' what you're doin', before. Whit's it a' aboot?"

The skinhead looked respectfully at Andrew's garb.

"Don't you mind, sir, you've nothing to worry about. We just don't want any Marys on the trains, do we sir? Carrying T.B. around with them, killin' innocent people like yourselves. 'ighly infectious, is T.B. sir, and it don't care who it hits."

"Marys? Whit's that?"

"Typhoid Marys, sir" the boy replied wearily. "Druggies, tarts,

230

poofs, all them. All dangerous to be near, sir, if you get my drift. You wanna keep well clear o'them. We're just helpin' you out, sir." He nodded deferentially and walked on. Terry breathed again.

They emerged gratefully into the sunlight at Hyde Park, and walked through the summer crowds towards the boathouse. It was good to see families at play around picnic cloths, to see children romping with dogs, to see young couples in denim shorts and matching t-shirts holding hands, walking barefoot in the park. It was what they needed.

"I wonder how long that's been going on, that evil nonsense on the tube" said Andrew, taking Terry's hand.

"Well...it's not really nonsense, though, is it? Any of that lot COULD have been T.B. carriers, couldn't they?"

"It's not that widespread yet!"

"But it would only take one, to kill both you and me, darling, wouldn't it?"

"And in the meantime, while we're carrying it, we can go onto the tube, or a bus, or to the theatre or the cinema, and spread it to thousands of people, quite the thing, because the brainless wonders we saw in the tube only intimidate the people who LOOK dangerous; not the ones who are."

"Well at least they're TRYING to help!" She dropped his hand and walked ahead of him.

He did not try to catch up with her. He was too depressed by her attitude. Though he could understand it, could understand it was based in fear, he could not share it nor condone it. Nor, he realised sadly, nor could he change it. He sat down on a bench, and watched her retreating back. When she turned and saw him, she too sat on a bench. And stayed there.

They stayed where they were for many minutes, each waiting for the other to cross the gulf between them. Then Terry got up and walked away, without looking back.

A most polite young man approached Andrew, carrying a stack

of handbills. Andrew tried to brush him off, but the young man insisted, saying

"Please do read it sir; it could save your life, and mine, and millions of others too. A very good day to you, sir." And he crushed one into Andrew's hand. It read:

IF YOU LOVE YOUR FAMILY, SAVE THEIR LIVES!
COME TO THE PEOPLE FOR PURITY RALLY THIS
SUNDAY, ALBERT HALL, 7.30pm
ENTRANCE FREE!
Come and join with thousands of others just like yourself; all political persuasions welcome, all religions welcome, atheists welcome too. What we have in common is simple common sense; we want to SAVE OUR FAMILIES from the terrors of AIDS and T.B.! We want CLEAN SAFE STREETS to live on, where our daughters are safe from RAPISTS, MUGGERS, MURDERERS! Isn't that what YOU want, too?
Come and listen, come and talk, with a live satellite link to the Usher Hall in Edinburgh, where People for Purity started! See and hear the REVEREND PETER SPENCER, live in Edinburgh, talking directly to YOU!
BE POWERFUL FOR CHANGE: HEAR HOW YOU CAN SAVE YOUR FAMILY. PEOPLE FOR PURITY CAN HELP YOU SAVE THEIR LIVES!

He crumpled it up and threw it away. It was a measure of his distress that he did not wait until he passed a litter bin. Walking back towards Hyde Park Corner, he noticed once again that there were many more beggars than he ever remembered before; he did recall hearing on some news programme on Radio 4 that their numbers were increasing as more and more people from all over the country swarmed to the 'golden pavements' when they were made redundant, could not pay their mortgages, and lost their homes. Their wives and families were mostly shacked up with relatives in any corner they could get, or on the miserable bed-and-breakfast trail. Daddy went to London because the rich South always seemed to have more jobs, but so many Daddies were doing it that most of them got nothing, not even enough for the train fare home. The various charities which doled out soup and bare essentials were getting very thinly stretched, as the recession bit deeper and deeper and contributions from a sympathetic public shrivelled and died away.

There were thousands of empty houses, repossessed houses, all over Britain: and thousands and thousands of homeless, evicted families. There were others who had not waited for the ignominy of eviction, but had put the keys through the letterbox of their building society, with a short note of apology, before setting out quietly, at night, on their journey to nowhere.

The building societies could not sell the empty properties, for the property market was in a complete slump. Even though lenders had slowed down their repossessions, well aware of the difficulties, the problem continued to grow. So the families wandered the country hoping for better luck, while the houses which had once been their homes stayed empty. Somebody, somewhere must have benefitted, else the insanity of the situation would presumably have been spotted and stopped. It was hard to think of who that somebody could be, though. Some vengeful god, bent on punishing the weak, perhaps.

Speaker's Corner was thronged, and on the soapboxes were men of a dozen stern and sterling convictions, all diametrically opposed to one another and all absolute in their rectitude. They had sparse audience, except for one pleasant-faced chap who was not haranguing but smiling encouragingly and gathering all in with his arms as he talked. Hoping for respite from his hurting, Andrew wandered over to listen.

The man sounded like a Slav, possibly Russian, with a thickish but charming accent, and quite easy to understand. His smiles were eager and honest, very winsome and trustworthy. He was a man who enjoyed talking to people, and making them happy. And he had some very happy news for everyone, he said.

Another evangelist thought Andrew. Not today, thank you.

"Because it is, are you happy here in London? Is it nice and clean, with nice people and good clean air and goodness for your little ones? No? But where can you go, good peoples? Where is safe for families now? With good jobs, and big nice houses very cheap, and all you can eat just for pennies? Nowhere? No, you are wrong! The Ukraine is waiting for you! Waiting to welcome you! That's right! Is a safe place with no HIV, no AIDS; we keep everybody hotel, nice hotel, three months before they go in; no work, nothing to pay, nothing to do but enjoy! So nobody get in with AIDS Virus! After that, plenty work, plenty houses, pretty ones, only cost little - and two years nothing to pay, loan from Ukraine Government, to say welcome!"

A lone heckler rallied to his calling.

"Oh yeah, mate, and is that when we get sent oft to Siberia then, eh?"

Nobody laughed.

Nobody laughed. Andrew looked at their faces; rapt. The speaker went on, about free schooling, free training for all promising youngsters, free health care and free everything for pensioners.

"You bring whole family, we are to be delighted! Ukraine endless wheatfields, endless beautiful; plenty room for everybody. We need willing workers, my friends. You can build things, you come. Doctor, nurse, you come. You make good shoes, we want to buy them you come! You teach children, you come too! Everybody welcome. And whole family; even dog! We pay everything; passage, hotel for three month, everything."

"Why?" asked Andrew. "Why do you pay for everything?"

"Not enough people" said the man, simply. "Ukraine big beautiful place but not enough people to make it live well. Need people to make a future. Good people. Decent people. British people are the best."

A small roar of applause.

"It like the first settlers, in America" the man was warming to his subject now. "New frontier, new world; only we got television and computers too, make life civilised! English language programmes too! Everything! All we need now is people, families,

families tired of sick living in West!"

That kind of remark would have got him lynched (verbally at least) just a few months previously. Now, there were rumbles of agreement, mutterings of 'Damn right' to be heard all through the crowd.

The speaker held up leaflets. "All details in here! If you serious about new life in beautiful land, all safe and healthy for family, you come get a leaflet. Then come see us in Embassy, near St James Park. We looking forward to meeting you!"

A few people shuffled forward, not wanting to be the first but wanting the leaflet. Then somebody called, quite politely,

"What about our own houses? We can't sell them, you know." The speaker slapped his forehead, as if he could not believe his own stupidity.

"I forgot to tell! We have new deal with your Government! They buy your house from market value price for you! Give you wonderful start in Ukraine, because houses much cheaper there!"

The surge forward was almost the whole crowd, and their eyes were sparkling. Most of them had already decided, and if the details on the leaflet coincided with the speaker's words, they would be going.

Twenty years ago, thought Andrew, I might have gone myself.

He walked on, ignoring the pleas of the beggars, and his mind was filled with confusing pictures of himself, aged thirty, with Ruth, aged seventeen, standing in a waving wheatfield...then it wasn't Ruth any more but Terry, just as she was now, holding his hand lovingly...

He hailed a taxi, not wanting any more crowds, any more people, any more problems. The driver leaned out of his window as he pulled up, asking "Where to, squire?" and Andrew realised he had nowhere particular to go until his meeting with the Prime Minister.

"79 Whitehall" he said, automatically, and climbed in. He might as well go and do some work, see what was happening. The driver prattled on about the traffic, Chelsea's chances next season, the terrible heat, and his wife's bunions, but Andrew was oblivious. The Ukrainian speaker's spell was wearing off, and his vision of himself in the prairies there, slowly fading. That last point before the crowd surged forward was beginning to bother him, though; why would the Government pay to lose its people? It was surely one hell of an expensive way to massage the unemployment figures and the homeless figures! And why hadn't he seen anything about it on tv, or in the papers, or heard about it on the radio? He made some rapid calculations, based on the current rate of Unemployment Benefit and Income Support, and the likely average number of years of unemployment between middle age and retirement, when the income from the State merely turned into the same thing called something else. He added in the average cost of health care for a couple, from middle years to death, and for the lifelong health care, housing and all State benefits of those children of theirs who might never get jobs at all.

He then thought about the true market price for a very average semi, two up and two down with a small garden. He was appalled to find that the price of the house paled into insignificance beside the previous figure...the Government was not only easing the statistics by doing this, it was saving a fortune.

There was much paperwork waiting for him in his office, and Sarah Kepple manfully trying to cope with it all by herself while the other two were on holiday. Grateful for the diversion, he rolled up his sleeves and got stuck in.

He met Terry on the steps of 10 Downing Street at the appointed hour. They smiled professionally at each other, and though they brushed shoulders when going through the door, the gulf was as wide as it had been in Hyde Park, and possibly wider. As they were announced to the P.M., she whispered quickly "We'll talk about us later" and he nodded.

Jim Brettles was not there, only the Prime Minister and Harold Sweeting. Beneath their normal urbanity, a certain nervousness could be detected. But the P.M. was a born performer, and his voice was steady and smooth and polite and assertive, all as normal. Terry had trained him well.

"Come in, settle yourselves down. Would you like coffee? No? Right then. I have some ideas I'd like to put to you, Andrew, and I want you, Terry, to tell me what you think the public reaction MIGHT be, and how we can swing it to our point of view; that is to say, how we can make sure they understand properly.'

'Now. Because of the increasing rapidity of the spread of AIDS, and the failure so far of educational programmes, and now this dreadful business of the cats, I feel that your job, Andrew, is growing into something more properly served by two people, rather than one. I need hardly say that this is no reflection on your abilities or your performance"

"Hear hear" interrupted Sweeting, somewhat to everyone's surprise.

"Yes... Anyway Andrew, what seems to me to be sensible is if we split the job into the two most obvious parts; the bringing together of all efforts to monitor the spread, and the dealing with the actualities of the epidemic. So I propose that Harold here, as Minister for Health, is most sensibly placed to collate and organise the dealing with the epidemic, the public health measures; and you, Andrew, I want you to really get on top of setting up mass screenings, and collating the resultant statistics. How does that strike you?"

Terry noticed that the P.M. was only addressing Andrew; clearly, Sweeting had been sounded out earlier. Had been informed earlier. Had accepted, earlier.

"Whatever you wish, of course, Prime Minister" said Andrew, slowly. "What exactly do you see as my primary role, then?"

"I'm giving you the Medical Corps of the Reserve Forces, to help you organise it all. It will be a massive operation, I do realise that; you'll need plenty of help, and I'll make sure you get it. And funds; whatever you need. I mean that; whatever you need. So what do you say?"

Terry's scalp was prickling again. Why was the Prime Minister so reluctant to spell out what Andrew's new duties would be?

"I'm sorry, sir" said Andrew "I must be being slow today. I still don't quite understand what it is you're giving me all these people and all this money to do?"

"National screening, of course! Sweeting here will declare HIV Positivity to be a notifiable disease, and we must set up a really tight screening operation to make sure we find each and every Positive. I would imagine you would start with, say applicants for mortgages...insurances...jobs...hospitalisation... all those things. Then draw the net tighter. It would be entirely up to you."

"But sir, being HIV Positive is not having a disease. The virus can sit there for decades, and not do a thing to the host, possibly stay quiet for the person's whole natural life. It isn't a disease, as such, at all. Neither is AIDS. How can we call them notifiable diseases, when they aren't diseases?"

"Don't tell me my business!" snapped the P.M. "Semantics is not going to get us out of this hole!

"I was not using sophistry; I was pointing out a genuine difficulty in our laws, sir."

The Prime Minister's anger was being cowled by his eyelids.

"We make the laws, Andrew; don't you worry about the laws."

Andrew bit back any remarks about democracy, and Terry saw him biting down on them and, with a struggle, remained silent herself.

The Prime Minister rose from his chair, walked over to stand in front of the fireplace. Though he was addressing Andrew, he was staring at the ornate plaster mouldings on the ceiling. "Look, be reasonable; all we are asking you to do is to find out the true figures out there; the real number of Positives floating about in the community, as opposed to the ones we happen to know about because they've come forward to be tested." He dropped his gaze to look down on Andrew, parent-to-child. "Are we asking too much of you, Andrew?"

Every instinct told Andrew to rise and be as pushy, as politely hostile, as the Prime Minister. But long years of political training kept him seated, kept his eyes down on the desk and not up challenging the man.

"It will be...a difficult operation. A massive operation. Have we thought through, yet, how long it's likely to take? And how many people will have become HIV Positive AFTER we've tested them and found them negative? It's not the logistics which worry me, Prime Minister; it's two things. Firstly, I have grave doubts about the necessity or even advisability of the screening because of what I have just said; to be effective, everybody in the country would have to be screened every three months or so; and if we think about that, we can see that it would take a huge percentage of the population working flat out to test the rest, it's just not do-able. And secondly, what are we going to do about it once we have the statistics? Assuming that they are all anonymous statistics, of course, and not...lists..."

"Oh no; not anonymous. It would be tantamount to murder if we found thousands of people who are HIV or AIDS sufferers, and left them to wander about infecting others with T.B. Or whatever else the virus throws up in the future. We must have their names."

"Then" and Andrew hesitated even to ask the question, for he felt he did not really want to hear the answer "what will be done about them, when the lists are complete?"

A look passed between Sweeting and the Prime Minister, and there was something unreadable in their eyes. But Terry's scalp told her that it had to do with the big story which hadn't broken yet. Alarm bells were screaming in every corner of her journalist's mind. She looked at Andrew to see if he had read the signals, but his face was quiet.

"It's way too early to answer that one" said Sweeting. "Until we have some idea of the numbers involved, and, for example, any geographical anomalies in the spread, or demographic factors involved apart from the sexual lifestyle factors we already know about...it will take some time to digest your statistics, once we've got them."

"So essentially, what you want me to do is to find out who has got the virus; every name and address; and report it to you. Is that it?"

"That's it" said the P.M. as if he was congratulating a child on successfully adding two and two and getting four. "As accurately as possible and as fast as possible. Well? Are you up to the job?"

And now Andrew did rise, and pushed his chair back tight into the table. He turned to face the Prime Minister and spoke gently.

"I don't think I am, actually. It was kind of you to offer it to me first; but I must decline."

This time Terry could not fail to read the look between Sweeting and the Prime Minister; it was fast and fleeting and quickly veiled, but it was one of triumph. She also rose, and spoke very pleasantly.

"I imagine you will not be requiring my services any more then, either; my relationship with Doctor Douglas might make the next incumbent a little uncomfortable, and I would think that the AIDS scenario would be the major part of my job from now on. Rather than cause difficulties, I will resign." She walked over to join Andrew and could not resist one last little dig.

"I'm sure you will be more than pleased with Frank Ainsley; he may not be as bright as I am, but he is certainly more malleable."

She smiled.

The Prime Minister affected a sad, disappointed expression. He walked over to them, and shook each of them warmly and sincerely by the hand.

"I'm so sorry you both feel that way. Of course I would not dream of forcing you, or trying to persuade you. I would like to thank you both, especially you, Andrew, for your sterling work. Always. So:" his tone changed to that of almost a normal human being "What will it be now? More gardening up in that paradise of yours in St Fillans? Or back to general practice? At least you two can finish your holidays now; lucky people. I think Harold and I have had all the holidays we'll be getting for some time."

"Something. It'll take a bit of thinking about." said Andrew.

"Yes. Well, then" said the Prime Minister. And he walked them to the door. As he opened it, the security guard was right there.

"Better hand your passes over now, I suppose" said the Prime Minister. "Of course we'll always be glad to see you visiting us, any time, any time at all."

They handed over their passes to Number 10 Downing Street,

which the guard shredded in front of their eyes, without expression.

"Bye, then" said the Prime Minister, and the guard ushered them out.

They walked away, in the direction of Whitehall.

"Might as well go and get my things from my office now, rather than later" said Andrew. "Coming with me?"

"I'll come with you to yours if you come with me to mine, afterwards" she said, and he agreed.

"Well" she ventured into the silence, as they walked up Whitehall. "We were well and truly fired, weren't we?"

"Yes. Shot ourselves in the foot, rather, didn't we?"

"Not only fired, but told to get out of London and stay out of the whole thing."

"Pardon? I must have missed that bit."

"Gardening in St Fillans? General practice, also in St Fillans? Holidays, also in St Fillans? Come on Andrew, you're not that naieve."

"Damn me. I never noticed that. You're right, though, you're right."

Without thinking, he reached for her hand. She hesitated for just long enough to remind him that they still had personal problems, before taking his hand in hers.

He gave it a comforting squeeze, and she smiled a little.

"By God but I don't like what they're proposing" began Andrew, hotly.

"Oh, don't be silly; they're not proposing anything of the sort.

They know as well as you do that it's unworkable and pointless and anyway, people wouldn't stand for it."

"The mass screening?"

"Yes. They've no intentions of doing it. That was just to get you to resign."

He stopped walking. "I'm a fool" he said. "A cretin. How did I manage to miss that? You're right again. Then...why...? Why so keen to get rid of me?"

"Same reason that you didn't see what they were up to. You're

241

too honest."

"That's no reason..." they continued walking.

"Not normally, no; so they ARE up to something, something you wouldn't touch with a barge pole, and so Sweeting will have to do it. He won't mind a bit. Well that's not true, actually. I was watching him. He obviously knows all about it already, and I would have expected him to be grinning like a Cheshire cat. But he wasn't. In fact both of them looked ...um..."

"Sad. I though both of them looked sad."

"Yes. I find that terrifying. What can be so major, so awful, that those two would be made sad by it?"

"The cats?"

"No. Bad enough, but not that bad. That would make them worried, concerned maybe, certainly appalled. But not sad."

She pulled her hand out of his.

"Nothing being said here, I notice, about how I feel, having just been pushed into resigning too. But then I'm just a Media Advisor. Or I was. So I suppose we needn't waste time discussing my feelings: they're always invalid, or inappropriate, aren't they, Andrew?"

She spoke without venom or bitterness, only with sadness. The sadness of someone who sees and feels a deeply loving relationship trickling through her fingers like dry sand, and blowing away in the wind. She knew this was a stupid time to make him argue about their relationship, and she knew that she was behaving in an unlikable, unlovable way, but she couldn't seem to stop herself.

Andrew wrenched her around and slammed her, not very hard, against the wall. He stood very close to her, and he spoke sternly.

"It's not going to work, you know; your campaign of brinkmanship. I don't know whether you're even aware you're doing it, but it's as plain as the very sweet upturned nose on your very sweet upturned face. You are pushing and pushing me, being more and more difficult and demanding and selfish, like a spoilt child, which I know you weren't. You're doing it to see when you reach my breaking point, when I'm going to turn away from you for good. Well it's not going to happen. Okay, I don't much like the way you pout and snarl from time to time, but it does not change how I feel about you, nor is it going to change that. I love you, I want to marry you, and I want to live happy-ever-after. If you insist on making that difficult by pouting and snarling every so often, you go right ahead. But until the day you tell me you do not love me any more, I will be right there beside you. Loving you. Loving you like anything, pouts and snarls and warts and all."

She slumped into the warm grip of his arms.

"I honest to God don't deserve you."

"Do you love me, Terry?"

"Desperately."

"Do you think you could learn to maybe disagree with what I say, or what I think, or even what I do, from time to time, without disliking me?"

"Hate the sin, but not the sinner, you mean?"

"I suppose that's about it, yes."

"Okay."

"Okay?" he grinned. "Is that it? Okay?"

"Well, I could have dressed it up a bit in moral philosophy and circumlocution, but it would have boiled down to 'okay' anyway."

"Oh" he said, his eyes shining again with love and merriment "I love you, you atrocious woman."

They walked on, hand in hand again.

"You were saying..." she prompted.

"About Sweeting?"

"No no, not that the part about getting married. Talk to me some more about that. I liked the sound of that part. Do I get to wear a huge big pretty white frock? Or would that be considered tacky, as we are now both unemployed?"

"You get as many huge big pretty frocks as you want, in every colour, and you can wear them all at once if you like. Just as long as you say "I do" nice and loud and clear, I'll be a happy man."

"You would, too, wouldn't you? You'd let me turn up in anything I liked and you'd still be pleased to see me, wouldn't you? Because you love me to bits, you adore me, don't you?"

She whirled him round to hug her again, and folded him up in her own arms.

"I LOVE you. First time in my life. Last time. Only time. Forgive me when I'm scratchy. I'll try not to be. I know I'm bitchy sometimes: no, I am. Oh, you weren't going to contradict me! Well. I won't pretend it's all a protective shell I've evolved to cope with difficult times and difficult people; maybe it was to start off with, but it's built in to me now. Part of me. But I will try to control it. No. I'll try to dismantle it, let it go. I don't need it any more. You know all about me, and you still love me. There's nothing else on God's earth that I could ask for. Thank you for loving me so much, my love."

Their kiss was so long and so softly, nuzzlingly loving that they got a round of applause from the passersby, and walked on, Terry giggling, Andrew blushing.

"It's been one hell of a day, hasn't it?" said Terry, contentedly. "Our first major quarrel...we both got fired...and we got engaged. All by two o'clock in the afternoon. What a day."

Two burly security men were waiting for them at 79 Whitehall. By their sides stood two small brown paper parcels. These, they informed Andrew, were the personal things from his office. It would not, therefore, be necessary for him to enter the building proper, as the formalities could be accomplished here in Reception. One of them asked for and shredded Andrew's pass for the building, while the other got Andrew to sign a receipt for his belongings. They were itemised right down to "Ballpoint pens, nonissue, 3. Paper handkerchiefs, one packet, one-third used."

There were no papers, nor computer disks nor printouts, included. No information, in short, not even his address book or telephone file.

Andrew quietly signed on the dotted line.

"This is shabby" hissed Terry. "Shabby treatment for anyone. But particularly to someone who.."

"Ssh" was all Andrew said.

She sshed.

Andrew picked up his parcels, and left with Terry.

"Well now" he said, outside, with an attempt at joviality. "How about the Ukraine? I hear it's lovely at this time of year, and they're very keen to have us."

"Personally, I was more attracted by the adverts for Australia, and Canada. They seem awfully keen on having us too: well not me, actually, because I'm in the media. Was in the media. Maybe they could train me up to become a useful member of society, after all. In the meantime, I expect we'll find the same reception committee waiting at my office. Shall we go?"

She was right. It was humiliating. But at least Frank Ainsley either had the good taste not to come out and crow, or he wasn't there. Some of the other staff came out, though, when they heard Terry was there. The Security men wouldn't let her talk to any of them. It was distressing for her, and it made Andrew very angry.

"Look, she can talk to them any time she likes outside this office, can't she? So why can't she talk to them now?" he harangued one of the Security men.

"Darling, ssh" she said. Andrew faced the small group of embarrased journalists, and spoke in loud, ringing tones.

"You're all invited to our engagement party, at Terry's flat, on Saturday night."

They grinned, and so did Terry; several of them gave her the thumbsup sign. The Security men were not amused, and hustled them out of the building, almost throwing Terry's parcels at her feet, but they felt triumphant.

They indulged in another long, comforting kiss at the front door.

Then they shuffled brown paper parcels between them till they were evenly laden, and walked off in search of a taxi. Terry gave vent to a kind of snorting chuckle, and burst into muted song.

"We're a couple of swells" she began, and started to walk in a passable imitation of the Chaplin tramp. "We live at the best hotels, In June, July and August, far away from the city smells, pa,rum,pa.."

A real tramp walked past them, staring uncomprehendingly with haunted eyes. She sobered up instantly.

"Where are we going, Andrew? Back to my place?"

"I suppose so. We've got a party to organise for Saturday."

"And an awful lot of talking to do. And a big fat diamond ring to buy. For the third finger of my left hand."

"This has been the most bizarre day of my entire life" said Andrew.

"I'm starving" said Terry.

"You would be. Chinese? Indian? Thai?"

"Morello cherry pie at Joe's, please."

This taxi driver gave up on conversation after five minutes of being ignored by the couple canoodling in the back. Some people, he told his wife later, got no shame at all.

———— • ————

The preUsher Hall meeting of the PFP in Edinburgh was not going well, that Wednesday night. Albert could see the Reverend disintegrating before his very eyes, and there was clearly some connection with Frankie in all this; every time Peter Spencer's eyes drifted over Frankie, his speech became more and more lame and halting. Albert became extremely worried about the Reverend's ability to perform adequately, never mind exaltingly, on Sunday.

With the extremely expensive live satellite link to the Albert Hall already booked and in place, and promises of a full house in both venues, a hitch, or a poor performance, was unthinkable.

The PFP committee was getting progressively more shuffling and nervous as the evening wore on, and it became more frequently necessary for Albert to interrupt the glorious leader to say things like "So what you're saying here is..." and "If I could just recap on that, to make sure I understand properly" and use the opportunity to say what Peter Spencer had not in fact said, but should have said.

"Yes, yes" was all the rebuff he got. Eventually, Peter Spencer pled an upset stomache and sat down, leaving Albert to finish organising everything. Which he had no trouble in doing, as he had already done it and fed Peter Spencer with the ideas.

All was ultimately agreed, and the committee went to their

various homes in high hopes of a splendid night of glory on the coming Sunday. Peter Spencer would usually have invited Albert and a few other key members round to the manse for a roundup talk over tea or coffee, but tonight he excused himself and wandered off. Albert collared Frankie as he was wheeling Grandad out of the hall.

"Frankie, have you got a couple of minutes?"

Grandad insisted he was well able to get a taxi, would use the phone at the back of the hall, and not to worry about him.

"You go and have your chat, son; actually on second thoughts I think I'd like to go an' see what's up with the Reverend; he can take me there, and I can get a taxi home maself afterwards. The drivers are aye willin' to see me up in the lift, dinnae you worry. You two go off an' enjoy yer chat over a pint or something, go on!"

But pints are rarely private enough; Albert followed Frankie's lead, down to the beach at Silverknowes, deserted at this time of night, even in summer. They parked on the promenade, and Frankie sat in Albert's car.

"So: what's wrong with the Reverend Spencer, Frankie?"

Frankie considered for a moment, but had expected the question and had already decided to tell Albert the truth. He had no particular reason to protect his father, after all, for his father had not protected him. And there was no advantage Frankie could see in Albert ever breaking the confidence, for Frankie did not really give a damn whether people knew or not, excepting of course for Flora; then again, he was sure Albert would realise it would not be good for his health to ever tell Flora. So Frankie told him the whole story.

"And you're going ahead with your marriage, then, even though she's your half sister? I see." Albert did not sound shocked, though he was, rather. This information was useful though; it put Frankie slightly higher on the sliding scale which went from normal up to psychopath. "Well, whatever the reason, Peter Spencer seems to me to have outlived his usefulness to the movement. We can't let him up on that platform on Sunday night, can we?"

"He's pathetic" said Frankie.

"Quite. Tell me Frankie, now tell me honestly, what are your feelings towards this man now?"

"Not much. Not real feelings, none at all in fact. I *think* he's a real shitehouse; but I don't *feel* anything."

"Good, good. Now how would you feel if he was to die, rather suddenly? Or let me put it another way, what would you think of that?"

"It would be good; there would be no chance then of Flora ever finding out, not unless he's told his wife, of course; but I doubt that."

"And if we could use his death to further the great cause, Frankie?"

"Even better."

"Good. Well, I think we should do it this Sunday."

"At the Usher Hall?"

"Well possibly, yes...but no, I think in the church. You see some innocent people are going to be hurt too, and it would be more useful to us, I think, if they were churchgoers; people would be more outraged by that."

Frankie looked at him sideways on.

"You're good at this, aren't you?"

"Thank you. Now do you want to help, or would you rather I did it myself? Or how about one of your...team?"

"You show me what to do, and I'll do it. I'll do it myself."

"You're a remarkable man, Frankie" said Albert. *And one fine day, when the job is done, I shall be able to get the hell out of all this, and I shall never have to spend another five minutes of my life dealing with sickminded psychopathic bastards like you, my friend. Oh God, roll on that day! And let me still have some shred of humanity left in me then to enjoy it...*

At nine o'clock on Thursday morning, Frankie was visited in his office by two plain clothes C.I.D. men: a Sergeant and a Constable. They wanted to see Tommy Bain's file, and they wanted to see it immediately. Frankie protested about confidentiality, but was pleasantly ignored.

Nobody could be more pleasant than Frankie Dunn when it

suited him. He got out the file, ordered teas from his temporary typist, and passed the file across the desk to his guests, smiling aimiably.

"Does Mr Bain have a problem, gentlemen?"

No reply.

One of them read the file while the other asked questions about the nature of Mr Bain's relationship with Mr Dunn. No relationship, as such, Frankie explained; just the usual one of advisor to client. Actually, he volunteered, Mr Bain had been in here just last week, was it? Yes, last week, a few days ago, anyway, and had asked to surrender all his policies. No, he hadn't given any reason. As they could see from the files, Frankie had (albeit reluctantly and against his own advice) acceded to this request; the liquidation of the policies was already in train.

No, Mr Bain had not told him why the money was wanted; they were not friends, and Mr Dunn would never press a client on a personal matter. Yes, Mr Bain had indeed seemed rather upset.

The officers seemed quite satisfied, but Frankie was not. He phoned Albert, met him at this week's appointed place (the rock garden in the Royal Botanical Gardens), and asked him if he could find out what was going on regarding a certain Thomas Bain, who seemed to be the subject of some police investigation or other. Frankie volunteered no further details and Albert asked for none.

Albert promised to see what he could do, and then talked Frankie through his part in what was to come on Sunday morning.

Frankie listened properly, nodded in the right places, clearly understood what he was to do and how he was to do it. It could have been preparations for a business deal, or a lesson on the flora and fauna of North Western Australia; it was simply a question of details to be absorbed, no emotions involved at all.

The children romping illicitly up and down the rocky steps took no notice of them. They were so ordinary, the tall young man and the stocky older man... and anyway the fun of escaping 'the Parkie' was the principal reason for being there, not the miniature Alpines or the flowering shrubs which rioted all around.

Even while driving home that night, Frankie's thinking about the

249

death of Peter Spencer was confined exclusively to how much support and caring Flora was going to require, and a slight unease as to the possibility of a spontaneous abortion due to the stress of losing her father, or, more likely, the shock of being in church when her father blew up in front of her eyes. Still, if that happened, the plans for the wedding could easily be dropped. There would be no particular point in marrying her after that. A woman who failed to carry his baby to full term was no use to Frankie.

Flora was proving more easy to influence than Frankie had anticipated; she had willingly agreed to give up her job at Radio Forth round about the seventh month, as she would not be entitled to maternity leave by then, and in any case was now working only as a researcher for other presenters, which she found frustrating. She and Frankie were of one mind on the importance of bringing up his child with 24-hour care and attention.

Their only current disagreement was on their married home; Flora wanted to stay in Bellevue Street, and Frankie wanted out of the city altogether and into a big house, with staff, in the country. This sounded too much like isolation to Flora, and she was digging her heels in. She had made friends at Forth, and wanted to stay close enough for the odd lunch together, during the week. Frankie did not want his child's mother to come under the continuing influence of media types, but his given reason was that he wanted her to be as free from stress as humanly possible, because he loved her so much.

She was weakening, her backbone crumbling under the weight of his love.

And then that evening Frankie played his ace. In a concerned, kindly voice, he invited her to confess that her 'real' reason for wanting to stay in Bellevue Street was that it only had two bedrooms, and there would not therefore be any room for Grandad. Whereas a country mansion, with staff, would be able to accommodate him with ease. He, Frankie, could understand this; and he was ready to give in. After all, what young bride or young mother wanted an aged relative hanging around, particularly a disabled one?

Though she quite liked Jock Dunn, she had not anticipated living with him; but Frankie's martyrdom, his preparedness to dump his poor old Grandad so that selfish little Flora could escape family responsibilities, was too much. The country house was adopted wholeheartedly.

————— • —————

Terry's flat was swathed in balloons and satin ribbons for the engagement party, and her left hand was suitably attired in a modest but pretty engagement ring. Thoughts of a big fat diamond had vanished as soon as she saw the antique rings in the jewellers, and she had fallen completely in love with a cabochon emerald set in ornate rose gold. Naturally this had necessitated the purchase of an emerald green dress to go with it, and a silverblonde rinse for her hair to give the ensemble an extra zing. She was looking ravishing, and Andrew was as proud as punch to think that this exotic creature was in love with him. They fussed round with boxes of wine and platters of canapes, all far too good for journalists, she kept saying, while adding more and more to the feast.

The doorbell rang, far too early to be a guest; it was Callum, come round early to help. Andrew was very touched, and Terry was delighted. They had told him of their engagement over the phone, and though he had sounded pleased she had thought he might feel a little put out. But he was very happy for them.

"Got some news of my own, actually" he said, ultra-casually, as he laid plates and cutlery on the sideboard. "I'm starting a hospital radio show next week. I've got the six to seven spot in the evenings. All requests."

"Well done, son" beamed Andrew.

"Not 'arf" smiled Terry. Callum turned to face her, smiling winsomely.

"Sort of wondered if you could give me a few tips; free, of course, now you're part of the family. I mean, you do media training, don't you? I've done a demo cassette, but I thought it was pretty duff, myself. As it happens, I think it's in my jacket pocket...?"

"Callum! Behave yourself!"

"No, no, Andrew, it's all right, I'm delighted to do it. But not free; my terms are, you put all your engineering skill into filling vol-au-vents for the next half-hour."

"Fair dues. So do you want them backfilled, straightfilled, or infilled?"

"I want a meaningful ongoing dialogue between the radical pastry and the rather conservative prawns, with an interface of mayonnaise. And stuff. Move it, slave!"

She followed him into the kitchen. Andrew experienced a warm glow, listening to them clattering cheerfully together, talking nonsense and enjoying themselves. He looked around the little lounge, screwing his face up slightly at the prettypretty decor, with too much gingham and lace and too many pictures of flowers on the wall. Terry was always willing to admit that she had no taste at all (except, now, in husbands), but that she knew what she liked. He tried to superimpose the gingham and lace over a mental picture of the lounge at St Fillans, and shuddered. The doorbell rang again.

It was Joe Cromwell and his wife Shirley.

"Make way for the Welsh!" cried Joe, and foisted a very large bottle of an ancient peaty malt upon Andrew. "We brought you this imported culture. We were going to bring you a bundle of leeks, but Shirley here insisted on whisky. The woman has no class, I'm afraid."

"It's good to see you again, Andrew" said the classless Shirley, kissing him on the cheek. "We're so pleased you've found happiness again; and thanks for the invitation to stay in your flat at Victoria tonight." Andrew helped them off with their summer jackets, and hung them away in the bedroom. Being Andrew, it had not registered with him that Shirley was wearing the same shade of green as Terry; when Terry came out of the kitchen, however, both women registered it immediately.

"Ah" said Terry, brightly.

"What a lovely...dress!" said Shirley, smiling at 40 watts. Joe

252

snickered.

"Come now ladies, claws in, you both look divine in a Celtic sort of way. And why is nobody upset that Andrew and I are both wearing grey trousers?"

The five of them got on well immediately. Which was just as well, for the time wore on and the doorbell did not ring again. Nobody came. The embarrassment was profound, though nobody mentioned that nobody had come, and vast quantities of food and drink were consumed, in a desperate effort to make it look as if those catered for had actually turned up.

————— • —————

Flora was not, after all, coming to church. Frankie had explained to her, on Saturday night, that her father did not want to call the banns until he and she had been reconciled; they were to go to the manse for dinner one night next week, and talk. Frankie thought the risk of miscarriage would be much lessened if Flora did not actually see what happened to her father.

Grandad was not coming to church this morning either; Frankie had crumbled two Phenergan tablets into his porridge that morning, and Grandad was feeling very pleasantly sleepy. Frankie valued his Grandad, and did not want him upset.

He was feeling good as he drove to the house of God in the sweet fresh morning air.

Inside the church, he took up his regular position in the back pew, which normally meant he was just in front of Grandad, and was where people expected to see him. The church was thronged, and the media were out in force, hoping for juicy vituperation from the pulpit with which they could preface their pieces later on about the Usher Hall rally.

The Reverend Spencer was not looking well. He laboured through the early part of the service, and the hymns were all of the mercy, mercy, meek and mild sort, which was not his style at all; his people expected rousing Sankey hymns, the gird-up-your-loins, fight-for-Christ type of thing which went so well with their newfound virulence. Still, it was their own hero, their brave champion, up there, and they went on worshipping him anyway.

Peter Spencer ascended the steps of the pulpit to deliver the sermon. He leaned on the lectern, and announced that today's text would be Matthew Chapter 5, verses 3 to 11, known as The Beatitudes. This was not his style either, and some concern was whispered among the faithful. The media types, more cynical, were expecting some twisted interpretations of the lovely verses.

"Blessed are the poor in spirit" he began "for theirs is the Kingdom of Heaven. Blessed are they that mourn, for they shall be comforted." Frankie made as if to scratch his ears, quickly twisting the yellow foam ear plugs deeper inside.

"Blessed are the meek" whispered Peter Spencer "For they shall inherit the earth." Frankie pressed the button on the calculator-sized object in his pocket. The radio wave travelled almost instantly to the detonator on the two ounces of Semtex concealed under the lectern on the pulpit, and Frankie opened his mouth as if to yawn, on the advice of Albert Kennedy.

The blinding flash of light produced an odd effect: for a nanosecond, it looked as if the Reverend Spencer, arms upraised to Heaven, was rising from the Earth in a blaze of glory. Just before the soundwaves hit the congregation, they saw that it was only the top of the Reverend which was rising. The blast had severed his head, neck, arms and upper torso from the rest of him.

Albert's advice would have been better given to those in the front few rows; people whose mouths had been closed suffered more from the shockwaves than the few who had been speaking, or yawning, or simply sitting mouth agape. There was blood running from many ears, and noses, and there was a lot of screaming. Frankie ran to help, swiftly passing the device to Albert Kennedy, who had been standing near the door in his own accustomed place.

"I'll get help!" shouted Albert, and rushed outside to telephone the police, having first tossed the device over the wall. The ultrathin latex gloves they had both been wearing were not noticeable, but prevented fingerprints; those, too, went over the wall, along with the two sets of ear plugs. And the man waiting behind the wall took all of this away with him, very rapidly, and disposed of them.

All the media vans and cars parked outside were disgorging their contents, as everyone and his photographer fought and ran and struggled to get exclusive pictures of the disaster. They, pushing to get into the church, were colliding with the people inside the church who were running and struggling to get out.

Albert used the carphone in one of the press vehicles, and the police, fire brigade and ambulances were there within minutes.

The Semtex had been expertly moulded and positioned; there was in fact very little damage to anyone except the minister, who was most definitely dead. There were, however, gratifyingly noisy scenes of panic and hysteria, very news worthy, and Albert joined Frankie in comforting and soothing the milling hordes, walking people to the exit and to the ambulances, taking especial care of the elderly and the very young, and those few who had been pierced by flying fragments of pulpit or lectern or, in one case, a very sharp rib from the Reverend. Several camera crews took footage of these two angels of mercy, and some of it went out live on air.

(A score and more of the congregation were very violently sick, once outside, but nobody took pictures of that.)

Frankie, who had been careful to get blood smeared on his face from one of the wounded, approached a policeman who happened to be standing near a cameraman.

"You must find them!" he cried, loudly, and the camera swivelled to find him. "These people are animals! Look what they've done!" His eyes were wild, and his hair photogenically dishevelled. The blood was most effective.

The policeman, a young man who was close to being sick himself, having seen what was under the two green cloths lying draped over two somethings just below the pulpit, in front of the altar, tried to calm this brave, Christian soul. But the cameraman's reporter pulled him away, eagerly, and the young policeman was not experienced enough to stop this from happening.

"What has happened here?" asked the reporter. Frankie covered his face with his hands, took them away, looked at the smeared blood on them, aghast. He held them up to the camera.

"Look! This is the blood of my father-in-law! They have murdered a minister of the church, and he was to be my father-in-law! They have murdered a minister of the church!"

"Who has, sir?"

"Those I can't say it. No Christian could say the words that would describe those people! The drug barons! The ones we've been campaigning against! The ones who bring death and destruction everywhere they go!"

"But sir, you've been campaigning against just about everybody, haven't you? How can you be sure it's the drug barons who've done this?"

"You're right, you're right. It could be homosexuals...or organised criminals of any kind...or just yobbos...or anybody who's foul enough." He turned, theatrically, to talk direct to camera. "Well you won't stop us! Those of us who loved the Reverend, who believe in the things he fought for - the things he DIED for - will be at the Usher Hall tonight. You won't stop us! You'll NEVER stop us!" He turned and looked behind him, then wandered off, to support an elderly lady who was walking with difficulty towards the church door. His tenderness and caring were fine to see, his devotion to the welfare of others, in the midst of his own personal distress. Yet the camera operator had a slight feeling of unease, watching him. Still, he'd got probably the most dramatic interview of the day, and he was well pleased.

———— • ————

Mark Tyme phoned Andrew's flat, looking for him, that Sunday morning. He was at Hyde Park, doing the soundchecks for this afternoon's live Concert in the Park, and he'd had an idea. Callum, thrilled to bits, gave him Terry's number, but said there was probably nobody home, as both of them were out with friends, having breakfast somewhere.

"Look, it's pretty urgent; do you know when he'll be back?"

256

"Um...about one, I think. His friends are driving back down to Kent, and they have to be there before four o'clock, so I would think...one, or thereabouts. Can I get him to phone you, if they come here first?"

"Yeah. Thanks." He gave Callum his Vodaphone number.

Breakfast was not going terribly well. Joe wanted to talk about their "resignations", which he had read about in the newspapers. He had been sad to read that they were throwing in the towel so early, and wanted to hear some more trenchant reason than that given out by the Media Office, which was that Doctor Douglas and Miss Aitken had both found themselves unable to continue because of 'other commitments' unspecified. But Andrew could only stick to what he had said when Joe phoned him, that this was true, both for him and Terry. Neither he nor Terry could even indicate that there might be other reasons; nor could they speculate on last night's absence of friends. There was much Andrew wanted to talk to Joe about, but could not; the conversation was awkward and stilted, as Joe clearly felt he was being frozen out, and did not understand why.

Even Terry's appetite was blunted, for once. And Joe and Shirley decided they really ought to be going, round about eleven o'clock, while the muffins were still warm and the coffee piping hot. They all shook hands, kissed cheeks, and separated outside the restaurant doors.

"We are going to finish up with no friends at all. Social lepers."

Terry was not joking. "Those we want to talk to either don't want to risk their careers by talking to us, or...we can't risk our own liberty by talking to them. At least, by saying anything worthwhile to them. I did like Joe. And Shirley. And we couldn't tell them anything."

"Thank God we have each other, then" said Andrew. "Imagine what this would be like if you were completely alone, and couldn't talk to anyone at all. At least we can talk to each other."

Having nothing left to stay in London for, they headed back to Tudor Court to pack up the rest of Andrew's things.

Mark Tyme was pleased to get Andrew's call.

"Listen, Doctor Douglas, we're doing this gig this afternoon at the Park; I wondered if you'd like the chance to come up on stage and talk to the audience? Should be useful for you they're sort of fifteen upwards. Younger, some of them. Just the kind of people you want to reach, yeah? We've got Rock Against AIDS leaflets being handed out by the ticket people, but I thought the personal touch... yes, I did read about your resignation, but I figured you could still come and talk as yourself; more effective now you're not a front man for the Government, I'd have thought. What do you say?"

He said no. He was not in the mood. Then he heard himself saying that, and was disgusted, so he said yes. What did one man's mood matter, when some young lives might just be saved by hearing what he had to say?

The concert was to start around three o'clock. They got there early, complete with Callum in tow, to have time to talk to Mark. The shockhaired star was welcoming and respectful, which put Andrew up another million notches in Callum's firmament. Callum begged to be allowed to go and be very quiet indeed behind the soundmen and the lighting men, and was dispatched with appropriate warnings. Terry, Andrew and Mark Tyme sat with lukewarm coffee in the group's "battle bus" behind the massive stage. Their talk was backed by the shrieking, complaining noises of guitars and keyboards being soundchecked on stage, and interfering with amplifiers.

"That was something in Edinburgh this morning, wasn't it?" said Mark. "Oh, you haven't heard? The church that crazy person preached in was bombed or something - there was an explosion, anyway - and Peter Spencer was blown to bits. Stone dead."

"People for Purity? *That* Peter Spencer?" Andrew was horrified.

"Yup. Nobody else killed..."

"Pity" said Terry, thinking of Albert Kennedy.

"...a few injuries, nothing fatal. Some poor little kid got a pair of burst eardrums though, five, I think they said she was. We had the telly on in here, and saw some of it. Rotten bloody business.

258

Who'd do something like that in a church, eh? I'm not a Christian myself but still, each to his own..."

"Any word on who did it yet?"

"No, not so far; there was some guy saying it was the drug barons or something, I saw, but he was like wildeyed and staring, Peter Spencer was about to become his father-in-law or something, he was out of his tree."

They talked about People for Purity, and about AIDS, and about tuberculosis. Mark had watched three close friends die of AIDS, and two were now in psychiatric hospitals, their minds dimmed and eaten away by the direct action of the virus on their brains.

"It's not that they don't know who they are any more...they don't even know what they are. The ones that died early were lucky. Though they didn't think so at the time. I hope, if I get it, I go quick..."

"You mustn't get it" said Terry, fervently. "You mustn't take the risks. Your fans... they've got to see you can be cool, and still keep alive. Half those kids think it's just gauche, just uncool and oldfashioned, to practice safe sex. The other half, they think it'll spoil the romance of the moment. We've got to make it streetsmart to use condoms."

"Look" interrupted Andrew "I'm the least streetsmart person on the face of the planet. Will any of them pay any attention to me, if I go out there? I doubt it. Mark, you should be doing the speechmaking, not me."

"Nah. You're the fatherfigure type, man! The thing is, you're not stuffy. You're the kind of father most kids would like to have but don't. If their real Dads said, take care, be sensible, they'd hoot with mirth, just to wind him up. But you come across like a human being, not a spoilsport. You're it."

"I don't know. I've never had much time for trendy vicars, or boring old farts like me putting on jazzy t-shirts and saying hey, too much, man; I don't talk the language of the young any more. I doubt if I ever did!"

"Stop putting yourself down!" Terry was crisp and to the point. "Get your act together, and make it good. How long have we got till showtime, Mark?"

He tilted his cornflowerblue contact lenses towards his Rolex.

"Not long; if you'll excuse me, I have to go change upstairs. You two help yourselves to coffee down here...I'll be passing through in half an hour, and at that point you'll need to follow me to the wings and then wait for my cue. Okay?"

"Fine" said Terry, as Andrew was staring fixedly at the floor and turning pale.

She clapped him on the back. "Hey: it's not nerves, it's excitement! Use it!"

"You haven't heard, have you?"

"Heard what?"

"The noise outside. A million weenyboppers gathered to shriek at Mark Tyme. And about to get me, instead. It's not excitement. It's nerves, believe me, it's nerves."

Half a dozen jumpered-and-jeaned young men whizzed past them on their way upstairs. Twenty minutes later, they descended again, changelings, gorgeous creatures every one, in brilliant colours and astonishing makeup. Behind them, Mark Tyme's white hair was echoed in a white bodysuit with pale blue lightning bolts on the chest. His face was matt grey, his lips bloody, his eyeshadow deepest blue. It was electrifying. He beckoned to Andrew to follow him, and Terry followed Andrew. She giggled as she saw them together the picture of raucous, abundant youth and energy, and the sober, lovat tweed suited gentleman. Andrew smiled wryly at her amusement.

They climbed the steep metal steps to the backstage area, and the band preened themselves one last time, waiting for the M.D. to announce them. When he did, the cheering began, and the boys wandered onto the stage in a kind of casual strut which drove the crowd wild. They took up their positions with their instruments then, after a suitably theatrical pause, Mark was announced and leaped onto the stage.

"Trrranggggg!" went the instruments, and Mark grabbed the microphone from the M.D. and waved at the crowd. They waved back, ecstatically. Andrew, watching from the wings, was fascinated.

"Hi" he said, in a long, throaty drawl.

"Not high enough!" yelled almost ten thousand voices.

"How high do we wanna go?"

"Over the top!" they screamed, and their idol nodded, grinning. He was in his element.

"Well now people, to get to the top, you gotta start..." he turned and wiggled his rear at them.

"...at the bottom!" they yelled, laughing.

"Right, as they say, on. Now before things get too, too vulgar, I want you to shut your delicious little mouths for a moment, and listen to a man in a suit; yes I do, I do, so just hush up now and be good. Or if you must be bad, be... bad... *quietly*." His audience roared with delight. "I want you to give a big, warm, sweaty hand to a man who's going to tell you how to go on being bad for years and years and years, without ever having to pay for it. Okay?"

"YES" they chorused, whether or not they understood a word he was saying.

And Mark Tyme waved Andrew onstage, and Terry got all excited and worried for him and proud of him all at once, as he walked towards the microphone as if he'd been doing it all his life.

Mark draped an arm around him and handed over the microphone, making kissing noises at him before winking largely at the audience and strutting offstage. Andrew looked out at an endless, undulating sea of faces, and felt somewhat seasick. Or was it stagefright? Either way, he would very much have liked to be putting a mulch down on his azaleas, at that moment. Or walking a tightrope across the deepest part of the Grand Canyon, without the benefit of a safety net. Anything, really. Anywhere.

"Ah" he said. "It's that condom moment." It was the witticism of the week, which Terry had reported hearing in the street, a parody of an old commercial for Condor tobacco. The audience roared and applauded, and Andrew began to enjoy himself.

"This is the bit of the concert where some boring old fart comes on stage to try to persuade you not to kill yourself for the sake of a good fuck" he went on, to everybody's astonishment, not least his own.

"But I, personally, am not going to waste my time or yours."
The audience was quieter now. "Because you don't care about living forever, do you? You're young, that means you're immortal, doesn't it? Nothing can touch you. You're free. You'll have sex with anything pretty that moves. And I'm not going to stop you. Nobody is going to stop you. If you're HIV positive, and you fancy a really good time, and some poor bastard is willing to go to bed with you without using a condom, well, why not? After all they won't KNOW you're HIV positive by looking at you, you, all young and freshfaced and healthy looking. You'll most likely kill them, yes, but...there are too many people in this country anyway. And not enough jobs. I mean, you know, five million unemployed right now, and more to come. That's serious stuff. So go ahead, that's my advice. For god's sake, DON'T use a condom. Keep doing exactly what you're doing now. Then, in five years' time, half of you will be dead or dying." He paused, and there was silence. "Half of you. Take a good look around you. Turn to the person on your right. Touch their shoulder. You're touching somebody who will be dead in five years' time. Don't let them take you with them. Or do: that'll mean more jobs for the ones that are left. So on you go, have fun; screw around all you want. We'll all be really, really sorry to see you dying. Really we will. We'll miss you. Goodbye."

And he turned and walked off stage, to Terry, to silence. And although it had not been planned, the band struck up the opening chords of "Keep Your Love Alive" and Mark Tyme came on stage and sang it. Andrew was standing almost shaking in the wings, being hugged by Terry. The audience, and the band, and the singer, were all subdued.

The first set had been planned to consist of five songs, and now consisted of six. By the time the sixth one was in full swing, most of the audience had rallied and were rocking in the aisles. But some, many, were still quiet. Mark Tyme and the band came off stage to tremendous applause. Mark shook Andrew's hand, but the drummer looked at him in fury.

"You really fucked them up for us mate, thanks! That's the deadest audience we've ever played!"

"They will be, yes, in five years" Andrew replied stonily. "I wasn't making that up, you know. Lots of those kids are dead meat already." The drummer looked at him, still savage, but now haunted too, and strode off down the metal steps towards the battle bus.

Another band was introduced, a lesser-known one, and many of the audience got up and headed for the icecream vans and hamburger stalls. Terry and Andrew didn't want to interrupt Mark in the middle of changing, so they walked slowly away, away from the back of the stage, away from the crowds, towards the restaurant at the Albert Memorial side of the park.

They ate ravenously, Terry having now recovered her appetite and Andrew having found one he didn't know he had. In between mouthfuls of steak, he told her he would never get up in front of a live audience again as long as he lived, and she nodded sympathetically and told him she was immensely proud of him all the same and there were going to be lives saved by what he had done.

"Nonsense; they were bopping and dancing about within minutes of my getting off stage."

"Those were the ones you saw, and heard, my love; you didn't notice the ones that were sitting talking. I did. It was worth doing, believe me. Pudding?"

She had her usual two puddings, and he managed a very large bowl of trifle, which Terry dipped into shamelessly as he ate. They had coffee, and talked of tomorrows. Callum was presumably still at the concert, they would just go back to the flat and pack, and leave him a note. The rent was paid in advance till the end of the summer anyway, so he might as well have the use of the place. They would take the Branson Pullman to Edinburgh in the morning, and on to Perth, and phone Isa to come and pick them up. The house at St Fillans would be ideal for a rest and recuperation break, and they had all the time in the world to sort themselves out. They might even get married there; Terry had visions of a real Highland piper at her wedding, and was entranced.

As they paid their bill, they saw the first trickles of people drifting homewards from the concert, whistling, talking, laughing. And, across the road, the first trickles of people queuing up to get into the Albert Hall for the People for Purity rally when the Hall opened its doors at six o'clock. Some of the concertgoers were flagging down the taxis which had just delivered the PFP people. Those in the queue were very huffy about this, and this did not go unnoticed by the concertgoers, some of whom started goading the 'goodygoodys' rather loudly. The goodygoodys were not in the mood to take this silently, not after the murder of their beloved leader that very morning. They retorted, verbally but sharply. Terry tried to tug Andrew away.

"This is going to turn nasty" she said, urgently. "Come on let's walk away very smartish, on this side of the road."

"No, no...what could happen here? There are policemen all over the place. Nothing's going to happen." Terry grimaced at his innocence. He insisted on walking calmly across the road, among the growing crowds of concert people, and standing patiently waiting for a taxi, letting others push ahead of him.

It only took one short-tempered concertgoer to push things over the edge. As a taxi pulled up, and a stout matron and her husband clambered out, this young man hauled on their arms in his impatience...perhaps he was trying to help them, perhaps not...and said "Come on, darling, let's be having you". Her husband, aghast, and perhaps misunderstanding and perhaps not, pushed the young man quite hard, and he fell back against the youth behind him. This youth pushed him forwards, and he cannoned into the matron, who fell against her husband.

Tempers frayed, hot words were hurled about, and the crowds gathered around the incident, each faction egging on their heroes and trading insults with the opposing force. It might have remained as an isolated incident of mixed drama and farce, had not a van pulled up outside the Hall at that moment and disgorged half a dozen toughlooking men in casual but immaculate dress, with PFP tattooed on their foreheads.

They waded into the fight without stopping to ask questions, and several concertgoers received damaging blows. Thereafter, things got more confused and much more serious. Terry dragged Andrew to one side, towards three policemen who were standing watching and doing nothing. She tried to drag him past them, but he stubbornly refused to move.

"Look what's going on there! Go and do something about it!" he harangued them. The oldest constable looked at him with mild reproof.

"I don't think we need you to tell us our business, sir; you just move yourself along there, keep safely out of the way, and get yourself home, sir."

"But it's turning into mob violence look!"

"I don't think so, sir; just a few young lads teasing some of the druggies from the free concert, sir, that's all. Just high spirits. That's what I see anyway, sir; lads, is that what you see? It is? Well then sir, there you go. Now you go home sir, before I have to do something about you wasting police time. That's a good gentleman."

The fighting was actually diminishing now, but Andrew could see several bloody noses and several people limping or clutching their faces or arms. He wrenched himself out of Terry's grasp and went to offer help; he was rebuffed in every case, quite rudely in some cases. Terry came across to get him.

"Come on. We're not wanted here. We're going home."

Back at Victoria Mansions, Andrew strode about the flat, convinced he should telephone the Commissioner of Police in the morning and make a formal complaint against the officers. Terry, who was more used to London life and the attitude of the Metropolitans concerning young people in general and young people gathered in crowds to sing or dance or demonstrate in particular, could not believe his lack of understanding, or his belief that a complaint would achieve anything.

"You've not been much involved then, in this kind of thing? Thought not. Look, forget it. It's not worth pursuing, believe me. Nothing at all will come of it. And had you considered that they might just have been following orders? Come on, love; will the guardians of public order be more on the side of the People for Purity, or on the side of a crowd of bopping young people, half of whom were probably mildly stoned? Well? Whose side do you think the Commissioner would be on?"

"But it isn't a question of sides; it's..."

"Oh, please. One day, I must drag you kicking and screaming into the nineteenth century."

"The twentieth."

"The nineteenth will do for a start. We'll try the difficult stuff later! Now are we going to get packed, or what?"

They packed, left a note for Callum, and took a taxi to Terry's flat. There, they packed most of her things, made a few goodbye phone calls (Terry lent her flat to a delighted cousin) a call to Branson Pullman and a call to Isa in St Fillans, and settled down in front of the television for some winding-down before going to bed.

The late night news did not let them wind down.

There was coverage of the Albert Hall rally, and more extensive coverage of the Usher Hall rally, at which Albert Kennedy was performing to a full house of enslaved adoring people, wringing their souls with his description of the carnage in the Church of St Andrew that morning, and his searing indictment of the depths of depravity in all who broke the public peace and the private joy of simple family life. The drunks, the drugged, the muggers and the buggers and the murderers and the rapists, the extortionists and the blackmailers, and every kind and class of criminal and lowlife, were all wrapped neatly into a package and delivered for extermination. The audience were invited to gasp with astonishment at the public service and devotion of Frankie Dunn, who was sitting on the dais on the platform, his head in his hands, those selfless, serving hands so newly washed clean of the blood of his father-in-law-to-be.

"Take back the streets. Take back the night. Take back the sweet family life we all want. Drive the evil ones out! Drive them from the cities! Drive them from the face of the planet!" The news programme cut him off, there, and switched to the audience in the

Albert Hall, hushed, rapt, watching the video wall on stage, which was carrying the live satellite pictures from Edinburgh. Albert's voice boomed out, exhorting them never to forget the sacrifice of the great, murdered, martyred Reverend Peter Spencer; and not to let his death be for nothing.

The feed now switched to live coverage of the crowds leaving the Albert and the Usher Halls. They were elevated, shiningfaced, enthralled. Andrew moved to switch off the set in disgust, but Terry's scalp told her the main story was only just about to break, and she prevented him. As they watched, as the cameras tailed the crowds along the streets, they saw mayhem begin.

The camera crews followed in their cars, as groups of PFP people chased late night revellers and party guests, assaulting them when they caught them. They moved on, baying for blood, loosed from all constraint for they were holy warriors, they were cleansing the streets, and anyone they caught up with was savagely beaten. The news presenter's voice faltered as he kept up a commentary, giving any details relayed to him from the camera crews, his eyes on the monitors on his desk. Couples walking homewards in both Edinburgh and London, even respectable looking couples, found themselves surrounded and hit. Any young men the crowds happened upon received far worse treatment. It was very evident that not all the PFP people were young, or male; there were people of all ages and descriptions doing the beating. It was a bizarre sight, as well as a horrifying one.

The end of the programme was scheduled for ten-thirty. At ten-thirty-five, the presenter turned his shocked face to the studio cameras again, and announced that the programme was now over, but more coverage would be given in a special bulletin later on.

"Well?" said Terry. "Did you see any policemen in amongst any of that, trying to stop it? Any squad cars? I didn't."

"I'm phoning the Prime Minister in the morning. This is disgraceful. He must do something about this."

"Oh, I think probably he already has" said Terry, very softly. "Who do you think controls the Commissioner of Police, my darling?"

They did not stay up to watch the later bulletin. There was nothing to be gained from it, and anyway the papers would be plastered with reports tomorrow morning, which they could read at their leisure on the train.

But once aboard the train and comfortably seated, when they opened their morning papers they found very little indeed about last night's "minor disturbances". What they found was that every newspaper was carrying very large amounts of copy on the imminent destruction of every cat in the land.

'My, my, bloody Frank bloody Ainslie. You're smarter than I thought' said Terry, to herself.

CHAPTER EIGHT

The talk on the train was all of cats...pet cats, zoo cats, wild cats, feral cats. The conductor on the Pullman, the clients in the dining car, the waiters, everyone, everyone greeted each other with "Terrible about the cats, isn't it?" or variations on that theme.

"I heard it on the radio this morning" they went on, or "I just caught it on breakfast telly" or "It was in The Times/The Sun/The Daily Star" or any other medium. Very little except a major war had ever caused quite such blanket coverage excepting, of course, for salacious tidbits about politicians or superstars. War, sex, and pets; the British obsessions. The dwindling power of the pound on the international markets, tucked modestly away in single column endpieces, occasioned no comment.

(In the rarified confines of the Pullman, expressions of dismay were civilised and restrained; this was not the case in any of the towns or villages through which the Pullman raced northwards. Most people started the day off feeling confused; they could see the necessity for the roundup, but/and they hated it. This conflict being too difficult for the average person to handle, they sought a nice, easy, prepackaged attitude which they would feel more comfortable with, and they found it anywhere there was a People for Purity chapter...in short, they found it all over the United Kingdom.

"S'disgusting, innit? Bloody government; if they'd of got their act together in time, this wouldn't of 'appened. Bloody poofters; they brought it in, you know; oh yes. Poofters and druggies and slags and blacks; effing Marys, every bloody one. S'a known fact, that. S'their fault all right; them an' the nancy Government. I don't care what party they are, they're useless. Poor little bleeders, all them kittens and such. What 'uv they ever done to us? It's the bloody poofters and druggies and slags and blacks wot they want to put down, that's what I say."

If enough people say the same thing often enough, it becomes accepted as the truth: if not intellectually, then still, certainly, in the

269

gut.   Those who normally referred more to publications like Scientific American, or Nature, or even Omni, for scientific verification of any current theory, found it impossible that month to find any copies of these publications in their newsagents, and those who had taken out subscriptions were informed with regret that obtaining American publications was out of the question for the moment owing to some international printers' union dispute. British titles were readily available; they contained nothing which would confirm or deny the origin of the new mutated virus. They showed a surprising tendency, at this time of heightened national interest, to run features on new strains of brewer's yeast, or the algebraic fractals inherent in the more primitive ferns indigenous to Korea.

In any case, a spirit of scientific enquiry tended to slouch when faced with a distraught wife or child, cuddling the family moggy and howling in distress.

"Poofters, druggies, slags and blacks" were so convenient to hate; they were not 'like us', and could therefore be hated with impunity, as no members of one's family were likely to be included (and if they were, one could probably do without them tolerably well).

People for Purity meetings became regularly overcrowded, spilling out of city hall and village hall alike. As the coloured and black members withdrew, more and still more white people filled their places. But we digress, we go too far ahead; back to the Pullman, and Andrew, and Terry.)

"I wish we'd met some other time" said Terry, putting down her fifth newspaper and demanding that Andrew did the same. "I wish we could have just been... in love, and happy. Doing something simple. You being a doctor, for instance, tending to little cute pies with measles and chicken pox, and me away through in the kitchen, baking bread in the Aga, wearing a Laura Ashley frock and with nice friends coming round to dinner that night. And people able to walk home on a pleasant summer's evening without licenced yobbos beating them up and then nobody giving a damn the next morning because some ratfaced little shit like Frank Ainsley has coordinated this so bloody well that everyone has, by now, forgotten it."

"When has there been a time when everything was all right, do you think?"

"Well...from the end of the Second World War till now."

"Nonsense. Maybe there was nothing that affected you, personally, but there has always been hell on earth somewhere, and some of it here in Britain. Look at us; we're unemployed but we've got no young kids to support, no mortgage to pay, and money in the bank. It isn't like that for most people. AIDS isn't something that's come along to spoil a nice party. It's just another hellish part of life, for most people. Life is very, very hard going for the majority of people in the world, including here. You and I have just been lucky up till now, that's all."

"I suppose."

"And if you think we're badly off now, you and I, think about some of the people directly affected. They're dying; we are merely inconvenienced. We're still lucky, when it comes down to it."

"You're right. Of course you're right. But still...I am afraid that we will never have a normal day again in all our lives. The kind of day you look forward to when you're growing up; safe, warm, in love, at peace. I don't believe there's going to be much of that in the years ahead for any of us. Gut feeling. We're going into a long tunnel...and the light you can see at the end of the tunnel is the light of an oncoming train."

Waverley Station in Edinburgh was fresh and clean in its new privatised colours. Multitudes of people thronged the main concourse, admiring the little shops with their individualised wares, taking advantage of the cafes and pubs.

There was almost an hour to wait till their connecting train to Perth; they dragged their baggage with them into the Cafe Complet.

"I'm suffering from trainlag. I want FOOD!" said Terry, loading her selfservice tray with chocolate croissants, ham-and-cheese crepes, and petit pains and butter pats and apricot jam.

They took a large cafetiere, with a jug of hot milk, and staggered

271

to the marble-topped table where they had deposited their suitcases. Another set of suitcases was crowding theirs; this couple arrived within a minute. It was Jan van Elsen and his wife.

After the requisite surprised-and-delighted smiles and nods and words and introductions had been effected, van Elsen quizzed them gently about their resignations, which he had been 'very sad to see' in the newspapers.

They were as unforthcoming as they could get away with politely, and he tactfully dropped the subject.

"So what now?" asked Mrs van Elsen, in a softly accented voice.

"Are you on holiday now?"

"Oh, forgive me - how did the fishing go?" asked Andrew.

"Most enjoyable, thank you. Salmon are really magnificent fish; both to battle with and to eat afterwards. Doctor Douglas, we only have a few minutes here; may I telephone you some time this week? I would like to talk to you at more length than is possible now."

"Of course" he answered, pulling one of his business cards out of his wallet. "Delighted". The conversation now switched to holiday topics, like the weather. Terry's concentration wandered and lit upon two black gentlemen in the full, gorgeous Sierra Leone national costume but with wellworn leather briefcases at their feet, sitting drinking tea together at a table nearby. It was a table for six, and the cafe was crowded, yet they were alone.

Her hearing stretched and focussed on the tables around the solitary pair; mutters of "Bloody Marys" and "Take their bloody AIDS back home with them" were rising, to a level where the targets could not possibly avoid hearing them. Terry hoped they did not speak English; she was embarrassed for them.

A young Asian man wearing British clothing jeans and a t-shirt brought his coffee and croissant to the table for six, and sat down to eat. He nodded and smiled to the Sierra Leoneans, and said "Good afternoon" to them, in a standard Edinburgh voice. They smiled slowly at him, saying "Good afternoon" back in very cultured accents. The watchers looked on.

"Lovely day, isn't it?" asked the young Asian man. The

foreigners, still not sure if they were being baited or not, nodded again.

The rest of the cafe was falling silent. Even the others at Terry's table were now aware of the atmosphere, and were listening.

"Staying in Edinburgh, then?" persisted the young man. One of the Leoneans replied "Yes. We have just arrived. We will be working in the Royal Infirmary, and are awaiting the person who will be here to meet us. This tea is delicious, and also the crepes we ate. We think we will enjoy your lovely city."

"His city?" asked one of the bystanders loudly. "That'll be right!"

"Yes, it's fine, is Edinburgh. A few morons here and there, same as everywhere. Some decent people as well, though. Doctors, are you?"

"Surgeons" one of them replied.

A young couple who had just paid for their meals and had been standing silent and still, watching this, started moving. They went to the table for six, and they asked if those seats were free, and they smiled and sat down and began to eat. They were white.

Two youths displaying PFP badges on their jackets sauntered lazily over to the table. One of them demanded the attention of the young white man.

"Colour blind, are you, sir?" he asked, pleasantly.

"Not blind at all" the young man blandly answered. "Not like some people, eh?"

He turned back to his food.

His lady was turning pale, but she smiled pleasantly to the two men from Africa.

"Did we hear you say you were surgeons? We're so pleased to have you, then; perhaps some of our waiting lists will get shorter now. Do you have a speciality?"

"Obstetrics" said one, and "Paediatrics" said the other. The two white youths looked disgusted. One of them turned and addressed the customers now ranged, carrying their food trays, along the walls.

"Well it's not goin' tae operate on any of MY kids, I can tell you;

or my wife neither. We want tae live!"

The obstetrician had had enough; he made to rise, but his companion stopped him. This goaded and frustrated the white youths. One of them pulled something white and oval shaped from his pocket, and handed it to the young white man at the table. He pulled out another and handed it to the young white woman. Pulling a third and fourth from his pocket, he handed one to his companion and donned the other himself; it was a face mask, such as cyclists sometimes wear, and people in cities with particularly foul air. But these masks had 'Free from PFP' printed on them, neatly, in the centre front.

"Dinnae you die of ignorance, pal" he advised the seated white man, who had tossed the mask away in disgust. "Them Marys are full o' T.B. an' AIDS. Ye cannae breathe near them, sir. It's no' safe. Nuthin' to do with racial discrimination, ye understand; jist common sense. Wan o' them sneezes; you die. Simple as that. Ye should try an' remember that, pal."

He and his friend, still sporting their masks, wandered away.

Andrew rose to speak to the Sierra Leoneans, but at that moment the London Express was announced and he and Terry had to shake hands and say goodbye to the van Elsens. When he turned again, the young surgeons were gone.

The veterinary surgery in St Fillans was run by a practice of four vets, three of whom worked with local farmers on their livestock, and one of whom looked after the domestic pets for the area. Sandy Allan, the 'pet vet', dropped in to see Andrew that first evening, for consolation and conversation. It was just short of eight o'clock when she arrived, and she was already drunk.

Terry and Andrew were tired and dispirited after their long journey and everything else which had happened recently. They did not really want company, but they understood her need for it, and offered her more whisky, and something to eat. She accepted the whisky and asked them not to profane it with water.

Sandy Allan was a very large lady, in all directions, and she had tremendous 'presence'. You could not fail to notice that she was in the room, however crowded that room might be. Her clients trusted her utterly, and she abused them regularly and roundly for overmollycoddling their pets, and they tolerated it because she loved their pets as much as they did, and was dedicated and devoted to the welfare of even the most unprepossessing specimen.

"It starts tomorrow" she said, downing half a glass in one gulp. "The supplies are all in...there's to be a van standing by to take the black bags to Perth to the nearest big incinerator. I suppose this was your idea, Andrew, was it?"

She toasted him laconically before downing the rest of the glass. "Nice one".

"No it wasn't; but I support it. It can't be avoided. You of all people must realise that; you know how quickly a virus can spread among animal populations."

"I don't care" she mumbled, holding out her glass for a refill, which Terry got her. "I don't think about it; I just feel about it. And I feel bloody awful. I spent all those years training to save their lives; tomorrow I start slaughtering them, the sick and the healthy alike. Murdering kittens. Murdering cats. Most of which will be completely untouched by this new virus of yours, Andrew. There hasn't been one case of it yet in Scotland, you know."

"Not that we know about, no. And it isn't 'my' virus, it has nothing to do with me."

"Oh no, right, yes, you, the Government AIDS man, nothing to do with you, eh?"

"As it happens, no. I'm not the Government AIDS man any more anyway, and it was the World Health Organisation which identified the new situation, and coordinated the worldwide action. Nothing to do with me; but as I say, I do support it."

"Well I can tell you, that's not how people in St Fillans see things. It's your virus, and it's your fault. Simple country folk like us are like that, you see; simple. Simply simple."

"Oh, great" said Terry. "We come all the way up here to get away from this kind of nonsense, and find you're Mr Popular up here too. This is going to be some holiday. Welcome to sunny St Fillans." She poured a large glass of whisky for herself and sat down heavily in her chair.

Andrew sighed. The two women were sunk in their own thoughts, downing his best Scotch like it was water, and saying nothing. He got up, stretched, went for a wander, through into the study. Out of habit, he checked his fax machine; there were three brief messages on it from Mark Tyme, saying that the band was playing the Glasgow Apollo next week as their last British date, and would be on holiday for a week after that before going to Germany to cut their new album. Could he come up for a day or so and talk? Would Andrew please phone him?

He tore off the messages, carried them through to show Terry, found Sandy Allan more or less upright and lurching towards the door. She peered at him through an amber fog.

"If I were you" she breathed "I'd stay home tomorrow" and she left.

He picked the mail up from the hall table, where he had left it. There was a leaflet headed 'Do you have a cat?' and he took it through to the lounge to read. It said:

"The termination centre for your area is St Fillans General Veterinary Practice, 3 Strontine Road, St Fillans. Reception times will be at 9am, 12noon and 3pm each day for the next four weeks. Please bring your cat or cats in secure containers. If you have no secure container, a suitable cardboard box may be obtained free of charge from either your local termination centre, or any main Post Office. Please do not give food to your cat for 24 hours before you deliver it for termination.

Be assured that the termination procedure is painless and instant. Your cat will feel nothing. Please remember that this procedure will help to assure the safety of yourselves and your children, as cats carrying HIV virus would be lethal to humans. DO NOT HIDE YOUR CATS. You would be doing them no favours by keeping them hidden, waiting to die in agony from the virus, possibly infecting your children. IF YOU KNOW OF OTHERS WHO ARE HIDING THEIR CATS, inform your local termination centre IMMEDIATELY. Do not allow these people to put your life at risk.

H.M. Government regrets the necessity of this action very deeply, but begs all citizens to show the fortitude and sense of responsibility which we know the British public always shows in times of trouble."

Yes, thought Andrew. It might be better to stay home, tomorrow.

———— • ————

The undertakers working for Gwendoline Spencer were finding it hard to find a slot at a crematorium for the Reverend. Cat carcasses were expected to keep the fires stoked twentyfour hours a day in a city the size of Edinburgh, for some time to come, and human customers were being turned away.

Eventually, they persuaded Gwendoline to settle for a burial in the new graveyard out at South Queensferry (the little Church of St Andrews at Corstorphine had no graveyard at all). It was surprisingly convenient, the opening of a new interdenominational graveyard, just in time for the feline roundup. Most convenient. Those few undertakers who were part of a national chain found that equally convenient new graveyards were opening up all over the country. Nice to see a bit of organisation, they said, among themselves.

Rumour had it that there were also plans for new crematoria all over the place too; now that would make life a lot easier. Actually, the undertakers could see a bit of an oversupply situation here, but better that than their current difficulties in squeezing their customers into shorter and shorter ceremonies at the crematoria, and more and more plots-per-acre in those graveyards still accepting new burials. Old Henry, their most phlegmatic embalmer, had already done the necessaries for the gentleman; he was unfazed by the business of putting bits together into a box, had already done that poor kid murdered a few weeks ago. Nothing bothered Henry. He was invaluable after a road smash. The only thing he wouldn't touch was an AIDS corpse. You could tell him and tell him that there was no danger; Henry would have none of it. So the younger ones, the trainees, stood in their white plastic moon suits and did the job.

Gwendoline had anticipated a service in the Church of Saint Andrews before the burial, and had expected that a minister from another church would officiate. But she had had to do battle with the sweet, soothing, sensible Albert Kennedy. He felt (and he was sure she would agree) that the vast numbers of People for Purity would want to do homage to their leader, and that a secular occasion would allow them to participate; somewhere capacious, he said, somewhere fitting.

Gwendoline was adamant: the church service. People for Purity could do what they liked, she said, but her husband had been a minister of the Church and would have a fitting send-off. The repairs would be completed in a week, she had been assured, and it was the right place, the only place, for his memorial service. What's more, it would be family and close friends only; not a political rally.

Flora was on her side and by her side. She had moved out of Bellevue Street, temporarily, and back home again. Radio Forth had given her compassionate leave. They had felt rather bad about the fact that Flora had learned of her father's death, had actually heard the explosion, through listening to the station. Lying there in bed, alone, hearing the awful reports continuing, Flora had avoided hysteria by going straight into shock. In this condition, she was able to sound sensible and levelheaded. The screaming was all going on inside her, deep inside her, and would have to come out eventually but for now, she was being strong and supportive for her mother's sake.

Frankie, too, was being strong and supportive. "A very present help in time of trouble" Gwendoline called him, and asked him to escort her and Flora to the funeral service. Frankie was humbly glad to be asked.

It was a strange time. The streets were unreal; in the summer sunshine, mellowing now into August, there were people openly

278

crying, carrying 'suitable cardboard boxes' with yowling contents. Pathetic queues formed at termination centres; most people had decided it was best to get it over with quickly, and over fifty per cent of the population of cat-owners had turned up at their local centres at nine am on the first morning. Having to go home again carrying their pets, having to see them again, stroke them again, only to try again later in the day, had been a difficult, a searingly difficult thing for most people to do. Anger against the Government for the ramshackle organisation of the event was growing; anger against the Marys was growing faster, for apparently causing the disaster in the first place.

Frankie had handed out face masks to all his staff, with a fatherly warning to watch themselves at all times. PFP volunteers had taken these masks round to most of the country's employers, to Personnel departments, urging that they be made freely available. Company doctors were inundated with requests for information on this; they went on denying that the masks would do any good, but were ignored.

The recently formed People For Purity Task Force used the masks to singularly chilling effect. For effeminately-dressed men, for young girls in flirty or vulgar clothing, or thick makeup, for coloured or black people, for young people dressed in dirty jeans who might be druggies, for all of these it was difficult to go out in public now. You might be just standing at a cash point, or sitting for a spell in the sun on a park bench; wherever you were, a small group of people was likely to form around you, all wearing white masks. It was unnerving. In the daytime, nothing else was likely to happen to you. But if it was night, you were attacked, silently, by the squad.

These squads became known as Cossacks, because they liked to make bloody Marys. Because of the danger of contamination from that blood, they tended to wear rubber gloves and plastic moon suits when they went out at night. Yet strangely, none of these attacks was ever reported in the media. Even stranger, no perpetrator of such an attack was ever tracked down by the police. On the other hand, the work being put into discovering the assassins of Peter

Spencer was quite phenomenal: the public demanded it.

The forensic chaps had established that a doubletiming mercury detonator had been used, which could have been triggered either by a timing device (and fragments of one of these had been recovered) or by a direct radio signal. They noticed, too, the expertise which had been used in the blast; it had been so carefully calculated to kill the minister outright while causing minimal damage around him. Why would any group bent on vengeance against PFP be so careful about the church congregation which was at the heart of the organisation? It didn't make sense.

The Edinburgh police were having a busy time of it; having used genetic fingerprinting to pinpoint the murderer of the young rent boy, they had thought an arrest and conviction would be swift and sure. But the bastard had disappeared; his mother had told them, tearfully, that he had sold his car, bought new clothes, but behaved otherwise quite normally... except that she suspected he had a new girlfriend (the police did not buy that one). And then he had just vanished. She had no idea where, or why. A man had telephoned him the morning of the day he vanished, and she thought Tommy had called him back, but she did not know who it was.

The cancelling of his insurance policies made it seem certain that Tommy Bain had planned the murder in advance, and intended using his insurance money to effect his getaway. Yet he had gone without waiting for the money to come through: very strange. The story had been told on Crime Night, there had been extensive work done by every force in the land, Interpol had been alerted, but Thomas Bain had vanished off the face of the earth. The police were not unduly worried: the amount of blood which had been spilled, and the amount of virus in that blood, meant that God would catch up with Tommy Bain fairly soon, even if the police did not. The file remained open.

Some of the younger men on the Force were perturbed about the new directives towards a softlysoftly approach to police work: it was being taken to extremes of inaction, and this was not why they had joined up. They fretted under the restrictions, and they objected (quietly) to being told to look the other way if well-intentioned groups of vigilantes such as the Cossacks were volunteering to do their work for them. Some of the more bigoted older officers were even joining in these fights, and not on the side of the defenders. Nothing was done about it.

The unwritten code of behaviour for situations where groups of whitemasked men were obviously frightening some lone person was that you walked straight past, as if nothing was happening. If that lone person cried out to you, you did not hear it. If bands of Cossacks were jumping on drunks, or flashers, or anybody, at night, you did not see it and you did not report it. It was all new and strange, and even the older officers, the less bigoted ones, thought it was all very wrong.

While enduring this inaction upon seeing members of the public humiliated, frightened and beaten by the Cossacks, the officers had further to endure a sad and upsetting duty which they were told to pursue to the hilt. This was the hounding and prosecution of anyone found concealing a cat. These tended to be the most isolated and vulnerable members of the community...elderly ladies whose cats were the only companions left...children, who found some hideyhole for their animals and fed them surreptitiously. The lonely, the ill, the strange and the unwanted, many of them clung to their cats as to life itself, offering pathetic photocopies of the Termination Certificates handed out at the centres as proof that Puss, or Chairman Miau, or Calico, had been duly despatched. Their premises were searched, their cats dragged scratching and yowling from the boxes under the sink (a favourite) or on top of the wardrobe, or under the bed, by the Reservists: the police were left to harangue and, in cases of physical resistance, arrest the culprits, who were often hysterical by now. It was a duty which every one of them would have avoided if possible, as it left the image of your friendly local policeman somewhat shredded when they were seen hauling some tearful wretch into their cars to be driven away and charged. It was not unknown for crowds of neighbours to gather around the police car, yelling abuse and sometimes rocking the car with the

281

police and the miscreant inside. The officers themselves found it odd that this was never mentioned in the media. It was certainly mentioned a lot at home, by their spouses and their children and their erstwhile friends, and not in glowing terms, either.

In short, it was a miserable time for every officer and not any better for the vets, or for the Reservists. But as anyone who passed an even mildly critical remark was invited to join the five and a half million unemployed as soon as they liked, very few criticised. The operation was expected to be largely completed inside a month; all that could be hoped for was that after that, the hostility and the shame would die down, slowly.

"But why, Frankie? I thought you were going to have a big oration, a big People for Purity meeting, your own eulogy for Dad?" Flora did not much care either way, but she was surprised at Frankie's news that the meeting had been cancelled. Frankie was hesitant, clearly concealing something.

"We just changed our minds, that's all. Must look to the future now, not to the past."

"But...?"

"Well it's Albert's decision, of course, not mine...well it's the Committee's decision really. I just go along with what they say. Just leave it, my darling, let's talk about something else, shall we? Have you decided where we're going to get married, yet?"

"No. I thought about a registry office, actually. But..well how would you feel about that? No, Frankie, wait a minute; there's something you're not telling me here, and if we're to be husband and wife there are to be no secrets between us. None. So talk. Please."

Frankie eased himself into Peter Spencer's favourite fireside chair, looking reluctant and sorrowful. He said that the truth of the matter was really no truth at all; that they were dealing with rumour here, but very powerful rumour, and though it was untrue it was so terrible that they must ignore it, not address it. Flora looked at him blankly. This did not sound like Frankie at all; it scarcely even looked like Frankie. There was something entirely new about him, a depth, a maturity. She wondered how long this had been growing without her seeing it, her being too sunk in her bereavement to see what was in front of her eyes.

"Look, it's your father's funeral tomorrow; can't we wait until after that before we go through all this? It's not fair to burden you with this awful nonsense when you've got to go to his graveside tomorrow and say goodbye to the man. It's not fair to him, either."

"You tell me now."

He sighed deeply.

"All right; but remember, I don't believe all this rubbish and neither should you. If I tell you, it's only so that you understand what's going on, NOT because I believe it, or Albert believes it. He doesn't."

"Yes, all right; all right. Tell me!"

"Well. You remember that murder of the lad who was a prostitute, recently... Alec Something, I think his name was? It seems the police managed to get a genetic fingerprint of the murderer." Albert's friends had proved very forthcoming. "Of course they won't say who it was; but whoever it was, they think he murdered your father as well. The guy has disappeared, you see; and they found some traces of Semtex in one of his sheds; he seems to be a farmer of some kind, out Penicuik way."

"Did he know Dad, then, when we were out that way ourselves?"

"They think so. Look, my love, I'd rather not go on. Honestly. Please."

"TELL ME!"

Flora's knuckles were white, gripping the arms of the other fireside chair. Gwendoline walked in, carrying a tray of tea and sandwiches for all three of them. She had lost a lot of weight, and her pallor was constant, and the dark circles under her eyes.

"Here we go: some afternoon tea for us all. Meat paste all right for you, Frankie? Flora's got a real passion for it just now. It was oranges, with me, when I was pregnant!" She smiled pleasantly, but her eyes missed nothing. "What's wrong, my children?"

"Nothing at all, Mum" said Frankie consolingly. "Just worried about tomorrow."

"Sit down Mum: Frankie has something to tell us about Dad and his murder." Flora briefly recapped what Frankie had already said, and insisted on his continuing. He evinced deep embarrassment, but agreed, reluctantly. The dead man's wife began to shake a little, again, but controlled herself well enough to sit down and look reasonably composed.

"The rest of it is pure rumour; vile rumour, I should say. I honestly don't think you two want to hear this. All right, all right; but remember, I did not want to tell you. They're saying that this farmer went to your Dad's church when he was a young lad, Flora, and that your father...oh God...it's not true, of course, but they're saying that he had some kind of sexual...that he turned this boy...you know. He turned him into a homosexual. He had intercourse with him, many times. I can't do this..." He hid his face in his hands. Flora's voice was trembling.

"Go on" she said.

"They're saying...the police think...that when this farmer had killed the young boy, he was so overcome with disgust at himself that he killed your father because he felt it was his fault that he had turned into a murdering psychopath. It's not true; of course it's not true; but somehow that vicious rumour has rippled all through People for Purity. And...there's some anger."

"Peter LOATHED homosexuals. Remember how he treated Gerry, Flora? He loathed them. He loathed them." The tremors were visible now, and Gwendoline felt herself on the brink of some deadly abyss.

"Of course he did, Mum! Like Frankie says, these are only vicious rumours! Surely to God, Frankie, people know how my father felt about these things?"

"Yes...but they're saying, you know, homophobia is one of the signs of a suppressed...homosexual. I'm so sorry, ladies. I'm so sorry." He rose and went to comfort Gwendoline. He sat on the arm of her chair and enfolded her in his arms and rocked her, looking helplessly at Flora.

"But the Semtex?"

"Well, yes, they did find traces of it at the farm, like I said. The police think he might have got it earlier this year, from the gangs that were widening the road near the farm; they apparently used it for blowing up trees. But my goodness there could be a million explanations for that, surely? Maybe he planned to blow up some shed, save money on proper demolition? Something like that?"

"But then why were there only traces there; there would have been a lump." Flora, too, felt herself tottering.

"Flora! For God's sake! You don't believe this do you?" Her mother was wild eyed. "You can't! Not your father! Of all the people in the world, not your father!" She whooped oddly, then gave vent to great gulping sobs, and collapsed, weeping uncontrollably, falling from the chair to the carpet.

Frankie tidied her clothing to retain her modesty, and waved Flora across to comfort her. He offered to call a friend, or an ambulance, but Flora asked only that he help her take her mother through to her bedroom, and then make some hot milk with a whisky in it. Flora had to put her own reactions on hold, along with all the other emotions swirling inside her, while she dealt with her mother's needs first.

The funeral, for 'family and close friends only', was not well attended. A very few members of the dead man's flock had not been reached and turned by the rumours so expertly set going by Albert and Frankie, and those few members turned up. Even they were there partly out of morbid interest, and from knowing that the television cameras would be around somewhere. The freshfaced young minister taking the service was surprised at the poor turnout. He had been expecting hordes, and he was disappointed.

His eulogy was inappropriate to the occasion; he had incorporated phrases like "a man beloved of thousands", but he could hardly deliver this to a three-quarters empty church. The smell of new wood put him off, too. He was not used to that, and it was a constant reminder that the last man who stood in this pulpit was now

285

lying in pieces in that coffin over there.

Being unable to give his planned speech, he had to busk it. He was not very good at this. There were certain things you could always say about a fellow minister, of course, and he more or less made up the eulogy he would have liked to have delivered by someone over his own coffin, the eulogy of an ideal and average Church of Scotland minister. It did not, therefore, have much to do with Gwendoline's husband, or Flora's father. The cameramen and reporters were as confused and surprised as the young minister at the poor turnout, and as lost for reasons why. The only reason given to them concerned Albert Kennedy, who had of course intended to be here but, as Frankie had explained, was ill.

Gwendoline alone saw that there were no other churchmen at the service, and she never forgave the Church as long as she lived. Whatever had happened to her beloved Peter in the last few months, he had given unstintingly over a lifetime, devoted to the Church and to God; this was a poor farewell from the organisation he had served so faithfully for so long. And the people he had served, also; so pitifully few of them there to give thanks for his life and his work. Gwendoline's heart cooled within her at that service. It turned (she felt it do so) from flesh to marble. Only Jock Dunn, sitting in his wheelchair at the front for a change, had tears running down his cheeks. Only he seemed to remember what friendship and love was about. Jock had always been a stalwart supporter of Peter Spencer: an admirer, even. He had scarcely missed a service in all these years.

She remembered so many services in this and their previous churches; so many upturned faces, listening, shining, joining their sweet young voices in the praise of the sweet Lord of All. So many children brought to Jesus by her husband, so many people helped. And now, an empty church and a murdered man to be buried, and no-one to care. She looked alongside her and saw Frankie take Flora's hands in his, keeping her safe. She would be all right. Gwendoline had nothing to leave her, as they had lived in manses all their lives and given any spare cash to the Mission funds. There was only the furniture, a few plates, some nice ornaments. But

Frankie was a good provider, that was for sure; she had no worries for Flora. It occurred to Gwendoline that there was not one single reason for her to continue to live. It would just be a question of waiting to join Peter in heaven. And it would be a new Peter, a cleansed Peter, her husband as he used to be, full of fire and vigour and love. Looking back she saw that this had begun to change at Roslin. She wondered why. She looked at Frankie. She remembered how specially kind Peter had always been to Frankie's grandparents, and the growing boy himself, how sad he had been for them at the running away of their errant daughter. There was a flicker at the back of her thinking, but she ignored it for it felt uneasy. She thought, instead, that it was meet and fitting that the boy Peter had so helped would now help Flora. Not all of the Reverend's good work, therefore, would have been wasted.

It rained at the burial site, and the few mourners huddled by the young saplings as if they provided some shelter. Only two camera crews were still with them, and they obviously felt as if they were intruding on a very small, very humble affair. This did not stop them getting some heartrending footage of the old man crying in his wheelchair, the rain and the tears dripping off his nose and his chin comingled.

———— • ————

The same rain was falling gently on Albert Kennedy and the tall, elegantly dressed man he had met last at Peebles. This time they were in Burntisland, a small town in Fife, just across the Forth from South Queensferry. They walked down by the breaker's yard at the harbour, looking at the decaying hulks brought here on their last voyages, here to have their proud hulls turned into scrap.

"The Good Ship United Kingdom of Great Britain" said Albert, without humour, as they passed one particularly fine vessel rusting with each passing wave, creaking her plates mournfully.

"Don't think of it that way; think of what the scrap is made into. Other ships, brave, new ships. Safe ships." replied the man.

———— • ————

At Terry's suggestion, Andrew had arranged for Mark Tyme and Jan van Elsen to visit him together. Each had readily agreed to the suggestion. Terry wondered how little St Fillans would react to the arrival of arguably the biggest rock star of the day, but she need not have worried. The Mark Tyme who arrived (early) sported a sober brown haircut and very ordinary clothes. Nobody recognised him, if anybody saw him. And van Elsen, instead of power dressing, had downgeared to tweeds on the flight to Glasgow.

A table had been set on the small patio at the back of the house; it was shaded from the sunshine, but showed off the garden. Pitchers of lemonade and sangria were there, and glasses, and plates of nibbles.

Perhaps it was natural courtesy...perhaps the warmth of Terry's welcome... perhaps their mutual interest...whatever it was, the rock star and the business tycoon met easily and quickly established a good working rapport.

Andrew had a vague, unformed plan to harness the powers of these two men, for they represented two major strata of society: the young and the business community. With their joint resources, contacts and influence, they could surely come up with something which would help. Help to do what, he was not sure; there was nothing to be done about the spread of T.B., which was already affecting hospital admissions in all major cities. They could probably do nothing to halt the chaos being caused by People for Purity. But just possibly they could influence enough people to slow down the spread of AIDS.

The conversation turned towards employment first; Mark was seriously interested in this, as it affected his fans directly.

"You know we started using the Wolfson circuit cards to test all our new employees" began van Elsen. Mark nodded. "You might be interested to hear that the rate of HIV positivity measured by the presence of HIV antibodies, not virus, that's the way these cards work, is one in twenty-three of all applicants." He nodded to their surprised faces. "That means, next year, perhaps one in twelve, *one in twelve* of our potential workforce unusable. Though the first collations are not yet in, we assume that this rate is roughly the same throughout the other industrial sectors. You will appreciate that our applicants are mostly, though by no means exclusively, young people. That will give you an idea of the current situation, Doctor Douglas, yes, Andrew, thank you, and I am Jan. We begin the routine testing of all our employees next month, and will be repeating the tests every three months after that."

"What is the median age of your applicants?" asked Mark Tyme.

Van Elsen smiled.

"How good it is to find someone who understands the difference between 'average' and 'median'! The average age is twentysix, but the median is around twenty-two. The cluster, if you like. Why do you ask?"

"Because we need to know how young the majority of people are when they get infected, so that we can target education to the age group below that" said a very un-rock-star-like Mark. "We get a lot of parents writing to Rock Against AIDS complaining that their innocent children are being handed condoms and sexually explicit leaflets, at our concerts. In fact the median age of our audiences is about seventeen, which is far from being innocent childhood these days. I just wondered if we should be looking at younger kids, for instance, maybe we should set up a pop group aimed specifically at weenyboppers, all handsome and wholesome, and use them to front an education programme? What do you think?"

"I think" said Terry slowly "That it's too late for all this. It's a good idea, but only if you can go back in time and do it ten years ago; then, by the time these people filtered into employment, they would be all right. As you can't do that; it's too late."

Andrew protested. "Surely not! No effort is wasted, it's worth saving any lives we can!"

"Of course" she replied. "But from Jan's point of view, it's still too late. Jan needs healthy productive workers now; and the group he recruits from is infected already to a level where in - let's see - a very few years time, he won't find hardly anyone free of infection.

One in twelve next year...maybe one in six the year after...one in three the year after that...then the year after that, bingo. Nothing. Nobody left who isn't infected. Not that the whole population of the country will be infected, but the particular generation needed to work, to produce; they'll be effectively finished. Waiting around, unemployable, waiting for AIDS or for dementia or for T.B., whichever comes first."

Each of the other three looked around the rest of the group, waiting for someone to gainsay this. But who could? It was true.

"This country's finished." Terry's voice was hollow. "The T.B. is increasing daily, and still no cure; it will affect bigger and bigger pockets of population. Did I say this country? Every country." She got up from the table and walked a little unsteadily into the house. Andrew went after her and found her standing in the study staring in front of her, unseeing.

"I don't want to stay here any more, Andrew. I want to go to the Ukraine, or Australia, or Canada, or any of these places they're offering a three months quarantine and an AIDS-free life. I can't take this any more. It's too late, and it's too much, and I want out." She clutched the back of a chair for support. "I want to live; I want to be happy; I want a kitten. But it'll have to be a puppy. No more kittens ever again.." she crashed down into the chair. "This bloody, bloody disease! What have we done?"

He hugged her tightly from behind and she dropped her head onto his comforting arms, but the tears continued to pour down. Van Elsen stepped gingerly into the room.

"Would you prefer us to leave, Andrew? We can easily do so, you know. We don't want to intrude."

"No: I'll be with you in a few minutes, if you would be so good as to wait for me. Please." Van Elsen nodded, and withdrew.

Terry continued. "I didn't tell you, but when I went to Isa's shop for the wine and things this morning, I got frozen out. She served me, but she looked right through me while she was doing it. Nobody said Good Morning to me. No wonder Isa can't manage to do your housekeeping any more; she'd be lynched. What kind of a life would it be for us here? They'll never forgive us for the cats. Never.

It may not be sensible, but when were people ever sensible? If they'd used a bit of common sense, we wouldn't be living in - living in hell, right now. I can't take any more, my love. I'm sorry."

For answer, Andrew just hugged her a little tighter, and kissed the top of her head. She smiled wryly. "I know, we can't talk about it just now; we've got guests. Forgive me. I think I'll go upstairs. Will you manage by yourself? Of course you will. We can talk later. Go on, Andrew, go on. I'll be fine."

She patted his arms, and he disengaged, watched her go from the room. He turned his troubled face to the patio, and rejoined his guests.

Before lying down on their bed, Terry switched on the television and kitted herself out with chocolates and a glass of milk. Using the remote control, she flicked through the channels, looking for something sweet and romantic. Some Fred and Ginger, with ostrich feathers and unlikely sets, and too much lipstick. That was what she needed. But not what she found.

She and Andrew had watched very little television since they arrived, and she was fascinated by the change in the kind of programming available. There were news bulletins here and there, but the news seemed very different to what she was used to. The foreign news, for example, was all about the great advances being made in building the strong, dynamic, vital economies in those countries whose names were becoming a familiar litany: Australia, the Ukraine, New Zealand, Canada. Van Elsen's company, ICI, was shown building new chemical tank farms in hitherto unexplored regions of the Australian outback, and great enthusiasm was being shown by the managers about the abundant sources of minerals and all kinds of raw materials. All they really needed were people, it seemed. The presenter recapped on the offers flooding in to Britain for families to relocate in these boom areas, and the substantial incentives being offered. She pointed out, with that kind of maternal sternness so beloved of Auntie Beeb, that although the British Government was willing to pay market price for emigrant's houses, it should be borne in mind that as the pound dropped and industry went into deeper and deeper slump, and more and more people were moving out of Britain, market prices for houses would continue to fall. The hidden agenda was only barely hidden: it was "Get out now, while the going's good".

Almost as an afterthought, and without much evident interest, the presenter finished by saying that Parliament had been recalled early from the summer recess, owing to the pressure of legislation waiting to be discussed. No details were available yet of this legislation, but a substantial cut in social security benefits was expected to be part of the package. Government sources had revealed that the amount of benefits being claimed was beginning to outstrip the amount of National Health and related tax income being gathered, and so some fairly drastic measures were necessary. The promised Privatisation Bill for the National Health Service was to be moved up, and most treatments would now be fee-costed, whether an individual was insured or not.

The AIDS Update, carried as a short after the main news so that you could switch off and avoid it if you wanted to, told of the fruitless search for drugs to treat the new strains of tuberculosis, and the continuing frustration of not being able to test any vaccines. Once again, it was made clear to the most unscientific viewer that a vaccine had to be tested to lethal dose first, either on massive quantities of chimpanzees, or equally massive quantities of people. As the chimp population of the world could not supply enough victims, and no human volunteers had yet come forward, the hunt for a vaccine was no further and not likely to get any further. Laboratories around the world were ready to go with promising preparations (mostly of deactivated HIV plus T-cell boosters of some variety, not exactly a novel concept by now) but without human testing the preparations were not usable. Raids on some labs were reported, by parents desperate to protect their children. The next and last item was an interview with a very proper lady, mother of four, who wanted to complain about the sexually explicit materials her children were being handed at rock concerts.

No, it wasn't very Fred and Ginger. It was exactly what would confirm her mood and her determination to get out of all this, away to somewhere clean and safe and civilised.   Terry rolled over, wrapping herself snug and tight in the quilt, and let herself be carried away by sleep.

She awoke in the twilight, abruptly, to the sound of breaking glass downstairs. In the lounge, at the front of the house, there was a big jagged hole in the window. In amongst the shards lay a large piece of rock. Andrew arrived behind her, and ran to the window just in time to see a figure vanish down the driveway, a male, probably, but in the gloom it was impossible to be sure.

Fred Hamilton came through from evening surgery and found them staring at each other wordlessly.   He saw the window, shrugged, hung his head a little and sighed.

"Nobody came to evening surgery tonight. Or last night. And nobody phoned for me to come to them. Not since the start of the terminations at the vets'. I didn't want to bother you..."

He waited, but neither of them spoke.   "There's a 24hour emergency glazier in Perth; I'll call him. Then I'll put the surgery kettle on and make you both tea. I'd appreciate a word, if I may." When he had left, Andrew went to the kitchen and returned with a handbrush and shovel.

"I'll do that" said Terry, quickly.

"No; you're not in any fit state. Go on, pour us a quick whisky each before we go through for tea and sympathy."

"Where are van Elsen and Mark?"

"Long gone. I'll tell you about it later - go on, whisky, please?"

She brought three, and they carried them through to Fred's consulting room. There was another consulting room, long unoccupied. Andrew had almost thought of moving in there again, fleshing out the practice. But perhaps he was too late for that. It was not sympathy which Fred dished out with the hot sweet tea; it was worry. He was apologetic about burdening them with his troubles, but things were coming to a head at home, and he had to do something.

"It's Stuart and Amy, my kids; they're getting stick at school because I work with the 'cat man'."

"This is ridiculous!" said Terry, but without surprise.

"I know. But it's happening all the same. And my wife, Andrew; she says she's beginning to find it hard going to make conversation with anybody. It's as if you are contagious. And we're becoming carriers of something very, very bad. Please believe me, old friend, this comes hard with me but I have to give you notice. I've hardly had a patient this week, and scores of people have asked for their cards every day. They'd rather travel to Comrie than walk a dozen yards up the road to this house. To be honest, the amount of patients we're losing, you won't be able to afford my salary soon."

Andrew still thought the situation was retrievable. Terry knew better.

"Look, Fred" he began. "There must be some accommodation we can come to; a holiday, perhaps? You must be due one. How about a month's holiday, till things blow over?"

"You don't understand, Andrew. Things aren't going to blow over. Not in a month, I doubt in a year, possibly never. You are irretrievably mixed up in the public eye with AIDS. With the death of an entire species from the whole world. With the killing of millions of family pets, most of whom were perfectly healthy. With the whole miserable mess...you've been involved, so it's your fault. Whatever happens next will be your fault too, as far as they're concerned. I'm so sorry that I have to go, but I do have to. And you have to let me."

They sipped in silence for a moment. Andrew looked at Terry with extra care, as if seeing her clearly for the first time. He smiled at her.

"There is an alternative, Fred, if you're interested. Terry and I will be moving on; would you like to consider buying the house and the practice combined? It's a fabulous garden for kids to play in. It's a fine house. And I wouldn't be asking a fortune...not from you."

Fred blushed with pleasure. His face, which had been wracked

294

with guilt, blossomed into relief.

"Are you serious? Well of course I'd have to ask the family how they felt about it, but...if the price was right, Andrew, I think you'd have yourself a deal!"

"Mmm" said Terry. "You could always disinfect the whole house after we'd gone, get the exterminators in, maybe? Recarpet and redecorate? We'll soon be completely unnoticeable, all traces gone, all fresh and clean and nice and respectable. That'll be all right then, won't it? My, my yes. You could soon pretend you'd never known us at all. Three times, maybe, before the cock crows." Her bitterness was crushing, and Fred blushed again, but this time with remorse.

Andrew got up and lifted Terry out of her seat by her upper arms. He was very angry. He walked her outside, through to the private part of the house, and to the foot of the stairs.

"I suggest you go for another rest. Or jump up and down and scream in temper if you wish; what you will not do is insult my guest, my partner and my friend. My loving you does not give you carte blanche to behave badly."

"He is rooking you" she said, determinedly.

He looked at her with pity, real pity.

"My god girl, the way you see things...it must be hellish to be you." He turned and left her, went back through to Fred Hamilton.

Tears ran down her cheeks as she watched him leave her.

"Yes it is, actually, at this precise moment" she said out loud. "It is fairly hellish to be me. But that still doesn't mean he isn't rooking you." She went upstairs, lay down again, facing the window, and watched the light die.

———— • ————

People for Purity had gone through a brief period of becoming a neoNazi organisation in which being white had assumed enormous importance, had then reached critical mass just at the time of Peter Spencer's discreditation and had now, in late August, fragmented into nothing. Without the modicum of restraint which PFP membership had imposed, those factions more disposed towards direct action (usually violence) had blossomed.

Those who leaned towards the pen rather than the sword had become equally noisesome; there was never a newspaper now without letters from the public and articles by journalists all of whom were convinced that the building of concentration camps for high-risk groups was the only humane and considerate thing to do.

"Think how these people are being hounded and abused by every sector of society" was the usual refrain. "They need a safe place, a haven, somewhere with people like themselves, where they can live with dignity and do useful work for whatever portion of life remains to them." A mixture of hospice and Butlins was portrayed, with nice remedial work like basketweaving available to soothe the poor frayed nerves of the poor frayed sufferers. It all sounded wonderful, even to some of the people who knew they would be first into the cattlewagons, but then again, who was going to fund it?

The Health Service was a shambles already, and had been so long before AIDS had increased the burdens on its resources. There was no fat surplus, no extra budget, not even a slim margin to draw upon, in the Treasury. And to increase the tax burdens and the interest rates in the depths of a recession would be murderous. So how could it be accomplished? Though there was no shortage of Disgusteds from Derby willing to push for the supercamps, none of them offered any sparkling suggestions on ways of resolving the financial problem.

Curiously, there was rarely any energetic reply to the paens of Christian solicitude urging the setting up of concentration camps. There was the occasional reply asking why the 'poor overburdened British taxpayer should provide such a soft option for such disgusting people?' But there was nothing in the way of truly liberal sentiment, or expressions of concern on the civil rights front. As Terry said: either the British public were awfully easily conned, OR the newspapers were arrogating to themselves once again their rightful position as absolute diktat of public mores, OR the Government had a hand in all this somewhere.

Personally she favoured the last of those three possibilities. And she resolved to find out if she was right. As a long-time journalist she had acquired the habit of always carrying her 'black book' of contacts upon her person, for without this any journalist is back to stage one, with years of work to catch up on. Other journalists do not look with favour upon one of their number who asks for a loan of their black book; Terry had therefore had hers on her when she and Andrew had resigned/were fired. In its depths there was the telephone number of a Detective Sergeant who had been a very useful source of stories in London when working for the Metropolitans, and who had transferred to the Glasgow force some two years back. She called him, pleading friendship and the desire for much gin-and-reminiscences. D.I. Charles Barker didn't believe her for a minute, but she had always amused and rather charmed him, and he agreed to meet her in one of Sauchiehall Street's more reputable wine bars on the last Wednesday in August.

Andrew drove her down and waited for her in a double room in the Central Hotel, not at all happy about his lady love being out for the night with someone else, with the avowed intention of getting thoroughly blitzed 'if necessary'. He had brought work of his own to do while waiting, as he had never been a man for propping up hotel bars, but it sat untouched on the desk and he spent his time gazing at the wallpaper, or looking out of the window.

Below him, on this August evening, he would have expected to see couples walking hand in hand, groups and families of people, people laughing and talking and sitting on buses, going to see friends, going out to dinner, going out for a drink. But the streets were half-empty, the buses few, the taxis very busy. He peered through the thickening gloom and saw the reason why: on every corner, two or three men stood silently, wearing Cossack hats. They scrutinised every passerby, but all the hour that Andrew sat in horrified fascination there was not one shortskirted girl or colourfully dressed young man or coloured or black person to be seen. To be harrassed. To be taken down the side streets and beaten up.

The Cossacks grew fretful as the evening wore on and they had found no victims. As pub closing time drew near, they started shuffling their feet and laughing, in anticipation. Yet when the pubs emptied, not a drunk could be seen. The people walked in straight lines, soberly, not shouting or singing, not fighting. They were mostly middle-aged people, all respectably and quietly dressed, and all in couples. All of them nodded deferentially to the Cossacks they passed.

Glasgow belongs to who?

A taxi drew up by the hotel door; two commissionaires rushed to usher the passenger inside. The new system was that the commissionaires paid the taxi, and retrieved the money from the grateful passenger, plus tip, in exchange for said passenger not having to stand fumbling for change while the Cossacks approached; two burly commissionaires, all known to be family men and irreproachable and having also some fighting experience, were more than the average two or three Cossacks would tackle. The passenger had been Terry; she was in the room five minutes later, and she was not smiling.

She gazed at the desk, her eyes taking in the sheets of notepaper headed "League Against AIDS" and the fact that there was nothing written upon any of them; and she saw Andrew flinch slightly and shrug his shoulders apologetically.

"Didn't feel much like working, tonight. I was thinking about you. How did it go?"

"I'm stone cold sober. Like everyone else was when they left the Vin Gogh. Nobody dares to get drunk any more. What the hell has happened to Glasgow? You told me about cheerful drunks patting little children on the head and giving them sixpence, in the old days. Well there are no cheerful drunks now. No drunks."

"I know; I saw the Cossacks all along the street."

She took her jacket off and slid out of her dress, turned the bath taps full on, got undressed as she talked.

"Weren't you supposed to be doing something tonight to fax off tomorrow to van Elsen and Mark Tyme? League stuff? I packed all your reference books for you to work from..."

"Yes, yes...och, I just couldn't be bothered. When I saw the Cossacks, it began to feel as if maybe it's too late for Leagues Against AIDS, whether van Elsen and Mark help or not. What you said at St Fillans; I think maybe you were right. It's too late. Things have gone too far."

"Good. You'll come with me then. To Canada, or Australia..." He sighed loudly. "Oh not tonight, my love, let's give that particular argument a rest for tonight, can we? Tell me how you got on with your policeman."

She wrapped a towel round her naked body and sat down again at the dressing table, creaming off her makeup. The peaches and cream of the decor made a jewel of her, with her peaches-and-cream skin tones and her blonde highlighted hair. He stepped behind her and stroked her hair while she worked and talked.

"Not my policeman, not any more. I've seen jobs change people, but not like this; he literally isn't the same man any more. He used to sparkle, you know? A bit of humour, a lot of sense, an intelligent man, ambitious. Now all he wants is to serve his time, retire early, and bugger off somewhere else. Like any sensible person." Her eyes met his in the mirror, meaningfully. "He hasn't an ounce of humour left in him. Nor hardly any personality to speak of. It wasn't just the business of the cats, though none of them much liked that. He's frustrated; he can't believe what's happened to police work; their hands are tied as far as the Cossacks are concerned, and THEY are taking over the cities. Of course it's not all bad." She turned, faced him, her face unreadable. "The crime rate is going down, sort of: if you stop classing muggings and murders as crimes. Drunkenness is slowing to nothing. You scarcely see a prostitute about on the streets, male or female. Muggings and murders by non Cossacks are almost eliminated, apart from the usual 'domestics'. I daresay the trains run on time, too." Her expression was bleak. "And the police can't touch the Cossacks, and the Cossacks know it."

She rose, walked through to the bathroom, turned off the taps, slipped into the steaming water. Andrew sat beside her and started soaping her back, absentmindedly.

"Thanks. So anyway...now that the Cossacks know they're untouchable, they've started branching out. A bit of the old enterprise spirit. You can guess most of it; extortion, so-called 'insurance' from shops; they've started erecting barriers across the entrance to some of the main streets when they feel like it, and they charge people money to get in. And out. It's like a checkpoint system; and if they don't like the look of you, you don't get in. Hm. If they don't like the look of you, believe me, you don't WANT to get in, 'cause you won't get out."

"How come we saw nothing of this coming here?"

"They haven't graduated onto the motorways and major highways yet...but they will. And so far they're only harassing pedestrians. They'll graduate to cars, though. Once they're organised enough. And that's the point...the organisation. Charlie said that things happen all across the country more or less together; not in a happenstantial, coincidental way, but definitely planned. And now that People for Purity has collapsed, who the hell is planning it? Who's running it? Charlie hasn't a clue. He says he's past caring. You ask about it, in the Force, and you get told to keep your nose out of State affairs."

"Nineteen Eighty-Four" said Andrew, rinsing his hands and drying them. "Only ten years out, after all."

She looked at him with great concern.

"I never heard you sound so weary before, my darling. I'm sorry; I've been rabbitting on."

"It's not you, love; never you. It's life. This country. Yes, I'm beginning to think you're right about getting the hell out of it. Once the sale of the house in St Fillans is through, and we've got the money, let's go."

Her reply surprised him.

"Not bloody likely!" she said, with considerable verve. "There's a story in all this somewhere, and I'm going for it. I'm not sure if I'm heading for the Pulitzer prize, or twenty years inside, but I'm going for it. And you're going to help." She rose from the steam and allowed him to fold her in the velvety peach towel. He lifted her out of the bath and deposited her on the mat, still holding her, looking down into her face. It was alive again.

"I'm going to help?"

"You're hired. Chief Assistant and bottlewasher to the gentry. And lover and friend and, one of these days, husband. And I promise not to put you on hatches, matches and despatches."

"Pardon?"

She smiled and snaked all over him. "Nothing. Take me to bed, minion."

So he did.

——— • ———

Edinburgh's budget for the Festival was even smaller that year. The notorious striped canvas, illuminated 'onions' were back decorating the railings along Princes Street Gardens again, to the dismay of both resident and visitor alike. These varicoloured monstrosities were lit up at night as if that somehow made them more attractive, despite the protestations of thousands, over many years, that it did not.

Scottish Opera was there, and Scottish Ballet, and the Covent Garden lot, and the Baroque Music Ensemble, and all the hordes of players and singers and dancers of music both esoteric and classical, from all over the world. The good burghers of Edin were usually fairly absent from the cultural gatherings, deeming them not only disgustingly expensive but also awfie boring; this year was no different. The Fringe, grown so that it was now four times bigger than the 'real' Festival, spilled out as usual into every conceivable venue and several inconceivable ones, from rooms upstairs in pubs miles from the city centre, to rooms in people's houses, with seating for almost a dozen people (few of which seats were likely to be filled).

Everyone assumed that the whole Cossack thing would be forgotten and out of sight for the period of the Festival. Everyone was wrong.

It began gently, with nudging of coloured or black visitors by people wearing the familiar white face masks. Then, over a few evenings, the nudging turned to mobbing, and the mobbing to beating. It mattered not to the Cossacks whether the victim was a tourist or a player; they were foreign. That was enough. Soon, even a French or German accent was enough to make you a target; the Cossacks were not racist, especially, just straightforwardly xenophobic.

A couple of days later, the Cossacks started invading concert halls, Festival and Fringe alike, and attacking any foreign-looking people who refused to leave. The police were called on every occasion, and on every occasion they were so late in arriving that there was nothing remaining to be done but ferry the injured to hospital.

Within a week the Festival was abandoned. The visitors went home. And the crowd loved it. Football fans started to demand that foreign players be sent packing - and they were. The few remaining American, Dutch and French oil executives in Aberdeen found reasons for moving back to Houston and the Hague and Paris in a hurry. Nationals of most countries, especially in the major conurbations such as London and Manchester, found themselves with sudden strong family reasons for heading home. As British nationals were bumped up into the new jobs, there was rejoicing. Settled Asian and black immigrants and their families moved into ever tighterpacked ghettos, and defended their streets...and still there was little or nothing about it in the newspapers, so that on the whole, the British populace was not aware of what was going on. Each person saw what was happening next door, and saw no further.

But Terry saw; she was too long in the trade not to be able to read between the headlines. And she was well able to extrapolate from the little information she had, towards a U.K. picture of intensifying isolationism.

The telephone is a wonderful invention, powerful when coupled with a journalist's little black book; yet she found it extremely hard to persuade old colleagues to talk to her at all, and none of them would fax anything to her or write to her or meet with her, even those who now worked in Scotland. She offered to fly down to London to meet people; they were all tremendously busy these days, and could not find the time even for lunch.

Only Flora agreed to see her. Terry's flattering comments on her performance during her last-ever radio programme had been a great comfort, and treasured; she would be delighted to help in any way. Flora was not on the news team, and had not therefore either seen the D-notice or signed it or even become aware of its existance and as for the R.D. notice, Clause 12 of Section 5, she did not know it existed.

She did not get round to mentioning Terry's call to Frankie because they had so much else to talk about at the moment that it hardly seemed sufficiently important to bring in to the conversation. There was their wedding, and their search for a beautiful country house, and now there was Flora's mother to be talked about. Gwendoline had thrown her daughter back to Bellevue Street, as Flora's presence did not lessen her grief or her mourning, and she thought Flora should be out there grabbing her happiness with both hands while she had the chance.

Though pleased to be her own mistress in her own house again, Flora was sad and sorry to think of her mother all alone in the manse until she could find herself a sheltered flat; Gwendoline had refused anything offered by the Church of Scotland and was determined to make her own way. But without funds, she was having a hard time of it, and the Church could not wait forever, with the new minister and his wife waiting in a modest hotel for her to vacate the manse. Frankie and Flora discussed it over a Chinese meal down in Stockbridge, in the same restaurant where she had first thought he might, perhaps, be courting her.

"There's nothing to discuss" said Frankie firmly. "She is very welcome to move in with us and Grandad, as soon as we're fixed up; in the meantime, why don't you have her to stay here with you? There's room; she needs a home. She needs you."

"She thinks she'd be interfering in our riotous love life" said Flora, playing with her food. "Of course she doesn't realise you don't come near me any more."

"You're pregnant!"

"I was aware of that, Frankie. It was me that told you, remember?"

His eyes narrowed very slightly.

"I meant.."

"Oh, I know what you meant; I'm not to be touched. I'm a plaster saint on a plastic plinth, to be worshipped 'cause I'm carrying your child. The problem is, Frankie, I still desire you. A lot." Her look would have melted mountains.

"Don't cheapen yourself. And don't come on to me in public; it disgusts me."

She put down her chopsticks.

"I'm too tired to care about you insulting me tonight, Frankie. You won't get a rise out of me tonight, any more than I will out of you, so to speak. Let's just pretend we're polite strangers, if you prefer."

He was instantly concerned. Was she tired? She could sleep in his arms. Was she afraid? He would protect her. Was she hungry? Was she cold? Frankie would provide food and warmth. Frankie would provide everything, down to her emotions, her thoughts, her friends and her enemies. And her family.

"We'll go straight home then, Flora, and you can phone your Mum and ask her to join us in the country. Then I'll tuck you up in bed and go home, let you sleep. I love you, Flora."

"Yes, Frankie. I know you do. I just wish we could sit and get guttered on red wine tonight, not hot milk. I daresay I'll get over it."

"When the baby's weaned, I will fly you to Paris and you can get guttered to your heart's content."

"Why Frankie: that's really romantic! I'll take you up on that. For now, I'll take you up on the hot milk and bed. You're right; I am tired. Thanks for caring, Frankie."

And he did care. He was rather proud of himself for caring. He did not suspect that his caring for her might not be quite the same once his son or daughter was safely delivered and weaned and capable of independent life. He thought it was real, his caring for her. He believed in it.

He was proud of himself later, too, when Gwendoline accepted their telephoned offer with thanks and happiness. Frankie was turning into a real family man, an honourable man. A happy man.

He kissed Flora goodnight, turned out the bedroom light, and walked softly down the stairs to his car. He drove to the street in Barnton where Albert lived.

The lift took him up the three flights to one of Barnton's most prestigious modern flats, built along Georgian lines and to Georgian proportions. Were it not for the newness and cleanliness of the plasterwork, you would have thought yourself in the New Town, Edinburgh's immaculate Georgian heart.

Albert's taste ran to the antique and the valuable, and the place shone with the subdued gleams of old oak, soft leather, rich gold and exquisite crystal. The thick washed Chinese carpet was in tones of gold, primrose, white and turquoise, giving the room a Louis Quinze atmosphere. It was sumptuous. At least the lounge was, and the bathroom; Frankie had never seen more than those.

Albert watched Frankie with an unusually quizzical expression as he poured his guest some ancient, crusty port from a crystal ship's decanter, into a crystal glass. Frankie would rather have had a pint of beer in a tankard, but would never say so. Port fitted much better into Frankie's vision of the fitness of Frankie's place in the scheme of things to come.

"Cheers" said Albert, sitting down to relish his port in comfort. "How are you doing, Frankie? How's the beautiful Flora? Good, good. And the troops?"

"They're doing fine. They keep asking for more money, though; I've given them some, so I'll need to recoup that from you. The PFP money is all gone, long gone."

"The whole two million? Surely not."

"Well, most of it; I've kept five hundred thousand in the current account, for emergencies."

"I do hope, Frankie, that there's no creative accounting going on here; not you, dear boy, of course not; but the troops. You do seem to have a very high-living brand of Cossack working for you. Other commanders don't seem to need quite the same level of funding. Is there something you could do about that, do you think?" The implication and the threat were very civilised.

"I daresay. Aye. It could be done. I'll just need to crack the whip a little."

"Good man. Those above us may have plenty of money, but all the same they are not to be regarded as a bottomless pit of gold to be plundered. You might perhaps remind your troop that they are supposed to be doing it for the Cause? Good. Now, to this evening's business. I have a cassette to play you which I think you will find interesting." He reached alongside him and switched on the machine. Frankie, expecting some kind of lesson in appreciation of classical music, affected attentiveness. But when Flora's voice came from the cassette player, the affectation became unnecessary.

"Terry!" said Flora's voice, in highly pleased tones. *"How nice to hear from you again. How are you both?"*

"Great" said a voice which Frankie only vaguely recognised, a female voice. *"Andrew and I were just talking about you the other day, about that radio programme...anyway, the thing is, Flora, Andrew and I are coming through to Edinburgh for a few days' holiday. Pity about the Festival...but still, we intend to enjoy ourselves. At the same time, I want to do a bit of journalistic digging into these damned Cossacks. Would you be interested in meeting us, and seeing if you could perhaps help us a bit? We'd be so grateful."*

"Of course I will; delighted. I did like Doctor Douglas. You give me a ring at Forth when you get here, and we'll organise some lunch. Okay?"

Albert switched off the player.

Doctor Douglas...Andrew...Andrew Douglas? Oh, the stupid bitch! And she hadn't told him? Then worse than stupid; traitorous.

Frankie's face was suffused with blood, with rage.

"Hold your horses" cautioned Albert, rising and gesturing for Frankie to calm down. "Flora doesn't know you've got anything to do with the troops, does she?"

"No, but.."

"So there would be no particular reason for her to tell you, would there?"

"No, but..."

"And if you say anything about this to her, she will know a) that you have somehow heard her private telephone conversation, and b) that there is some reason you don't want her to meet them and talk about Cossacks. Am I right?"

Frankie's breathing was harsh and laboured. But the burning in his cheeks slowly condensed to pinpoints of scarlet as he thought through what the older man had said.

"Yes" he answered, eventually. "So what do I do? You didn't play that to me for the good of my health. What do I do?"

"Cover yourself" said Albert crisply. "Douglas and his woman are getting too close. Make sure and drop into your conversations with Flora that you and I despise the Cossacks, that since the kindly and well-intentioned restraint of PFP has vanished, they're just a band of brigands. Shame, tut-tut, all that."

"I've already done that. She thinks you and I see each other out of friendship. Nothing more. She trusts me. Like I trusted her. Till tonight."

The death of Flora was writ large upon Frankie's countenance. Albert remembered nightmares he had had as a child after reading the Classics Illustrated version of Oliver Twist, and seeing Bill Sykes' twisted face as he murdered his Nancy. Albert swithered over interfering and not interfering, and knew his instructions but could not follow them.

"That lady would not betray you for her very life. It's perfectly obvious from looking at her that she loves the ground you walk on.

You'll never be more loved than you are by Flora Spencer, Frankie. You're a very lucky man" he said.

"She's let me down" replied Frankie, staring at the floor. "She's let me down."

"Rubbish; she'd die to protect you. You've just done a very good job on her, that's all. She really doesn't believe you have anything to do with the Cossacks, otherwise she'd have simply put off Andrew Douglas and Terry, refused to see them, said she was busy. I think you know her well enough to know that that is the truth. Women are wonderfully loyal, and Flora is an exceptional woman."

"Well. Maybe. I suppose you're right, again. Do you not get tired of being right all the time, Albert?" A note of warmth was de-icing his voice, and Albert relaxed.

"Good man. And just as well; there are plans afoot for you, Frankie, and they would suit a married man, a family man. In fact it would be essential for you." It was far too early to be mentioning this, but Albert knew Frankie's limitations on loving, and did not trust the defrosting of his voice. To save Flora it was necessary to remind Frankie how invaluable she was to him.

Frankie relaxed, as much as a cat ever relaxes.

"What plans?" he asked, smoothly.

"Ah" said Albert. "I can't tell you too much just yet, but there is a place in the sun reserved for a strongminded, dedicated man. A family man, with family values, just like Barbara Bush used to talk about whenever George was losing ground with the electorate. You're my candidate for it, Frankie; don't louse it up."

"A place in which particular sun, Albert? The Canadian sun? The Australian sun? Or maybe the Ukranian sun? Should I be going to night school to learn conversational Russian, maybe?"

Frankie enjoyed his moment of triumph. Albert was shocked at his commander's sudden leap of imagination, straight through fantasy into the truth.

"I...er..."

"Aye. I figured it out. Like I just figured something else out, Albert my old friend, my chum, my pal. You've got a wee crush

308

on Flora, haven't you? Don't let's waste time on denials, pal, I'm really not at all stupid. You've got the hots for my sister. And I'm about to marry her. Funny old world, isn't it?"

Frankie's voice was sugar sweet, and Albert felt the first drip of sweat fall from his brow.

"Now then" Frankie went on "Is there any more on that tape you want to play to me?"

Without a word, Albert switched the player back on and Frankie listened to a cascade of telephone calls all emanating from, or arriving at, Andrew's house in St Fillans. Van Elsen and Mark Tyme, Joe Cromwell and Fred Hamilton, and a dozen remarkably uncommunicative journalists were all there on the tape. Frankie listened in silence, eyes closed, nodding from time to time. When the tape finished he turned his gaze, his quiet, steady gaze, back onto Albert.

"Van Elsen's a real star performer, isn't he? He's got Douglas dithering down all the flowery paths imaginable. He's tying Mark Tyme in knots as well. I tell you what though, Albert: it's Terry Aitken we've got to worry about."

"Yes. That's why I played you the tape."

"No it isn't. You played me the tape to impress me, to make it clear that you have a lot of powerful friends; but I knew that already."

"No no; I meant it; you have to do something about Terry Aitken. At least I thought you might."

"Sure, Albert, sure I will, if you want me to. After all, you're the boss" said Frankie, rising. "Aren't you?"

CHAPTER NINE

Jan van Elsen tracked Andrew and Terry to Edinburgh via Callum. He telephoned them there on the night of their arrival for their short 'holiday', and asked Andrew if he might fly up from Heathrow on the morrow's redeye, to spend the day with Andrew and talk something over with him. As it happened, this was perfectly convenient, for the next day was when Terry would be having lunch with Flora, and she did not particularly need Andrew to be there.

"We're starting to get somewhere at last" said Terry happily as she dressed on Thursday morning. "Jan's obviously got something hot to discuss with you, and Flora's our best lead to that slimeball Kennedy. Today is the beginning of our Pulitzer Prizewinning series in The Guardian." She hugged him, her journalistic instincts taking over from her innate loathing of the subject matter she was pursuing. They breakfasted at a cosy table for two in the vast diningroom, and Terry's appetite (an infallible indicator of her general state of mind) was healthy. Terry had a built-in radar which detected any plans on the part of any hotel or boarding house to fob her off with anything which sounded remotely like 'Continental breakfast'. If offered croissants, she would ask sweetly that these be brought, hot, along with the bacon and eggs and sausages. And kidneys, she would add, and mushrooms and tomatoes. It was most unfashionable, and frequently brought sighs and eyes turned heavenwards by waitresses who anticipated trouble in the kitchen because the chef had not bothered to turn up for breakfasts for five years now, and the sous-chef used the early shift to catch up on his sleep.

Watching her fork up her usual large helpings, Andrew wondered if he could ever become so settled with Terry, so used to her, that her movements and her smiles would cease to be the delights they presently were. He hoped not. Though he rarely allowed himself to think of comparisons with Ruth, there was no doubt in his mind that his first love, his first marriage, had been a very different thing altogether; it had certainly been a mature and stable thing, a love built on companionship and similar interests, but it had rarely been as exciting, or disconcerting, as this. He meant no disloyalty to the shade of Ruth when he thought this; they had been happy and close and his grief when she died had been so real he thought it would last his life long. This new love which had crept upon him all unnoticed was almost an obsession: it was merry and sober and loving and sensual and deep; it was an all-encompassing love which he suspected few people were ever lucky enough to find outside the covers of romantic novels.

He had been so pleased when Terry's bleak fears and misery over the AIDS epidemic had been transmuted by her policeman friend in Glasgow into journalistic fervour; it had also helped to stave off his own increasing feeling of helplessness, of trying to put out a forest fire with a water pistol, or standing with his finger in the dyke while the flood waters raged over the top of it, drowning him along with the rest.

He kissed her farewell at the front desk and waited for Jan. The redeye from Heathrow...the taxi from the airport...Jan should be here before ten, and Terry was off to the Central Reference Library to research the last known details on People For Purity, as a background for her questions to Flora at lunchtime. Andrew sat in the Reception area and read a Scotsman, waiting.

Mid September can be beautiful in Scotland; Terry walked along Princes Street to enjoy the views of Princes Street Gardens, with the Castle beyond and above. She had passed three groups of Cossacks before she noticed she had not noticed them: nor had they noticed her, for she was sensibly dressed for a crisp early Autumn day, in suede trousers, matching tunic and a soft cashmere sweater, all in shades of turquoise.

The fact that she had not noticed them stopped her in her tracks, and she pretended to be admiring the view of the Castle while she collected her thoughts. Had the Cossacks become part of the scenery...already? She looked sideways at the pedestrians; none of them paid a blind bit of notice to the Cossacks, excepting for those who smiled and nodded affably at them. She looked closer at the people; it was a repeat of the scene in Glasgow when the pubs shut. There were couples, there were families, there were respectably dressed young people, and they were all white. There were no punks, no bikers, no lazing louts leaning on street corners (except the Cossacks). There were no men dressed in any of the homosexual call-sign clothes; no little gold earrings in the left ear or the right ear, to denote preference or services offered. None of the women wore makeup, none of them wore short skirts. She tried to find a word which fitted everyone and could not; you would have to use several. 'Asexual' was the first that came to mind, followed by 'white'.

It was like wakening up to find you were taking part in a play, and nobody had given you a script or told you what the plot was. She felt weird, displaced, and slightly panicked. She listened to the passersby, and her alienation was increased; everyone sounded impeccably British, and nobody was arguing. There was scarcely a disagreement to be heard; when someone proposed a point of view, their companions hastened to assent. And she had been wrong about people not taking notice of the Cossacks; if you looked closely, you could see all eyes darting constantly to these guardians of public morals, seeking approval, seeking anonymity.

The only thing which seemed normal was the noise of the traffic; yet when she focussed on this, gratefully, even that was different. It took a few moments to pinpoint what that difference was: it was the absence of horns. She watched the cars, and saw that it was not a play she was living in, but an old Government film from the fifties, a promotional film about good manners on the road. She saw a car duck into a bus lane, and she saw two Cossacks detach themselves from a shopfront a few yards ahead and walk in front of the offending car, and wag a remonstrative finger at the driver, very politely, and she saw the driver mouth 'sorry' and pull back into the proper lane, without a cheep, and all the other car drivers waited and let him back in.

But no, looking across the street to the shopping side of it, no,

t was not a film from the fifties, it was from some science-fiction
horror of civilisation's decay: almost every third shop had 'Closing
Down Sale' banners screaming across the windows. Those shops
had a trickle of customers busily going in and out: the others had
hardly any. The recession was biting deep, here.

She wandered on as far as the Mound, where she had to turn up
to the right to reach the library. But by then she had seen that even
some of the major chain stores, Boots and Littlewoods among them,
were closing down. She walked up past the two art galleries which
housed some of the world's finest pictures, and wondered what
pictures would be painted of this time, this place, these people. She
was no artist, but she wanted to paint a portrait which would last;
she would use words.

And how many people would there be left to read them, these
powerful words of hers? It didn't matter. Just a few would do, as
long as they were of mixed sex and could start the whole pointless
experiment off again. It was not going to be a series of articles for
The Guardian: at the back of her mind she had always known that
they would not, now, be able to print what she wanted to write. The
stamp of the D-notice was everywhere. No, not articles; a book.
A book that would last, that would prevent the progenitors of the
next generations from being so criminally stupid ever again. Yes.
That, she realised, was what her life was for (if you believed in that
sort of thing). It was something she could do; not something to stop
what was happening but perhaps, just perhaps, something to stop it
from ever happening again.

Now this, this book, was something worth living for. Somewhere
between her blacker moods and her highs was a serious-minded
woman, intellectually alert and unusually well-informed; this was
the Terry who had been an outstanding investigative journalist
before the Government had lured her to Downing Street. This was
the Terry who walked into the Central Reference Library; the Terry
who walked out again later was the cute, happy, friendly Terry who
would have a nice lunch with nice Flora from nice Radio Forth - and
pump her dry.

She arrived early at the Baroque, and treated herself to a red wine spritzer while she waited. Flora arrived a few minutes later, saw her, waved, walked across the room and had a man with her. He was tall, blond, elf-thin, grey suited, with an almost visible magnetism. Terry was hardly aware of hauling her stomache in and setting her shoulders down and straight; Frankie saw it immediately, and so did Flora. Flora merely grinned, inwardly. She was perfectly sure of Frankie.

She did not even mind when she saw Frankie hold Flora's hand for just longer than was absolutely necessary, when she introduced them; or when she saw that Terry did not pull her hand away, but waited for Frankie to drop it. She did not mind any of it, for she and Frankie were to be married the next week and they had just secured a dream house in the country, with ten acres of grounds and a separate cottage for the staff. She was almost entirely happy that day, was Flora, with only the unresolved and unreleased grief for her father still firmly tamped deep down inside. She was feeling magnificently pregnant, even though so far her belly had swollen so little she could still wear all her normal clothes. She was aching to wear the maternity clothes Frankie had flooded her with money to buy, but she would not do so until after the wedding. The wedding gown was a standard size 16, her usual size: nobody could guess, from seeing her in it, that she was pregnant. She would have a lovely wedding. And then a lovely life.

Pregnancy was dulling Flora's normally lively curiosity and energy; all she wanted to do was crochet little bonnets, and think thoughts of babies and teddies and sweet yellow potties that played tunes when Baby widdled in them. She was driving Frankie crazy, she knew, but he understood about pregnant women and humoured her whims...he would make a wonderful husband, and together they would make whole dozens of wonderful children.

It takes some women that way, pregnancy. No point in bitching about it; when the hormones shout their orders, the body responds and so does the mind. A similar undesirable state of hormone-induced behavior was fomenting in Terry, at that lunch; but not the bovine torpor of pregnancy. No; it was the straining, blushing ache of desire.

314

She was fighting it down with every ounce of intellect at her command. She did not like this man, and had not trusted him since she clapped eyes on him: a man like that, a man with such power about him, such smooth manners and such an obvious sexuality, a man like Frankie was never to be trusted. There was a slight cruelty about him, too; and dammit, it was exciting. While they chitchatted around the menu, she reminded herself that this was a Neanderthal reaction to power, this sexual attraction to a man who would hunt and kill successfully to protect one's offspring: that this reaction had no place in a civilised society, for this was not a civilised man. She had known too many women who had suffered at the hands of uncivilised men with winsome smiles, and (apart from Charlie) she had never fallen into the trap.

But oh dear, this trap had jaws of velvet-covered incisors...

And he kept smiling at her, knowingly but with a veneer of pretence, a veneer of politeness, enough to save her blushes.

Almost.

While they waited for their food, Flora smiled serenely and assumed Terry would forgive her for bringing her fiance, for said fiance knew more about People for Purity than she did, and she didn't want to disappoint Terry (for which, read, could not actually be bothered talking about anything much at the moment). It had been Frankie's idea, in fact: such a helpful man, wasn't he?

I just bet he is, thought Terry, smiling and nodding affably.

"My Flora told me how supportive you'd been to her at that broadcast" said Frankie, pulling a breadstick out of his mouth with shockingly blatant suggestiveness. "Any friend of Flora's is automatically a friend of mine." He pushed the breadstick back through his moistened lips, and the room temperature went up five degrees around Terry. "So you fire away with your questions, and I'll do what I can for you."

"Um...about Albert Kennedy" she began, and had to clear her throat. Flora smiled encouragingly.

"A very fine man; I'm proud to know him" said Frankie humbly.

"He's taught me a great deal about morals, about family values. I mean that; I do."

He slid the last morsel of breadstick into his mouth slowly, his eyes fixed on Terry's. She cleared her throat again and continued.

"Well let's see...ah, would you mind if I recorded this chat? I always carry a Walkman Professional with me, habit of a lifetime—and I always forget to bring a notebook." She smiled self-deprecatingly, just as if she couldn't see immediately that Frankie knew perfectly well that a taped interview would save her from being sued by him later on for misrepresentation. "I'm not researching for an article in the papers, actually" she went on "This time, it's for a book. A book about AIDS, and how it's all been handled, worldwide but particularly in Britain. And your Mr Kennedy has been very much involved in all that, hasn't he?"

"Now that's a real shame, Miss Aitken, that you're not doing a piece for the press. Because I had a scoop for you; quite a good one, as it happens, and I held on to it when I heard Flora was having lunch with you, because I always believe in returning a favour. You cheered up my Flora after a very difficult programme, which she certainly handled very well...so I thought I'd give YOU this scoop by way of showing my gratitude. Still, if you're not interested in that sort of thing any more, I can just phone up the Scotsman..."

She knew if she took the bait she would, somehow, be suckered; but she couldn't resist.

"No, no, not at all, Mr Dunn; I would be delighted, of course I would! What is it, this scoop of yours?" She brought the Walkman out of her bag and switched it on as she talked.

Flora was watching them from some far distant shore where fluffy rabbits bounded around in long grass studded with wildflowers, and a chubby baby sat chuckling merrily to see the fun, while his adoring mother stroked his baby blond hair and smiled sweetly.

"I am very proud to announce the birth of a new political force in this country; a new political party. We are launching nationwide as from right now, and we will be contesting every by-election till the General Election rolls round again. By then, we should be able to field candidates in pretty well every constituency. What do you think of that, Miss Aitken?"

"That rather depends on the party, Mr Dunn. What it's for. What it stands for."

"I do wish you two would call each other Frankie and Terry" pouted the pregnant one. "It's much nicer."

The food arrived, but only Flora seemed to have any appetite.

"So tell me about this new party, Frankie; is it People for Purity, again?"

"Not at all, Terry: or hardly at all. We would anticipate that some of the more responsible people from the PFP would join us, but it's not for Cossacks, or any other kind of hooligan."

"And the name?"

"The Moral Majority"

"You're kidding" she said, with a laugh in her voice, before her brain had time to stop her mouth from opening. The hardness of his glance turned her knees to jelly.

"I am not, actually. Perhaps your slick, cynical media friends will laugh at something which sounds so simple and homespun."

"And American" she added, helpfully.

"And American, and none the worse for that, I think. It's the right name."

"It's a rightwing name" she retorted.

"Not at all; it's just a name. It describes what we're about. We intend to try something really new in this country. It's called democracy."

"These potatoes are soooo buttery and delicious" said Flora, and returned to her meal, her social duty done for the moment.

"I'm not entirely with you" said Terry, hesitantly.

"I don't doubt that" and he smiled and her knees melted again. "But I'm serious all the same; when did the people of this country really have a say in how it was run, do you think?"

Honesty compelled her to reply "Never".

"There you go. We'll be offering something really new and really different; the chance for people to affect governmental decisions."

"How?"

"By a cascade referendum system. Whenever a motion is tabled for the House, the M.P. will send details to his constituency team and it will be circulated to ten people, each of whom will send it to ten more, who will all send it to ten more, and so on; it will take only a few days for every voter to be reached. And every one of them will vote on the issue and send that vote back to the person they got the information from, and they'll collate their ten and send it back along the line, until the M.P. has an actual democratic decision - the people's decision - before the House sits. And then he uses his vote according to the wishes of his electorate. Now what do you think, Terry?"

"What about emergency debates?"

"The same system, but by telephone."

She considered for a few seconds, but was extremely impressed and saw no reason to hide this.

"It's brilliant. Simple, effective...maybe a bit expensive?"

"No. According to the research results, people will do their bit for nothing, and even pay for their own postage; it's only ten stamps a time, so it's not exorbitant. Or ten local telephone calls. And for people on limited income, we will cover expenses."

"It's like all essentially simple ideas" said Terry slowly. "Once somebody has thought it up, you can't believe nobody thought of it before. It actually sounds like democracy. The voice of the people."

"And would you call that rightwing, then?" he teased her.

"Hardly. It's not any wing. It's unique."

"He's clever, isn't he?" asked Flora proudly. "I knew you'd find all this interesting. Anybody else for pudding? Oh, you haven't eaten a thing, either of you! I don't know...politics, politics, that's meat and drink to Frankie these days, isn't it, dear?" Her pride was luminous. "Tell her the really good bit, Frankie, go on!"

Terry raised her eyebrows politely. Frankie dropped his head modestly and shrugged.

"Och he's too shy; well I'll tell you. Guess who the first candidate's going to be? That's right: my Frankie."

"Which constituency?" asked Terry.

"Glasgow East" he answered, without inflection.

"Easterhouse? Bandit country! Surely there's more Cossacks there than ordinary Moral Majority type families: is that ideal for you, do you think?" Terry was surprised at the choice.

"It's available: Tom Sheddon died two days ago. And as for, 'is it ideal?', well, forgive me for saying this quite so simply, but you really haven't got it yet, have you, Terry? It doesn't matter what constituency it is, or what kind of people live in it. Does it?" He waited while she digested this. And saw the light dawn on her face, and saw that she found that light very, very cold.

"Dear God, you're right; it doesn't matter a damn, does it? Because it isn't a political party at all; not like one with policies. You've actually managed to dream up a party which is literally all things to all people. You don't need policies, do you? In fact they'd be a drawback. You are offering people a direct line to Westminster, for all their own personal views and ideas and... you can't lose, can you?"

The smile on the face of the tiger was a wide smile.

"No, we don't think we can, either" was all he said.

"And...you're going to be nationwide right away? Fight every by-election? You'll be able to force a general election in...months. Won't you? And then, if you can actually fight every seat...you'll...you'll fill both sides of the House, won't you?"

"We believe so. We hope so. It's time that government really was by the people, for the people. That's what we offer. And we'll have no difficulty fielding enough candidates to fight every seat, believe me. We already had a national network of decent people, in People for Purity. That had to go by the board, for some very unpleasant and difficult reasons, but the moral force it created is out there, still waiting to be used. Waiting to serve."

Terry gave a small wry smile. "And you? You want to serve...Frankie?" She managed to subtly inflect it so that it meant you want to serve Frankie, Frankie? And his answering smile was almost warm.

Jan van Elsen picked Andrew up from the hotel just before ten, and drew him into his taxi outside. The driver already had instructions to take them to Edinburgh Castle, and in minutes the two men were standing on the battlements looking out over the stunning view of Edinburgh. Not far below them, just beside Waverley Station, was the Baroque winebar. Just down and to the right of them, though out of sight, was the library Terry would be using right now. Andrew felt close to her and it relaxed him enough to ignore the small group of Cossacks idling by the sentry box.

"I'm glad to see you, Andrew, and looking so well too! Are you enjoying your holiday?"

"Hmm. I'm enjoying spending time with Terry, but being on holiday doesn't actually suit me too well. I've never been good at holidays...always fidgetting for something to do. It used to drive Ruth - my first wife - up the wall. How about you, Jan? Things getting any better?"

Van Elsen turned and faced inward, looking over the Esplanade, his face turned away from Andrew's.

"No. Well yes, they will be much, much better, before very long. But as they are now they could hardly get any better, could they? They could only get worse. That's what I want to talk to you about, Andrew."

"Something I want to say to you, first, though, if I may; I'd say you're about to talk about the League Against AIDS...you and Mark Tyme and me...and propose some thing for us to do. But I've been doing a lot of thinking, recently. Terry was right. It's too late to achieve anything worthwhile. This epidemic is continuing to increase whatever we do. It will continue until...I don't know. Till all those who are going to get it, get it. Or maybe the virus will mutate into something harmless. It happens. Either way...I'm sorry, but I don't see the point of trying to swim against the tide any more. I want out. Out of the League. Out of the whole ballpark." He was still facing seawards, still gazing far, and he stayed there to hear van Elsen's reaction.

"I agree" was the surprising reply. Andrew turned to face him. "You do?" he asked. Van Elsen smiled.

"I do: that's exactly why I needed to speak to you. And I'm glad to hear that you hate being idle, for what I am proposing will mean a great deal of work for you, and very worthwhile work at that."

"He wants us both to move to Australia" Andrew told Terry later that afternoon, as he opened the door of their suite and found her wrapping herself in a huge bathtowel. For once, he scarcely noticed her state of undress.

"The crazy so-and-so is moving the whole of ICI out of Great Britain, and taking every worker who wants to go with them, and their immediate families, and splitting the new operation between Australia and the Ukraine!"

"And no, I can't tell the press? Is that the next bit?" Terry tugged her impromptu negligee around her so as to look properly professional when she sat on the edge of the bed to blowdry her hair. "I mean, I presume this is all off the record for the moment, as it hasn't been in any of the papers yet?"

"Oh. I never thought to ask..."

"Fear not; it shall not drop from my lips. But wait till I tell you what IS going to be on tonight's newscasts, my love!" Her eyes were shining, and she opened her mouth to continue, but he interrupted, standing up suddenly and starting to pace the beige velour carpet.

"Wait, wait, I'm not finished; you don't seem to have taken in what I said! The whole of ICI decamping from Britain? Over six thousand workers, and their families, moving out in one fell swoop? What kind of example is that to set the rest of the country? I asked him that; he said, the only example left to set, for a responsible employer. He said, the country's finished, done for, no hope of recovery for so long that it would be criminal to stay here and rot."

She shrugged. "Sounds fair enough to me."

He ignored her. "I asked him, what about their grannies and cousins and friends and so forth, and he said, you won't believe this bit, he said every worker was entitled to bring not only their immediate family - spouse and children - but up to four blood relatives as well, and that's supposed to take care of the grandparents problem. Good god, it doesn't BEGIN to address the problem! I said that to him; he said, that's where you and Terry come in. He wants me to be some sort of Medical Director for the new settlement town in Australia, and you he wants you to set up the town press and media! He seems to think that if we go there and do that, then people won't HAVE any major problems because I'll keep them all healthy and free from trauma, and you'll keep them happy and amused and informed. What a neat little package, eh? Two of us to keep two and a half thousand families from going stark raving mad, finding themselves in some frontier town a million miles from home. The man's crazy! Crazy!"

Terry stood up, dropped the wrap, and started picking out clothes from the wardrobe.

"Crazy like a fox, as they say. The blue or the shocking Schiaparelli pink? Or the green? Or...okay, the pink." She pulled on her lingerie. "Van Elsen knows what he's doing. And after all, you and I have both been saying this country is finished for some time now. You can hardly disagree with him."

Andrew was getting really rattled. "Oh, I can disagree with him, and I do! Individual rats deserting the sinking ship is one thing; deliberately taking out huge numbers of healthy productive workers, when the country needs every penny it can get in tax revenue, is something else altogether. You must see that?"

She pulled the shimmering pink silk upwards, fastening it at her shoulders. "What tax revenue would that be, then, my darling?" she asked, all innocence.

"His workers! Their tax revenue!"

"I didn't know people paid Income Tax on their Unemployment Benefits but perhaps I'm wrong. Or have you forgotten all he said about the company hitting the skids because of shrinking world markets, an incredibly weak pound, and a diminishing workforce? Or maybe I just imagined all that? Or maybe I didn't; in which case ICI might go to the wall inside the year. So I say again; what tax revenues?"

322

Andrew sat down heavily on the bed. "It can't be that bad. Not yet. Surely."

"It can be and it is, and it's getting worse by the day. Have you read the financial sections recently? I have. The pound has plummetted way down past its European floor - again - and is so low at the moment they'll have to devalue. And put interest rates up. Again. More companies going bust, more mortgage repossessions, more unemployment...more every kind of misery. And, of course, more AIDS and more T.B. I can hardly wait, myself. Sounds yummy." She dragged his evening suit out of the wardrobe and thrust it upon him. Reluctantly, he started to change. "And now may I please, pretty please, tell you what you are missing right now on the radio and television news? Seeing as how it's my scoop, I did think you might just possibly be interested."

He was. Very.

Later, at dinner, she was fretful.

"I want to celebrate. My first media scoop in YEARS and here we are in this mausoleum! I want wine, song, champagne and laughter. I want you to tell me I'm wonderful, and support my head on your shoulders when I get blind drunk. Can't we go out to play, Andrew? Like, now?"

"Great idea; you get drunk, we get beaten up by Cossacks on the way home."

"Rubbish; anyway I bet I could get us into the Press Club - it's only just round the corner from here in Rutland Square, you told me first time we came here, remember? The commissionaires could come and walk us back to the front door, and we could get as drunk as we like! Oh come on, Andrew; let's live a little before we die! It's very historical: got great precedents (unlike America): look at the Middle Ages and the Black Death and all the dancing and drinking and general mayhem that went on then!"

"This is a singularly bad idea, but if you want to...okay."
She leaped to her feet, walked round to him and planted a big kiss on the top of his head before dragging him upstairs for their coats.

The Press Club was buzzing with talk of the Moral Majority. Mature gentlemen in rumpled clothes were propping up the bar, shaking their heads while carefully cradling their beers and whiskies with all the expertise born of long experience. Cub reporters and sub-editors and editors and assistant editors were all there, and the place was more crowded than was usual for a Thursday night. Terry was swiftly recognised and lionised, sat on top of the bar and poured more than half-full of drink. She was absolutely at home here, and Andrew was absolutely out of things.

"A toast!" cried one plump and mellow fellow, with the ruddy cheeks and the broken veins of a devoted toper. "A toast to the lady who brought us the first real, actual news we've been allowed to print for about six months!"

"Hooray!" came a ragged cheer, but most of the journalists were looking worried and trying to shush the toper. He was having none of it.

"Oh, get a grip, laddie! She's still got her NUJ card! She's one of us!"

"No she ISN'T" insisted one of the shushers, trying to wrest the man further back in the crowd, away from Terry. "She's one of THEM, remember?"

"Oh yes, so she is..sorry boys." The toper lifted himself heavily from Andrew's shoulder and was borne away.

"One of WHAT?" Andrew asked himself silently. He moved towards the front of the crowd, suddenly concerned for Terry. She was sitting on the bar top still, swinging her legs and looking quite absurdly glamorous in her shocking pink silk dress and matching satin shoes. Very 1950's, he thought in passing, and was horrified to realise that that was forty years ago, almost half a century ago, before she was even born.

She was regaling her audience with stories they could all identify with, stories about stories, stories about people impossible to interview and others all too eager with nothing much to say, stories about lying in wait like a paparazza in long grass for dramatis personae, stories about editors who cut all the interesting wellwritten bits and left only the bare bones of a beautifully fleshed tale.

Andrew looked round covertly and observed two gentlemen whose clothes were not in the least rumpled and whose demeanour was, though extravagantly casual, stone cold sober. They were smiling and nodding as if thoroughly entrained with the rest of them, raising their glasses and shifting from foot to foot and thumping the table and cheering...but they were not drinking. From time to time they spoke a few words to each other; Andrew walked casually over to stand close behind them. In that position he could not see the significant glance they exchanged when he arrived.

"Look at the legs on it" said one of them, in a stage whisper.

"Sexy little piece, isn't she?" agreed the other. Andrew became restive.

"See them legs of hers?" enquired the first. "I hear she's still opening them for that geriatric bastard Andrew Douglas."

"What, the one who got the Government to kill off all the cats? When they were all perfectly healthy? That bastard?"

"All the cats except his own little bit of pussy, up there on the bar...yeah, that Andrew Douglas."

Andrew's left hand was already curled into a fist, and he drew it back now to club the speaker nearest to him but it was caught and held by a short man in a dark brown tweed jacket. This man looked meaningfully at him, and shook his head warningly before nodding it in the direction of another man, taller and fatter, who was now standing, holding his pint, beside the two sober strangers.

"Starting to believe your own smear campaigns now, chaps? Bad sign, that. Like film stars believing their own publicity." He shook his head sorrowfully.

The two sober men visibly relaxed, and Andrew felt a small stir of fear. He had seen only one other man relax when challenged: that man was a black belt in Shotokan karate, and he had minced his opposition without blinking. The incident was far back, in medical student days, but it had never left him.

"Away home and climb in bed with your teddy bear, sonny; you're out of your league here with the grownups. Piss off, eh?"

said one of the sober men. Their challenger smiled.

"You don't frighten me, Clem: not with all these people around us. And not a microphone or a notebook in sight. Or any of your friends, except Clem 2 here. Or are you Clem 2? You two are so...interchangeable. Faceless. Pointless. Do your mothers know what you do for a living, boys?"

"At least" said the other sober man "we do SOMEthing for a living. Which is more than you'll be doing, come tomorrow." Their challenger laughed in his face.

"Too late, Clem, too late; I'm off to pastures new in a couple of days. Australia. New life, new land, and...not a Clem in sight. Must make your fingers itch, you two, to think of all the countries where you don't have any power at all. Must...gar you grue, to use a traditional Scots expression. Puir wee laddies. Only got a wee playpen. And now the big boys are going somewhere else to play. I just thought I'd come and say goodbye, Clem, and thanks for all the Attlees."

This whole bizarre conversation had been conducted sotto voce, too softly to carry as far as the bar; Terry was still holding sway, and at that moment the crowd roared with laughter. The two sober men chose this instant to kneecap their challenger, each man aiming a perfect and strong kick at one kneecap so that both legs buckled, broken, and the man fell to the floor in agony. Before he had time to scream, however, one of the sober men fell beside him and did something to his neck which caused him to lose consciousness. He then straightened up and shouted: 'Jeff's passed out again! We'll take him home, you lot carry on, okay?'.

The crowd, their attention fixed on Terry, made hardly a murmur as the two men heaved the unconscious man up and hustled him out of the door between them.

There was not a ripple left in the crowd where a brave man had been, seconds before. Andrew looked around for the short man who had caught his swinging fist, expecting him to have disappeared as well but he was there, and his face was drawn, just for a second; then, it lit up again with pleasure and bonhomie and drunken goodwill.

326

"What the - what was - ?" Andrew began. The little man in the brown jacket pulled him aside, back to a quiet corner of the room.

"It's time you knew. Jeff was trying to tell you; that's why they shut him up. He'll wake up in a hospital bed tomorrow, having apparently been mugged on his way home, too drunk to remember. He won't say anything. There wouldn't be any point." His face was still jolly, but his tone was dry and cold.

"This is criminal!"

"Quiet man; there are more Clems about here somewhere. And nothing's criminal if they decide it isn't. Look as if you're enjoying yourself, if you can. Laugh at your lady's jokes; you don't have to listen to her, just laugh when they do. And listen to me."

The little man joined in some general laughter, and Andrew endeavoured to do the same, with limited success.

"That's it. I'm John, by the way; you're Andrew Douglas, yes, I know. Keep drinking, Andrew. Keep smiling. And ask me any questions you want, only we'll have to make this quick or they'll be on to us. And I like my kneecaps facing the front, myself."

"I'm completely lost; I don't know where to begin. What to ask first. I don't know enought about what just happened to know how to frame questions so I'll get answers I actually understand!"

"Okay. I'll talk you through the principal points first and then we might have time for a couple of questions before Miss Aitken starts to miss you and comes over here. Right? Right. Jeff was one of the good guys; those kneecapping bastards are the bad guys, the Clems. The Cossacks of the media. The thought police."

"Why 'Clems'?"

"Clement Attlee. You heard Jeff say, thanks for all the Attlees? Okay. If a story is Attleed, it's got to go in the paper whether it's true or not."

"I still don't understand."

"I'm not surprised. It's a bit convoluted, but it makes sense when you get there. Attleed: reverse that, you get Delta more or less. Delta is.."

"The Greek letter D."

"Correct. You know what a D-notice is, I presume? You must,

with Terry Aitken as a friend. Well, guess what a reverse D is...that's right, a story which MUST be printed. A D-notice means you mustn't print it, an Attlee means that you must. So: Attlee: Clem. It's childish. A silly in-joke among newspaper people."

"Why did they do what they did to Jeff?"

"Because he used the words Clem and Attlee in front of you quite deliberately. Those two knew you were there: didn't you realise they were baiting you, with all that talk about Terry's legs? They were waiting for you to swing a fist at them, and then they'd have had you all over the front pages, drunk in a club with a drunken mistress. Discredited in the public eye, both of you."

"That wasn't worth him risking injury for. He shouldn't have..."

"He didn't; it was to make sure you'd want to find out what those words meant, so that you'd be sure to find out what's going on in Britain right now. Not that any of us know; but we sure as hell know something is happening. The press has never been so muzzled in its entire history, not even in the World Wars. There are Clems on every newspaper now, and in every newsroom, radio or television. That should make you worried. It worries the hell out of us."

"Are they not just keeping the more frightening stories out of the public gaze?"

The little man laughed outright, but the laughter had a desperate edge to it.

"Quite the reverse, my friend! The more death and disease, the more AIDS, the more T.B. the story has in it, the more certain it is to be printed! Every shop and factory that closes down, in it goes. Any new businesses starting up, forget it; good news isn't news any more."

"What sort of thing is Attleed, then?"

"Letters and articles that toe the party line, obviously. Stuff about bloody concentration camps in particular. You didn't think all those letters were really from the public, did you? The ones that say, give the AIDS sufferers a nice holiday camp to live in, free from persecution? They come straight from the Government Media

Office. All the articles about the brave new worlds abroad, and how the Government will buy your house from you to get you started...straight from the Media Office. Stuff praising those thrice-damned Cossacks, praising them while appearing to condemn them for attacking innocent people somewhere. Anything signed by Frank Ainsley - Terry must know him - that's automatically an Attlee. And you can bet it'll be on the radio and tv news too."

He drained his whisky glass dry. He was still smiling. Andrew offered to buy him another drink but the little man was nervous.

"Been nice meeting you" he said jovially and loudly. "Congratulations again on the scoop, please tell Miss Aitken. And enjoy the rest of your holiday!" He rose, patted Andrew aimiably on the back, and walked away, still smiling.

Andrew could see Terry's face wearing the signs of incipient collapse; he phoned for the commissionaires from the Caledonian, walked to the bar and waited a few moments until she swayed gracefully into his arms; carrying her Tarzan-style, to assorted cheers and encouragement, he walked out and was escorted back to the hotel. There was no chance of talking to her about all this tonight.

———— • ————

Nowadays Frankie drank beer, in Albert's flat. Albert still had his port, but this no longer impressed Frankie. And nowadays, Frankie was very much at his ease there. On the same evening that Andrew was having the hairs on the back of his neck raised in the Press Club, Frankie was sitting talking to Albert in the ornate sittingroom in Barnton.

"Are you sure she fancied you?" Albert asked.

"She was creaming herself for me" said Frankie, very relaxed and sure of himself. "Just like the effect Flora has on you, I suppose. And just as pathetically obvious."

His sneer caused the older man to cringe slightly. He had to ignore it.

329

"Okay. What I suggest, if you do feel that she's sniffing round too close for comfort, is that you pull her into the organisation."

"What? Are you losing your grip, Albert? Pull in the very person who's likely to...cause us embarrassment?"

"But she won't, will she, Frankie? Not if you persuade her smoothly enough... and not if she fancies you and you...lead her on a bit."

"Fuck her, you mean?"

"Well I didn't mean for you to...I mean...if you think it would help?"

"Sure. Tell you what, Al, I'll let you know what night I'm going to have her, and you can nip round and try your hand with the fair Flora. How would that be? Of course if you try it when she's NOT carrying my child, I'll kill you. But at the moment, well.." Frankie sounded magnanimous "...where's the harm, eh? 'Long as you use a sheath, of course. I don't want your mess on my woman. I don't want to smell you on her when I get home."

He pretended to peer at Albert's face with concern and care.

"No? Well then, I'll get you a girl you DO fancy, if you like. I have several, you know. And I'm sure you do know, even though I've never told you." He raised his eyebrows in polite enquiry.

"How young do you like them, Al old pal? Fifteen? Thirteen? Younger than that? No? What do you fancy then? A boy? No, you wouldn't fancy Flora if you were into boys. Go on, Al; have Flora. I won't mind. Honest."

The sweat was trickling down Albert's forehead again.

"I keep telling you, I don't fancy Flora. I don't. I like her and admire her, but I don't fancy her."

Frankie rose and stood over him.

"Why not? Are you telling me she's not fanciable? She's ugly, is that it?"

"No no, not ugly at all, she's a lovely girl. A lovely woman."

"So you DO fancy her then?" Frankie was enjoying himself. Albert sweated and swivelled in his seat trying to think of an answer that would stop this.

"Okay Frankie, I'll tell you. The truth. Whether you believe it or not is up to you." Frankie sat down to listen, head at forty-five degrees, all attention, smiling encouragingly.

"I don't fancy anybody. I'm just not that interested in sex. I've travelled most parts of the world in my time and when I was a young man, yes, I dabbled. I must have tried just about everything. Even you wouldn't believe what's available in some parts of the world. But after a few years, it all comes down to the same thing; an orgasm in some orifice or other. It all got to be just more of the same, after I realised that. And I lost interest. So I can honestly say that Flora, or any other woman, is beautiful or attractive - but it doesn't do a thing for me. Not any shape, size, age or sex. Not even my own good right arm. I'm just not sexually active any more, or interested in ever being so again. Now you can believe that or not: I can't make you believe it, even though it's the truth. It's up to you."

He sagged back into the depths of his chair, from the edge, and drank deeply of his port. Frankie was looking reflective, and when he spoke it was calmly and seriously.

"Aye well, there's something in what you say. I've felt a bit jaded myself from time to time. But..." he looked straight into Albert's eyes. "But: I got my appetite back, each time. If you do, and you look at Flora..." He hardly needed to finish the sentence. Albert started to breathe easy again.

"Fair enough, Frankie" he said. "More beer?"

"No. More talk. You serious about my getting Terry Aitken involved?"

Albert rose and poured himself another port, wiping his brow when his back was turned to Frankie, and imagining Frankie did not see this.

"I am indeed" he said. "And I think I have the perfect way of doing it. You're going to be an M.P. in seven weeks or so, my boy you could do with some media training. Facing the camera, doing interviews well, that kind of thing. And who better to train you than Terry Aitken?"

"And you don't think she'd be just the tiniest bit suspicious if

I asked her to do it?" said Frankie sarcastically.

"Oh she'll be a whole lot suspicious. But she's a born investigator that one, and she'll not be able to resist. Especially if she's got the hots for you. She'll know perfectly well that you'll be trying to sell her a bill of goods; but she won't think she'll fall for it."

"And you think she will?"

"Well, you said she was impressed at the setup, the Moral Majority cascade referendum. That's a good start."

"That and my body" grinned Frankie. "Okay, it might work; and I might enjoy making it work. It would amuse me to shaft the fiancee of the impeccable Doctor Douglas, especially when he finds out about it. And he will find out, because she'll tell him, she's the type. She'll feel guilty. I'll make sure she enjoys herself enough to feel really, really guilty."

Neither man even considered the possibility of Frankie's feeling guilty for betraying his beloved sister in the very weeks of their wedding and honeymoon. That kind of sentiment belonged to some other kind of human being.

Albert rotated his glass slowly in his hands, revving up to something. He spoke slowly.

"My friends and superiors...the people who back us..."

"The CIA" interrupted Frankie, grinning.

"The people whose organisation I cannot name...those people...they want to be very sure that neither Dr Douglas nor Terry Aitken will have any remaining credibility in the eyes of the public. They have to be disgraced."

"Why?"

"Because they are two very clever people, one with a background in medicine and one in journalism, and both spent years in politics. That makes them very dangerous."

Frankie shrugged and went to the drinks table, a beautiful black lacquered Chinese cabinet several hundreds of years old.

"I don't see what the problem is. Nothing they could ever say or think is going to be printed or published. No chance." He poured a large whisky into his pint glass and took it back to his chair.

"But they have such a wide variety of friends, between them.

People in power of various sorts, people who are not aware of our plans. People who might talk to other people and try to stop what we are trying to do."

"Then why don't we just get rid of them?"

"We may have to."

"Nobody would know; their deaths wouldn't be reported. There would be no fuss."

Albert sighed patiently.

"Their friends would notice. Even if it was disguised as the most natural of accidents, there would be some suspicion. That wouldn't matter if their friends were labourers or plumbers or...whatever. But they are politicians and public health administrators and journalists. So: no violence. They have to be kept quiet and kept well away from the truth, though."

"Bringing Terry into the heart of things is hardly keeping her at arm's length, is it?"

"Tut tut; you haven't been reading 'The War of the Flea' enough. The safest place to keep an enemy is in your pocket."

"Or in your bed" smiled Frankie.

Albert finished his port.

"Hmm. If your affair with her might break up her affair with Andrew Douglas, so much the better. United they stand...divided, they would be less of a problem. Mind you, once she's on the loose, she may be capable of causing more damage, without his age and experience to rein her in. And a woman scorned...is a dangerous beast to have on the loose. If you do seduce her, maybe you should keep things going with her for a longish time."

Frankie thought of Terry's neat little body, and mentally undressed her. He failed to become interested until he thought of Andrew Douglas being distressed, at which point more than his interest became aroused.

"Okay. Anything in the line of duty, boss. The sacrifices we make, eh?"

"Yees. That's something else I have to speak to you about, Frankie; the sacrifices. The girls you run, and your red file in your office...they'll have to go, I'm afraid. And no more incidents like Tommy Bain again. Ever. M.P.s can't be seen to be quite so...corrupt. Sorry."

"Christ, what's the point of having someone like Frank Ainsley out there looking after us if we can't get away with murder?" Albert walked across to the window, gazing down at the rooftops of Barnton and all the garden trees so golden in their September glory.

"There's been an increase in underground freesheets recently. They're stamped out pretty fast, of course, but still, it makes things like your covert operations a bit dicey. Most of these freesheets only reach a couple of thousand people before they're found, but a couple of thousand here and there... it's not safe, Frankie. And it's not worth the risk any more, not when you're about to be elected to Parliament."

"You're very sure about me getting in, aren't you? You got the ballot boxes being rigged or something?"

Albert turned, smiling faintly.

"Have more faith in yourself than that, Frankie. Have more faith in the Moral Majority. Remember what impressed Terry Aitken? You told me she said you couldn't lose. She was right." He walked to the door. "I'm going to the kitchen for some cheese and biscuits. You want anything? No? Okay; help yourself to a drink, then. Won't be a second."

Through in the gleaming galley kitchen, all mahogany cabinets and terracotta floor tiles, a heavyset man was listening to something on headphones. When Albert came in, the man nodded deferentially to him and removed the phones. Albert spoke in low tones.

"If he refuses to lose his subsidiary interests, waste him on his way home tonight. We can always use a martyr, but not a fool." He picked up the tray of cheese and biscuits and carried it away with him. The other man replaced the headphones and resumed listening to the sounds being carried to him from the microphone in the vase of silk flowers in the lounge.

——— • ———

Joe Cromwell, too, seemed to have a sudden urge for a day's break in Edinburgh. He telephoned Andrew the morning after the Press Club incident, and in tones of great bonhomie announced that he was pining for the old Alma Mater, and could Andrew see his way clear to spending a day of his holiday away from Terry, going round all their old boozing haunts? The bonhomie inadequately masked a tinge of anxiety in the Welsh lilt, and Andrew said yes, of course, what a splendid idea.

Replacing the receiver, he rolled over to see if Terry had been wakened by the phone call. She had not. The bedside travelling clock said tentwentyfive; he pushed her gently, kissed her ears and tickled her nose until she sputtered into some semblance of life.

"Oh" she whispered, as the hangover nibbled at her brain. "Oh."

"Pork sausages for breakfast, my dearest?" he enquired kindly. "Or lovely fatty fried bacon, perhaps, and some pale runny eggs?" She groaned and pulled the covers up over her head. He pulled them right back down again, and all the way off her. She curled up into the foetal position and groaned some more.

"Get me a doctor" she moaned. "No wait a minute, you're a doctor; DO something!"

He phoned room service and asked for two light breakfasts with plenty of strong coffee. While he was doing this, she pulled the covers back up and went back to sleep again. He gave up, showered quickly and was dressed just in time to let the maid in with their breakfasts. The maid looked over at Terry, looked questioningly and sympathetically at Andrew, and produced two aspirins from her apron pocket, which she handed him without a word. They smiled at each other, and she left.

He clanged the lid of the silver coffee pot as loudly as possible, and reluctantly she emerged from her cocoon to stare at him with blackcircled eyes.

"I don't feel very well" she said.

"You look a lot worse than that!" he retorted crisply. "Get some orange juice down you to rehydrate the brain, and then some of this coffee to stimulate you into some semblance of humanity. Come on."

"You didn't actually get sausages, did you?"

"No"

"Okay then, I'll risk moving a bit."

Every step, however gingerly taken, bounced her brain around inside her skull. She did not so much sit down as subside by inches into the chair, groping for the arms to steady herself.

"Oh" she said again. "Now there's an interesting little-known historical fact for you; Louis Quinze didn't drink alcohol."

"What?"

"If he had, he wouldn't have had these damn silly little chairs to sit on in the mornings. He would have had big soft stuffed ones you could disappear into and get back to sleep without anybody noticing. Do I really have to drink this coffee?"

It was over an hour before he could persuade her to venture forth into the September sunshine, and even then she was leaning on his arm a little more than was usual. They walked along Princes Street, down into the garden paths, and drank in the fresh air: a tonic for Andrew, torture for Terry.

"When are you going to be fit to talk to?" enquired Andrew. "We have to talk; there are things going on you'll want to know about, believe me."

"Give me till lunch-time, but don't, for God's sake don't give me lunch..." she managed. "I'll be all right by this afternoon. Can't we sit down on one of these benches so I can die in peace? Or in pieces, whichever you prefer."

They sat in the increasingly chill breeze, silent, their only communication an occasional tug on Terry's arm to stop her drifting off to sleep again, and her muted complaints about this. Then it got too cold to sit still, so he yanked her to her feet and walked her about the gardens till a suggestion of pink coloured her ghastly cheeks again and she started complaining with more of her usual verve.

"I'm FREEZING! You don't love me any more. If you loved me you'd take me somewhere warm and find me a teapot to curl up in. I want to go back to the hotel. I want..."

"I'll do you a deal: we'll find a cafe and I'll buy you an expresso and we'll talk in the warm, okay?"

"Yes boss."

They crossed Princes Street, hoping to find a cafe, but had to go up to George Street and down the other side again before they found a place which had not fallen foul of plastic and laminates. It was good to see an open coal fire, and white linen tablecloths and three-tier china cake stands festooned with roses and gold edging. Terry headed for the table nearest the fire, and they sat down gratefully. The waitress, in black top and skirt with a frilled white apron, took their order and retreated to the kitchen.

Though they were the only customers there to begin with, the lunch trade started drifting in almost immediately, and soon the little place was buzzing with people, chatter and savoury smells. Terry emerged from her hibernation and found it was, after all, very nearly good to be alive.

By her second expresso she felt able to tackle a scone and jam, and Andrew judged her ready to talk. Or rather, listen, and not fall apart. Or asleep. He told her about the Clems and the Attlees, and waited for her to show shock. She did not.

"I guessed something like that was going on. There's been far too much public assent recently in the letters columns, far too many people all with the same opinions. And the features...too much like each other. Oh, each paper's writers and subs churn it out slightly different, with their own flavour, but they're still essentially all saying the same things."

"Why are you not horrified by this? I am."

"I expected it, that's all." She looked down into her cup and quickly looked back at him. "Would you like a scone, at all? Or some lunch?"

At that moment, he knew that the reverse D-notice had been her idea.

And he wondered whose side she was on, and why she was by his side. Just in case, he said nothing, only that he would have the steak pie. Something within him died at that moment. Perhaps, belatedly, it was his youth.

"It's finally got to you, then, my friend" said Joe Cromwell the next morning, as they sat down in the Gown and Mortar. "You look more like I feel, now. Sad to see. Let's have a couple of whiskies to start with, shall we?"

"Too early for me: get me a coffee, would you? And...what do you mean?"

"Oh, I wouldn't have said it, but for all you were totally immersed in AIDS and T.B. before, you still had that bit of happiness in you that insulated you from feeling it all. It was an intellectual exercise before. Now, I think you feel it, like the rest of us." He went to the bar.

No, thought Andrew, *it's not that. Not that at all. Terry...*

His coffee came in a glass, with cream.

"A drop of Irish in it" said Joe cheerfully "Just to complete the Celtic triangle. Anyway, laddo, you're going to need it." The bonhomie vanished. "I've been hearing something on the grapevine recently. Something I thought you'd want to know about." He waited for a cue to begin. He got none. Andrew was staring down into his Gaelic coffee.

"You know something, Joe? I don't think I do want to hear it. Whatever it is. I am...sick of the whole subject. Sick and tired. It's with me every single minute I'm awake, and in my dreams, it's worse. Maybe I'm cracking up. Or maybe I'm just becoming sane. Whichever, I don't like it. I don't like myself much at this moment, and that's a hell of a burden to drag around."

Joe's voice was cold.

"Well now. That's a first, and no mistake. First time I've ever been disappointed in you, Andrew. First time in all these years. Do you really think it matters a damn what you feel, or I feel? In the middle of all this? Get a grip, man. If this is how feeling affects you, go back to seeing it as an intellectual exercise. Then maybe you'll be able to think straight again."

He swigged his whisky down in one.

338

Andrew continued to stare into his glass, hurt. He had hoped for some sympathy, or at least empathy, from his old friend, not this icy blast.

"Obviously something's gone wrong between you and Terry. As your friend, I'm sorry about it. But as the Public Health Administrator talking to the AIDS specialist, believe me, it doesn't make a pinprick of difference compared to what I have to tell you. Me and Shirley breaking up and all the kids walking out on us wouldn't matter either, comparatively speaking. Andrew, we are way past the point where personal feelings can be indulged in. We're right in the middle of the biggest crisis this world has ever seen...and you want to hide away because your love life is suffering? My god man, what has that got to do with our work?"

"I'm not in the middle of anything" Andrew pointed out, reasonably. "I'm out of the ballpark, remember? On the fringes. Not even that. Just...out of it."

"That's why you're in Edinburgh, is it, where the Moral Majority is being hatched? Sheer coincidence, is it? Sheer coincidence that Terry got the scoop. Sheer coincidence that according to Terry this morning, Frankie Dunn has invited you two to his wedding next week? You call that being out of it?"

"I don't know why we're in Edinburgh. I thought I did, but I don't."

"Listen to me Andrew; I don't care. Now you know perfectly well how much I've always admired you, so does my not caring about your emotional welfare give you some kind of insight into the importance of what I'm waiting for your gracious permission to tell you? Oh, the hell with it, I'll tell you anyway. Then, if you still don't want to know, believe me I'll get up and walk out of this bar and you won't be troubled with me any more, and it won't cost me one wink of sleep either. Wait there while I get another drink."

He ordered, he stood waiting for his order, he did not look back at Andrew.

Feeling awkward and slightly ashamed, Andrew glanced across at him and saw two shorthaired young men in grey suits rise from the table to his right and stand close at either side of Joe at the bar.

Andrew remembered these men arriving just after himself and Joe One of the young men had his hand in his pocket, the hand which was next to Joe. A few words were exchanged and the three of them walked out of the bar. Joe did not even turn to look at Andrew. Andrew barely had time to register surprise when the barman came across with an envelope, which he handed over, explaining in a puzzled voice that the gentleman who had just left had given him this when he ordered the Gaelic coffee, to be given to Andrew if the gentleman should leave suddenly.

The young barman pocketed Andrew's tip and walked back to the bar, still trying to walk like a heterosexual. He was doing well, recently; hadn't been assaulted for weeks. Had to take a taxi home after work, of course, and have no social life or sexual life at all: still, he was alive and well and not in hospital, and these days that was all he asked.

The two young men and Joe came back into the bar and walked up to Andrew. Joe spoke easily, calmly.

"Sorry about that, Andrew; these two here are old friends of mine, couldn't believe it when I bumped into them at the bar! Look, would you mind very much if we put off the Alma Mater reunion till another time? Euan and Alan here, I haven't seen them for donkeys...we'd really like to go and paint the town red, and I know you're not much into drinking. Would you mind if I deserted you?"

The two 'old friends' were smiling pleasantly, and Andrew hoped the white envelope was not sticking out of his jacket pocket.

"Well that's friendship for you!" he bantered. "Terry was looking forward to having dinner tonight, the three of us - oh, never mind. See you in London when we get back, eh? Go on, you old reprobate, I'll survive." He realised that Joe had been removed when the other two heard him about to tell Andrew something, and he tried to defuse that. "What were you about to tell me, anyway?"

Joe smiled gratefully. "Shirley and I are going to have another one: well, we're going to try, anyway. I was going to ask you to be godfather. Would you do that for us, Andrew?"

"Of course, delighted. That's splendid news!" They smiled at ach other, clubbed each other on the back, and shook hands.

"See you soon, then!" called Joe, as he was ushered out. At least, hought Andrew, the two young men looked less tense than they ad. Maybe they had swallowed it. Maybe.

Andrew went to the toilets to read Joe's note. It was short and astily scrawled.

"I am writing this at home before flying up to see you. You're the only one I can tell, must tell, and I don't know if they'll let me. Andrew, they ARE planning a concentration camp, but not just for Britain; for the world. They are planning to dump all HIV Positives, AIDS and ARC sufferers, and T.B. carriers, all together. All the senior people in Public Health have been invited to send in our suggestions about hospital provision and health care in general, and I gather that the SeaBees from the States and thousands of others will be building the damn place. Don't bother looking for it in the newspapers yet; you won't find it there. But I'm telling you the truth. I've had to sign away my soul on my promises of silence. Shirley's coming downstairs: she doesn't know. It's Madagascar, Andrew. And it's soon."

He shredded the note carefully and flushed it away. He walked out in a daze, turned towards Princes Street automatically, heading back to the hotel. He saw nothing as he walked. Though his face was immobile, his mind was racing.

Madagascar? What did he know about Madagascar? He was at this moment walking past the Central Reference Library; he went in, and upstairs, and he got out half a dozen textbooks and piled them all beside him on one of the old tables, polished by a thousand student elbows down the years. The smell of the place was exactly as it had been in his own university days; he liked that.

Madagascar. It was certainly big enough. He computed the likely number of people in the categories Joe had outlined, computed them on the basis of available statistics worldwide, and then multiplied that up to the likely true total right now and doubled it to allow eight months or so to fit in with Joe's concept of 'soon'. About fifty million. Madagascar?

He peered at the various maps. At about twice the size of Britain, Madagascar certainly had enough room. But there seemed to be a drastic shortage of habitable land, mostly confined to the coastal strips. Inland was much swampland, marsh and bog, and a mountain range which spread almost everywhere else. How could you possibly build enough towns and centres, roads, schools, hospitals and everything else that would be needed, to turn a country which presently housed six and a half million into one which could cater for fifty million people arriving soon? And as for those parts of an infrastructure which are not made of bricks and mortar, who would build those in? The newspapers, the television, the music and the song, the education system, all the cultural and social and political life of the place?

Even the legendary SeaBees and all the construction battalions from the world's armed forces would take years to fill every inch of coastal strip with buildings; and even then, there would not be enough. Joe was wrong. It was not possible. Not in Madagascar.

As he returned the books to the counter and went downstairs and back out into the street he tried to convince himself that Joe was completely wrong, somehow. Not just wrong about Madagascar, but wrong about the world having one collective concentration camp. Surely Andrew and a hundred other specialists had said often and loudly enough that this was not the way to deal with the epidemic? And yet, it made a certain amount of sense. Or was he succumbing to the whole nightmare scenario? Having spoken out so long and so loud against the idea of segregation for AIDS sufferers, it was difficult to persuade himself that there might conceivably be any merit at all in this blackly absurd idea. A whole island - not Madagascar, but some island, maybe, with the right infrastructure already in place. Yes, if you didn't care how any of the sufferers felt about it, and you didn't care about dragging victims from their beds and tearing them from the arms of their parents or wives or lovers or children, if in short you stopped caring about individual people like Darren Harrison and Miss Hislop, then an island containment would be quite an attractive proposition.

There would be incredible problems upon that island, and intractable ones too; for example would you sterilise every female occupant, to be sure the damned disease stopped with the present generations? And how would you staff such a place? With fellow sufferers? Or would they finish up turning and trying to escape? For millions would try to escape, would try to go home, however many musical evenings you put on. He remembered the old black and white film taken of the Jewish musicians at Belsen, grimly smiling to show to the world what a wonderful place they were living in and how well they were being treated.

Escape would be the national pastime; but on an island, that made life for the guards much easier. They would simply mine the beaches and patrol the waters, in comfort, by powerboat or by air. Guards could even be based elsewhere, not having to risk living/dying upon the island. There would, certainly, be people willing to gun down in cold blood the wretches trying to swim for their lives from a living death. The way world hysteria was going, the problem would not be finding enough people to do it but selecting from the applicants, the volunteers, the murderous.

He turned the corner of the Mound, and saw Princes Street and the gardens spread out beneath his gaze. He saw the shops closing down, and he saw the Cossacks everywhere, and he thought of van Elsen taking ICI out of Britain, and he suddenly knew for certain where the world's concentration camp was going to be.

CHAPTER TEN

Monday, the day of Flora's wedding to Frankie Dunn, dawned cold, damp and drear. In Flora's house, her mother was anxiously putting the finishing touches to the wedding dress and veil. In Frankie's house, Grandad was brushing imaginary fluff from Frankie's magnificent blue velvet jacket, which frothed with Jacobite lace at throat and cuffs, and set off the blues in his MacNeil tartan kilt.

In the Caledonian Hotel, Andrew and Terry were still pretending that all was reasonably well between them, and they were both utterly miserable. They had breakfasted in their room, and Terry had barely touched anything, pleading an upset stomach but suffering in truth from an upset mind and heart. She saw her beloved withdrawing from her, inch by inch, into cold hostility, and she did not know how to stop it.

"We're going through one of THOSE phases again my love, aren't we?" she tried, as she dressed and he did not watch her.

"Pardon?"

"You remember; when I was miffed with you in London and we were being far too polite and charming to each other and really wanted to kick each other into the middle of next week, and then we had our fight, and then we were all right again. I'm not sure what it is we're quarrelling about this time; but please could we have our fight and then be all right again, my darling? Please?"

"I don't know what you mean" he said, calmly and coolly, as he fiddled with his tie at the bathroom mirror.

"Yes you do. All weekend you've been damper than the weather; yes dear, no dear, three bags full dear, and never actually said anything to me and hardly ever kissed me and THEN only on the cheek and a pathetic attempt at a hug in bed. You're awfully angry at me about something; was it me getting drunk at the Press Club, darling? You've been like this since the day after that."

"You did make rather an exhibition of yourself." He stood in the bathroom doorway, looking at her pinning her hair up inside her at, and he wished he still felt moved by her, still felt all that love...but he felt nothing. Only irritation at the fact that she was still here, irritation at himself for not tackling the final scene with her, when he would tell her to go. He was a coward, he knew; at his age he should have known how to do it, but he did not.

Their phone rang, and Reception announced that their taxi was here and Andrew promised they'd be down momentarily. He shrugged on his raincoat and helped Terry into hers.

"A gentleman to the end" she quipped in a wavering voice. She darted him a look of panic. "I didn't mean..."

"Maybe you did. And maybe it would be for the best. We'll have time to talk it through later."

In the taxi, she reached for his hand to squeeze it, to comfort them both; he did not withdraw his hand but he did not close it over hers and he did not look at her. The tears began to run her mascara down her cheeks.

All the way to the Registry office, her mind threw up flashbacks of their happiest moments, and contrasted them with the bleak, cold man beside her now. She remembered backing into the lounge at St Fillans dressed in huge tweeds, and Andrew's smile of wicked merriment when she saw that he had someone with him. She remembered the time in the bedroom at St Fillans when she had first seduced him from the toes upwards. She remembered the day he proposed, in the street, and said she could wear as many pretty dresses to their wedding as she liked, and she remembered the shining love in his eyes.

Oh but she loved him; she had to do something to keep him. Perhaps if he, too, remembered these things he would be flooded with love again. She had to try.

"Have you decided how many pretty frocks I'm to wear to OUR wedding, darling?" she said, and her voice creaked a little.

He turned his head towards her then, and the look of chill disdain on it was enough. No words were needed to tell her that there would be no wedding. She let go his hand as he turned away from her, and found a packet of tissues in her handbag and muffled her howls into a handful of them. Andrew looked steadily ahead.

Had she been less steeped in her own distress, she would have noticed that Andrew's icy manner extended to all they met. His normal gentlemanly politeness and pleasant manners had been stopped dead. His caring nature had been clubbed to death by his revelation; he had not even telephoned Shirley to talk about Joe.

As Joe himself had said, personal feelings hardly mattered any more. He was withdrawn, disinterested and uninvolved. Even when he saw Flora, whom he had rather liked, he did not smile.

Even when he saw Albert Kennedy, whom he had rather hated, he did not scowl. He was unmoved by everything and everyone. He was watching these people perform like marionettes upon a stage, and he could not understand how they could laugh and be happy when their world was so nearly at an end. Of course some of them did not know this; but some of them, Albert Kennedy and Frankie in particular, surely did know and were deeply involved in making it happen.

The registry office was packed with celebrants and well-wishers, all dressed in their best. Frankie and Flora were brought in last, and stood together facing the Registrar. A cousin of Flora's had been drafted in to give her away, even though this was not a necessary function at a registry office, and Albert stood as Frankie's best man. Just behind them, Gwendoline Spencer sat with Jock Dunn, each looking proud, holding each other's hand.

The Registrar intoned his words with his usual solemnity, and they made their brief responses, and in a few short minutes the brother and sister were husband and wife. They made a lovely couple; Frankie magnificent in his kilt outfit, Flora romantically beautiful in her sweet girlish broderie anglais dress with the pale pink ribbons threaded through sleeves and neckline and hem, and the bouquet of pale pink roses and white roses and bountiful fern.

They were the ideal couple, the picture of youth and love, and even the bloom of pregnancy upon Flora merely underscored their contentment and their joy in each other and the promise of a bright future. It was a pleasure simply to look upon them, and as only

Albert Kennedy (and Frankie) knew that they were brother and sister, the crowd was almost unanimous in its applause and cheering and approval.

Cameras both still and video were pointed at them throughout the brief ceremony, for Frankie was news; the principals gathered on the steps of the Registry Office afterwards, beaming proudly, for the official album pictures and the last shots of the departing press and television men. Among these, Andrew saw 'John', who had told him so much at the Press Club that night, and for the first time in days, he became animated; he walked swiftly to stand beside John, and he asked to meet him again soon because there was something happening John ought to know about. To his surprise, the man turned dull eyes towards him.

"If I ought to know about it, they'll tell me. If I didn't ought to, I'd rather not."

"What's happened to you, man? You were..?"

"I was" he replied, closing up his camera. "But then I remembered I have a family. So I was, but I am not now. Please leave me alone, Doctor Douglas; you're not good news to be seen with, right now. Please."

Andrew dropped his voice to a whisper.

"If there's any way we can meet secretly, get in touch."

John looked at him despairingly.

"There is no way, and no way I'd want to. Please, move away from me, please!"

Andrew pretended to help him put the camera back into its case, and his whisper now was very low, and very fast.

"Have you heard of a Joe Cromwell? Does Madagascar mean anything to you?"

Aloud, he said "Marvellous things, these modern cameras, aren't they?" and he smiled up at John. John said, low and fast to match Andrew's whisper;

"No, and no; what are you talking about? No wait, don't tell me; not now not ever. Leave me alone! You're a prisoner in a glass cage, man, don't you know that? And I'm not climbing inside there with you." And aloud, he said "Terrific: wait till the new 3D printing gets organised, you'll be rocked on your heels by what the 3D cameras can do. Incredible!" And they smiled vacuously at each other, and Andrew wandered away. He did not see the two young men with short hair and quiet suits approach John behind his departing back, and escort him down the steps.

Terry smiled as Andrew came back to her, but he did not return the smile.

"I don't know what I'm doing here; I'm going back to the hotel. You stay; you'll no doubt want to talk to people here for your ace reporter story in the Guardian, eh? Find out lots of things you didn't know about at all, eh? Or maybe just catch up on the gossip with your chums Frankie and Albert?"

"My chums? They're my enemies, aren't they?"

"Oh, really? You invent the reverse D-notice, they use it; I'd say that puts you on the same side, wouldn't you?" He turned on his heel and tried to push through the crowd. She caught up with him as he descended the steps.

"Andrew! Is that what's wrong with you? The reverse D?"

"No. That's a very small part of what's wrong. But it's enough."

"Enough to make you hate me?"

He looked straight in her eyes. "I don't hate you. Don't be too childish, Terry. You turned out to be one of the bad guys after all, that's all. So now I don't feel anything about you. You should be proud of yourself; that front you put up was excellent. Cute, loving, with just a hint of bite in it; very convincing. You and van Elsen; great performances, both of you. Had me completely suckered. Well done. Who else was in on the joke, Terry? Mark Tyme? Jasmine Elliot? Callum, maybe?"

Terry put her arms round him, crying openly.

"Darling don't DO this to yourself! You're wrong! Nobody is taking you for a fool! Don't start hating everyone just because of me!" She pulled back, to look at him. "Listen; you're right about the reverse D-notice well, partly right. I did sort of invent that; but I had help. In fact, I really only took up an idea that Frank Ainsley came up with: I mean I thought he was joking, and then I thought why not? It was about the cats; I only meant for it to be about the cats. If it's still running, that's nothing to do with me, darling, honestly. Oh my love, please believe in me again! I believe in you so desperately much, and I love you. I love you."

The crowd surged down the steps, turning right towards the long line of gleaming black cars waiting to take them to the wedding breakfast. Andrew pulled away from Terry and turned left. She followed him, caught his arm, walked with him.

"Andrew? Darling?"

His voice was still cold, though less lethal. And it was tired.

"Go back to the wedding, Terry. It doesn't matter any more."

"What doesn't, my love?"

"You and me. We don't matter. Even if you're telling me the truth, it doesn't really change anything."

"But surely it changes everything, if you believe me?"

"No. In fairy stories, maybe. Not in reality. Okay, I believe you; now what? We kiss and make up and live happily ever after? I'm afraid not. Maybe I just don't feel romantic any more."

"But why?"

He turned to face her, and there was a certain amount of pity in his face.

"Because there are other things going on now which are more important than personal feelings. Which kill personal feelings. If you are telling me the truth, then I can't tell you about them because they are dangerous to know about; if you are still lying to me, then you know already. Either way, we have nothing to discuss, you and I. Not any more. I'm sorry."

He disengaged her arms from around him.

"Go back to the wedding, Terry. Go back." He turned and walked away.

Frankie was in his element at his wedding. So many pleasantly smiling faces turned towards him, as he sat beside Flora at the table. His speech was a model of eloquence, full of love for his bride and hopes for a bright future for them both. He thanked the bridesmaids most courteously, he thanked everyone for attending, but most of all his thanks and his gratitude went to his Grandad, for bringing him up well enough for him to win the love of such a wonderful woman as Flora Spencer oops, Flora Dunn! He blushed and smiled at this point and everyone laughed and clapped and Flora looked up at him adoringly.

Of course he did a little modest electioneering; his candidature for Glasgow East was now official, and he hoped to do well. His guests applauded enthusiastically. He talked of real democracy, and the voice of the people, and the desire of the people to clean up this once-great country and restore her to world prominence. While the guests cheered, Terry was silent. All she could think of was Andrew, all she saw was the empty chair beside her.

Later, Frankie sought her out. She was at the bar, downing her fourth vodka tonic. These were mixing well with the three champagne cocktails she had already consumed, and the large dry sherry with which the hotel had welcomed each guest. She was drunk, and maudlin, and feeling badly done by and neglected. He drew her aside to a quiet corner and he leaned closely over her, the velvet of his jacket almost brushing her face.

Despite everything, the smell of him aroused her.

Each of them saw the dilating pupils of the other. Neither of them referred to what was happening between them.

"I was sorry to see you and Doctor Douglas having a fight, earlier on" he said, all concern. "Are things all right again?"

"Things are fine, thank you. Lovers' quarrel, usual sort of thing" she smiled wanly at him.

"May I talk to you about something in private, Terry? Just now, I mean?"

"Of course"

"Right. Come with me there must be a place we can talk somewhere in this hotel."

He found one remarkably quickly a small lounge bar currently unstaffed and empty.

"One good thing about the recession, then" he said, smiling. "You'd never have found an empty bar in Scotland before it!"

They sat together on the upholstered bench seat by the window. He clamped his hand firmly on Terry's knee.

"Now then; you are someone I need, Terry. Professionally, I mean, of course."

"Of course" she said, removing his hand equally firmly. He managed to take it away in such a manner that the flimsy skirt of her dress was moved up her thigh a little. And she did not move to replace it and he knew he had her, in that instant.

He talked about media training, but his eyes were talking about something quite different. She talked about microphone technique and camera technique, but her eyes were exploring his and saying yes.

As her breathing became deeper, the swell of her rising and falling breasts under the thin fabric kept dragging his eyes downwards. He saw the points on the dress where her nipples were engorged and pushing through, and she knew he saw this. She began to squirm slightly in her seat so that her breasts were high, and he carried on talking about interview technique while he moved both his hands to cup her breasts and finger the nipples with his thumbs. He did not move to kiss her. She answered his query about television studios while he lifted her to her feet and pushed the bulging front of his kilt against her groin.

This was a game new to both of them, and it excited the hell out of them.

While she talked of studio lights and the need for make-up, he lifted her dress and slowly pulled her panties down to her ankles. She stepped out of them. His hands moved up her bare thighs and he asked her if she would work with him to prepare him for media interviews because he did, truly need her, he needed her quite urgently...because he was already being asked for interviews...he needed her very urgently...and she lifted up the front of his kilt and he was wearing nothing beneath it. And she said yes, she could see that he needed her urgently and in fact, as she was without a job at the moment, really, she needed him as much as he needed her. Urgently. She leaned backwards against a bar table and opened her

351

legs wide. He plunged into her without any further preambles. Her hips thrust forward eagerly to receive him, and still they talked about media training, her voice strained, his cool and professional.

He placed a hand under each of her arms and lifted her off her feet, gently bringing her down impaled upon him, sliding her up and down and up and down until she could no longer speak of media training or anything else. Her head fell back and she arched and bucked until he could stand it no longer and brought her down and shot into her, the two of them standing still, locked together, legs trembling, holding on to each other for support.

Outside the window, in the rain, Andrew turned sadly away. He knew Frankie had seen him there, but of course he could not know just how much this had added to Frankie's pleasure.

The Branson Pullman NightStar had one berth left, and he booked it. Callum was worried by his father's voice on the telephone, but as Andrew left no opening for discussing anything other than that he would be home in the morning, Callum said nothing. The desk clerk took Andrew's money without comment, and nodded when he said that he was paying the bill till the end of the week to give Miss Aitken time to find her next accommodation. Such a shame, the clerk thought; they had seemed so in love, this couple; the favourite guests of all the staff.

Andrew still had eight hours to kill before the NightStar pulled out from Waverley Station. It seemed to him unlikely that he would ever come back to Edinburgh, though he had no idea now where he would go or what he would do. He decided to take one last walk around this most beautiful city, take one last sight and smell of what had been the treasured city of his heart, the place of his studying, the place of his heady youth and, latterly, his lost delight in Terry.

He took a taxi to Waverley Station and deposited his suitcases in Left Luggage lockers. He started to walk along Princes Street with a view to turning up the Mound and walking round his old University haunts, but he lost heart well before he reached the Mound. For the days of his studying were woven in memory with Joe, who was now God knows where...and Ruth...and his love for

Terry was deader than Marley's doornail. His memories had been oil paintings, not photographs, and some vandal had now slashed those precious paintings to ribbons.

The rain had now stopped, and the clouds were rolling away and the lemon yellow sunshine of September set its pale fire to the autumn leaves of the trees around the Walter Scott memorial. In his mind he saw the empty gardens filled with AIDS victims, their haggard faces bleak in the sunlight, no hope in their eyes, walking like automata. The vision became less dense with people, so that fewer and fewer people walked this green place and, eventually, none. In his vision, Autumn turned to winter, and the gardens became overgrown, for their was nobody now to tend them, for there was nobody. Nobody left, in the whole country.

And then what? It was the first time he had turned his thinking to after the holocaust. What would happen afterwards?

Human Immunodeficiency Virus is a fragile thing; these islands would not remain contaminated, like a place infested with anthrax, or radiation. There would have to be a cleansing, of course, but on the whole, the country would be intact and could be recolonised.

Except...except for the new strains of T.B. They were an unknown quantity; those bugs could be lying in wait for the new incoming generations, to decimate them again. The small hope died aborning. Britain would be a plague country for the foreseeable future.

And who in their right minds would want to come back, anyway? Not Britons. How could any family face coming back to their old house, knowing that AIDS sufferers and T.B. victims had lived and died in it since they left, and knowing too that half their friends and relations had never left because they were still here, in the form of a handful of ashes blowing about somewhere?

No. That would be unbearable. So, not Britons. Then who? Which people would want this desolate land to bring their families to? He could think of no-one. The very name "Britain" would be anathema for centuries, a word used to frighten small children...if you don't behave, we'll send you to Britain.

Oh, dearest God. That was it. If you don't behave, we'll send you to Britain. If you steal and are unrepentant, if you murder, if you have no regard for the safety and privacy of other people...we will send you to Britain. From plague country to penal colony, an easy transition. Death is not the ultimate deterrent, for many; life on Plague Island would be infinitely more horrific.

And along with the murderers would come the disaffected, the dissidents, the rebels and revolutionaries. And the Jews, perhaps, or the Arabs, depending on who finally settled the Palestinian Question. There might be Protestants, or there might be Catholics; there might be Moslems. Or none of these, if religious tolerance ever actually happened. And even then, it might be the atheists who got shunted safely off to die.

A dumping ground for the unwanted, as well as the unrepentant. Such a bold and shining future. Such a symbol of Man's humanity to man. The perfect achievement for the Age of Aquarius.

The meek inheritance? Weren't the meek supposed to inherit the earth? Well, perhaps that was what was happening. The people who did not screw around, who used condoms when they were told...they might be classed as meek. And later, the people who believed and acted exactly as their respective States demanded that they believe and act, they could certainly be classed as meek. And the others? The lovers, the pleasure-seekers, the sick and the dying, and later the criminals, the political activists, and perhaps the insane? They would inherit the whirlwind.

Not just the evil and the psychotic, but also the bold, the adventurous, the fighters for justice; they would come here, sent from every part of the planet. The suppressed, the oppressed, the repressed, would be offered freedom in the penal colony. What kind of a civilisation would erupt from this volcanic mixture? Would the world bother to pay for keeping hospitals going? Maternity units? Accident and emergency services? Probably not. And would the world bother to put courts and prison to use, in a penal colony? If not, then the truly criminal would flourish here like the green bay tree, and take over quickly.

And before all that, while the HIV and the T.B. took their tolls in the plague country, would the world supply medicines and treatments to the plague victims? Had anyone thought of that? Of course they must have. Nobody, no body of men, could have dreamed up this plan without having a fascinating time playing with logistics. That was why they had risked telling Joe, and others like him; men who could dream up a Public Health care system for a plague colony. Andrew wondered if Joe was the only one who had risked breaking silence. And, inevitably, he wondered anew where Joe was right now, and if he was alive, and if he was safe. On balance he thought Joe would be all right; he was needed. They - whoever They were - would need men like him to stay and make this insane idea work well. So what about Shirley and their kids? Would they have to stay here, ultimately to become infected, probably with the irreversible new T.B., and die here?

How many would have to stay here to administer the various systems? How many men and women would have to wave goodbye to their families at quaysides and airports, to stay here and die, alone, in the line of duty?

Would anybody do it? Voluntarily?

He was only dimly aware of the fact that he was slumped forwards on the wet bench, his head in his hands, feeling and looking ill. Slowly he realised that five Cossacks, wearing impeccably polite and concerned expressions, stood around him. One of them spoke a pleasant-faced lad of around twenty.

"Are you well, sir? Can we do anything to help?"

Half a dozen venomous answers fought to reach his mouth, but he tamped them down.

"Kind of you; but no, thanks. I'm not sick, just rather depressed. Woman trouble, you know. I'll be okay."

They nodded in evident sympathy.

"Hope your troubles are over soon, sir" said the twenty-year-old, and the group moved on.

My troubles, thought Andrew, won't be over till I'm dead. Neither will yours, or anyone else's in this country. Terry was right about us all going into a long dark tunnel. Well, she would be, wouldn't she? I wonder how long she's known about it. Something like this...it must have taken a while to even get to the stage it's at now.

He thought back over the last ten years, seeking clues. There was no shortage of them, with the benefit of hindsight. The way the pound had kept sinking, and nobody had ever propped it up. The way industry had been left to go to wrack and ruin, even though subsidising it would have been much cheaper for the state than paying out thousands of unemployment cheques every week. The way the police force had been gradually pulled back from the duties which made city life bearable, like stopping noisy parties before neighbours started screaming, and picking up swearing, violent drunks on Friday and Saturday nights, and generally keeping the streets safe by having adequate foot patrols.

Perhaps he was becoming paranoid, for everything, now, seemed to point towards this conspiracy; even the way that British children and young people had been given greater and greater freedom and choice, and less and less discipline, so that they grew up convinced that what they themselves wanted was all that mattered in the world and all they had to do was reach out and take it. Given that kind of an upbringing, it was scarcely surprising that crimes, especially crimes against the person, had mushroomed from isolated incidents into a part-time industry.

But then the older generation was supposed to think that of the younger one, it was traditional, and you could find that sentiment in books as old as the Bible. He tried to smile at himself but found he could no longer smile.

The rain came back on, and he wandered back to Waverley Station, to shelter till the train came in.

Terry was very much more sober by the time she arrived back at the Caledonian hotel. She did not notice the desk clerk give her a sympathetic look as she picked up her keys from him.

Up in their room, Andrew had left a clean pair of panties out for

356

her, on their bed. The note beside them read "You'll be needing these, won't you?" and nothing else at all. There was not a hair of him left, not a smell, not a handkerchief. He was very completely gone.

"Oh Andrew: you came back for me, after all! And you saw me...with Frankie? Oh, Andrew! Andrew!"

She did not cry, she howled. She rolled on the bed, howling, dragging the covers up around her and creasing them in great handfuls and stuffing them into her mouth to stop the noise of her heartbreak from disturbing the neighbouring guests. The howls took a long time to subside into racking sobs, and she wailed her self-hatred aloud, crying out "You stupid bitch! You stupid drunken bitch! Look what you've lost! Look what you've broken now! The best thing that ever happened to you in all your life..." she stopped suddenly, and lunged for the phone.

"Hello? Reception? Did Doctor Douglas leave a forwarding address? No? Oh. Till the end of the week? Oh. Thank you." She replaced the receiver. "Damn. Wait; Callum!" And she dialled him and got him and he told her, the Pullman Nightstar, and she thanked him hastily and put the phone back down and raced to the bathroom to clean up her face, repair her make-up and brush her hair...her hat was somewhere in The Auld Reekie Hotel's Celebration Suite, where the rest of the guests were still whooping it up for the lovely Flora and her loving swain.

There was only the faintest of chances that Andrew would already be at the station; there were still five hours to go before the NightStar left, although it arrived a good hour beforehand. But it was the only place she could try to find him, and she did find him, seated on a quiet bench opposite the NightStar platform. When she turned the corner and saw him, she started to run towards him; then he happened to turn towards her, and saw her, and turned away, expressionless. She stopped running then, and stopped hoping, but still walked towards him, just in case there was some point, some purpose she might achieve, something to take hold of and build on again.

She sat down beside him and for a few moments neither of them could think of what to say. Terry tried first.

"I love you, Andrew." He made no move to turn towards her, but spoke.

"Fine" he said.

"I don't know how to do this!" she burst out. He still did not turn towards her.

"There's nothing to do; nothing to say. Go away. Please, go away."

"No" she said, on the verge of tears again and sounding petulant rather than tragic. "I love you; I want to mend this, if I can. Please let me try."

At last he turned towards her, and she was shocked to see how old he looked, for the first time since she had met him.

"Terry, you've got to grow up sometime" he said, without rancour or unpleasantness, without affection, without anything in his voice. "Some time, you have to start taking responsibility for your own actions. What you broke today was already falling apart. What you broke today can't be mended, Terry. Love isn't like a wooden toy you can bludgeon to death and then stick together again with superglue. When a feeling is finished, it's finished; dead. There's nothing so dead in the world as a dead love. There isn't anything there any more, for you to mend. Do you understand?"

"Yes, but I..."

"No. You don't understand. I wish I cared about that. But I don't. I do remember caring about you; I just can't remember...why."

She gasped as if he had physically hit her. She tried to hold on to his arm for some warmth, some support, but he picked off her fingers as if they were mildly ugly insects. At that moment, four Cossacks wandered towards them and stopped. The pleasant-faced lad of twenty or so, who had talked to Andrew earlier on in the Gardens, spoke again.

"Is this your woman trouble, sir?"

Terry became acutely aware of the fact that she was wearing make-up and a short skirt, and she was being rejected by a respectable-looking middle-aged man in a public place.

358

"No trouble, lad. The lady was just leaving. Weren't you?" His eyes were glacial. Terry sobbed and rose to her feet.

"Can we escort you from the station, madam?" asked one of the men. "It's not a place we encourage..ladies...to hang around." Andrew felt guilt stir within him.

"She's not a prostitute, gentlemen!" Terry looked piercingly at him.

"That's right, Andrew: I'm not. Remember that, when you remember me." And she turned and walked away from him, and the Cossacks let her go when Andrew raised a hand to stop them.

——————— • ———————

When Joe Cromwell had been escorted from the Gown and Mortar, he had been afraid. His oath of secrecy was luridly explicit, and the Clems clearly knew he intended to break that oath to tell Andrew about Madagascar. He had fully expected to be thrown into prison, and the key dropped in a river somewhere.

But the Clems had merely taken him down a small alleyway, and talked to him. They had reminded him of his duty and his oath, and pointed out that personal friendships and old loyalties were inappropriate compared with the magnitude of the plans to contain AIDS. They pointed out also that Joe, and the other few men entrusted with the secret, had been taken into confidence because they were needed to ensure a high quality of care for the AIDS sufferers in Madagascar, and that the Government would be sad to lose his services. He was privately unrepentant right up until they said that if the information leaked out ahead of the planned release date, a great deal of panic, and possibly riots and bloodshed, might ensue; the Government had to have time to prepare the way. There was no possibility of a change of plans, said the Clems, and so the only responsible thing to do was to help ensure that those plans were implemented with the very minimum of upset, hurt and harm.

He believed them. And so when they asked him if he had already told Andrew Douglas, before they removed him from the pub, he told them that he had. He was then driven back to

Turnhouse Airport, and put on a normal scheduled flight back to London, with firm handshakes all round and no further caveats other than that they were glad he now understood fully.

For most of the time, therefore, during which Andrew had been wondering where Joe was and imagining him cast into some utter darkness somewhere, Joe had been safe at home, wondering where Andrew was, and if they had picked him up and explained things to him properly yet so that he understood the need for absolute secrecy about Madagascar. Had Andrew been his normal self, he would have telephoned Shirley; in his present shocked state, however, he had come to his drab assumptions and just stayed there.

Joe felt rather proud and privileged, now, to have been entrusted with this important piece of information, and proud and privileged to be one of the few valuable men who could make it all come out right in the end. He, like Andrew, had been thinking through the logistics of the enterprise, and he, too, saw some bedevilling problems such as the care and education of any progeny produced on Madagascar who were not HIV Positive. It would be a difficult exercise, this, but worth putting one's whole self into. And he would be helping to keep this country and all other countries clean and safe for people like him and Shirley, and their kids.

Still, at the back of his mind, he did wonder; how in God's name could they ever persuade people to move to Madagascar? Even under duress, which Sweeting had personally assured him would not be used? Ah well. They would sort that out. Marvellous, what good advertising agencies can do.

It would be up to him, and the others, to make sure that life on Madagascar was as sweet as possible, for the years which would remain to some of the HIV Positives, and the months which might remain for the AIDS, ARC and T.B. sufferers. There would be a lot of hard work involved, but it was worth doing. He hoped very much that Andrew would prove tractable, so they could draft him in. He would wait to hear about this through official channels.

It never occurred to Joe, not once, that the Minister for Health had lied to him.

———   •   ———

Frankie Dunn had rented a small house in Callander for their honeymoon, as from here it was easy to drive to Glasgow to do his electioneering, and here it was safe to leave Flora on those days he had to be away. Grandad and Gwendoline Spencer had been installed in the country mansion near Peebles to supervise the electricians and the joiners and the plumbers and the stonemasons and the decorators, all of whom had promised faithfully they would be finished and out by the end of the second week in October. Grandad and Gwendoline would also be responsible for hiring the staff; Frankie wanted a cook, a manservant and a nurserymaid to be resident in the staff wing, and he wanted reliable cleaners and some helps on call in Peebles. The only room to remain undecorated and unprepared was to be the nursery, as Flora wanted to be there for this. There was plenty of time, as she was only just into her second trimester.

The Moral Majority (Glasgow East Constituency) was in full swing and ready for action, waiting only for the divine Frankie Dunn to arrive, to set the whole thing in motion. There were interviews booked already with the various media, and plenty of meetings organised in the few community halls and church halls available in the area. Red, black and white had been selected as the party colours, and buttons, badges, streamers and balloons were already being handed out at children's parties and the Saturday morning cinema.

Three spontaneous outbursts of public emotion had been orchestrated to arise once Frankie had started to tour the grim streets in the open-topped car which had been rented. The first would be a rushing forwards to shake him by the hand as the car crawled forwards; the second would be the heartfelt response to the words of the pretty little girl who would present him with a bouquet of flowers and say "Please Mistur Dunn, could we maybe huv a wee playpark?" And Frankie would bow low, kiss her on the cheek, and say loudly "You get your maw to phone me at Westminster, my lass, and we'll get you your playpark. I promise!" At that, half a dozen mothers in the audience would burst into applause, hopefully dragging the others with them. The third spontaneous demonstration of joyful confidence was to happen the night before election day an all-night vigil of party workers outside the primary school wher voting was to take place, singing songs of Scotland and democrac and the old millworkers and the old sailors and the old fishermer That one was sure to be televised.

It was an odd party, to an observer's eye; there was every kin of person in it from far right extremist youths with hedgeho; haircuts and aggressive chins, through chainsmoking Communit; Action mothers from Govan, Partick and Easterhouse, to committe ladies in Swan Lake hats who were clearly on the verge of Knittin; for Victory in their awfully nice houses in Bearsden. Yet eve among this heterogeneous assortment, there was one who stood ou was treated differently, and felt acutely uncomfortable at Part; H.Q. Her name was Terry Aitken and she was the new Medi; Advisor to the Moral Majority.

She had been importuned and cajoled by Frankie as the; rearranged their clothing at his wedding; she had said no. Ther after leaving Andrew at Waverley Station, she had sat alone in the Baroque, nursing a black coffee, thinking through her situation an calling on every reserve of fortitude within her. Lacking ar hysterical nature, she could not, like Flora, or Scarlett O'Hara conveniently dump her turmoil into some pigeonhole in he subconscious, labelled 'to be examined later'. She was cringing and miserable, and desperately sorry for herself and for Andrew. Yet she had to survive; even her financial situation was rocky, fo she had spent her way through her salary from Number 10 as fast as she had earned it, and any surplus had been quietly sent to her brothers. She needed a job; she needed something she could sink her teeth into; she needed something to take her mind off Andrew. For those less than glorious reasons, more than because she still wanted to write her book, she then walked unsteadily to a taxi rank, went back to the Auld Reekie Hotel, and found Frankie, his arms wrapped lovingly around his sister in her bridal finery, dancing a waltz. She waited, she accosted him at the bar, and said she'd changed her mind; he followed her, this time, to a quiet table.

"I'm pleased" he said, his eyes deep in hers. "You do please me ery much, Terry...by your decision, I mean." But this time, she as not in the mood for games.

"There will be no more sex in our relationship; it'll be strictly usiness. I mean that!" she said firmly. He grinned at her, very sure f himself as always.

"Of course. I promise you, I shan't touch you again. Ever. If ou want me, you'll have to do the chasing next time."

He knew she would, in time, when she was ready again. She new this, too, though naturally she did not admit it to herself.

And so she found herself in Glasgow, waiting for Frankie to tear imself away from his bride in Callendar and come to his adoring onstituency party, the morning after his wedding.

———— • ————

That was the morning Andrew got home to the flat in Tudor Court of course. Callum was shocked to see how pale and haggard his father had become, and belatedly wished he had not told Belinda o stay and meet him.

"Dad? Wow, you look..I mean..are you tired? Are you ill?"

"Tired. And surprised. Who's this, then?"

"I'm Belinda Murray, Doctor Douglas: Callum and I are engaged to be married." The girl walked towards him as he dumped his suitcases, expecting a warm handshake and a smile and speech of welcome to the family; that was what Callum had promised her. Instead, the old man seemed hardly to notice what she had said.

"Really? That's nice. Well, if you'll excuse me, I'm going to bed now. Didn't sleep a wink on the train." He stared ahead of him into nothingness, swaying slightly. Suddenly really worried, Callum took hold of his elbow and steered him into the main bedroom and helped him slip under the duvet the second his hat and coat and shoes were off.

"Thanks, son" said Andrew, turning over to go to sleep. But Callum was still worried.

"Dad... when was the last time you ate anything?"

"Mmm. Dunno. Yesterday morning, I think. Goodnight son."

Callum walked briskly to the kitchen, explaining to Belinda as he went; "His blood sugar's all to hell: lack of food. I should ge something into him now, before he conks out for the day."

"He's not a diabetic, is he?" asked Belinda.

"No, just borderline hypoglaecemic. Needs fairly regular food or he gets tired. If he missed his food yesterday, and didn't slee all night...well, no wonder he's a bit woozy. He'll be fine." Whil he talked he warmed up some milk, put plenty of hot chocolate an sugar into it, and took it through to his comatose father. Muc joggling and nipping was required to drag the errant spirit back t earth, and Andrew was not amused, but he sat up and drank th mixture, and did seem to derive some benefit and comfort from i before he snuggled back down again to sleep.

Just before he fell asleep, he heard Belinda say seductivel "Well love; if he's sleeping for a few hours, that gives us a few hour more, doesn't it?" and Callum said "I haven't any more sheaths lef you wonderfully wanton hussy!" and Belinda said, low and swee "Oh, who cares? We're getting married anyway. Come on..." an they walked away together. But Andrew was too desperately tire to keep his eyes open long enough to stop them though, God knows he tried.

At around five o'clock, Callum roused him saying in awed tones that the Prime Minister's Office was on the phone, and the P.M wanted to speak to him. Andrew struggled up, and walked groggil through to the lounge, where a very demure Belinda was sitting reading a magazine.

"Hello? Yes, this is he. Yes, I'll hold. Good evening, sir; how are you? Yes, thank you, I'm fine. When? Oh. Yes of course, Prime Minister; I'll be there. Goodbye." He replaced the phone and sat down, wiping the sleep from his eyes. Callum had made coffee while he was talking, and he sipped it gratefully.

"You didn't sound very respectful, Dad" said Callum, pride and doubtfulness vying in his voice.

"I don't feel very respectful. But I have to go there...Downing Street...at eight tonight. For dinner. Bloody farce." He looked at

364

ist over to Belinda, who looked so deliberately relaxed she was obviously tense, and waiting for him to take her on.

"So. You're going to marry Callum. And you're called Belinda. Belinda Douglas. Yes, that sounds nice. Are you nice, Belinda?"

"What do you mean, Doctor..?"

"Just that; are you a nice girl? Can we believe in your niceness? Have you always been nice, or did you do an Open University degree in it? Or have you only got an HND, or maybe a GCE in niceness? Because believe me, Belinda, you're going to need all the niceness you can get your hands on in the years ahead. You too, Callum."

She was upset and Callum raged to see it, his voice barely controlled.

"Stop it, Dad! Stop needling us! We don't want to hear about bloody AIDS, not tonight! Keep your bloody Doomsday scenario to yourself for once, will you? Nice? When did you last know what that meant? You should try it yourself some time! Belinda, we're going out for a meal - get your coat on. We'll see you later Dad - maybe. Have fun at Number 10, do, with your cronies. Talk the world into a raging inferno of doom and despondency, will you? Me and Belinda are going out to have a nice time, so there!"

They slammed the door behind them. Andrew looked at it.

"Gather ye rosebuds while ye may, children. For the days of wine and roses are not long. And especially not now." he said, softly, sadly. And went to bathe and dress for dinner, not so tired any more but still weary, worldweary, to the bone.

He was shown to the private diningroom used for family occasions by the Prime Minister, and also, occasionally, for small but important State affairs. The P.M. was pouring sherries at the drinks cabinet; around him stood Harold Sweeting, Jan van Elsen, Senor Juan Romero de Boca Negra from the World Health Organisation, and the man with the aquiline nose and clear blue eyes who had once passed Andrew on the steps outside. None of them was smiling.

"Ah, Andrew; good of you to come" said the Prime Minister, bringing him a sherry. He gesticulated at the group of men now turned towards them. "You know most of the gentlemen here tonight, I believe?"

"The whole rogues' gallery: apart from that man there" said Andrew. "Where are Albert Kennedy and Mark Tyme and Terry Aitken, then? Or are they out of favour now? Shame for them to miss such a fine dinner as I have no doubt will be put on tonight."

He peered into the sherry glass. The Prime Minister smiled sourly.

"You can drink it. It isn't hemlock, Andrew."

"I don't think I'd much care if it was" he replied, sinking the entire contents of the glass in one, and handing it back to his host with outrageous insolence. The Prime Minister drooped his head a little to conceal his annoyance, took the empty glass, walked Andrew to join the others.

Van Elsen extended his hand to Andrew but it was not taken. Nobody else moved.

"Do you know" said Andrew slowly "I don't actually think I can stay in the same room as you. I don't think I can stand it. You are the most despicable human beings this planet has ever seen. Have dinner with you? I'd sooner kill each one of you with my bare hands. If I had any energy left. You disgust me." He walked towards the door. "I give you fair warning; I will do anything and everything in my power to stop you. I will tell everyone I meet what you are doing to this country, and to all the poor bastards in the world who you want to drag out of their beds and ferry here to die in a strange land without family or friends." He paused, turned so that his back was to the door, opened his arms out wide. "Why don't you pass me a blindfold and shoot me now, gentlemen? I advise it. Because one way or another, I am going to stop you. So you can take your dinner and shove it."

The handle on the door would not turn. He sighed, and sagged against it.

"Of course you won't let me go. You can't afford to let me to, an you? I came here hoping to reason with you, you see. Then I saw your faces. You? You're way past reason. God damn you."

Van Elsen spoke.

"We're all on the same side, Andrew. You...us...all together."

"I would tear out my own heart if I thought I was on the same side as you."

"And how would you be if you discovered that we are on the same side as you?"

Andrew allowed himself to be led to a chair at the elegantly set dining table, and sat down, but he did not reply. The others brought their sherries and were seated. The Prime Minister did not sit at the head of the table; the man with the clear, cold blue eyes took that position, and he took it as if he were accustomed to it. He looked at Andrew and smiled gently.

"Doctor Douglas" he said, in his soft, hint-of-Irish voice. "I am Sean Keys, of the World Council. I am glad to make your acquaintance at last."

"The World Council?" ridiculed Andrew. "Did you bring your Daleks with you, then? Tell you what, Sean old boy, it isn't Doctor Douglas you want at all, it's Doctor Who: but then, I suppose that would be the good Senor Boca Negra here, wouldn't it?"

The Irishman continued as if nothing had been said. "I am Chairman of the World Council, Doctor Douglas, and Jan van Elsen, whom you know, is Head of the British Table of the Council. I - we all understand your distress. You won't believe that now, but perhaps in time you will understand that each one of us here has been through what you are suffering now. I wish I could say it gets better" (hadn't Joe Cromwell said that, too?) "but it does not. It just gets easier to swallow it down, and carry on, and do what must be done. As you will, also."

Andrew looked at him steadily, and his voice was very serious now.

"That may be; but then, what I think must be done will not necessarily be what YOU think must be done. So you will have to kill me, to stop me. Please, may we dispense with the last supper here, and just get to the part where you kill me? Or are you enjoying stringing it out like this? The condemned man ate a hearty supper Jesus, you sicken me."

Beside him to his left, Harold Sweeting spoke, curtly.

"Shut up, Andrew; a bit less self-pity would be good, and a bit more backbone. It's tough to face up to all this, yes; but it's not impossible. It isn't the world going to pot that's demolishing you it's Terry Aitken having it away with Frankie Dunn. And if you think we're going to sit here listening to you snivelling about your love life, when we have so much bloody difficult and deeply disturbing work to do...oh, go to hell. I thought there was more to you than this. Wrong again."

Andrew rose in one fluid motion, grabbed Sweeting's lapel twisted the pasty face towards him and raised his fist high and hard But by the time the two nearest men had got there to stop him, his face had already worked its way through rage to shock and then shame, and he slowly dropped his fist and sat back down in his seat. The other two men returned to their places; Sweeting ran his hands over his collar, making all smooth again. He was sweating.

Sean Keys poured Andrew a glass of red wine from the decanter nearest him.

"Drink up, Doctor Douglas. It's going to be a long night...there is a great deal to tell you and a great deal to do. We hope you'll decide to help us, but it's entirely up to you. I think we might have our soup now, Mister Prime Minister?"

At a touch of the button concealed under the tabletop, a secondary door opened and servants brought in the silver tureen and the silver ladle, upon a mahogany dumb waiter. They served in silence and withdrew, leaving each man savouring the superb aroma of beef and claret, onions and herbs rising from his exquisite Flora Danica soup plate. They supped with pleasure...even Andrew, who by this time was starving and would damn near have supped with the devil. If indeed that was not exactly what he was doing.

"Well now, Andrew" began the Prime Minister, after a nod from Sean Keys. "From the state of your mood and your behaviour after ou came away from researching Madagascar in the Edinburgh brary, and from what you've said since you arrived here, you have bviously come to the conclusion that Britain is to be the world's AIDS hospital."

"Hospital? I'd have said concentration camp. There's no ospital that I know of that cares for fifty million people. There's o way of caring for fifty million people in one place, without maybe another thirty million people staying here to care for them. So it won't be a hospital - will it?"

The Prime Minister sighed. "Andrew, you're letting your feelings get the better of your intellect again. All fifty million will not be sick all at the same time; we will need a great many more hospitals, yes, but remember that only about ten per cent of the total population here will actually require hospital treatment at any one time; and of course as the total number decreases, that ten per cent will be an ever diminishing number of people. It is workable, Andrew, and we have already thought out the major infrastructures. Some time ago."

Andrew put down his spoon and wiped his mouth on finest Irish linen.

"Still wrong. You're working on the AIDS statistics there; about ten per cent of HIV sufferers get full-blown AIDS, so ten per cent of your captive population will require hospitalisation? No. You've forgotten three whole categories of people in your calculations: the T.B. sufferers; the people who will be slowly losing their minds as the virus attacks their brains; and the ordinary toll of mumps and measles and broken legs...the normal sick and injured. Those three groups are going to double or triple or quadruple your imaginary ten per cent needing hospitalisation."

"Not quite" said Sweeting. "Not all of those will need hospitalisation, after all. The new T.B. viruses are untreatable, so there is no point whatsoever in putting those unfortunate people in hospitals. They won't get any better. As for the dementia patients, well, again, hospitalisation is no help to them. So although ten per cent is not entirely an accurate figure for hospitalisations, it won't be far off the mark."

"I'm sorry, but this is sheer sophistry; logodaedology of the highest order. Your T.B. patients may not benefit from an actual hospital, fine, nor your dementia patients but they'll still require institutional care of some sort, whether you call it a hospital or not. A rose by any other name..."

The other men seemed very interested in their plates of soup. A cold feeling stole across Andrew's soul. "They will receive care of some sort, won't they?"

"Yes of course they will" said Sweeting crossly. "What do you think we are? It's just that we deem institutional care for them to be inappropriate. We intend to provide care in the home. Peripatetic nurses and doctors will have endless house-call duties, going round the sick and the dying, making them as comfortable as possible."

"But the infection rate! These nurses and doctors...they'll be picking up and carrying the viruses around with them, through the streets...! And then they'll die themselves...so where will the care come from then?"

The secondary door opened; the servants removed the soup plates and served each diner with three different fruit sorbets before withdrawing, silently, as before.

Andrew still looked, pointedly, at Sweeting, who reluctantly answered.

"The medical staff numbers will...decrease...at approximately the same rate as the patients. The ratio should therefore stay the same. Workable."

Juan Romero de Boca Negra spoke, for the first time. His tone was firm, with a small sadness in it and a certain amount of sympathy for Andrew.

"Senor, this is all at early days for you still. You are still thinking, what is the best care we can provide for these poor people? You are still thinking, primarily, about the hospital population here in Britain. We all did, in the beginning. This will sound hardhearted to you, Doctor, but it is time to begin thinking about the rest of the world instead. There are more of them. The people who will be left, the healthy ones. The ones we are trying to protect. You must

370

understand this fully right now: the principal concern for everyone must be the survival of the human race. The protection of all peoples from the HIV virus and its associated ills. It seems people refuse to protect themselves; so we must do it for them. Our first duty is to make sure that Britain functions properly as an isolation unit; that all infected persons brought here. We have no intention of leaving them to die, untended, once they are here; but there will be hardships, there is no avoiding of that. There will be misery here, Doctor Douglas. But if we do not do this, then humankind is finished. We must protect the living, in all the other countries. Here, we will do what we can."

Andrew put down his sorbet spoon, rested his elbows on the table and buried his face in his hands.

Sweeting took pity on him. "It's not all bad, Andrew, though it seems that way to you right now. We'll be trialling vaccines, at last, once Hospital Britain is up and running." This startled Andrew from his slump.

"Here? How? Everyone who comes here will be already infected!"

"Um..no. No, they won't. For a start, there will be the medical and other staff who will stay or come here to help. Then many of the victims will want to bring family here with them, and some of those families will come. The vaccines will be trialled on the uninfected population."

Andrew hadn't thought he could be any more shocked but now he was.

"So those that come here uninfected will be deliberately infected with lethal doses? Because that's how you have to start vaccine trials, remember? Jesus God, Sweeting!"

Boca Negra came in again, speaking soothingly. "Not any more, Doctor Douglas; we have solved that particular problem. No lethal doses will be required. Not for any vaccine, ever again. We have had a project running for some years now in America: Silicone Valley in California, actually - where medical scientists and computer scientists have been working together on a computer modelling programme for this very task. We had hoped to discover a way of

371

trialling any vaccine purely by computer modelling, but this has not proved possible. However, I am glad to tell you that the early stages of lethal dosages can now be simulated quite perfectly. It is after the dosages cross that threshold that the problems begin with the modelling process. The subtleties involved, the range of variables, are difficult for either an analogue or a digital computer to handle efficiently, dependably. We did experiment with a stochastic model, with a digital input and output and an analogue processor, but the results were not consistent. We even tried it the other way round and got equally unreliable results. Still. We no longer have to fear killing the very people we are trying to save. It is a great step forward."

"How long" asked Andrew, as mildly as his anger would permit, "How long have you had this capability?"

"Not long, senor. And we have only just begun to be able to use the programme properly. I assure you, the various major forms of HIV are already being trialled against half a dozen different possible vaccines."

"The variations....will we not need a different vaccine for every one of the thousands and thousands, the millions of variations of the virus?"

"We hope not; we are concentrating on the three major types, and the envelope protein configurations which are common to most, or all, of their principal variants. If we can teach the body to recognise something which is even vaguely like HIV, and attack it...we are halfway home."

"And the vaccines? Still mostly killed virus with T-helper boosters?"

"Hardly. Those were the favourites before we understood that boosting the immune system was also boosting the virus. No, Doctor Douglas, things have moved ahead considerably since then. There are several interesting avenues being explored now; one of them involves chemically binding the HIV virus to one the body knows well as an enemy; preliminary modelling sequences do seem to indicate that the defence system learns to recognise the secondary virus later, even without its original host primary. We will see."

Andrew's interest was quickened. "This has implications for cancer research too, does it not?"

Boca Negra smiled. "It does. And for many other diseases...including the new T.B.s."

Sean Keys indicated quietly that he was now ready for his main course; the Capon Orientale was brought, and rice, and chutneys. This kept them all busy for a few minutes. Despite himself, Andrew was becoming almost excited.

"I presume this research will not be confined to these islands?"

Boca Negra replied; "Not the research, no; but of course the clinical trials of any AIDS vaccine will have to take place where infection by HIV is a possibility. And once Hospital Britain is in place, that will, hopefully, be the only place in the world where the infection is rife. Would you care for mango relish, Doctor Douglas?"

"Thank you no; but I would care for a lot more information. On every aspect of this miserable business. Like...how long have you all been working together? What the hell is the World Council...and who elected you to it?"

"I'll field this one" smiled Sean Keys. "Not everyone here is on the Council, Doctor Douglas; everyone here is involved in the British Table of it, of course. Its proper title is the World Economic Council, and it was born in 1983, in Brussels. A group of influential European business-people and money-market people had collected there to lobby the EEC to do something about the spread of AIDS; they got nowhere. Instead they spent several days by themselves in their hotel, deeply worried about AIDS, not just because their own organisations were going to be so dramatically affected, but also, I assure you, from humanitarian points of view. But the EEC wasn't ready to listen, at that point - at least not in public. So the Council was set up to monitor things worldwide. Other countries, that is to say, leaders of industry in other countries, were gradually brought in, and most of the leaders of the big financial houses...banks, merchant banks, insurance companies and the like; and then

373

eventually, some governmental officials of various kinds.

'By 1988, we had persuaded most of the big players - the USA, Brazil, China, and the EEC, and most of the Arab world, - that Hospital Britain was the only sensible proposition, as people were clearly not going to start using condoms, even if they died for their stupidity later. Stupidity is not supposed to be a capital offence, after all, so it was felt that we would have to save them from themselves. Isolation was the only way. Britain was the only candidate area which fitted all the criteria.

'Of course individual governments and companies had already started putting the mechanisms in place which would support the project; public opinion had to be solicited, all over the world. I regret to say that we are responsible for a good many deaths. Some of the gaybashing and the general hatred and tension were our fault; we encouraged it. It was necessary. A few deaths now to avoid very many deaths later. We needed some kind of positive image to arise on isolation policy, so that we would not face massive public insurrection when it happened. When it happens."

"Surely that will still happen. You can't change the face of the world without people getting a little upset about it?"

"You would be amazed, Doctor Douglas" Keys replied. "All our market research, in every country in the world, tells us that the Positive population wishes for somewhere to go, and the healthy population wishes that they would. There will be pockets of resistance, of course, but nothing major."

"Market research...reminds me...why isn't the very wonderful Albert Kennedy here tonight, gentlemen? Surely he's your blue-eyed boy in Britain. Isn't he?"

Sean Keys had his mouth full of chicken and could not reply.

"Still sarcastic about us, Andrew?" asked Jan van Elsen. "We hoped that by now you would be beginning to understand. But I will answer your question, because that is what all of us are here to do, tonight. Answer your questions. Albert Kennedy does not come to us; we go to him. Or Sean does, anyway. Sean visits all the Albert Kennedies, to support and guide them in their work. That work will be done soon, and Albert and all the others will have their reward."

Andrew grimaced. "As opposed to Frankie Dunn, who's got his eward already; big house in the country, seat in Parliament..."

"And his sister as his wife" added Sweeting, bitchily. Andrew blinked.

"Pardon?"

"Flora Spencer's father, the good Reverend, fathered little Frankie too. Flora doesn't know that, yet, but Frankie does. He's married to his own sister, and she's going to have his baby. Nice, isn't it?"

Andrew's mind raced back to that sight of Frankie plunging into the willing Terry, while Frankie's pregnant bride...his sister?...danced with their guests in the room next door.

He had to hold his hand over his mouth to stop himself from vomiting over his dinner. He rose unsteadily, but gained control, and sat down again. All the faces turned towards him were sympathetic, apart from Sweeting, who seemed to be enjoying the effect his words had caused.

Andrew faced Keys and spoke in a quiet, uninflected voice devoid of self pity.

"Tell me" he said "Why me? Why was I picked, why was Terry given to me on a plate, why was I ever involved in all this, put through all this? I was quite happy gardening in St Fillans. I was no threat to anyone. Why did you see fit to destroy me, Mr Keys?"

"You credit us with too much foresight, Doctor Douglas" he replied, kindly. "None of what has happened to you was our doing except getting you to resign. That is to say...you seemed like the best man for the job, for the AIDS Committee, but after your television appearances we thought - we realised - you were too honest. We could not risk you getting any closer to the Council, for you would have spoken out. As you are probably still planning to do... Anyway. Terry Aitken: nothing to do with us. She fell in love with you, you fell in love with her. It was not our doing. She is nothing to do with the Council, which is why she was fired. Frank Ainsley is a good worker on our behalf. Terry, like you, would never have swallowed the medicine. She is quite a character, Terry

Aitken. We rather admire her."

Andrew refused to be drawn. "Hmm" was all he offered in response. And then "I see". He twisted the stem of his wineglass this way and that, wondering what he could trust himself to say next. His food was almost untouched before him, and van Elsen noticed this.

"Chicken not to your liking, Andrew?" he asked, as if they had been at an ordinary dinner, in some ordinary universe.

"Drop it" said Andrew, very short and harsh. "Drop all this civilised crap, will you? What do table manners mean any more? Now?"

"They mean a great deal" sighed van Elsen, as if explaining long division to a child. "If it is not to preserve all that mankind has attained, all the culture and the science and the social niceties too, why do you think we would bother doing what we are doing to save this not very important species? All of us here are in fact more acutely aware of what man has achieved than we ever were before. I visit art galleries regularly - never made the time, before. Sweeting here is studying philosophy...your own Prime Minister collects Meissen porcelain and writes poetry...Sean..." but Andrew was shaking his head in disbelief.

"You're insane, all of you! Fiddling while Rome burns while your own men are torching it! Meissen china? Doesn't matter any more. Poetry? So what?"

The Prime Minister tried pouring oil on troubled waters. "Maybe you're right. Galbraith said, the only sane reaction to an insane society is insanity. So maybe we are..."

The oil on the troubled waters caught fire. "A quote from a pop psychologist in the 'sixties does not exactly justify what you are doing to the world."

The Prime Minister was getting rattled now. "Cool it, Andrew!" But Sean Keys smiled, and the P.M. subsided.

"He's not angry at us, not really" said the leader of the World Council. "It's not us he's fighting. It's his own dawning realisation that we are right. That Hospital Britain is the only sensible step ahead. Isn't it, Andrew?"

Andrew got up from his chair and walked to the drinks cabinet. He poured himself a very large Scotch, threw a couple of ice cubes into it, and stayed where he was, drinking deeply. When he turned towards the dining table, all could see the tear sliding down his cheek.

"Yes" he said. And turned away again, to pour more whisky in his glass.

It was, as Sean Keys had warned, a very long night. A very long nightmare of unbelievable plans and incredible logistics and desperately tragic figures. From the infrastructures of Hospital Britain they moved on, inevitably, to Operation Brittania; the removal to Great Britain of every person in the world who carried either the virus, or its antibodies, in their tissue.

There was still much to be discussed, even though plans had been broadly formulated for years. Each country was being left to plan its own roundup, though help and advice was always available through the World Health Organisation or the World Council. At this point, Andrew dared voice a suspicion which he found growing within him. Had any cats really been infected with HIV? Or was that a practice run for the roundup of human beings?

"No, no, Andrew, we're not that devious" said Sweeting. "Or that wicked, either. That was real enough."

"How did your wife react, Sweeting? I remember you said she was devoted to her Siamese."

Sweeting's face went slack. "She tried to set them free, into the woods. Silly little buggers kept coming back, so the Reservists got them. Then she left me."

The man was wretched, and Andrew felt a surprising sympathy for him. He too had lost his love, and he too had evidently only recently become part of all this.

Sweeting sensed the sympathy, felt irritated by it at first and then grateful for it. Nobody else round this table seemed capable of genuine sympathy any more, though they were all expert at slapping it on their faces when required. He looked at Andrew and said solemnly "Get Terry back, Andrew. It's plain as the nose on your face that you two love each other. That's worth hanging on to. It's all that's left to hang on to."

"I'm afraid I'm not that romantic" said Andrew. "Not in the face of all that's to be done. Terry would never sit on all this; she'd blab to somebody. And I wouldn't want to live a lie with someone I love."

"Well said" soothed Sean Keys. "All of use have either already come round to that, or" and he looked straight at the Prime Minister "Or else we soon will. So you're with us, Andrew? Finally?"

Andrew felt as if the eye of everyone he had ever known was on him at this minute. His mother, his father, his schoolteachers...Ruth...Callum...Joe.

"Yes" he said. "I loathe this with every fibre of my being, but it is necessary. And if it has to be done, I want to help make it happen...*right*. With some dignity for people. With some hope of happiness. I want to stay here and work with the AIDS victims."

"No, Andrew; you don't need to do that. We want you to go ahead with each new settlement, like van Elsen's new ICI settlements...help people to adjust. Make them happy. Set up systems to take care of them. The healthy people need help too, you know. There's no need for you to stay here and die!" Sean Keys was urgent in his persuasiveness. "We didn't ask you here tonight, risk telling you all this, just to lose you to AIDS or T.B. We want you to live: and work with us."

"I'd quite like to live too; but not abroad. Too British for that! Too stubborn, too. No. Give me some kind of overseeing job here. Let me work as a doctor again, or at least an administrator of doctors. That's what I want."

"Senor; Doctor Douglas; there will be no shortage of martyrs, I assure you. We have enough volunteers already! Please reconsider."

"You miss the point, Senor Romero; I have no intention of being a martyr. None. This computer modelling...the new vaccines...all tremendously exciting. I want to be here when the breakthrough comes. Because just possibly, after the vaccine is eady, a cure might just be found. I can think of nothing which would give me more personal satisfaction than being here, helping to stop the deaths, bringing life and hope back to people. Please; let me stay."

Every face round the table was reluctant, but Sean Keys finally gave in and agreed on condition that Andrew accepted the post of overall Controller of Public Health in Hospital Britain. Andrew accepted.

The discussion, the surreal statistics and plans, went on. It had been necessary to invent an almost entirely new social structure and economic strategy, for a whole country full of walking wounded. Should they have to work? Or would the world provide endless food and supplies? Two years ago, agreement had been reached: the basics would be provided by the Hospital Board, which would replace the Government (which would by that time be the Moral Majority, and could say and do anything at all by virtue of the fact that every voter would 'know' that all decisions truly were the wish of the people) and would be funded by a new tax on all workers all over the world which meant very little cash input from each healthy worker in exchange for living in a country guaranteed to be free of AIDS.

Luxuries would have to be worked for or gone without, if the person was capable of work. Every effort would be made to match the person to the right job; journalists would work on newspapers, secretaries in offices, businessmen would be set to run supply lines and distribution points (most of which would simply replace existing supermarkets and corner grocers). Alcohol would be made extremely cheap; marijuana would be legalised, and sold in the form of prepacked joints, like cigarettes.

The hidden agenda was, despite the newness of the plans, a very old one; it was basically bread and circuses. Entertainment would be given very high priority, to keep the people happy. And docile. As to housing, that would be offered on a parity basis as far as was reasonable. The man who was being removed from a three-bedroom bungalow would be given something equivalent; only the later and last arrivals would find themselves shunted into damp tenement room-and-kitchens in Glasgow or London or Liverpool.

"Are we to have ghetto situations?" asked Andrew at this point. "Brits in London, for example, Europeans in Manchester, Africans in Birmingham..?"

Sweeting looked scornful, although such a suggestion had been put forward by several countries which felt that home-from-home might be easier to live in than a racially mixed land where nobody spoke their neighbour's language.

"Hardly" he said. "That might lead to fights. No, there will be language and cultural classes, and get-togethers organised, by the Cultural Club leaders. They'll be AIDS sufferers, or volunteers, who come with each batch of intake from whichever country, and make sure their lot integrates as well as possible."

"I see" was all Andrew said. Some of his questions definitely made his hosts uncomfortable, during those long hours of talking. For example, the question of sterilisation of all females in their fertile years: was this to be policy? They sidestepped this by saying it had not yet been decided, but clearly it had been decided, it had been decided upon. Logic dictated: if females were allowed to reproduce, more HIV Positives would be born, and their progeny also would continue the deadly line; therefore no female could be permitted to bear children. Not even those who arrived as children themselves; they too would undergo sterilisation. Though vasectomies for men were easier and cheaper there were still more men infected than women, so it would be a shorter, if more bloody, business to sterilise the women. This way, the generations presently infected would be the last generations of the virus. Unassailable, this kind of logic, once you allow it to overshadow basic humanity.

There would be many children brought, and caring for them would be a special kind of hell for the nurses and doctors and social workers...and Cultural Club leaders. Few of them would reach maturity. What need, then, for schooling? Or training? No need. No education. No hope.

The subject of extradition was danced round with delicacy and finesse; every country had already been saturated with positive propaganda to the point where a good many Positives would volunteer the minute Hospital Britain was announced, and for the others, those who did not volunteer?

"A certain amount of friendly persuasion might become necessary" admitted Senor Romero de Boca Negra. "But it will be done with great tact and diplomacy." Later it transpired that this tact and diplomacy would include screening 100% of the world's population, using the Wolfson circuit cards, and a discreet tattoo being applied immediately a Positive reading was obtained; there would be no hiding place.

Chiefs of Staff of all the various armies had met and constructed, over three years, detailed extradition procedures for the incomers, expatriation procedures for the outgoers, and timing mechanisms to make all safe meantime. It was generally felt that although it made sound sense to have an incoming boat, once emptied, filled with outgoers, there was a distinct possibility of mass fighting breaking out between the two groups; a very lacy plan now existed to ensure that as one lot was being 'welcomed' at one port, the boatload of outgoing Brits would be departing from quite another city. The same plan, in reverse, was in place for the other countries, where 'voluntary' departures would be kept well away from the planeloads and boatloads of hopefuls waiting to start their exciting new lives in the homes so recently vacated by people 'persuaded' to leave.

The whole plan was calculated to take two and a half years from the time the truth was announced; but that truth was nowhere near being announced just yet. The Prime Minister explained that the British temperament seemed to offer peculiar resistance to propaganda, and it would be far too risky to announce Hospital Britain until they were more sure that virtually everyone in Britain wanted out anyway.

"People might get hurt" he explained, in tones of deep concern. "If there was some sort of uprising about it all, and we had to suppress it."

"Your thoughtfulness does you credit" said Andrew.

It had to arise some time during the discussion, and it did voluntary euthanasia. Psychologists working for the World Council had warned them that the suicide rate would be high; on purely humanitarian grounds, therefore, they had recommended that special places be assigned where people could go to die with dignity. It had been suggested that some sort of bonus be paid for each suicide, the money to go to their families back home, but some spoilsport had called that inhuman and the suggestion had been abandoned. Shame, really, Sweeting had thought; with the costs envisaged for each sufferer's terminal phase, a bonus encouraging people to do the decent thing could easily have been accommodated in the budget, and would no doubt have proved most successful.

Voluntary euthanasia would, just by being there, save the Hospital Board considerable expense; not least in the terminal wards, where the drained and exhausted living skeletons, men, women and children, would beg for merciful release. And be given it. On humanitarian grounds, of course.

"Of course" said Andrew. He thought of Ruth in her last days, and how hard it had gone with her, and how much morphine she had needed just to get through another hour. She had begged him to help her die, and he could not do it. He had never forgiven himself for that, and had kept a very open mind on euthanasia ever since, like most doctors. But to hear it spoken of, openly, as a cost-saving exercise...it was hard to swallow. He had to remind himself that Sweeting was Minister for Health, with budgets to worry about, not a doctor; not someone who had sat, hour after hour, with a dying patient, sharing those precious irreplaceable last hours of confidences and worries and beliefs.

Sweeting talked very easily of thousands and millions of deaths; Andrew wondered if he had ever seen even one. It is less easy to talk of millions of deaths if you know to your very bones what each death is like.

Well after midnight the talk turned to 'afterwards'. Andrew had been right about that; when the plague was over, Britain would be the world's penal colony. At this point, he was blithely assured, his ob would be over; penologists would replace medical staff, and the social structures would change all over again. All in all, Sean Keys said pleasantly, it would work out to the world's advantage. Imagine, he said, safe streets to walk on everywhere. Who would risk being sent to Britain? And those that did would most richly deserve what they would find here. No more soft options of medical care and Cultural Club leaders: oh no. It would be a true prison. But of course, as a medical chap, no doubt Doctor Douglas would not care to hear of their plans for that. He agreed. He did not want to know. And he asked only that, when that time came, he might be given free choice as to which country he wished to emigrate to. Much nodding of heads and smiling of reassurances was done, all round the table. It was all tremendously civilised. There were even jokes: Sean Keys was especially tickled that Hospital Britain would finally solve the Irish question, which was, of course, dear to his heart; as Eire had agreed to vacate her soil along with the rest of Great Britain, the Irish question was finally settled, and for good. And in such a truly unforeseeable way, my goodness! Everyone smiled at that one.

At almost two o'clock in the morning, the meeting was broken up. Everyone shook hands (particularly warmly with Andrew) and the coats were soon brought and the cars called to wait outside. Andrew's car was first.

He turned up his collar against the cold, and folded himself gratefully into the padded warmth of the black limousine. The driver touched his cap deferentially, said "Tudor Court, is it, sir?" and drove off smoothly. Sitting back comfortably, not yet really tired after his long sleep today, Andrew began to plan how he would bring these callous bastards down. Callum was sure to know of some underground freesheets somewhere...that would be a start. A good start. And he would find Terry, and get her back. She had been drunk; she had been stupid; but she loved him and he loved her. Sweeting was right. It was all that was worth hanging on to, in the end. And he would apologise to Callum, and be nice to Belinda. He would help them get away, make sure they had a good future.

383

Somewhere. He was elated, full of plans, full of beginnings. These dehumanised men in that elegant diningroom might have logic on their side; but they had forgotten that every living being matters. They had forgotten their humanity, and replaced it with intellect. There had to be a way out of this mess which did not require fifty million people to die away from their families; there had to be a way, some way, of persuading people even now to start using condoms. Sweet Jesus, he reflected, it was so simple. So simple for the world to avoid the catastrophe. With enough information surely, surely people would listen? If they found out what was being planned for them, surely they would listen. And act. For when it came down to it, the threat which was decimating the people of the world was not HIV or even the plans being hatched at Number 10 Downing Street. It was a much older enemy than that. It was complacency.

Back in the private diningroom of Number 10 Downing Street, the other men stood talking.

"He didn't buy into any of it, you know" said Harold Sweeting.

"I know" replied Sean Keys. "The chauffeur has his instructions. Credit us with some sense, Harold; it was all arranged. If he had accepted it all, we would have got one of our men to order him a taxi. As it is, it's the chauffeur." He sipped a last liqueur, appreciatively. "Pity. He's a good bloke. Ah well. You can't win them all. So, gentlemen, same time next week?"